Praise for *Heartstone* (Book 1)

"If you're into Austen retellings, or if you like talking dragons with your regency romance, or if you're just looking for an upbeat, light-hearted change to your fantasy routine, *Heartstone* is for you."

—The Book Smugglers

"It is a truth universally acknowledged that adding dragons to *Pride and Prejudice* is the best idea I've heard in a while."

—*B&N Sci-Fi and Fantasy Blog*

"Wow, where do I even start? I *must* address the stunning world-building that lies within these pages. This is White's debut novel, but her imaginative and addictive world feels as if it was written by a seasoned writer. Elle Katharine White is an author to watch."

—The Speculative Herald

"Elle Katharine White has managed to blend the classic elements of *Pride and Prejudice*—the characters, the social commentary and financial issues, and the conflict between Lizzie Bennet and Mr. Darcy—with wonderful, monster-filled fantasy. It has all the lovely romance with a hint of heartbreak from the original, but combines it with fantasy in a way that feels utterly unique."

—All About Romance

"Honestly, pick up and read *Heartstone*. Even if you don't much like *Pride and Prejudice*, this fantasy retelling is accessible, does a very nice job creating a fantasy world, and has a fine analogue Elizabeth Bennet in the form of Aliza Bentaine."

—Culturess

Praise for *Dragonshadow* (Book 2)

"White's 2017 debut, *Heartstone*, fused epic fantasy with the manners of Jane Austen so perfectly, she basically created a whole new sub-genre. The sequel picks up the charm offensive where the first book left off."

—*B&N Sci-Fi and Fantasy Blog*

"*Dragonshadow* is the second book written in the beautiful world that follows the lives of Alastair and Aliza Daired. The counterparts to the beloved *Pride and Prejudice* by Jane Austen. The fantasy novel brings out all the stops—romance, fighting, and a war that's only just beginning . . . The story was breathtaking. Absolutely breathtaking. I enjoyed following the lovely couple battle together and grow as characters. White was able to keep me engaged with the story from beginning until the very end. I recommend this book—and series—for those that like fantasy and for Jane Austen fans as well. Everything about the story was rich and romantic."

—*San Francisco Book Review*

"This book is very much about digging deep. . . . The writing and world-building here are very much the stuff of classical fantasy novels. While there is enough that is new to captivate and delight fans of the genre, there is also enough that is typical to give them that pleasant feel of familiarity. . . . *Dragonshadow* is a good sequel novel."

—All About Romance

"White delivers another warm-hearted tale of romance and fantasy adventure. . . . Another fun foray into a land of dragons and mystery."

—*Publishers Weekly*

Flamebringer

ALSO BY ELLE KATHARINE WHITE

Heartstone

Dragonshadow

FLAMEBRINGER. Copyright © 2019 by Laura Katharine White. All rights reserved. Printed in the United States of America. No part of this book may be used or reproduced in any manner whatsoever without written permission except in the case of brief quotations embodied in critical articles and reviews. For information, address HarperCollins Publishers, 195 Broadway, New York, NY 10007.

HarperCollins books may be purchased for educational, business, or sales promotional use. For information, please email the Special Markets Department at SPsales@harpercollins.com.

Harper Voyager and design are trademarks of HarperCollins Publishers LLC.

FIRST EDITION

Designed by Paula Russell Szafranski
Title page and chapter opener dragon art © VectorNes/Shutterstock

Library of Congress Cataloging-in-Publication Data has been applied for.

ISBN 978-0-06-274798-3

19 20 21 22 23 LSC 10 9 8 7 6 5 4 3 2 1

FLAMEBRINGER

A HEARTSTONE NO[VEL]

Elle Katharine White

HARPER Voyager
An Imprint of HarperCollins*Publishers*

For Ryan, Crystal, and Amanda
brother- and sisters-in-arms

the GREAT ICE

the SINGING SANDS

BANSHEE
BAY

NORTHERN
WASTES

HOLLOW
HILLS

the BARRENS   Castle
                 Sevorn   Mortunton

LAKE MEERCA

Lunquind

RUSHLESS
WOOD   Lukoina

WIDDERMERE
MARSH
              Widdermere
              Marsh Hall

the OLD WILDS

                              WINTER
                              SPEAR

AN EDANNATHAIR

HARBOROUGH RIVER
HATCH   Selkie's Keep
       Hatch Ford   RUSHLESS

RIVER   UPPER
HATCH   DEAH   Hallowsdean

       Cloakeep   LOWER
                        DEAH
DRAGONSMOOR
   Shepherd's Vale

     House
     Bearhaqua
Ramshead Landsley   Cloven
                                      Cairn

                  ARLE

TYNE
          MIDDLEMOOR   North Fields

                                      the FENS
          HART'S RUN
   Little Dembley   Bleayhourne
                    Manse
          bellhedge   EASTWICH

                    RIVER
   Upper   MERYLL   LESSER
   Westhall   EASTWICH

   Westhall   WESTWICH

         Edan Rose   Edonnie

   Lower   RIVER
   Westhall   Hunted   MAN   WASH
                  Forge

         WAIH   LESSER   BAY of
                          WESTWICH   MAN
     Whin-on-the-Water   Wsh

                                 ISLE of
                                 KINE

Flamebringer

CHAPTER 1

THE LONG WAY AROUND

We had made a terrible mistake.

I felt it in every beat of Akarra's wings, in every white-clouded breath that rushed back to sting my face with ice crystals, every tear drawn out on the knife-blade of the wind. The storm was getting stronger. Snow was falling thick and fast, though *falling* was no longer the right word. Falling implied verticality. This snow drove toward us with single-minded horizontal fury, *Tekari*-like in its efforts to unseat Alastair and me. Worst of all, it was getting dark. I gripped Alastair's waist with fingers I could no longer feel and squinted over his shoulder. Through ice-rimed eyelashes I could just make out the ground far beneath in patches of white and dirty gray where the snow had scraped its frozen claws over the Barrens of the Old Wilds. Still no trees in sight. Or hills or mountains or landmarks or anything. We were lost.

"Alastair, we have to turn back!" I shouted. The wind spun my voice away. I tried again, pulling down my scarf and clumsily waving one hand in the hopes he would see it.

He turned a little. The length of cloth wound around his mouth and chin was frosted with snow. "Can't land here," he

1

shouted back, each word fighting its way through the wind. "Not . . . cover . . . shelter . . . wait."

Wait for what? I wanted to scream, though I knew it was useless. The storm had long since swallowed our bearings, and landing in weather like this would be a near death sentence, dragon companion notwithstanding. No shelter, no wood for a fire, with night falling and our food stores already low, and no guarantee we'd be able to get in the air again if the *Tekari* of the Old Wilds found us, we had no choice but to keep going. No storm could go on forever.

But then, no dragon could either. Ice glistened on Akarra's scales, her saddle, and the edges of her wings. We no longer flew straight but dipped and swayed with every draft, and in the lull between gusts I heard her labored breathing. It had been a long time since she'd had a proper meal. It'd been a long time since any of us had eaten. I closed my eyes and pressed my forehead against Alastair's back. *Janna have mercy, why did we do this?*

The gods didn't answer. They didn't need to. It had been almost two days since we flew from Morianton on the shores of Lake Meera, chasing the Wydrick-*ghastradi* and his valkyrie mount. His words from the tavern still burned in my ears, vicious, poisonous, louder than the howling of the storm. *"The summons comes for the House of Edan Daired and old things will be called into account. The ledger will be brought forth, and when all Arle kneels before our master, then you'll know I've won."*

All through the night we'd flown after him, blindly, furiously, Akarra's dragonfire burning through the swirling snowflakes like the avenging sword of Mikla himself.

It was a sword that proved blunted and faithless in our foolish hands. The first rays of dawn had found us in the mountain pass west of Lake Meera, illuminating the whole lake valley and the Old Wilds beyond. At Alastair's command Akarra landed, breaking the crust of snow that spread all around us in a smooth white blanket, unmarked by any sign of Wydrick or his valkyrie.

"We've lost them," I said.

Alastair's voice came muffled from beneath his scarf, the single word short and sharp as the wind. "Yes."

"What now, *khela*?" Akarra asked. "The *ghastradi* warn of a war that is coming, we are many leagues from our allies, and you"—she looked over her shoulder at the empty scabbard on Alastair's back—"have no sword."

We'd tried, even in our haste, to find a sword for Alastair in Morianton, but our bad luck had held. The blacksmith had nothing beyond a hunting axe, and the local regiment of Rangers had made themselves scarce since the flight of their captain. Alastair had fairly thrown a pair of silver dragonbacks at the blacksmith in return for the axe. It was a crude thing, bereft of the razor-edged elegance of Alastair's Orordrin-wrought blade, which was now sunk in the depths of Lake Meera, but still better than nothing. Or so I'd thought. That little delay had cost us our quarry.

Akarra must have seen our dark looks at the mention of weapons. "Do we return to the town?" she'd asked.

I looked behind us. Watery sunlight poured from cracks in the overcast sky without warming anything. Far below us the waters of Lake Meera caught it like a wintery mirror, shattered on its northern shore by the promontory and battlements of Castle Selwyn. Save for the steward Mòrag and a handful of servants, the castle was empty now, bereft of its mistress after the madness of its vanished lord. I thought of what else it held, intangible but no less real: grief and silence and the hollow condolences of the midwife. We'd left nothing behind there but heartache and loss.

I turned from the lake and looked out over the pass, toward the

Old Wilds. The horizon stretched in a solemn gray line farther than I could see, any landmarks lost in the haze of distance. Clouds like leaden curtains were already gathering in the south.

Alastair shook the snow from his cloak. "We need to regroup and take council. If Wydrick was sent to Lake Meera to recruit allies for the coming war, then we need to do the same."

I'd agreed, trying not to think of the kind of allies Wydrick had tried to recruit. An ancient vengeful spirit from the Old Wastes, a creature that thrived on fears and drove children to their deaths, a shadow of a shadow of the first darkness that fell upon the world. I thanked the gods the Green Lady had fled in the end, but that was still little comfort. We had no idea if Wydrick had succeeded with other creatures like her, or what on earth we could do if he had.

"Akarra, how far is An-Edannathair?" Alastair asked.

"Edan's Crest? You want to speak to the Vehryshi?"

"Your people may know more about the *ghastradi* than human lore can tell," he said. "Where they came from, whom they serve. They may even know how to kill them."

The dread weight of his words and their unspoken corollary settled over me like a snowdrift. *And if they didn't know? Or worse, if the* ghastradi *couldn't be killed at all?*

"I've never heard tales of the ghost-ridden in the eyries, Alastair," Akarra said at last.

"Other dragons might have."

She shifted beneath us and studied the sky. A few snowflakes settled on her back and evaporated in a hiss of steam. "The peaks of An-Edannathair are many leagues' flight south and west, and I don't like the look of those clouds."

"It won't be any easier taking the eastern route back through the mountains," I offered, thinking of Rookwood and the *Vesh* ambush we'd escaped on our way to Castle Selwyn. "I agree with

Alastair. If there's a chance we'll find answers with the dragons, we should take it."

"Very well. But the wind is shifting, *khela*, Aliza. It'll be hard going, and we'll have to take it in stages. You'd both best wrap up."

We'd obeyed, hunkering down in our fur-lined cloaks as she caught the updraft and soared out over the pass, toward the Dragonsmoor Mountains and home.

The snow started soon after that. It hadn't seemed dangerous at first: stronger winds, a few snowflakes, a deepening chill, but nothing life-threatening. Akarra predicted the storm would move east, spending its wrath on the mountains surrounding Lake Meera and the Langloch and leaving us a clear path through the Old Wilds.

She was wrong. It grew worse.

Not an hour after we'd set out the wind turned and all direction lost meaning; *up* meant deeper into the heart of the storm and *down* was blinding whiteness and struggling dragon and numb fingers clinging to any handhold I could find. Shards of ice drove through my cloak, knifing through my riding clothes as if they were silk. My hair had stopped whipping around my face only because it was frozen in place. The sweat and melted snow streaming down my neck soaked into my collar, only to freeze again. My lungs burned with the cold.

I opened my eyes and regretted it at once. More tears welled up as the wind scoured bits of ice across my face. Even Alastair's back was no shelter anymore. He'd refused to switch places when we set off, insisting on taking the full force of the storm, and my heart ached as I felt him shiver through the layers of cloak and armor.

Janna, if you're listening, give us strength. I mouthed the names of the Fourfold God with all the faith I had left and willed my arms to warm him. *Mikla, protect us. Odei, make a way out. Thell—*

Akarra faltered. Dark shapes rose out of the snow ahead, faint but growing clearer as we hurtled toward them: sharp, spiky things that looked like they'd hurt if we hit them, and *oh gods, we're going to hit them.* The world tilted. My scarf slipped and powder filled my mouth, stinging like a thousand wasps and silencing my scream. I slid sideways, scrabbling for purchase on Akarra's saddle, but I was no longer master of my limbs. Akarra roared and somewhere Alastair was shouting, but the dark prickly thing loomed out of the storm, and in ducking to avoid it I lost my grip on the saddle. I fell.

There was whiteness and blowing cold and pain. My side throbbed and I gasped for air, choking on snowflakes as I fought to catch the breath knocked out of me. For a second everything swam: frozen tears and trembling shades of blue and white and violet and more of those dark prickling shapes and the biting, driving, howling, ever-present snow.

"Aliza!"

Sensation returned slowly, in gasps and aching *everything.* Rational thought came next. *I fell. I fell and I'm not dead.* Akarra must have been close to the ground.

Dark shapes much like the ones I'd seen before falling now swayed crazily in my peripheral vision. I rolled to my side and looked up, realizing as I did that the snow was no longer blinding and the wind had lessened. For a second I stared at the shape above me, numb brain trying to make sense of it. Straight, with bristly bits coming off. And green? *Is that green?*

"Pine," I muttered, then louder, "A pine!"

It was the first tree we'd seen since leaving Lake Meera. Hope warmed me like nothing else could. We were still lost, grounded in the midst of a blizzard, and very nearly frozen to death, but at least we'd made it across the Barrens.

"Aliza! Where are you?"

"Here!" I struggled to my feet, wincing at a pain in my hip. The snow was thin beneath the boughs of the tree and I could see bare earth and pine needles underfoot. It was only after I'd taken a few limping steps toward Alastair's voice that a new thought tempered my excitement. We'd found trees on the border of the Barrens, yes, but which border? I racked my brain for a mental map of the Old Wilds. Our route to the dragon's Keep at An-Edannathair should've taken us southwest, back across the treeless marshes of the Widdermere. If the winds had pushed us southeast, these would be the forests surrounding Lykaina and direwolf country. If we'd been blown north or northwest, we'd be deep in the heart of the Northern Wastes and undisputed *Tekari* territory. If we'd been driven west . . .

Cold that had nothing to do with the snow filled my heart. "Alastair?" I cried as loudly as I dared.

"Aliza!"

"Here! I'm here!"

Alastair shuffled into sight. Akarra followed, clearing the way with the occasional blast of dragonfire. I caught his arm and pulled him into the protective shadow of the tree. The lowest branches dropped pine needles around us as he crouched next to me, breathing hard and covered in snow. "Are you hurt?" he asked.

"No, I'm fine," I said. "But, Alastair, look! We're through the Barrens!"

He peered through the branches as Akarra dropped to her foreknees outside our little copse. "Do you know where we are, Akarra?"

"I'm not sure."

Alastair growled something in Eth and Akarra looked at him sharply.

"No, I *don't* have every corner of Arle memorized," she said. "You can't expect me to keep track of landmarks in a storm like that."

More Eth.

"It was all I could do to keep us in the air!" she snapped.

"You should've turned around when you realized the storm was too much for you," Alastair said in Arlean.

This time Akarra responded in Eth and their voices rose, fiery words mixed with the slither of falling snow and the howl of the wind, loud enough to set my head pounding. I pressed cold hands to my temples. *For Thell's sake . . .*

"ENOUGH!" I cried, no longer caring if there were any *Tekari* around to overhear. "This isn't helping! Alastair, we wanted to come this way, remember? Don't put this on Akarra."

"Listen to your wife," she growled.

I whirled on her. "And Alastair and I are about to lose our noses to frostbite, so don't *you* start either, all right?"

Akarra looked away. Alastair straightened the hunting axe in his sword-belt and ran a hand through his hair, shaking free beads of ice. His Rider's plait had long ago come undone. "*Fine.* Akarra," he said at last with exaggerated civility, "what's your best guess as to where we are?"

"I can't say for certain."

"I said *guess.*"

Akarra snorted. A heap of snow slid off the nearest branch with a wet slumping sound.

"Please," he added.

"The storm pushed us west, *khela*, fast and far. You know where we are."

Alastair flexed stiff fingers in front of him and said nothing. My heart sank as understanding crept through the cracks in their silence. "Rushless Wood. That's what you're both trying not to say, aren't you?"

"We can't be sure," Alastair said.

"Even if we're not, it doesn't matter," Akarra said. "We can't keep flying in this weather. You two will freeze to death and I'll drop from hunger by the time we reach anything like a landmark." She sniffed the wind and peered up into the darkening sky. "It's too late to do anything more tonight. We'd best make camp here."

Alastair pulled off his sword-belt and harness and hung them over one of the lower branches, and after several minutes' struggle with the buckles, I did the same with our panniers. Together we cleared the dusting of snow around the tree trunk. The ground was cold, hard, and knotted with roots, but it was dry, or at least drier. There were even enough pine needles and dead twigs for a small pile of kindling, which Akarra lit with a carefully aimed blast of dragonfire. Three times it fizzled and smoldered before catching, and the cheers Alastair and I gave at the tiny tongues of flame were loud enough to make Akarra shush us.

"Until we know where we are, I'd rather not advertise our presence any more than we already have," she said with a frown toward the darkening woods. She shifted closer to the fire and wrapped her tail around the trunk, enclosing us in a living, anxious fortress. Ice sloughed off her, running in little rivulets between scales. "I'll take first watch."

"I'll take second," Alastair said in a considerably less peevish tone. "Wake me in a few hours."

Akarra tucked her head under her opposite wing. Alastair fished a bit of bardsbread from our panniers and sat with his back to her steaming side. I sat next to him, taking the chunk of bread he offered without enthusiasm. We chewed for a minute in silence.

"I was wrong," he said at last.

"Hm?"

"To follow Wydrick. We wouldn't be out here if we hadn't chased him from Morianton."

"We couldn't just let him fly away."

"Yes, we could have," he said firmly. "I should've known he was taunting us. On the road north, in Morianton, even now. That's all he's ever done, all he's ever been: a *taunt*. From our earliest days as boys together. Any time he trained longer with my father or bested me in a Sparring or mastered something before me, he would never let me forget it." He exhaled long and slow, his breath suspended in a frozen white cloud in front of him. "We should have taken the long way around."

I went back to gnawing at the stale loaf. Argument, justification, sympathy: whatever he was looking for, I was too tired to give. My jaw worked up and down, cold muscles moving mechanically as I navigated the crust of coarse seeds that stuck in my teeth. I no longer remembered what real food tasted like. Everything was chill and grit and cramp and numb hands and throbbing head, and still Alastair went on, chipping out icy monuments to his regret from the frozen air.

"I should have known he was playing with us. He—"

"Alastair, stop. I wanted to catch Wydrick as much as you did, all right? We *all* decided to follow him back there," I said. "Stop trying to take the blame."

His silence took on a grudging edge as he pulled off the length of cloth that he'd been using as a scarf. It'd once been one of his spare shirts, sacrificed to his dagger when we'd started up the mountains. I'd donned the other half beneath my hood like a cowl, though it hadn't helped much. Breathing through the thin cloth had transformed it into a frozen shell that chafed my nose and did little to block the cold. It now lay slumped in a soggy circle around my neck. I tugged it off and hung it on a branch above the fire, hoping rather than believing that the fitful flame would dry it out by morning.

When Alastair's silence continued, I settled against Akarra's side and negotiated a more comfortable sleeping patch. The living furnace at our backs kept enough of the cold at bay to prevent our freezing to death, but Akarra could warm only that which she touched, and the cold found other ways in. It worked through my clothes like a dull needle, pricking my face, my arms, my feet. The enormity of my folly in taking four walls and a roof for granted for so many years struck me once more, the Old Wilds' birch rod to the back of my spoiled complacency.

You brought this on yourself, you know. Before the words had come only in a whisper; now they thundered inside me, an unyielding magistrate sitting in judgment over my folly. I squeezed my eyes shut. I had been afraid, and in my fear I had lied, claiming readiness to accompany Alastair and Akarra with all the unthinking enthusiasm of the *nakla* I was. And I had paid for my naiveté. Holy gods, how I had paid for it. I was paying for it still.

I drew my knees up almost to my chin, curling reflexively inward against the question that I knew was coming, that would always and forever be coming for me in the dark place between sleeping and waking.

What if?

What if I'd stayed at Pendragon? What if I'd not forced my body through weeks of physical hardship, terrible food, and the terror of the trek across the Old Wilds? What if I'd never seen Castle Selwyn, never faced the horror that was the Green Lady? What if I'd not fallen on my stomach in the ruined abbey? What if I'd never been on that beach when Wydrick and his ghast came to survey their murderous handiwork? *What if, what if, what if, if, if?*

If I'd stayed at Pendragon, would our child have lived?

Neither the fire nor the woods nor the winter silence had an answer. A tear slid down my cheek, warm as blood.

"Do you remember what Tristan said?" Alastair asked.

I opened my eyes.

"*You've tasted the lifeblood of one of the Great Tekari,*'" he murmured. "He said there would be consequences."

"Aye, I remember."

He touched my heartstone on its chain around his neck. The deep green gem had formed from the last drop of lifeblood of the Greater Lindworm, spilled from the heart Alastair had eaten to cure himself of its poison. Getting the heart had cost him the life of one of his oldest friends, and I didn't doubt that it was that knowledge as much as the physical reminder of the Worm's sting that slowed his sword arm and gnawed away at his confidence. "Aliza, I need to know what's happening to me."

"You're still healing, that's what's happening." I rolled over again. "Give it time."

"What if you're wrong?"

"Alastair, please."

"North Fields changed something in me. I can feel it. What if I'm never the way I was?"

Yes, what if? What if? "You know I don't know the answer to that."

He drew deeper under his cloak and pulled his hood over his eyes. I tossed a few more twigs onto the fire and wondered how much longer it'd keep up the pretense. It was smoking in earnest now, the flames no larger than my hand. I sank into my little bearskin bundle and fought my way back into darkness.

It wasn't sleep that waited for me within that darkness, though—merely cold and panicked restlessness. When Alastair shook me awake a few hours later, I felt more tired than I had been when we'd lain down. The fire had long since burned out and snow was sifting in through the branches, dusting our panniers in white. By the rhythm of Akarra's breath at my back I guessed she was asleep, though hers too was a restless one. Her wings fluttered above us, fighting dream-winds. I stretched my stiff limbs, wrapped my cloak around my knees, and listened to the howl of the storm.

Hours crept by. I measured them by the accumulation of powder along the branches just visible in the distilled moonlight. Snow still fell, but the storm had finally slackened, and here and there the clouds parted long enough to show a glimpse of sky beyond. Apart from the sound of our breathing, all was deathly still. Shivers ran icy-nailed fingers along my arms and down my back. Akarra no longer felt as warm as she had when we had lain down. I forced my eyes open and sat rigid beneath my cloak, but my mind drifted like the snow and I wondered, not for the first time, how many nights it would take to get to An-Edannathair. Many more like this and we might not make it at all.

The soft crunch of snow sounded outside our copse. I forgot about the cold.

"Alastair!" I shook his shoulder. He stirred and opened his eyes. "There's something out there," I whispered.

I could see his struggle against the cold and clinging fog of sleep as he stared at me, trying to make sense of my words or perhaps just to remember where we were. A second later he was on his feet, axe in hand. He nudged Akarra's wingtip and spoke softly in Eth. She too took longer than usual to wake, but her sides flared with sudden heat when she did. She peered out into the snowy darkness.

"I don't see anything," she said. "What did you hear, Aliza?"

"Footsteps," I said.

Alastair drew back the curtain of branches and looked out. "From where?"

"I'm not sure."

He muttered something and ducked under the boughs. I followed the crunch of his steps as he circled the tree. "There's nothing," he said. "No tracks anywhere."

"And I don't smell anything," Akarra added. "You must have heard the snow falling off the branches."

Alastair returned and sat next to me with a grunt. "Or you may have been dreaming."

Akarra shielded us with one wing and exhaled a thin stream of dragonfire into the pile of blackened kindling, which sputtered and caught with a crackle. "Better you sleep now, Aliza. I'll take the rest of your watch."

"No, you sleep," I muttered. "I'll finish my own watch."

Neither of them argued, and that worried me most of all.

The moon slipped behind the clouds. I focused on tending the fire, breaking off dry twigs from the boughs overhead and tossing them onto the kindling with clumsy fingers. After nodding off a third time, I finally gave in and woke Akarra for the final watch. She said nothing, only stretched her wings and set her face toward the Barrens and the Wood and whatever waited for us there.

I was glad when she shook us awake at dawn. A dream had troubled me during that second sleep, but I couldn't remember the details, only dark trees and blood and somewhere close by, the thump of a fourth heartbeat.

DAYLIGHT PROVED A BLESSING AND A CURSE. SORE BACKsides and numb fingers combined to make both Alastair and me less than cheerful, and with no hope of breakfast beyond a few bites of bread, I was rapidly heading for irritable by the time we stumbled from the shelter of the tree. The scene outside our make-shift camp improved my mood a little. The pine grew on a ridge overlooking a valley so thick with trees there was no ground visible, and through the trailing snow we caught glimpses of mountains to the south. One peak stood above the others, shining white for a moment before the clouds swirled over the sun and veiled it from our sight.

"Dragonsmoor," Akarra said without the enthusiasm I expected.

"Isn't that a good thing?" I asked.

"Rushless Wood stands between us and the peaks of An-Edannathair."

"At least we're not in direwolf country," I said, reaching for a lightness I didn't feel. *Just somewhere that may be much worse.*

"It's farther than it looks."

I felt the westward wind on my face, remnants of the blizzard that had blown us so far off course. If it didn't change soon, Akarra would have to fight it the entire way to the mountains. Silently I calculated. *A fortnight on the road to Lake Meera, another few weeks at Castle Selwyn, a night and a day across the Barrens, one night on the border of the Rushless, and how much longer through the Wood?* We had been away from home for almost a month. I wondered when Alastair's staff would start to worry. "How far is House Pendragon from here?" I asked Akarra.

"Farther than that. Several days at least."

"Can you fly?" Alastair asked her.

"I'm unsteady enough as it is, *khela*. I wouldn't trust myself to keep you from falling." She hung her head, and he rested his forehead against her side. "I need to eat," she said in a faint voice.

At the mention of eating, my stomach growled loudly enough

to draw both their gazes. I busied myself with gathering our scarves, now more frozen than dried, from their branches and pretended nothing had happened. I'd been able to push the hollow feeling away for minutes at a time by thinking about how very little food we had left, but hearing Akarra admit her own weakness broke down that defense. It felt as if a lifetime had passed since our last meal at Castle Selwyn.

"Then we'll go on foot." Alastair donned his scabbard and threw one of the panniers over his shoulder. He must have seen my despairing look. "For now," he added. "There are bound to be wild animals in that forest."

"I'm not leaving you to hunt, *khela*," Akarra said.

"Then we'll hunt with you."

She raised one horned eyebrow.

"We'll go quietly."

"If you say," she said. "But stay close, both of you. I don't like the look of those trees, and there's a strange smell."

I sniffed and inhaled a snowflake. "What is it?"

"I don't know. Not something dead but—well, not something alive either." She looked over at Alastair, who'd left his axe within easy reach at his hip. "Keep that ready, will you?"

THE RIDGE WAS SLIPPERY WITH SNOW-COVERED PINE needles. Akarra conceded after the first nearly turned ankle and flew us down to the border of the trees. I tried not to think of the Marsh-Rider Lydon Tam and his description of the inhabitants of Rushless Wood, nor of his foster sister Johanna Mauntell, of her wild laughter and bared teeth and the symbol of the Bleeding Tree carved into her back. If he was right, there was danger here that had nothing to do with the *Tekari*. We kept close to Akarra as we entered the Wood.

The pines petered out after the first few yards. Trees of a kind I'd never seen before took their place, growing so thick it took careful maneuvering for Akarra to move through them in places. They had the look of poplars, but their trunks were several arms' lengths around and the bark smooth and silvery, like birch. What branches they had grew high above the ground. It was quiet under the trees and solemn, as if we'd entered an endless pillared hall in the ruins of an ancient overgrown palace, and the trees deadened the sound of the wind enough to make me uneasy. *Something* was off about these woods. For midmorning, there were a few too many shadows.

"Do you feel that, Aliza?" Alastair asked after a few minutes. He kept his voice low.

"What?"

"The cold. It's gone."

Now that he pointed it out, I realized I'd stopped shivering. The air was still. I looked up. Interwoven branches formed a roof overhead that blocked most of the snow and the few flakes that made it through melted before they reached the ground. We continued in silence for a long time, alternately walking and sitting on Akarra's back. The knot of anxiety in my gut did not loosen. Light took on a curious quality beneath the trees and it was hard to judge how long we'd been in the Wood, though by the ache in my feet and the rumbling of my stomach I guessed it was past noon when an odd sight brought us to a halt.

"Akarra, wait a moment." I slipped down from her back.

"What is it?" Alastair asked.

I stopped in front of the tree that had caught my eye. A dark streak at chest height marred its silvery bark. At first I'd thought it was fire damage, but on closer inspection the bark proved unharmed. The stain had grown with the wood. It ran up the side of the trunk like moss, but there was no moss to be seen, and it was dark reddish, not black or green. *Odd.*

"Alastair, get off my back," Akarra said quietly.

No sooner had he dismounted than she sprang upward, jaws snapping. Twigs fell around us. She landed clumsily, wings hitting tree trunks on either side, the remains of a squirrel's drey sticking out from her teeth. With a crunch and a spurt of flame she bit down, then spat it out.

"Empty," she growled. "And tastes foul."

Alastair said a few conciliatory words in Eth and remounted. I didn't.

"Aliza?"

I stared at the place the twigs had fallen. Bloodred sap leaked from their broken ends. The uneasy feeling crested as I turned to the tree again. "Just a moment."

"What is it?" Akarra asked.

I waved for quiet and moved closer, pressing my ear to the silvery bark. Perhaps I was only imagining it. I *hoped* I was only imagining it.

I wasn't. I made the fourfold gesture and backed away, stumbling over leaf litter and exposed roots.

"The *trees.* The trees have heartbeats."

CHAPTER 2

RUSHLESS WOOD

Akarra took a turn listening, then Alastair. "Those can't be real heartbeats," he said. "Can they?"

"I don't know," Akarra said. "I've never heard of anything like it."

I crossed my arms beneath my cloak, willing another layer of something between me and that awful *thud-thud*. "Can we keep going?"

We pressed on with new urgency, keeping our distance from the trees as much as possible. It wasn't easy. The woods grew thicker the farther south we went. There was no snow on the ground anymore, and the branches were woven so tightly overhead that even the worst of the storm couldn't get through. *And neither can we*, I realized. Even if Akarra had been fit enough to fly, the sky was closed to us now. I could tell by their grim looks that they'd realized it too, and probably had long before I had, though neither of them said anything. The unspoken consequence of our decision hung over us like a personal storm cloud. *Too late to go back now.* Alastair walked beside me with one hand on the hilt of his axe.

Dead leaves muffled our footsteps, ankle-deep in some places, making walking treacherous. They turned the forest floor beneath us into a patchwork carpet in the colors of late autumn decay. I picked up a leaf. It was shaped like a beech leaf but mottled with patches of pale yellow, deep purple, and one spot near the stem that was almost translucent. The same dark red sap from the broken twigs had dried in the leaf, most noticeable in the translucent section where it veined through it like blood. *The Bleeding Tree.* Perhaps Johanna Mauntell's scars weren't so figurative after all. I let the leaf fall and wiped my hand on my cloak.

Soon the quiet began to bother me. We saw no squirrels or winter birds or forest creatures of any kind. The woods even swallowed the sound of Akarra's heavy tread. It made it that much harder to ignore the heartbeats, which continued as we moved deeper into the Wood. Gradually I noticed a pattern. Not all trees had them, but those that did were the ones that also had the strange dark streak running up the side of the trunk. More than once I thought I saw movement from the trees out of the corner of my eye, but when I turned to look, there was nothing but the trees and the deepening shadows.

"How long until we reach the mountains?" I asked when we stopped for a rest.

"Not sure," Akarra said. "Unless we reach River Rushless in the next hour I don't think we're going to make it out before nightfall."

"There aren't settlements in this corner of Arle, are there?" I knew even as I asked what the answer was. Alastair pulled me close and rubbed some life back into my arms, his expression grave with understanding.

"No, *khera*. Not this far west."

I shivered. The prospect of spending a night within earshot of the heartbeat trees sat in my stomach like the corpse of a toad, cold, slimy, and nauseating, but what choice did we have? I dug through our panniers and drew out what remained of our food: two half-full waterskins, still mostly frozen, one small loaf of bardsbread, and a greasy packet of dried saltfish. We each took a small piece of bread—Thell, how I hated the taste of it now—and a bite of the fish, mentally calculating how often we'd be able to repeat this before we ran out. The result was not comforting.

A rumbling from nearby made me jump and Akarra looked abashed. "Sorry. My stomachs."

"We'll find some game soon," Alastair said. "There must be something alive in these woods."

Akarra frowned. "Too *much* is alive in these woods. Do you hear that?"

I listened. It was a subtle change, hard to notice until pointed out, after which it was hard not to notice. The heartbeats within the nearest trees had quickened.

Akarra sniffed the wind. Her wings rose like the hackles on a cat. "On my back! Now!"

Alastair leapt into the saddle, pulling me up behind him.

"Hands to your weapon, *khela*!" she growled.

The words were still on her lips when I saw them. The shadows retreated like a creeping black curtain, revealing human figures between the trees. They watched us with narrowed eyes, their sharpened teeth drawn back from bloodless lips. Those that wore clothes were dressed in furs and flayed leathers; those that weren't wore stripes of blue woad, dark against their pale skin. All carried weapons, and every weapon was pointed at us.

I fumbled with my dagger as Alastair drew his axe. The hot, crackling scent of dragonfire filled the air, fading into a moment of breathless silence.

"Who are you?" Alastair demanded.

A man stepped forward. His pale hair fell in ropes to his

waist, and he wore little besides a pair of trousers and a quiver strapped to his hip. A longbow hung loose in his hand, its recurve smooth and white. "*Our* woods, Rider, not yours. You do not demand anything of us here," he said in heavily accented Arlean. "Who are *you*?"

"My name is Alastair Daired," Alastair said without lowering his axe.

A murmur ran through the gathered crowd.

"We're just passing through," Akarra said. "We have no quarrel with your people."

The man gave a short, barking laugh. "Who are you to say, dragon? Have you any idea who we are?"

I remembered what Lydon Tam had told me at Widdermere Marsh Hall. *The Guardians of Rushless Wood, and the most dangerous things within its borders.* "Mauntells," I said quietly, then louder, "You're the Mauntells, aren't you?"

"You know of us?"

"We've heard stories. You're the Guardians of the Wood."

He snorted. "You southern folk know nothing but lies and legends of the bards. How did you come so far into the Rushless?"

"The blizzard drove us to your borders," Alastair said. "We hoped we could find shelter here until it passed."

"Did you?" The man smiled slowly, his lips stretching wide like a dry worm, splitting a little at the corners. Akarra tensed beneath us. "You must be truly desperate."

I never saw him notch the arrow. The sound came before my brain registered the motion of the draw. There was a hiss, a whiz, and the world turned upside down. My stomach plummeted as Akarra reared, roaring, and snatched the arrow meant for Alastair from the air in her teeth. The air boiled, and for an instant I was blinded by scorching, searing white as Akarra spread her wings and sprang into the air. Bone-dry leaves crisped and crackled around us—

And then we were on the ground again, cut off from the sky by the impenetrable roof of branches above.

A laugh rose from among the Mauntells. Their leader hefted his bow again. "You do not pass the borders of the Rushless without our permission, dragon. Coming *or* going."

Alastair spoke to Akarra in Eth and she drew back, still snarling. Akarra opened her mouth and arched her neck, ready to flame. "You're going to regret that, Mauntell," he said.

"Burn the trees, dragon, and it is you who will regret it," the man said.

The shadows between the trees moved, cloaking the Mauntells around us in an unnatural night. Only the bowman remained visible, his smile shining white as bone in the gloom.

Every instinct within me cried a warning as Alastair raised his axe. No one could grin like that in the face of an angry dragon. Not without good reason. I caught Alastair's arm. *"Don't do it!"* I hissed. He fixed me with a furious look, but I held on. "Can't you see he knows something?" I said in his ear.

Alastair looked again at the grinning bowman, looked at me, and lowered his axe.

"Tell us what you want, Master Mauntell," I said, "or let us pass."

"Even we have heard whispers of the great dragonriders of Arle, my lady." He pointed to Alastair with the tip of his bow. "Your family's battle prowess is said to be unmatched, Alastair Daired. I should like to put that to the test."

"A duel?" he said.

"Aye. Formal and proper, according to the ancient customs. You alone and I alone and none to interfere." He cast a scornful glance at Akarra. "Human *or* dragon."

Alastair narrowed his eyes. "To the death?"

"Alastair, no!" I whispered, but he drew his arm out from under my hand. The bowman gave a little snorting laugh.

"Your companion fears for you! Perhaps tales of your battle prowess have been exaggerated?"

"When I kill you, Mauntell, your people will lead us to the southern edge of the Wood," Alastair said. "Those are my terms."

"*If* you slay me, then yes. My family will escort you to the border of the Wood with every honor we can bestow. I swear it."

I felt the dreadful tension in Alastair's touch, sensed the furious reeling back and forth as he felt his way forward against the unknown. "And if I refuse?"

"Then you shall wish you took your chances in the blizzard."

I leaned close. "Don't you *dare*."

"I agree with Aliza," Akarra murmured. Sparks poured from her mouth with each word. "*Khela*, don't risk it."

The bowman smiled again, showing canines filed long and sharp. "Do not think dragonfire will end your worries, dragon. You may bring down a score of us in one breath, but we are threescore, and one breath is all we need. You can't catch every arrow."

A faint creaking made me turn again. A dozen Mauntells stepped out from the eaves of the forest behind us, bows drawn and arrows on the string. My stomach dropped. There was no way all of them would miss.

"I shall make it easy for you, Alastair Daired," the man said. He set his bow down and drew a short knife from his belt. "I won't fight to the death. Kill me if you can, but I'll do no more than maim."

"I accept." Alastair was on the ground before I could stop him. The bowman opened his arms wide with a manic grin.

"Good! Come on then, Fireborn. Show your mett—"

Alastair ducked. In one smooth sweep of his axe, he cleaved the bowman open from hip to armpit.

A gasp rose from the other Mauntells as their leader fell to his knees, mouth wide in a silent scream as he tried in vain to hold his entrails inside. Alastair stepped away, wiping the axe blade on his sleeve as the bowman collapsed face first into the leaf litter, groping blindly at the trunk of the nearest tree.

"Our bargain?" Alastair cried, looking around to the woad-streaked faces around us. "Lead us out of the Wood and you'll never see us again. You have our word."

The only answer was growls from among the Mauntells.

"He swore it!" Alastair said, and pointed to the dead man.

Only he wasn't dead. Akarra hissed as the bowman lifted his head from the leaf litter. I swallowed my scream. Something was *happening* to the tree where he touched it. Beneath his fingers, dark tendrils like snakes flowed from the bark and into the man's body, weaving in and around the gash, seaming it in shadow and drawing the flesh closed. *Just like a ghastradi.* I clutched at the saddle, desperate for an anchor in a world once more turned inside out.

The bowman rose unsteadily, brushing leaf litter from his side. "I said *kill* me, dragonrider, not inconvenience me. Our duel isn't over yet."

Alastair raised his axe, but Akarra threw out one wing to hold him back, dragonfire dancing around her bared teeth. As one of the Mauntells raised their bow.

"So much for oaths and honor, eh, Daired?" the bowman said. "You heard the terms! Tell your dragon to step aside."

"A corpse has no honor," Akarra growled. "We do not bargain with the ghast-ridden!"

"Then it is fortunate we are not *ghastradi.*"

A new voice rang out through the woods, and the smile fell from the bowman's face as an old woman emerged from the trees, her silver hair bright against the shadows that flowed like living ink between the trees. She wore a direwolf pelt and held a greatsword almost as tall as she was. Bone-white bows dipped all around her as the Mauntells hurried to look anything other than threatening. She surveyed the scene before turning to the bowman with a raised eyebrow.

"Grandson, what is this?"

He shifted his weight and did not meet her eye. "Intruders, Grandmother."

She examined the smeared pattern of woad across his chest, the sole remnant of the wound that should have killed him, and clucked her tongue. "You are a reckless, foolish boy, Goryn, and I'm ashamed of you. This is not how we treat guests."

"They're not guests!"

"That is not for you to decide." The old woman turned to us. "Even so, I do not blame you for your interest. Well, Daireds? Explain yourselves."

Alastair swung up onto Akarra's back, axe still in hand. His voice was calm, but I could feel him trembling. I was too. "I am Alastair Daired. This is my wife, Aliza, and my dragon, Akarra. We have no quarrel with you and your people. We only wish to pass through your woods in safety."

"No quarrel? Then I suppose it was out of kindness that you struck down my grandson?"

"He challenged—" Akarra began, but the old woman waved a hand.

"The boy is a hopeless show-off. I do not hold you responsible." She sheathed her sword and motioned for her family members to do the same. They obeyed with varying degrees of embarrassment, and none of them looked at us as they did. "I am Frega Mauntell and I offer you the guest-right. You will stay with us tonight."

Alastair glanced over his shoulder. *Ghastradi* or not, the thought of sleeping within a league of the Mauntells and their ghastly trees made me more eager to face the Barrens. I shook my head.

"We just want to pass through," he said again.

Frega Mauntell shook her head. "It is late and the shadows are long. The storm still rages beyond the Wood. You had much better come rest and refresh yourselves. Tell us your story and we shall tell you ours, and when the storm has passed, we will escort you to the border of the forest with all due honor. You'll not receive such an offer from the snow."

I shook my head.

"Let them be, Grandmother," Goryn said, resting a hand on her shoulder. "Can't you see that they don't want our help? Let them find the border themselves."

She shrugged him off. "Brash boy," she muttered. "Are you certain, Daireds?"

Alastair nodded.

"Very well then." The rest of the Mauntells began to slip back into the dark forest as Frega gestured to the surrounding trees. "I offered in all good faith and you refused, which means I cannot protect you. May the weald-wraiths grant you a swift and painless death."

"What?" Alastair and Akarra said together.

"You have shed the blood of Old Maun, and while I may forgive, the Wood does not. Farewell, Fireborn," Frega said with a bow, and disappeared into the shadows.

I exhaled, long and slow, and sheathed my dagger. It took two tries. "Alastair?" I looked to him, hoping for reassurance, but he was staring at the trees. The shadows deepened. Against the pale trunks of the trees nearest us, the strange dark streak writhed like a snake before sinking into the bark and out of sight.

"Akarra," he asked slowly, "what are *weald-wraiths*?"

"I have no desire to find out."

The leaves trembled overhead. One drifted down, just brushing my cheek. I yelped and swatted it away, making both Alastair and Akarra jump, but before I could apologize I saw my fingers. They were bright with bloodred sap. Alastair swore and helped me wipe it away with one hand, his expression tight with a new kind of fear. With the other hand he drew his axe.

The heartbeats within the trees quickened.

"Akarra, find the Mauntells," Alastair said. "Now!"

She ran. Nameless terror followed. I clung to Alastair and tried not to listen to the crash of branches and stirring of leaves and the strange, high laughter that seemed to come from everywhere and nowhere, hidden just beneath the heartbeats. *Weald-wraiths, not ghosts*, I told myself in a vain attempt at comfort. They had given life to Goryn at a touch. Could they take it in the same way? *A swift and painless death . . .*

Akarra stopped hard, throwing me into Alastair. The shadows around us withdrew in a wave of, not light exactly, but the same kind of muddy twilight we'd seen when we first entered the Wood. A weight went with it. Beyond the rustle of leaves I thought I heard a sigh as the darkness withdrew, like a petulant child torn from its plaything.

"Second thoughts?" Frega looked up at us with a bemused expression.

"We accept your generous hospitality," Alastair panted.

"A wise decision, Master Daired. Well then, come! Our fires will be the warmer for your company. I look forward to hearing your tales."

"And in the morning, you'll lead us to the edge of the Wood?" I asked as Akarra started forward.

"Morning is a long way away, young mistress. Rest first; then we shall talk of mornings."

I didn't need the pressure of Alastair's hand to remind me how little choice we had. Akarra followed Frega deeper into the woods. The old woman walked close to us, her greatsword nearly brushing Akarra's wing. Neither Alastair nor I dismounted. I wondered if Frega could feel the waves of heat roiling off Akarra's side, or hear the low growl deep in her throat at every leaf that drifted across our path. Frega offered no conversation and neither did we, and in the intervening quiet I heard another telltale rustle behind us.

I leaned close to Alastair. "Two hundred paces to the right. Look."

He looked. A trio of Mauntell archers kept pace with us beneath the shadow of the trees, their bows within easy reach. Not threatening, but not friendly. Akarra hissed.

"Something wrong, dragon?" Frega asked.

"You lie, Mauntell. We are not guests; we are prisoners."

Frega glanced back at her archers and laughed. "Believe me, we have no use for prisoners. They are for you, and . . . not for you."

"What do you mean?" Alastair asked.

"You have seen what would happen if you were to travel unaccompanied through these woods. Or you would have seen it soon, if you had not returned to me," Frega said. "As I said, the weald-wraiths have long memories. If you wish to cross Rushless Wood from now on, you must travel with the blood of Old Maun or not at all. This is the price of the blood you shed, Master Daired, and Goryn knew it." Her look grew thoughtful. "I'm sorry he goaded you into it."

Alastair straightened in the saddle. "Lead on, Madam Mauntell."

My head felt light, my stomach hollow as Akarra reluctantly

followed Frega. I imagined we made for a strange procession: two humans, weak with hunger and terrified but pretending not to be, and an angry dragon who put on no pretense at all, ushered by what felt in one moment like an honor guard and in the next like a scouting party returning, despite what Frega said, with prisoners. The trees grew denser and the land sloped downward. Time meandered beneath the shadow of the Wood, but I guessed nearly an hour had passed before we spotted our destination. The glow of fires pricked the shadows ahead of us, and domestic noises filled the silence: the clank of a cooking pan, the sound of pouring water, the murmur of voices. My heart sank as our escorts ushered us into their settlement. I'd hoped for a clearing, perhaps a glimpse of the sky and a chance for Akarra to make good our escape, but we had no such luck. The trees of the grove grew farther apart here, but the roof of branches overhead was as thick as ever.

We followed Frega past rows of tented fires. Peat fires, I noticed. In fact, there was no wood anywhere. The shelters built against the trees were made of peat too, or animal skins draped over ropes. Torches burned in earthenware bowls, licking up oil instead of kindling. I glanced at the rows of archers marching next to us, Goryn at the forefront, and wondered again at the color of his bow. In the midst of this monstrous forest, among trees that protected their own, what had the Mauntells used to make such a weapon?

The other Mauntells looked at us as we passed, some with confusion, some with shock, some with outright hostility, but none offered a challenge. Frega stopped before the largest of the trees, directly in the center of their encampment. A low peat hut encircled the trunk, its roof draped in animal pelts and dead leaves, and high above the door, carved deeply in silvery bark, was the sigil of the Bleeding Tree.

CHAPTER 3

WRAITHS OF THE WEALD

Frega swept back the pelts covering the door and ushered us inside. "My own hut, Daireds. Rest here," she said. "I will have my grandchildren bring *ghrish* and water for you shortly. And for you, dragon," she added, leaning out of the doorway to speak to Akarra, "I have nothing yet, save my apologies. My hunters left this morning for meat. They'll be back before nightfall."

Akarra settled down against the wall of the hut so that her head was even with the door and Frega's face. The old woman took a step back to escape the unapologetic heat dancing around her open mouth.

"As you please," Frega said. "In the meantime, guests, refresh yourselves. Sleep, if you can. You will not be harmed. When you are ready, I will hear your tale."

Alastair followed her to the doorway and watched as she headed for a distant fire. When she was out of earshot, he rested one hand on Akarra's neck. "I know that look. You smell something, don't you?"

"Yes, I do." She sniffed again. "Familiar, but I can't place it."

"Dangerous?" I asked, even as Alastair whispered, "Wydrick?"

31

"Not Wydrick, but I can't tell if it's dangerous either." She shook her head and nudged Alastair back through the door. "I'll let you know as soon as I do. For now, rest and get your strength back, both of you. I'll keep watch."

I looked over Alastair's shoulder toward the camp, which had resumed its usual pace. A few Mauntells gave us the occasional glance, but most ignored us, intent instead on questioning Frega or others in her scouting party. The words *hunters* and *game* came up most often in what conversations I could hear, but I caught a handful of *strangers* and even one *prodigal*. A flash of something pale drew my eye to the far side of the encampment. Goryn sat on a protruding root, his longbow on his knees, fingering the string as he stared at us. He was smiling again.

"Come on, Alastair," I said.

The inside of the hut was smoky and dim, the peat fire in the corner throwing off more heat than light. Furs and dry leaves covered the floor, and Alastair had to duck beneath the bunches of drying herbs, ropes of grass fibers, and earthenware jugs hanging from the ceiling. Besides the herbs, there was no sign of food or water. I swallowed my disappointment. It was all I had to silence my grumbling stomach.

The bole of the great tree formed the fourth wall of the hut. We kept well away from it, settling our cloaks in the far corner by the fire. I wondered how Frega, or Akarra for that matter, expected us to get any sleep with that strange presence looming so near. In the firelight it looked harmless enough: silvery bark like a birch, the usual swell of roots poking through the leaf litter, the faint scent of decaying earth, but each time I closed my eyes I saw those dark tendrils moving through Goryn's body, restoring life where Alastair had taken it, and I couldn't help but shudder.

The ring of steel forced my eyes open. Alastair sat cross-legged by the hearth, cleaning his axe. He didn't look up as I moved next to him.

"Alastair—"

"I know what you're going to say and I don't want to hear it."

I blinked. "Sorry?"

"You were right. Goryn knew something I didn't. You don't need to remind me."

"I wasn't going to."

He looked up. "But you were thinking it."

It took real effort not to roll my eyes. *Now? You want to do this now?* We were trapped in a haunted forest, prisoners in fact if not in name of a family with a mysterious connection to the ghast-like creatures within the trees, with only the tentative promise of both food and escape, and Alastair thought it a good time to invite an argument.

"What do you want me to say?" I said. "Aye, I was thinking it, and so were you."

"He would have killed us if I hadn't accepted. I had to fight him."

"Probably."

"He . . . what?"

"I know you had to accept it," I said, suddenly weary. "It might've been a stupid choice, Alastair, but it was the right one. And lest you forget, you won."

"No, I didn't."

"I saw his *entrails*," I said before immediately shoving the image out of my mind. "You won, dearest. He cheated."

He sat up a little straighter and set down his axe, his maimed hand resting on the shining blade. Not a trace of Goryn's blood remained. For the first time since we'd landed at the edge of Rushless Wood, he looked me full in the face, and I him. The marks of hunger and weariness, dread and desperation were traced deeply in his features, as I imagined they were in mine, but at least we understood each other.

"So then," he said after a moment, "what are these things in the trees?"

"*Weald-wraiths*, whatever those are."

"But are they *Tekari*? They healed like a ghast."

Yet not like a ghast, I thought. The weald-wraiths might have patched Goryn's wounds in the same way Wydrick's ghast had patched his, but these tree creatures had withdrawn when the job was finished, leaving Goryn quite human. Dangerous, and perhaps unkillable within the Wood, but still human. "Maybe so," I said, "but I think Frega was telling the truth. I don't think any of the Mauntells are *ghastradi*."

There was a long, fire-flecked silence. "Just something like them," he said at last.

I had no answer to that. Instead I settled my chin on my fist and stared into the smoldering embers. After all, what did we know of ghasts and where they came from, or even what they really were? Old wives' tales had always placed them firmly within the category of *Tekari*, but perhaps that had only been for lack of any better title. Bard Henry Brandon had sung of the origin of the Oldkind once, how the Fourfold God had molded them from water, air, earth, and fire, but no ballad I'd ever heard had mentioned the birth of ghasts. Like an evil echo I heard the voice of the Green Lady again in my head, taunting and terrible. *A shadow of a shadow of the first darkness that fell upon this world . . .*

Alastair raised his head as the pelt covering the door drew back and Frega ducked inside. "Settled, are you?" she said.

"We're fine," Alastair said stiffly.

"Famished, you mean. No need to deny it. I'm familiar with every kind of hunger, Daireds, and I see its marks on the both of you." She deposited an earthenware jug between us and sat with a creaking sigh. "*Ghrish*. Not much in the way of a meal, but it will keep you upright until the hunters return. Goryn will bring bread shortly."

Alastair and I glanced at each other. The drugged meal in Langdred was still fresh and painful in our memories, as was the bandit Rookwood's attempted theft of our heartstones. As unlikely as it was that word of the *Vesh* bounty had spread to the Mauntells, I would approach strange food and drink with caution.

Frega sighed at our hesitance. "Four preserve us," she muttered, and took a long draught from the jug. "Does that satisfy you, Daireds? Your caution is wise but unnecessary. There would be no use in poisoning you, and if my family wanted you dead, there are easier means. Now," she said as Alastair took a sip and passed it to me, "tell me of the world beyond our borders."

I sputtered, my response tangling with the foul taste of the *ghrish* as it slid down my throat in some combination of coarse bread soaked in vinegar and sour milk.

Alastair managed a much more discreet cough, but he didn't take a second sip. "What do you want to know?"

"Why, everything!" she said. "We hear whispers, of course; echoes of your great tales: Edan Daired and his dragons, the great Saints and their Accord of Kinds, the birth of the *Shani* and their Riders; but they are whispers only, filtered through many minds and many mouths. Brave traders will occasionally venture close enough to the banks of the Rushless to exchange a song across the water, but our family does not go beyond the protection of the Wood. We have not since Old Maun came to live here a thousand years ago."

I swallowed convulsively to rid myself of the taste of *ghrish*. *Maun. Mad Maun*, he'd been called in all the songs Henry had sung about the founding of Arle. Once Edan Daired's lieutenant, Maun abandoned Edan at the height of his campaign against the ancient *Tekari* and wandered north with his wife and young son into the unknown wilds, never to be seen again in the south.

"Why not?" I asked.

"Old Maun never told us why he fled the Fireborn's army. The Wood provided his family the sanctuary they desired, far from the machinations and monsters of the south. They made peace with the wraiths of the weald and became caretakers of the Wood, even as the wraiths became their guardians. We stay for the same reasons he did. It is our home."

Not for all of you. "Why did Johanna leave?" I asked, thinking of our encounter in the Widdermere.

Frega gave a violent start, nearly upending the jug. "Where did you hear that name?"

Alastair leaned forward in a conciliatory gesture that only just disguised the hand resting on his axe hilt. "We met her in the Marshes. She saved us from a harbinger of valkyries."

The furrows in Frega's brow deepened.

"Madam Mauntell?"

"My granddaughter has no part in our family anymore," she said at last. "We do not speak her name within the Grove of Maun."

"She said she comes back here once a year," I tried.

"She serves her penance every year before the Long Night, it's true," Frega said with a dismissive gesture, "but we do not speak her name. I did not give you the guest-right to tell me of the exile. Give me news of the world, Daireds, or leave."

Curiosity gnawed at me, but I ignored it, conscious of the warning in her tone. Between the two of us, Alastair and I gave Frega a halting account of the War of the Worm and the events that had brought us to Castle Selwyn. She had surprisingly little interest in the rise of either the Greater or Lesser Lindworms, but our news of *ghastradi* unsettled her.

"When you mentioned the ghast-ridden earlier, I thought you were speaking in jest," she said, "but now I see you were not. You say you've met not one but *two*? And these walking freely through the kingdom?"

"Aye."

"These creatures spoke to you with one mind, one voice?" she asked.

"Not exactly," I said, "but they did both warn us—"

She rose as if I hadn't spoken, her gaze turned inward. Her gnarled hands tugged at the direwolf pelt she wore around her shoulders as she paced. "I don't understand. This evil was broken ages ago, sundered and separated, buried and unmade," she muttered. "Thell's circle is complete; what was bound cannot walk the waking world again. Not now, not ever."

Movement across the hut caught my eye and I drew in a sharp breath. "Alastair."

A dark shape was moving beneath the bark, moving in an agitated rhythm that matched Frega's furious pace. Alastair sprang to his feet. "Madam Mauntell, what is *that*?"

She stared at him as if she'd forgotten we were there. "Eh?"

"The weald-wraith." I stood and backed toward the wall as the dark stain spread across the wood. "The thing that healed Goryn. The thing you said was *not* a ghast." I pointed. "That . . . *thing*."

Frega brushed her fingers across the trunk. The shadow rose slightly and wove dark tendrils through her fingers before sinking out of sight. "I ask you here to share with me your tales of the world, but it seems you know less than we do. I shall have to teach you your own history. What do you know of the *An-Eskatha*, Lady Daired?"

"The what?"

"The root is in Eth. Surely the Rider knows it."

"It means *the eldest*," Alastair said carefully.

Eldest. Where had I heard that before?

"They were the creatures that came before humans, *Tekari*, *Idar*, and *Shani*, old before even the oldest of the Oldkind," Frega said. "The *Eskatha* came from the first things the gods shaped from emptiness, the four great guardian spirits bound to the world at its birth. We call them Elementari, for their true names were banished in their breaking and— You scoff, dragonrider. Do you doubt me?"

"There are no creatures older than the Oldkind," Alastair said.

"And why should there not be?"

"If there were such things, the Nestmothers and the Vehryshi would know of them. My family would know of them. There'd be stories, histories—"

"Yet there are none. Telling, this silence, is it not? Why do you think dragons have put it from their minds? Do they wish to be replaced as first among the gods' creations? No, dragonkind has chosen to forget. Even the dragons of the Ruined East, who forget nothing, have put it from their minds. Humans are no different. The Oldkind who do remember do not speak of them anymore, for the Elementari rose against their makers, and for that, they were unmade. Broken without remedy, their sundered spirits faded into the wood and water, stone and storm. They became *An-Eskatha*: the Tohu and Ummerue, weald-wraiths and the Woman of the Waste, elemental ghosts surviving on what life they can borrow from the living." She tapped the tree. "Whatever form that takes."

The Green Lady. I remembered now where I had heard the term *Eldest* before. "What about ghasts?" I asked.

Frega shifted and the weald-wraith fluttered beneath her touch. "*An-Eskatha* were born of the breaking of the three great Elementari," she said slowly, then stopped.

"And the fourth?"

She spun on me with sudden violence, "No! We Mauntells might not know much of the outside world, but we know better than to speak of that. Do not mention these creatures again."

I opened my mouth, but Alastair put his hand on my shoulder. Anger swelled inside me, not at him, but at the answers that Frega dangled before us, only to snatch them away at the last second. We'd come too far for that. "You say the weald-wraiths aren't ghosts," I said, "yet they healed your grandson's wound like a ghost. How do you expect us to believe you?"

Frega snorted. "Because our wraiths demand neither hearts nor heartstones for their protection, girl. They asked nothing of us except that we guard the trees that keep them alive. It is a fair exchange." She moved to the door. "I am keeping you from your rest, Daireds. Good evening."

"Madam Mauntell, wait."

Alastair caught her arm as she raised the door-pelt, then dropped it just as quickly as the weald-wraith leapt from the tree, its snarling shadow form diving between him and Frega. He fell back with a cry. From beyond the door Akarra growled.

"Khela?"

"Do not harm me and it will not harm you," Frega said, watching as the wraith took on a wolf-like form and stalked closer to Alastair, its tail drawn out long and thin to keep it tethered to the tree.

"Khela!"

Alastair spoke to Akarra in Eth and her growling subsided. The wraith stopped and looked to Frega. She made a motion with her hand and it retreated, its shadow-stuff spooling like black wool back into the tree.

"Well?" Frega said with a raised eyebrow.

"You said the wraiths don't demand your heartstones," Alastair said after he was sure the weald-wraith was gone. "What did you mean by that?"

What anger had filled her expression at the mention of ghasts drained away, replaced by surprise. She looked from Alastair to me. "You don't know? You understand, of course, the nature of heartstones."

"They're gems," I said, "formed from the last drop of lifeblood—"

Frega laughed. "*A drop of lifeblood?* Is that what the holy scholars of your kingdom have taught you? A tale fit for children, that. A heartstone forms from the last drop of blood, yes, but they are so much more than pretty trinkets. They are the gift of the gods to all living beings: all the beauty, all the pain, all the little hatreds and loves of a life condensed into a gem, faceted like the Godself and given to remind us of our mortality."

Unconsciously I felt the outline of the heartstone brooch on my shoulder, pinned beneath layers of linen and leather. "Why would the weald-wraiths want heartstones?"

"They do *not* want them!" she growled. "Can't you understand? To steal the gods' gift, to consume it and corrupt it while its host still lives, to trap a soul within a broken cage and refuse them entry to the Fourfold Halls . . ." She shuddered. "The weald-wraiths would not dare do something so vile. I have already told you they are not ghasts. The trees sustain them, my family protects them, and they are content." There was the sound of raised voices from outside the hut. "That is enough for now. If you'll excuse me," Frega said, and swept out.

"*Khela*, Aliza, come!" Akarra said.

It was nearly dark outside. Cooking fires pricked the shadows around which the Mauntells moved with an air of agitation. "What's going on?" Alastair asked.

"The smell. I remembered," Akarra said, her voice low and urgent. She pointed with one wingtip toward the thickest knot of Mauntells, which grew louder and angrier and closer by the second. "And she remembers us."

Johanna Mauntell walked through the crowd with head held high, ignoring her family's jeers and curses in both Arlean and a guttural tongue I didn't recognize. She stopped suddenly when she caught sight of Akarra.

"Grandmother?" Johanna's voice rang out clear and hard through the grove, leaving silence in its wake.

Frega stepped forward. "Is your penance served, prodigal?" she asked.

"I have paid what was owed."

"Let me see."

Johanna removed the wolf pelt she wore over her shoulders, turning so her back was just visible. There, dark red against her white skin, were fresh wounds, branching out from the scarred sigil of the Bleeding Tree carved into her back. Frega nodded.

"Blood for blood, child. It is well. You are free to leave."

Johanna shrugged her furs back on and turned to us. "What are they doing here, Grandmother?"

"They are not your concern. Go now."

Johanna spat. Various cries and snarls rose from the crowd behind her. "You have given them shelter, haven't you?" she said. "Grandmother, don't you know what follows them? Don't you know who they are?"

"They are guests. Now—"

"They are not your guests!" Johanna cried, and let out a torrent of words in her family tongue.

The snarls melted into gasps, then died away altogether. Slowly, one by one, the Mauntells turned to look at us. Inky stains writhed on nearby tree trunks and dry leaves fell around us with a rustle. More than one hand started for a weapon as Johanna went on.

"Aliza," Alastair whispered without taking his eyes from the Mauntells, "get on Akarra's back."

I swung up and he followed, moving with a dreadful deliberateness, palms raised in a desperate show of the good faith I could feel drying up all around us. A growl started deep in Akarra's throat as the Mauntells pressed closer to Frega and Johanna. I tightened my grip around Alastair's waist. He was as taut as a bowstring, every muscle trembling with the need to run balanced against the hopelessness of it. We were backed against the wall of the hut, with armed Mauntells surrounding us on every side and the living cage of branches overhead, so retreat was impossible.

Johanna stopped suddenly, her shoulders heaving. "Darkness hunts them, darkness and ancient hatred. Can't you feel it? They will bring down on your heads everything you fear," she said in Arlean. "You must send them away!"

"They have the guest-right—" Frega tried faintly, but Johanna cut her off with a violent gesture.

"*They are not your guests!* Grandmother, they are your *doom*," she said, and added a word in Mauntell.

Frega whirled on us and drew her greatsword. "You! You lied!" she cried.

"Madam Mauntell—"

"I will not hear it! You deceived me, dragonrider. You are cursed, Daireds, you and all your blood. Get out of our woods and never return! *Go!*" She stepped forward. "GO!"

Akarra roared, tucked her wings to her sides, and ran.

CHAPTER 4

AN-EDANNATHAIR

I couldn't tell how long she ran. Minutes or ages later, she slowed in a hollow beneath the canopy of four great trees, panting and blowing out jets of steam and smoke. Alastair slouched in the saddle. His face was pale, his breathing noisy. My hands wouldn't stop shaking as I watched the shadows. Was it my imagination, or were those wraiths slinking out from the trees?

"Can't stop here long," Akarra said. "Have to . . . keep going."

"Just a minute," Alastair said. "Catch your breath."

The trees around us rustled. A few leaves drifted down.

"Alastair, we need to go," I said.

A twig snapped behind us. Akarra spun around with a roar, neck arched and mouth open, but no dragonfire came. A few sparks fell sizzling onto the leaves, then a rush of hot air, then nothing.

"You waste your strength, dragon," Johanna said as she stepped into the clearing. The shadows receded a little. "You've burned it all up."

"Johanna?" I said. "Are you following us?"

"Didn't have to, fool. You've been going in circles. Another minute and you would have been back in the Grove . . . *if* the wraiths let you get that far."

"Why?"

"Shh!" She tilted her head and put one hand on her sword, facing the darkness with bared teeth. "*Listen*, little bird! They're coming."

Wood creaked all around us. More leaves fell. The heartbeats within the trunks quickened.

"I am of the blood of Old Maun!" Johanna cried. She touched her back and raised a bloody hand toward the shadows. "I have not harmed you or your trees, and by your oath to my family you must let us pass."

The darkness around us congealed, pouring from the stained tree trunks like tar. The air went very still, thick like the shadows and hard to breathe. Slowly the darkness took form: three feature-less human-shaped figures, each tethered to their own tree by a thread of absolute black. One was about my size, clearly a wom-an's silhouette, but the other two were smaller, childlike. Johanna shrank from them until she was nearly touching Akarra, but she did not lower her hand.

"You know who I am, then."

The largest wraith dropped to one knee and reached out to the taller of the two smaller shadows, miming a gentle gesture, tuck-ing the child's hair behind one ear. The shadow-child cocked its head. A dark shard appeared in its hand.

The strike was soundless, but I heard it in my mind. Alastair winced as the shadow-child struck again, burying the nonexistent blade deep in the heart of the wraith-woman while the smallest shadow looked on. Johanna's hand faltered.

"You don't need to—" but the figures did not let her finish. The wraith-woman sank to the forest floor, dissolving into a puddle of darkness, which the older child watched with interest. It gestured the smaller shadow to its side as if to share in its discovery, but the second child was already reaching for the knife.

Johanna turned away.

"I did justice," she said quietly. "I did justice and I have served my penance. I serve it still. My offense was not against your kind."

The smallest shadow strode over its fallen sister and stood in front of Johanna. Cautiously, hesitantly, it stretched out one hand and touched her bloodstained fingertips. Johanna shuddered and closed her eyes, but what she could not see Alastair and I did. The wounds on her back closed over, leaving only reddish scars that looked weeks old instead of hours.

All at once the wraiths drew back, their tethers recoiling into the trees. Johanna's shoulders sagged. "Come." Her voice sounded faint and far away. "They'll let us pass, but we must hurry. You cannot be here when the sun sets."

She darted into the woods on our right. We followed. There was no more discussion, no debate. Treachery would hardly be worse than lingering here, and we were too tired to argue. Johanna ran ahead of us, her Rider's plait streaming out behind her like the lash of a whip. Trees rushed by on either side of us, an endless stretch of shadow-streaked trunks and breathing darkness and ancient creatures with long and terrible memories. Johanna never faltered, never lost her footing. She ran, and Akarra ran, and the world narrowed until there was only panting dragon and rustling leaves and the ache in my knees and calves and the chafe of saddle and the endless, endless trees.

The pale colonnade blurred. A snowflake stung my face, then another. I blinked away the pinprick of cold before thought at last caught up and I realized the ground was growing white around us. It was lighter too. Here and there streaks of green rushed by, tossed and shivering in the wind that blew down from the mountains. And then, gloriously, the sound of water.

Johanna didn't slacken her pace. She charged toward the gurgling and vanished with a loud splash. Akarra drew up hard, throwing out her wings for balance as she backed away from the crumbling edge of the embankment.

"You wanted the world beyond the Wood." Johanna's voice drifted up from the river below, where she stood knee-deep in the shallows. Beyond her the water of the Rushless flowed in a sluggish, snow-choked ribbon. Shards of ice sloshed against her bare legs. Across the river the land rose again, much rockier than on the eastern bank, and there were hardly any trees. I nearly wept with joy to see the first slopes of the Dragonsmoor Mountains marching toward the clouded sky just a few miles away. "Here it is, dragon, dragonrider. Little bird, your sky beckons. Farewell." She turned toward the trees.

"Johanna, wait." I slid from the saddle, found my legs had turned traitor, and caught Akarra's wing for support. "What happened back there?"

"You have eyes," she said. "You saw what happened."

"You killed someone, didn't you?" Alastair said.

Johanna clambered out of the water without looking at us. "A long time ago."

"Who was it?"

"Why do you care?"

"Because you just saved our lives," I said.

"Save you? You think I *saved* you?" Johanna laughed. "Oh, little bird, don't you understand? I saved my family *from* you! All I have done, all I have ever done, even when I was a child, was to protect them. You wish to know why I was banished, why my family will not speak my name?" She nodded to the trees. "My sister met a trader at the edge of the Wood in her fifteenth winter. He told her of your Arlean traditions, of what it meant to wear another's heart-stone, and she wanted one of her own. Oldkind are thin within the Wood, so that night she stole Grandmother's bone knife, drew our mother to a place far from the wraith-trees, and stabbed her through the heart." She held out her bloodied hand with a bitter grimace. "Just so she could see what a heartstone looked like."

"Oh gods," I muttered. "Johanna, I'm sorry."

"Your sorrow does no good, and neither did your gods. They did not stop my sister." She faced us. There was a hard, proud light in her eyes, as blue and icy as the river. "I avenged my mother, and it is for that that Grandmother Frega sent me from the Wood."

Alastair dismounted. "You protect the people who banished you, who carve their sigil into your flesh?"

"They are my family," she said simply.

For a moment they stared at each other, two warriors from different worlds, and I heard in that silence the true language of the Riders, shared, as it always was, without words: the language of blood, of loyalty and vengeance. *No, not vengeance*, I thought. *Justice.*

"What did you tell them?" Akarra asked, and the moment broke. Alastair swung back into the saddle and helped me up. "Back in the grove. You say you were protecting them, but what were you protecting them *from*? Ancient darkness, you said—"

Johanna whirled around, sword drawn. "Do not speak of it! There is evil tied to the bloodline of the dragonriders—old evil, older than you know. I felt it the first time I saw you three in the Marshes. Shadows chase you, shadows with stolen faces nursed on ancient hatred, the servants of the Fourth. The circle is bro-ken, and I must hide and you must run, faster and farther than you've ever run before if you wish to escape it. Now go!" She sheathed her sword and sprang onto the bank. "We won't see each other again," she said, and disappeared beneath the shadows of the trees.

NO ONE SPOKE AS AKARRA NAVIGATED THE RIVER crossing. After the stillness of the Wood, the wind along the Rushless bit like a living thing. It caught her wings as she dipped toward the river and her tail grazed the surface of the water as she steadied herself, sending up an icy spray that had Alastair and me dripping before we landed safely on the opposite side. A cloud, invisible and intangible but no less weighty, stayed behind on the other bank, with the weald-wraiths and their fearsome guardians. I drank the air in great gasps like an infant first finding their lungs. Alastair slipped out of the saddle and touched four fingers to the earth. "*Shai shurran'a An Tyrekel*," he said softly before helping me down.

"Thank Mikla indeed," Akarra said. "The Drakaina herself couldn't order me to go back through those woods."

"What did Johanna mean, Akarra?" he asked. "What evil is tied to our bloodline?"

"I've no idea."

I tried to remember everything Johanna had said to me at Widdermere Marsh Hall. *Madness, and such ancient hate*, she'd said of what we brought, but she couldn't have known about Wydrick. *Or could she?* Was that the evil that followed us?

A cold gust swept down from the foothills, carrying with it the remains of the storm in stray snowflakes and the memory of frostbite. I scanned the sky. The clouds were flat, dark, and heavy. It was early evening by the light, but nights came on quickly on the open moors and I guessed we had only one, maybe two more hours of daylight. I shaded my eyes and looked toward the slopes of the mountains. The blizzard had dusted the landscape with snow, drifting across the swells and hollows of the moorlands before us and making distance difficult to judge. "That second peak is An-Edannathair," Akarra said.

"The Vehryshi will need to know what we've seen," Alastair added.

Akarra's wings fluttered at her side.

"You don't think we should tell them?"

"It's not that," she said. "If Arle is in danger, then they must be told, but *khela*, I know my people. I heard your conversation in the hut, and while I don't like it, Frega was right about dragonkind. These *An-Eskatha* creatures, the Vehryshi have kept no records of them. They may not believe us. The *ghastradi* have not been seen in Arle for centuries, after all."

"They'll believe us." Alastair tightened his scabbard in its harness across his back and helped me to my feet. "They must."

I looked up at the peak Akarra had indicated. The foothills weren't far, but the summit was lost in clouds. "How far is it to Pendragon from here?"

"Two days. Maybe two and a half, depending on the wind. The gusts turn treacherous this side of the peaks. It'll be difficult going as it is."

It was a foolish hope anyway. If we were to face the mountains, I'd at least not let us go on empty stomachs. A fleeting smile touched Alastair's lips as I broke the last stale slice of bread and with a look of loathing handed it to him.

"I feel the same," he said.

"Tell me Madam Gretna doesn't keep any bardsbread in the larder at Pendragon," I said. "I never want to see another piece as long as I live."

"Consider it banished."

Akarra inhaled the rest of the smoked fish. We took turns sharing the waterskins, and once we finished, I filled the empty skins with snow and hung them beneath the saddle flaps to melt as we flew. The meal hadn't touched the yawning hunger in the pit of my stomach, merely outlined it, calling attention to how large it really was, but it was better than nothing. The knotted ache that had been growing in the back of my head for the last few hours began to unravel. That we'd now consumed the last of our stores was a fact I tried to ignore. *Food, warmth, rest. It's all waiting right up there,* I thought. *Just make it up the mountain.*

THE DRAGONSMOOR MOUNTAINS WERE TALLER THAN they looked.

"How long—do you think—to the peak?" I managed, squinting against the reflected light from the snow below. Even under overcast skies it hurt to look down, and I cringed to think what it would've been like in full sun. My knees and thighs ached from gripping the saddle and I was starting to lose feeling in my fingers again. Before us the mountains rose to the very roof of the world, already growing violet with the evening.

"Half an hour if the wind holds," Alastair said. His breath was warm against my ear. Since the snow had stopped, he'd consented to sit behind me, though I soon realized it was less of a concession and more of an attempt to keep me firmly in the saddle. Akarra hadn't exaggerated; the winds here were unpredictable, and they snatched at us each time she banked. I was glad of his arms around my waist.

"Twice that," Akarra said. Her voice was thin and strained. She didn't try to speak again.

Slopes of icy scree passed beneath us. A few tenacious pines clung to the higher crags, but they grew thinner and farther between the higher we flew, until we passed the tree line altogether and the world faded into shades of gray and white. We flew in silence, filled only by the sound of Akarra's laboring wings and the rush of wind and the frosty rattle of Alastair's breath in my ears.

After a few minutes he leaned close again. "How's your nose?"

I checked. "No blood yet."

"We'll have to—"

An updraft caught Akarra on her downstroke, and I cried out as the world slid sideways. Her wings beat the air madly. We dropped, were flung back, and were driven upward before a sudden gust.

"Akarra, *reqet!*" Alastair shouted.

The saddle shifted. Tears stung my eyes as the wind tore at us, tossing Akarra between updrafts like a cat batting a moth. Up became down and down became blinding white and unforgiving blue and the steel-gray of stone. I grabbed Akarra's shoulder spikes. The saddle slipped another inch.

"Don't let go!" Alastair bellowed. "Whatever you—"

There was a jerk. His words trailed off into a scream that cut me to the bone.

"ALASTAIR!"

I flung myself after him, reaching for leather, for bearskin, for anything. My hand found the edge of his cloak and I held on as if the life of the whole world depended on it. With a jerk that nearly tore my shoulder out of its socket, he stopped falling.

"Akarra!" I screamed. "Land *now!*"

A shadow fell across her back.

"*Let go!*" a new voice said, deep and rolling as thunder. The saddle twisted beneath me and I saw wings and scales and tongues of fire burning away the clouds. Alastair shouted something, but another gust of wind swept the words away. New pain pierced my shoulder and my strength gave out as the saddle tore from my grasp. We fell.

"Alast—*ow*!"

Something hard dug into my ribs, driving the breath clean from my lungs as it arrested my fall. Half blinded by the wind, I felt around to see what had caught me. *Scales?* Scales and talons and . . .

"Aliza? You—all right?"

I swung toward the sound of Alastair's voice and my heart nearly burst with relief. He hung a few feet away, looking equally relieved, though it was difficult to make out his exact expression. The strange dragon had caught him upside down.

"Mind your Riders, *kes-ahla*!" that voice boomed again. "I'll not have you dropping them on our doorstep."

I looked up. Iron-gray scales gouged with many years of battle scars blocked the sun. The dragon peered down at us. His eyes burned pale blue, the color of marshfires.

"Well now, *two* Daireds! Lykasha!" he cried, and a smaller bronze dragon dipped out of the clouds to our left. "Fly ahead and tell the Vehryshi to assemble." The bronze dragon disappeared. "I assume that's who you're here to see, young Daireds," he said, "unless this is just an honorary visit?"

Akarra answered in Eth. Her voice was distant, tired. She struggled to keep up. The older dragon made a conciliatory sound in his throat that rumbled in all my bones.

"We'll have you sorted soon," the dragon said in Arlean. "Hold on now, and *kes-ahla, quret*!" A single upstroke sent the ground spinning into nothingness below us. The wind screamed in my ears and frost crystallized on my eyelashes. There was warmth beneath the dragon's scales but none in his talons, which held my arms pinned to my side. I squirmed, trying to free a hand. "None of that now, little one!" the dragon boomed. "We'll be there soon."

I gave up and slumped over his claw. Wind whipped ice-sharpened strands of hair into my face, my eyes, my mouth, and I tasted sweat and blood—*blood? Oh, blast.* Of course the nosebleed would wait until now. I closed my eyes. We'd be there soon and this would all be worth it. *Food. Warm beds. Solid ground. Food. Warm beds. Solid ground. Food—*

Burning golden sunlight pierced my eyelids. "Ah! Here we are." The light dimmed and the wingbeats on either side of me ceased. There was a bump, a bit of grunting, and the claws loosened. I felt warm stone beneath me. "There."

I opened my eyes. I lay facedown next to Alastair on the floor of an enormous cavern. Firelight danced across the uncut stone in front of us. I squinted over my shoulder to see Akarra land at the lip of the cavern, her silhouette black and weary against the darkening blue of the sky beyond. She hurried forward and touched Alastair with her snout.

"*Khela,* are you all right?" she asked. "And you, Aliza? I didn't mean . . . the wind caught me by surprise. I thought—Aliza, you're bleeding!"

"S'nothing," I said, and dabbed at my nose with my last swatch of clean sleeve, of which there was little, then none. "It'll pass."

"No thanks to you, *kes-ahla,*" the scarred dragon growled, and Akarra shrank into herself. With her head bowed and wings tucked to her side, she looked like a kitten caught in the reproving glare of a great hunting hound. "You should know better than to attempt an ascent like that when the *Tanar-Al'eketh* is blowing!"

Alastair went forward and bowed to the older dragon. "We didn't have a choice. *Shurraneth shan,* my name is—"

"Alastair, son of Erran, son of Seraphina, heir of House Daired. Of course we know who you are," another voice said. "Stand aside, Tanar, and let me see them."

The sentinel drew back and a female dragon came forward, crested and crowned with an iron circlet. Her scales were dark, almost black, but in the torchlight they glittered midnight-blue and her eyes were the same fire-opal color as Akarra's. Other dragons flanked her, more than I'd ever seen before, all straining to see us over one another's shoulders and whispering among themselves in Eth. I felt very small.

Akarra bowed with her wings over her head. "Vehrys Neheema," she said. "*Shurraneth shan.*"

"Well met, little daughter. And you, Lord Alastair, and your lady—my fire, have you been in a battle?"

I curtsied, wobbled, and straightened, still scrubbing at my chin and cheeks. "No, just the mountains. Aliza Daired, your, um . . ." I trailed off, my mind suddenly blank of the proper address. This dragon was not the Drakaina, and I knew no other dragon honorifics. *Madam* didn't seem to fit and she was certainly no lady. *Shurraneth,* Alastair and Akarra had said. That stirred a distant memory. "Your Honor," I tried.

"I am *Ahla-Na-Katar-Lys-te'an Neheema,* She-Who-Brings-Light-to-the-Dark, Chief Keeper of the Sacred Hearth," the crowned dragon said. "Vehrys Neheema, you may call me. But Tanar, for shame! Can you not see our friends are at the end of their strength?"

"Forgive me, Vehrys Neheema, but Akarra had not—"

"There'll be time enough for scolding later, if a scolding must be had." Neheema raised her wings. "Attend me, dragonets! Bring roast meat and water to the Daired chambers." There was a stirring deeper in the cavern and a handful of smaller dragons appeared. "Tanar, return to your guard. Akarra, come. I will speak to you as you eat."

Tanar rumbled his reply and retreated to the mouth of the cavern. Akarra headed after Neheema with a meaningful look in our direction.

"Is she in trouble?" I asked Alastair when they'd gone.

"Not once she tells Neheema what we've seen." He looked around. "Shield and Circle, *khera*, I didn't imagine the Hearth would look like this."

"You've never been here before?"

He shook his head. "Daireds rarely visit. My grandmother did once and Aunt Catriona might have come with Herreki, but I've only heard stories. I've always wanted to see it."

Out of the glare of the setting sun, my eyes had begun to adjust. What I'd thought were mere shadows took on architectural depths. Pillars rose from floor to ceiling all around, carved in the silhouettes of dragons and leaping flames. The source of the firelight came from deeper in the cavern, a bright circular glow roaring beyond the largest of the pillars, but it was too far away to make out the details. Everywhere there was a sense of *immensity*. Not just in space, but in years as well. The very shadows felt heavy with the weight of centuries.

"It *is* beautiful," I whispered, "but right now I wouldn't care if it was a hole in the rock with a dirt floor and a gargoyle infestation. Just as long as there's food."

"Ask nicely and you may get a hot bath too," he said, grinning that dimpled grin I'd missed so much. I hadn't seen it since the Morianton midwife had delivered her fatal news. "Maybe even a real bed."

"All right, we ask nicely. But whatever happens, food first."

"My lord Daired?" One of the smallest dragonets came forward.

She was about the size of a draft horse, watery silver with beautiful golden eyes and a strong Eth accent. She dipped her head almost to the ground. "And lady. Come please. I will take you to the quarters of the Daireds."

She led us in the opposite direction from where Akarra and Neheema had gone, watched carefully by the rest of what Alastair had called the Vehryshi. The main cavern branched into dozens of smaller tunnels, though smaller meant that they were only several stories above our heads instead of dozens. The smell of dragonfire was strong here, sharper than it was at House Pendragon, wilder and more metallic. It sent the hairs on the back of my neck prickling. Our guide walked with her wings bent out a little at her sides, wingtips nearly touching in front of her. She said nothing as we walked.

"What's your name?" I asked after a few minutes, keen to take my mind off the disappointment as each turning failed to reveal any human-sized rooms or, more distressingly, any sign of food.

She jumped. "My name?"

"Er, yes."

"You wish to know my name?" she asked.

"Is that allowed?"

"I—oh, yes. Of course," she said. "*Ahla-Na-al Hsetek-an-Sanar,* my lady. She-Who-Rides-the-East-Wind."

"Sanar? Like Niaveth Daired's dragon?"

"My Nestmother named me for her honor, yes," she said. Her wings rose a little.

It made sense that the lone dragon in Arle's greatest epic would hold a place of honor among the dragons of An-Edannathair, but this namesake still intrigued me. Here above the clouds, in halls of living stone lit by wild dragonfire, even the tragedy of Marten,

Princess Ellia, and Niaveth Daired seemed somehow small and unimportant. Apparently, however, the dragons remembered the tale as well as we did. I thought of the steward Mòrag's recitation on Martenmas. The chilly shadows of Castle Selwyn seemed ages ago, but I couldn't forget her unflattering description of House Daired. She'd spoken of greed and corruption, of the blood of the Fireborn watered down in the generations between Edan and Niaveth, who had pledged her sword to protect the princess in her great task: winning over the Oldkind of Arle to an alliance with humans, as Niaveth's ancestor had once done with dragonkind. As the song had it, it was in the service of the princess that Niaveth's dragon Sanar was slain. A tragic end, but a noble one. No wonder the Nestmothers christened their dragonets in her honor.

Sanar stopped at the end of a long corridor. There was no door, just an archway into darkness. "Here are the quarters of the Daireds," she said, and breathed a column of dragonfire to the right of the arch. "We keep it in readiness for times of such visiting."

Flames rolled down the oil-filled channel along the top of the walls, filling the room with golden light. The pile of ancient and dusty furs, the ewer basin full of steaming water, and the little table laid with roast wild goat seemed in that moment a glimpse into heaven itself.

"Eat and rest," Sanar said. "Someone will come to summon you when the Vehryshi have made ready."

Alastair thanked her in Eth and she bowed again before leaving us alone.

We were at the food before the sound of her footsteps faded. The meat was blackened, stringy, and the best thing I'd ever tasted. The ache inside me shrank with each bite. Neither of us felt the inclination to talk. We ate, drank, shed our armor, and splashed clean in silence, the warmth and wonder of our surroundings soothing my exhausted muscles as well as any bath. I collapsed onto the furs next to Alastair with just enough consciousness left to appreciate the fact that we *had* human bedding, though I wouldn't have minded if we had boulders for a headboard and a stone for a pillow. I was asleep in seconds.

CHAPTER 5

HE-WHOSE-BREATH-IGNITES-THE-MORNINGSTAR

I woke in the exact same position I'd fallen asleep. There was no window and no way to tell how long we'd slept, but by the stiffness in my limbs and the crick in my neck I guessed the better part of a day. The quiet flames burning in the channel cast the highest part of the ceiling into shadow. I rolled over, wincing at newly discovered bruises on my shoulder. Unsurprisingly Alastair was already up, and looked as though he had been for a while. He'd washed, dressed, and rebraided his Rider's plait, and now sat atop the pile of furs with his axe on his knee.

"Morning," I muttered, "or whatever it is."

"Evening." Carefully, with an eye to something I could neither see nor feel, he ran a whetstone along the edge of the blade. The air trembled with the silvery *ting*. "The dragonets brought dinner," he said, and he sighted down the blade in the direction of the door. A stone tray piled with more charred meat sat next to the arch. "Neheema and the others will be ready for us soon."

I got up and splashed my face in the ewer basin. The water was the same temperature as the air: warm, almost too warm, and still as dust. Compared to having our faces scoured off in a blizzard it was delightful, of course, but also a trifle stifling.

"What will they do, do you think?" I asked as I set into the meat. "The Vehryshi." Visions of a fiery phalanx of dragons filled my head, raining down wrath on the enemies of Arle. Even the *ghastradi* would quake in the face of such formidable allies.

"I don't know. They have to decide if they're going to help first."

I looked at him over a blackened goat leg. "*If?* What do you mean, if? Isn't that why we're here?"

"We're here to ask for help."

I set the meat down. "You think they'll refuse?"

"I think we'll have to make an excellent case. Akarra may have been right to doubt them."

"But, Alastair, I don't understand. Why wouldn't they help us? Even if they don't believe everything about the *ghastradi*, they know your family. I mean, they're *dragons*, for Thell's sake! They're already our allies." A new and terrible thought seized me. "Aren't they?"

"These are dragons of the mountains, Aliza, not Daired dragons," he answered after a moment. "They honor my family and abstain from hunting humans and other *Shani* out of respect for Edan's legacy, but they are not sworn to anyone." He bent his head and continued sharpening his axe.

The weight of his words filled me like lead, and I felt again as I had when I'd slipped out of Akarra's saddle: the warm solidity of certainty torn from underneath me, leaving only the terror of the fall. If war was coming and our friends were no longer our friends, what chance did we have? I groped around for a new subject, any subject, to take away from the horror of that idea.

"How's your shoulder?" I asked.

"It's fine."

"Are you sure?"

"I can manage," he said.

"Thou won't be able to for long, young master, if thou continuest that *wretched* noise!"

I nearly upended the water basin in surprise. Alastair leapt to his feet. "Who said that?" he demanded.

"One who will tear thine arms from thy sockets if thou insistest on such racket!"

The sound of grinding stone and a trickle of dust drifted down from the shadows overhead, and something crawled out into the light. No, not crawled; it *waded* through the stone like a swimmer through shallow water. A head appeared just above the archway, a grinning, malformed head with goblin ears and a nose like a bat's. Its eyes burned like live coals.

"As I thought," the gargoyle said. "Wastrel youth! No respect for the repose of thine elders. And very ill dressed too." It extended an arm, all knobs and sinews of stone, and pointed to Alastair with a claw that sparkled like diamond in the firelight. "Mark my words, thou—"

"Mephistrophomorphinite Ignaat, what do you do here?"

The gargoyle leaned down to see Sanar standing in the corridor, her wingtips crossed above her head as a human might cross her arms. "Er, Friend Sanar," the gargoyle tried, "I was—wast—just—"

"None of your excuses. Out!"

"But they have—hast—no manners!"

"*You* have no manners. *They* are honored guests of Vehrys Neheema. Bother hatchlings if you must. They need always a sharp tongue."

The gargoyle grumbled and slid back into the wall. Alastair slipped the axe back into his belt.

"Out," Sanar said. "All the way! The Vehryshi will not stand again for your eavesdropping!" A shiver of dust fell from the archway and the grinding sound faded. She sighed. "Deepest apologies, my lord, my lady. Ignaat is—how do you say—*yeksha,* something of a relic. He is old and harmless. Pay him no mind. Now, Lord Daired, you are ready? Vehrys Neheema wishes to speak with you."

Lord Daired? My heart sank, then rose again at Alastair's touch on my arm. "We're both ready," he said.

Sanar blinked. "My lord? I don't know—"

"Lead the way, *kes-ahla,*" he said firmly, and I smiled.

To her credit, Sanar did not protest, ushering us instead out into the corridor. I kept one eye to the walls, expecting grinning faces and diamond claws to leap out at any second, but the gargoyle did not make a reappearance. That sense of immensity pressed down on me again as we passed into the main chamber and the ceilings soared overhead, now invisible in the dark. Stars like points of ice pricked the sky beyond the mouth of the cave and a cold wind stirred the air, fresh but frigid. From all around came the rustling sound of wings and whispers. Dozens of dragons had already gathered around the central fire and more were coming from other doors around the chamber. Akarra stood at Neheema's side. Her eyes were bright and her wings no longer drooped. Neheema raised her head when she saw us. The whispering stopped, and I felt a sudden wave of unease. Dozens of eyes reflected the glow of the fire, their stares piercing me like hot coals, and I wondered if I'd been right to come after all.

After a pause, Neheema came forward and greeted us in Eth. My cheeks burned as I curtsied. "I'm sorry, Vehrys Neheema. I don't speak much Eth."

"Ah. Well then, welcome to the Council of the Vehryshi. I trust you are both recovered from your ordeal?"

"Thank you, yes," Alastair said.

"Sit."

There was a stone slab on the opposite side of the fire pit. The fire had been banked for the night, but the heat was still intense enough to warrant strategic sitting to avoid singed eyebrows.

"Akarra tells me quite the tale," Neheema said. "It seems you've come to us the long way around. It has been a hard road."

"It has, Vehrys Neheema," Alastair said. "Not one we'd wish to dwell on."

"Tell me, what do you make of this thing you saw, this ghast-spirit that rode the body of the Ranger Tristan Wydrick?"

Alastair's jaw tightened. "I thought I'd killed him, but it turns out he'd already sold himself to one of those creatures."

"Was this before or after he crippled *Ah-Na-al Hon-she'an-Mar'esh?*" another dragon asked with a hint of a growl.

"I don't know for certain," Alastair said, "but it must have been after, when he fled Arle. I'm sure the Drakaina has told you of the years my family spent searching for him."

"And found nothing, yes," Neheema said. "You believe he left the kingdom and sought out this ghast-creature, then."

"Or it sought him," I added.

"Nevertheless, he returned possessing the half-life of a *ghastradi*. But for what purpose?" she asked.

"He—or it, I'm not sure which—warned us of war, something of which the Battle of North Fields was only a foretaste," Alastair said.

The dragon to the left of Neheema interjected in Eth, but Neheema stopped him. "Speak the human tongue, Vehrys Rheshek, for Lady Daired's sake."

Again my cheeks burned, more fiercely this time.

"This ghast-creature spoke lies," the dragon Rheshek said. "The Worm is dead. Its *Tekari* following have scattered."

"There is scattering, *shan'ei*, and there is regrouping," Akarra said quietly. Rheshek grunted and flicked his tail.

"If ghasts are rising in Arle again, the war cannot be over," Alastair said.

"What do you propose, Lord Daired?" Neheema asked.

"The king must be told."

"Told what?"

"What we have seen. And the Ranger-*ghastradi* must be found and made to tell us what he knows. We cannot be caught unawares again," Alastair said. "Arle's defenders must be ready. The Riders, the Free Regiments, the army, everyone must prepare for—"

"For something you cannot describe, moving against the kingdom you know not when, attacking you know not where," another dragon said. "You come with vague warnings from untrustworthy messengers, Lord Daired. This is no threat; this is speculation and hearsay."

"You don't believe us?" Alastair asked.

"We do," Neheema said before the other dragons could answer. "We do, my friend. There is truth in your face and Akarra does not lie. Whatever you saw in the Marshes and Lake Meera is certainly an enemy of the kingdom, but he is only one man."

"He's not a man anymore."

"Nevertheless, he is but one. You cannot expect the king to raise all Arle's defenses against a single creature, horrible as it may be."

"He wasn't alone," I said. Dozens of searing eyes turned to me. I swallowed and stood. "Vehrys Neheema, Wydrick wasn't the first *ghastradi* we saw, and he wasn't the only one to warn us. There was a man in Hatch Ford who spoke of war too. He said the Oldkind know something, that they've sensed what's coming for several years at least. He said it was something powerful enough to wake both Greater and Lesser Lindworms." I glanced at Alastair, who nodded encouragement. "We think it might be one of the . . . *An-Eskatha?*"

There were murmurs in Eth as the dragons tasted the word. Neheema frowned. "*The Eldest?* What do you mean by this, Lady Daired?"

"It was something we heard when we passed through Rushless Wood," Akarra explained. "Family Mauntell told us of creatures older than the Oldkind, powerful creatures they called the Eldest. One of them may be behind the *ghastradi.*"

"But surely we would know of such a power," a female dragon said, "if it existed. We have never heard of such a thing."

"Did either of the *ghastradi* you encountered name their master or hint at its intentions beyond war?" Neheema asked.

I could feel the heaviness in the intervening silence, could feel Alastair's reluctance like a buckler fending off the arrow-tipped suspicions of the Vehryshi. "No," he said at last.

"Then we remain at an impasse. You do not know, and we do not know, and there is no way to discover what threatens the kingdom save the word of this Wydrick. Do—"

"A moment, Vehrys."

Neheema drew back as an older dragon with faded gold scales walked into the circle of firelight. Akarra's wings twitched at her sides. There was a small, sharp sound from Alastair, as if he'd suddenly had the wind knocked out of him. Without any conscious effort, my hand found his as the old dragon fixed his eyes on us. They might have once been violet, but now they were clouded by age. Nevertheless, something about him seemed familiar.

"*Ghastradi* or not, this *Ranger,*" he growled the word, "became an enemy of House Daired the moment he maimed your sister's dragon. Even if he does know what you think he knows, Lord Alastair, why would Wydrick warn *you?*"

Alastair's throat worked up and down. No words came out.

The old dragon narrowed his eyes. "You do not know."

Alastair shook his head.

"Vehrys Kaheset is right," Rheshek said. "Might this not have been mere idle boasting, young man?"

The cool, dismissive tone in which they both spoke set my blood seething and my teeth on edge, and I forgot my embarrassment. We'd passed through storm and hunger and undead horrors to get here, and no dragon, no matter how high-ranking, was going to speak to Alastair that way.

"Boasting, maybe, but not idle," I said. "The *ghastradi* in Hatch Ford had no reason to taunt us, Vehrys Rheshek. Both he and Wydrick said the same thing."

Rheshek raised a horned eyebrow. "The point remains, Lady Daired. If there was war coming to Arle, why warn the staunchest defenders of the kingdom beforehand?"

"To make us afraid," Alastair said, his jaw tight as he surveyed the Vehryshi around us. The old dragon's gaze alone he avoided. "I see it now. They knew you wouldn't believe it."

Another dragon made a chiding sound in her throat. "Now, Lord Daired, before you accuse us, you must understand the gravity of your claims—"

"I know what I've claimed, Vehrys. War is coming to Arle. When or from what quarter I don't know, but if you're true descendants of the Flamespoken Sire, you'll stand with our people. If you won't," he said, "we'll go find others who will."

Neheema's growl silenced the Vehryshi's cries of protests. "*Shurraneth shani*, fie! Are your scales so thin that mere words pierce them? Lord Daired speaks with courage and candor. We should expect no less from the Blood of the Fireborn." The grumbling faded and she turned back to Alastair. "In short, my lord, you wish us to pledge our fire against this threat."

"Yes."

"That is no light vow you require of us, but we will consider it. Vehryshi, come. We will take counsel in the Inner Hearth. Akarra, attend on us, and you, Lord Daired, as you please." She retreated into the shadows. The other dragons filed after her until the chamber was empty save for the old dragon. He nodded stiffly to Alastair and went back the way he'd come without a word.

Alastair sat on the bench and rubbed his temples.

"Who was that?" I asked.

"My father's dragon."

Those violet eyes. *Of course.* The painting in the family gallery at House Pendragon had shown Lord Erran Daired as a handsome, imposing figure astride a mighty dragon the color of sunset, together daring the world to challenge their claim as masters of House Daired. And now? The crown fashioned from Lord Erran's skull rested on the charred head of the Broodmother Crone of Cloven Cairn and his dragon was a twilit shadow of his former magnificence. I touched Alastair's arm, searching for words and finding none. He covered my hand with his.

"You should go back to our quarters," he said heavily. "I need to be with Akarra."

"You think you can change their minds?"

"No. But we have to try." He stood. "Can you find your way back?"

"Aye."

He kissed my cheek and hurried after the dragons.

It was not only the draft from the mouth of the cavern that

set me shivering in his absence. I drew my collar up and went to the edge. The mountain fell away steeply beyond the threshold, the crags and ridges shining gray and ghostly in the light of the young moon. Clouds like silver horsetails scuttled across fields of stars and my breath hung frosty in the air. It was beautiful, but with a cold and terrible grandeur that left me feeling strangely bereft. Some lingering subconscious hope had been whispering over and over in the back of my mind since the borders of Rushless Wood, though I just now recognized it: *we need only to get to An-Edannathair and all will be well.* That was the true battle, I'd thought. The Vehryshi or the Nestmothers or *some-one* would rally around our cause and sweep from the mountains in a glorious wave of righteous wrath, hunt Wydrick and the other *ghastradi* down and, if war was inevitable, stand shoulder to wingtip with Arle's defenders as we prepared to fight this unnamed terror.

That belief lay shattered now, that hope embittered. *All this way.* We'd come all this way—but no. It wouldn't be for nothing. Alastair and Akarra were fighting their own battle in the Inner Hearth; hopeless or not, I could do no less.

I went in search of Kaheset.

HOW THE ANCIENT DRAGONS HAD CARVED THE LABY-rinth of tunnels through the peak of An-Edannathair was a mystery, but whatever the means, the purpose was clear. They intended for guests to stay where they put them. The alternative was to wander until death at the hands of weariness, starvation, or boredom. Or all three.

I paused at the branching of the fifth identical tunnel to gather my wits and silence the nagging fear that I was lost. *How far could it really be?* I asked for the third time, realizing as I did that I had no idea what "it" was. Some vague, half-formed concept of a dragon's nest had lodged in my brain, some cozy chamber strewn with shed dragon scales and the remains of their last meal, but as yet I'd seen nothing but tunnel, torch-channels, shadows, and rock.

I looked around. The floor was stone, worn smooth by centuries of taloned feet and scaly bellies, and it showed no tracks. The walls too were unmarked. Sight would not help. I closed my eyes. Besides the crackle of the torches and the sound of my own breathing, all was quiet. I opened my eyes and felt the nearest wall. A dragon moving anywhere in the vicinity would surely send vibrations through the stone. Nothing but a distant grinding, and then not even that. Dust slithered down the wall where I'd touched it. *Blast.* I'd have to retrace my steps.

I started back the way I'd come, rehearsing the explanation I'd give to any wandering dragon I happened to meet. *Am I not supposed to be here? My mistake. I must've gotten lost while looking for our chambers and— What's that? Our chambers are on the other side of the Keep? And we're near Vehrys Kaheset's quarters? Fancy that. Well, now that you mention it, could you give me directions?*

I stopped. The grinding fell silent an instant after I did. A little shudder of dust trickled down from the dark overhead.

"Master Gargoyle?"

More dust fell. I folded my arms.

"I know you're there."

Two points of light glowed deep within the wall on my right. "And what's it to *thee* if I am?" a muffled voice said.

"Are you following me?"

"Ha!" The gargoyle sprang from the rock and landed on all fours in front of me. Knobby knees rose higher than his head, giving him the look of a heavyset grasshopper. "Accuse me of *discourtesy*, maiden, hmm? Will, er, *wilt* thou?"

I hid a smile. Relic, was he? I curtsied. "Of course not, Master Gargoyle. I wanted to thank you for your protection."

He peered up at me. Stony ridges drew together over those glowing eyes. "Truly?"

"Truly."

"You speak of protection. Are you—I mean, art thou afraid of danger? Here?"

A little flattery would do no harm, surely. "Not with you keeping a weather eye, sir."

He stood a little straighter.

"In fact, I bet you know all these passages," I tried rather lamely. "I bet you couldn't get lost in here even if you wanted to."

"Indeed. Pray, lady, what is thy name?"

"Aliza Daired."

"*Daired.*" He made a sound in his throat like pebbles in a mortar and pestle and narrowed his eyes. "Bound to that wretched warrior-lord, art thou?"

"He's my husband, yes."

"Hmph. Well, 'tis not the accustomed practice of those belonging to the Honor of Ignaat to rejoice in the plight of the unfortunate. You have my sympathies."

"Alastair's not so bad."

"Then I see thou hast fortitude as well. As it says in the Epic of Eldrunna, *'Tis the great of heart and not of strength who stand under the yoke of adversity.'*" He sniffed. "Hmm. I suppose thou art not half so odious as thy lord. I am Mephistrophomorphinite Ignaat, my lady," he said, and executed a complicated bow, which culminated in the top part of his head disappearing into the floor. "Your humble servant."

"Pleased to meet you. Mepho . . . Mephi . . . Master Ignaat, do you know how to get to Vehrys Kaheset's chambers?"

"I beg pardon?"

"Kaheset. Golden scales, violet eyes."

"The Keeper of Records? For what purpose shouldest thou wish an audience with him?"

"Do you know where he is?"

"Contain thy impatience, Lady Daired. As you said, I know where all things are in the Great Keep. I merely wish to know what makes you imagine he will speak with you. Er, thou."

"Is he an important dragon?"

"Important? Ha! Hermit-like and sullen as stone-grubs at first thaw, but for his service to thy husband's clan, the Keepers do him honor. Rarely have I seen him stray so far from the Hall of Records as he has tonight."

"You were listening to the council?"

"Perhaps." The brightness of his eyes dimmed and he sank a few inches into the floor. "Oh, very well. Yes, I heard. Mere chance, you understand. I was passing by and happened to overhear."

"Naturally."

"In truth I couldn't help it."

"Of course not."

"You won't tell, er, friend Sanar, will you?" he said, in a quite different accent. "Or any of the Vehryshi?"

"Won't breathe a word."

"You have my thanks." He looked over his shoulder and cleared his throat. "In that case, as you are a lady of circumspection, it would be my honor to show you to the Hall of Records. Come. This way."

He set off at a lope along the corridor, sometimes wading in the stone, sometimes walking on top of it. Every turning looked the same to me, but he went forward without hesitation, his diamond claws *click-clacking* on the ground loud enough to disguise the sound of my footsteps.

"Master Ignaat, are there any other gargoyles in the Keep?" I asked.

"Oh no, my lady, not here. There are scattered boulderings in the southern peaks, but they have little commerce with me, nor I with them." He lowered his voice. "Young fools, the lot. Still mired in the sediment of their first century. No respect for their elders. Here we are." He stopped. "Just around that bend."

"Aren't you coming?"

He shifted from claw to claw. "The Hall is most strictly forbidden to me. I, ah, daren't."

"Who's there?" Kaheset's voice boomed out from the passage beyond. "I hear you, Mephistrophomorphinite!"

Ignaat shrank into the floor until only the top of his head was visible.

"Thank you, Master Ignaat," I said. "You're a true gentlegargoyle."

He rose a few inches from the ground. "I am?"

"The best I've ever met."

There was a thud of heavy footsteps from the inner chamber. "*Ignaat!*"

"Will you wait for me?" I whispered. "I don't know if I can find my way back without you."

Contorting that stony visage from its set expressions of disdain must've been difficult, but he made an honest effort at a grin. "May I be ground to dust and scattered to the *Al'eketh* before I leave my post, my lady!"

"Thank you," I said, and entered the hall.

It spoke to the size of the room that an irate dragon was not the first thing I noticed. Like the Hearth Chamber, the ceiling of the Hall of Records was lost in shadow, but unlike the other rooms in the Keep, the walls here were filled with carvings. The trembling light of the central fire made them look almost alive. Kaheset stopped short when he saw me.

"What are *you* doing here?"

I curtsied. "Aliza Da—"

"Don't waste your breath, I know who you are. We all know who you are. What do you want? Did Alastair send you?"

"No. I just—"

"If you wish me to change Neheema's mind, you're wasting your time." He looked away. "I am called *Vehrys* as a matter of honor, but I am not one of the Keepers. It is not up to me whether the dragons go to war."

"I'm not here for that. I'd like to know what happened between you and my husband."

"He hasn't told you?"

"No." It wasn't a lie, but it wasn't the whole truth either. I wanted to hear Kaheset's version of the story.

His wings drooped. "Has he . . . mentioned me at all?"

"Not really."

With a deep sigh he beckoned me forward. "Come into the light, child. Let me look at you."

I obeyed. The Hall was silent as he circled, studying me with an intensity that left me feeling mentally stripped.

"I see why you are really here, Aliza Daired. You wish to ask what I mean, living out my days as a chronicler in solitude instead of defending the children of my *khela* alongside Herreki and Akarra and little Mar'esh. Is that not so?"

"Aye, I suppose."

"And yet you are the *nakla* that married a Daired."

I frowned. "What does that have to do with anything?"

"It tells me a great deal about you. We have heard of you from Akarra and Herreki, of course, and I confess that you have been something of a puzzle to the Vehryshi. You gave up the tranquility of your people to unite yourself to a bloodstained House. It is a strange choice to those of us who know what the life of a Daired looks like. Are you sure you're not here to ask what *you* mean?"

"I just want to understand."

"As well you should. You should know the House to which you've bound yourself." He started toward the far side of the Hall. "Has Alastair ever spoken of his father?"

"Aye," I said quietly. "He told me about Cloven Cairn."

"Then you know why Erran died."

"It wasn't Alastair's fault! Kaheset, you must know it wasn't. He tried to save him—"

He whirled around. "You think I *blame* Alastair for Erran's death?"

"Don't you?"

"Of course not! I know Alastair wasn't responsible. It's not *him* I can't forgive."

Then who? The words filled my head, my mouth, but he continued in a low voice, as if he'd forgotten I was there.

"It cannot be an accident, your arrival. Not with such tidings as you bring, not if the Ranger has returned. Perhaps it is time." He gestured with one wing. "Come with me, Aliza. There is something I should like you to see."

I followed him to the farthest wall. Torches blazed on all sides here, illuminating a series of carvings more ornate than all the rest. A single line of red followed certain channels, branching and connecting again like the root of some ancient gnarled tree. A bowl of water sat on the ground before it next to a small pile of crushed stones. Kaheset bent over the stones and breathed out a stream of dragonfire hot enough to make my face smart and the stones crackle and break apart, leaving a chalky reddish stain in the circle of black. He scooped some of the pieces into the bowl, waited for them to stop sizzling, and dipped the point of his tail in the dye.

"This is the accounting of the Fireborn's bloodline," he said, and daubed fresh crimson over a faded portion of the channel. "Few humans have seen it. Few dragons either, besides those who are charged with its keeping." He pointed to a section near the bottom, where the red line stopped. "There. Read."

There were names carved above the sketch of two human figures.

ERRAN DAIRED (AH-NA-AL JESHKE-HESHEK'AN-KAHESET)—
ISOBEL ORANNA-DAIRED (GREYTHORN GRIMSPIKE)

Between them branched two lines.

ALASTAIR DAIRED (AHLA-NA-AL KANAH-SHA'AN-AKARRA)—
ALIZA BENTAINE DAIRED (NAKLA)
JULIENNA DAIRED (AH-NA-AL HON-SHE'AN-MAR'ESH)

There was nothing else. "I don't understand."

Kaheset pointed with his wingtip to Lord Erran's name. "Look harder."

The letters of his name went deep, carved with time and talon. The stone around it was smooth and bare, but there was a patch just to the left of his name that looked different. The stone wasn't so smooth and there was an indentation there that didn't match the rest of the wall. At a nod from Kaheset, I ran a hand over the section. I could just make out the impression of other letters, letters that had been carved or chipped away. Impossible to read in the shifting light, but still there. I closed my eyes and tried to string the letters together by touch. *Y. O?* No, not *O. D?* Yes, that was a *D. Y-D-R-I* . . . *Y-D-R-I-C-K* . . .

I jerked my hand from the wall. I didn't need to feel again for the first letter to know it was a W. I looked up at Kaheset, aghast.

"Yes. Even with my best efforts, the truth cannot be hidden forever." His head drooped. "I know little of her. Erran told me only that her name was Merranda and that she was a Ranger from Antward-on-Tyne, but his actions spoke the truth when he would not. My *khela* loved her as no man I've ever known has loved a woman."

"Then Tristan Wydrick . . . ?"

"Yes. He is Erran Daired's son."

CHAPTER 6

A PLEDGE OF FIRE

"That is a *lie*."

I whirled around. Alastair stood beneath the entry arch, his face pale, his fists clenched at his side, eyes fixed on Kaheset. His words parted the air of the cavern like the shaft of a spear, quiet and deadly. Yelling would have been less frightening.

"It's a vile slander and I will not allow it," he said.

Kaheset sighed. "You are in the halls of the Vehryshi, Alastair, in the Keep of the Chronicler. It does not rest with you what will and will not be allowed," he said. "I have kept this secret far too long."

"Tristan Wydrick was the bastard of a Ranger and a bard from Upper Westhull. He—"

"He was Erran's *kyshakyn* son and you know it. You've suspected it since you were a child. Your father wouldn't have fostered Tristan if he was not his own."

"My father took him in because he was a good man. A *good* man, Kaheset!"

"It is the best men who make the worst devils."

"You *dare?*" Alastair cried. "He was your brother-in-arms! He fought for decades at your side, and this is how you repay him?"

Kaheset inhaled sharply, then turned aside. "Oh, curse me as you will; I care not. Continue believing that your father was honorable, upright, the very picture of integrity, whatever you wish. Only leave me out of it. I am weary of the affairs of humans and I will have no more of this."

Alastair's eyes blazed. "*Ah-na'shaalk.*"

Kaheset spun around. His growl shook the Hall. "You speak to *me* of shirking my duty? Of cowardice? I kept his secret for years, boy, against the laws of both our kinds and my own conscience. *I* was the one who disguised his absences, who claimed a contract every time he went to visit Merranda. I lied to the world for the sake of my *khela*, Alastair, and it cost us everything. Your mother—"

"My mother knew?"

"Isobel was an intelligent woman. Of course she knew. I did all in my power to keep it from her, but the years had worn through her patience and her suspicions would not be allayed. She learned of it after your sister was born. Why else do you think she took that contract in the Fens so soon after the birth?"

"She . . . the Fen-folk needed her protection."

"Your mother could have taken any contract in the kingdom. She had no duty to the Fen-folk, yet she chose to fight the lamias in that stinking, poisonous swamp. Why do you think she did that? A young warrior, brokenhearted, betrayed by the man she loved but unwilling to shame him publically, she saw no other recourse. She was already weakened from the birth. When that sickness came on her, she embraced it."

"And my father *died* avenging her!" Alastair cried. "He swore an oath before Thell at her pyre. A blood oath, Kaheset. Or don't you remember?"

"You think he made that promise out of love? Don't be naive, boy. That was guilt, not love."

"You're lying."

"Erran cared for Isobel, yes, and he knew his duty, but he only ever loved one woman. He'd broken all his vows to his wife save one, and that oath was the last balm he could muster for his guilt. I know very well it was a blood oath; nothing else would atone. Think of the years it took him to fulfill it! Your father was the greatest warrior Arle had seen in generations, Alastair. You must know it wasn't the lamias who defeated him."

Alastair took a step back, hands half raised as if to fend off the blow he felt coming, that I felt coming, that hung in the still air of the Hall like an invisible hammer.

Kaheset followed him step for step. "Why do you think he swore to Thell and not Mikla?"

"Kaheset, don't."

"Your father never intended to leave the Cairn alive."

The silence pressed on my ears, a living, terrible thing. Alastair turned and walked from the Hall.

Kaheset sighed as he watched him go. "He is so like Erran. Stubborn, and a fool."

I wanted Akarra's strength or the Drakaina's authority or anything besides the weak and pathetic body that was all I had to hold my anger. "Do you have any idea what you've done?"

"I have unleashed the wind of truth, Lady Aliza, which only the strong of wing can ride. Better he brave the storm now than live any longer under the pretense of calm." Perhaps he saw the fury in my expression, for he was quick to add, "But do not despair.

The boy may be a fool, but he is a Daired too. He will weather this."

I stared hard at the great dragon beside me, drinking in the broken pride in his marshlight eyes, and wondering if there was some of his Rider in him as well. "His father was everything to him."

"Then that was his mistake."

"It was a mistake to love his father?"

Kaheset scoffed. "You humans with your saints and heroes. Learn the truth as I did, both you and your husband: they will always disappoint you. If Alastair returns to Pendragon a wiser man for my honesty, then I will have done some good. It is all I have left to offer House Daired."

The chill in his tone set my teeth on edge. I tugged at my trousers in a mock curtsy. "You needn't worry. We won't be bothering you again."

He looked at me then, face to face and eye to eye. His breath was cool and smelled of age and decay. "You think me cruel, do you not?"

"Well, you're certainly not kind," I spat.

His golden head drooped. "Believe what you will of me, my lady, but no matter how foolish or stubborn he may be, it was never my wish to cause Alastair pain. It is not his fault his father was faithless."

"He'll still carry that burden the rest of his life." I turned to go. "Goodbye, Kaheset."

"Lady Aliza, wait."

"I have nothing more to say to you."

"You need only listen. I spoke the truth in the Council Hall: I do not know what it is you faced out there in the Old Wilds. All the gods forbid the *ghastradi* have returned, but if they have, and if

Tristan Wydrick has fallen thrall to the brotherhood, he will not stop until he has destroyed House Daired."

I stopped in spite of myself. "You knew him, didn't you?"

"All too well. Erran took him as his ward the year Isobel died. I watched him grow to manhood in the Pendragon halls, and I saw how love blinded my *khela*. Even after his disgrace and demotion, Erran could not bear to send him away. The boy reminded him too much of his mother."

"Did Wydrick know he was . . . is a Daired?"

"I do not know. Erran never told him, but he was always a clever lad, and no boy with half his wits about him could doubt there was something to his ancestry. Whether he knows for certain now I cannot say, but even if he does not, I fear we have handed this unknown enemy a great and terrible weapon."

"What do you mean?"

"The boy was raised to be a Rider, Aliza. Erran trained him himself, and in those days Wydrick thirsted for nothing but his approval. He was baptized in the ways of war before most Rangers touch their first weapon, and now you tell me that he's been given not only the undying strength of a ghast, but also the brotherhood of an ancient evil that even we dragons do not fully understand. What time and hatred have warped that desire for approval into, I do not know, but I fear it. I fear the damage he is capable of inflicting on Alastair and Julienna and their dragons. If given the chance, next time he will not stop with a maiming."

Anger and desperation crested in a wave and crashed over me in a sudden impassioned torrent. I seized Kaheset's wingtip. "Then come help us fight him! Kaheset, listen to me. I understand why you lied, but take this chance to make it right. Come *with* us."

"Aliza . . ."

"Please, Kaheset. Don't abandon the Daireds again."

He breathed deeply and drew himself to his full height. For one bright hopeful moment he seemed to consider it. Then he shook his head. "I cannot. I have made my vows to the Vehryshi. Here I have sworn to stay, and here I will remain. My regret is my penance."

My heart sank and I released him. It struck me then that I preferred an angry Drakaina to this cold and willful betrayal. I flinched as he rested his wingtip on my shoulder.

"Perhaps this has shown you the price of the life you've chosen as a Daired, Lady Aliza. I wish you the strength to bear it. Now return to the Council Chamber. The Vehryshi will be ready with their verdict, and you'd do well to be at Alastair's side when they deliver it. *Hysehkah*, my lady. May the Four watch over you."

I started for the door, dreading what lay ahead even as I wondered if it could be worse than what lay behind.

IGNAAT LED ME BACK TO THE MAIN CHAMBER, APOLO-gizing again and again for bringing Alastair to the Hall of Records. "I thought if he wished to see thee, he must have some sense about him, and he looked in such distress—but wherefore did he leave so suddenly? And without thee? Has the cad proved ungentlemanly? Upon my stone, dear lady, if he has treated thee in an infamous manner, thou hast but to say the word and I will avenge thy honor."

I let him talk. There was too much to think and too much to feel; my feet moved without any direction from my mind, and my gargoyle guide seemed satisfied with the occasional nod or shrug. I thought of Wydrick's face. Any mental image of the man was shadowed now by seething, heaving darkness, but his eyes would be forever etched in my memory. Not like Alastair's at all, and yet somehow familiar. Green instead of brown, but the shape was the same, as was the intensity. Fairer of hair and complexion too, but such were the forest-folk of Antward-on-Tyne. He must've looked very much like his mother.

The click of diamond nails stopped. I came to myself on the threshold of the Council Chamber. The central fire had burned low, stretching the shadows of the dragons near the Inner Hearth up the walls and onto the distant ceilings. The hum of conversation hung in the air. I didn't see Neheema. "Thank you, Master Ignaat," I said.

"'Twas a pleasure, my lady," he said, and shrank out of sight just as one of the shadow-shapes looked in our direction. It broke off from the drove, resolving into the silver scales and timorous face of Sanar as she approached me.

"Lord Daired is there, my lady." She pointed to the mouth of the cavern. "He went to fetch you but returned alone. It would be good for you to go to him, I think."

The stars were fading in the eastern sky, but the moon was still high and bright, illuminating Alastair's silhouette. He sat on an outcrop a little above the cavern mouth, hunched like a gargoyle and perfectly still. An-Edannathair fell away just inches from the edge of the outcrop; one false move, one strong gust, or one loose stone would send him tumbling into the emptiness. The foothills, or what could be seen of the foothills through the carpet of clouds, were many thousands of feet below. I shivered. "Come inside, Alastair."

He shifted on his perch and said nothing.

"The Vehryshi are almost ready for us."

"You go," he said quietly. "I'll be there in a minute."

"Kaheset shouldn't have told you that way," I said. "Dearest . . ."

"Aliza, please. I need a minute."

I wanted to stay; I knew I couldn't. I left him to his musings.

Sanar drew me aside as Neheema and the others emerged from the Inner Hearth. "All is well with the Lord Daired?" Sanar asked in a whisper.

"He's fine," I lied. "Sanar, what are they saying?"

"There is among them divisions. Some wish your claims to believe. Others do not."

"What about Neheema?"

"I do not know."

"And you?"

She raised one wing in a dragonish shrug. "There is in your faces truth, and Akarra is to me as a Nestsister, but such things you claim! The dead-that-are-not warn us of a war-to-be? I do not know what to think."

"We saw what we saw, Sanar."

"Yes, but hush, my lady," she said as Neheema drew near the fire. Akarra followed her, her wings drooping, her head lowered. What little hope I'd dared to keep alive dried up inside me.

"Where is Lord Daired?" Neheema said.

"Here." Alastair moved into the firelight at my side, his expression set and unreadable. "Have you decided, Vehrys Neheema? Will you help us?"

"We have given careful consideration to your claims, my lord, fantastic though they may be. You know we are your allies. We shall always be your allies, but until we know more about this threat, we cannot pledge our fire. Return to the lowlands and take counsel with the Drakaina. She will advise the best course of action in this matter."

I wished her words surprised me. I wished I could feel anger or frustration or anything beyond weariness, but I could not. From the moment I saw Akarra I'd known their answer, and Kaheset's revelation had worked like slow-creeping ice, numbing me to everything but exhaustion, bone-deep and inescapable. We had failed and failed and failed again, and now all I wanted was home. I wanted to go *home*.

Neheema's voice came as if from a great distance, apologizing once more and ordering the dragonets to bring supplies for the journey back to Pendragon. Alastair's farewell was perfect, formal, and bitter as wormwood. Akarra said nothing at all. Attendant dragonets brought our gear from our chambers and we resaddled Akarra without a word. The Vehryshi walked us to the mouth of the cavern and bid us goodbye.

Akarra spread her winds to catch the waking wind. We did not look back.

IT WAS A QUIET FLIGHT THROUGH DRAGONSMOOR. THE mountains rushed by beneath us, dark at first, then dazzlingly bright as the sun rose, and it came as a relief to my aching eyes when we at last plunged beneath the layer of clouds that lapped the lower hills. Akarra stopped for the night at the village of Shepherd's Vale, where the old innkeeper welcomed us warmly and showed us into the same room we'd stayed in on our way north. I sank onto the bed without undressing, too tired to care about anything beyond pillows and blankets and warm, unfeeling darkness.

Alastair did not join me. The last thing I saw before sleep enveloped me was his silhouette against the fire as he knelt on the hearthrug, flexing his maimed hand at his side. When he turned to loosen his scabbard, I saw, very faintly, the gleam of tear tracks on his cheeks.

WE HAD BEEN AWAY FROM HOUSE PENDRAGON FOR AL-most a month. A lifetime would've felt less long. I wondered if the servants would see the new lines in my face, would be able to trace the marks of loss and fear and regret in the dark circles under my eyes or the hollowness in my cheeks. Perhaps they wouldn't. Perhaps there was nothing to see; I hadn't looked at myself in a mirror since leaving Castle Selwyn. If the truth reflected the image I held in my head, no part of the woman who'd left Pendragon all those weeks ago had survived the journey.

Akarra landed in front of the main gate. In my earlier life I might have taken pride in the difference a month had made, in how smoothly I was able to dismount now compared to my first attempts, but pride was a luxury both of us could no longer afford. Alastair's silence had begun to worry me. Feelings beyond grief pulled his jaw tight and kindled a fire behind his eyes, feelings I didn't recognize and wasn't sure I wanted to.

Our arrival brought Pendragon to life. Shouts from the servants who'd seen us land carried into the house, which a minute later produced the plump, beaming figure of the housekeeper, Madam Gretna, and the graver but no less relieved steward Barton. Alastair handed Akarra's saddle and our gear to one of the stable lads with directions to have them cleaned and ready by morning.

"You don't mean to stay?" I asked Alastair as the boy hurried away.

"The Vehryshi were right," he said, and I realized as he did that it was the most he'd spoken at once since we'd left An-Edannathair. "We need to see the Drakaina. We'll stay the night and start for Edan Rose tomorrow morning."

He'd said *we*. Fear, sorrow, and uncertainty weighed too heavily on my heart to allow anything like a leap, but for a moment I felt the burden lift. *He'd said* we.

"Aliza, Alastair, I'll meet you here at dawn," Akarra said. She sniffed the air. "Dress warmly. The winds are changing again. The *Al'eketh* is rising. It'll be a long flight to Edan Rose."

Madam Gretna clutched her cap to keep it from sailing off as Akarra rose from the ground. "Welcome home, my lord and lady! I can't tell you how glad we are to see you. We were beginning to worry."

"Any letters for me?" Alastair asked.

"Indeed, sir," Barton said. "Quite a number, in fact. I've arranged them on the desk in your study."

Alastair loosened his scabbard harness and handed it to the steward. "Thank you. Send word to the armorer and swordsmith in Lambsley. I'd like to see them today."

"Yes, sir."

"Until they arrive, I don't want to be disturbed. There's something I need to attend to," he said, and hurried into the house. I watched him go, the slow ache of shared sorrow settling deeper inside me with each footstep of his tactical retreat.

"Begging your pardon, my lady, but is the master well?" Barton asked.

"He's fine. It's just been a long journey."

"I'll ensure your chambers are ready." He bowed and followed Alastair.

Madam Gretna stayed with me as I started up the stairs, feeling anew each minute of our journey in every aching bone, every sore muscle. It would take much more than a single contract to toughen me to the Riders' life.

"If you don't mind me pressing, are you *sure* everything's all right, Lady Aliza?" Madam Gretna asked.

"Hmm?"

"It's just that, well, we were expecting you last week and the master seems in a bit of a state, and begging your pardon, you look rather out of sorts yourself."

"We're fine, Madam Gretna," I said firmly.

She peered at me over half-moon spectacles, and I saw the shrewdness of every mother I'd ever met, weighing the words of a tired child she knew was lying and no longer cared if he was discovered. "Very well," she said at last. "Never you mind me. I can't help but fuss when the family is out working. It's been that way since the master was just a lad."

I gave her a sidelong look. Had she known of her old master's affair with Wydrick's mother? Madam Gretna was no fool; surely she'd had her suspicions. Little details, the unexplained absences, the things perhaps only a housekeeper would notice and then dutifully put from her mind. *Poor woman.* I wondered if Lord Erran had ever fully grasped the thousands of small deceptions his faithlessness would demand, not only of him but of everyone who loved him.

"I'll tell the chambermaids to have a hot bath waiting for you, my lady," Madam Gretna said after a pause. She turned down the hall toward the servant wing, then stopped abruptly. "Oh, and a few letters came for you while you were gone. I've set them out on the desk in the mistress's study."

I found them just as she said, neatly stacked on the rosewood table in the study off the Pendragon library I'd used only twice since the wedding. I leafed through the stack of letters. My heart warmed to see Aunt Lissa's handwriting on one and Anjey's on another, my sister's sealed with the twin wyverns and crossed axes of Family Brysney. I set the folded parchment aside and picked up the third letter. From my friend Gwyn, by the address and handwriting, and I smiled at the crest imprinted in the yellow wax. It was, of all things, a wheel of cheese. I broke the seal and pulled the chair closer to the window to read it.

Hunter's Forge
Lesser Westwich, Arle
1061 SE

My dear Aliza,

Thank you for your letter. I'm glad to hear you are settling in well at House Pendragon. If the rest of the place is half so grand as what we saw at the wedding, then you're bound to have months of exploration ahead of you.

There was a splotch of ink on the next line, which had been crossed out. The letter began again beneath it.

You must forgive little William. He does fuss so when he's not being held, and he finds quills fascinating. I will try to keep it out of his hands. Wynce would have me start afresh on a clean sheet, but I think it adds character and I'm sure you won't mind. Anyway, you know what they say about old habits. I can hear my father's voice in my head whenever I so much as think about wasting paper.

Alas, I'd promised myself not to mention my father. How quickly that man can spoil pleasant thoughts! Perhaps it is a fortuitous segue, however, as you had a particular question that touched on him.

I have put off thinking about it again and again since receiving your letter, and for that I beg your forgiveness. The truth is, Aliza, I don't know what to do. To answer your question in short: yes, Father's debt to the Silent King's moneylenders has been repaid. It took a hefty loan on Wynce's credit and what little family honor my father had left, but we paid it back a week or so after your wedding.

I would like more than anything to leave it there, to assure you that all is well and this unpleasant business is over, but I cannot lie to you. The longer answer is not so neat.

Another splotch.

Apologies. After Wynce and I married, I began receiving correspondence directly from the Elsian moneylenders. I believe I showed you the first note. They correctly deduced my motives for marrying into a magistrate's household and named me my father's surety. How they came to such a conclusion, and from what close proximity they must have been observing my family's concerns to do so, still upsets me to think about. Nevertheless, it was done. I promised them full repayment, with interest, within a year's time. It was a foolish thing to do, but I had no choice. I had neglected to ask, and my father had not told me, exactly what the terms of interest were.

A third splotch, this one smudged along the edge with a tiny fingerprint.

It seems William has decided I shall not finish this letter. He is a wise child, as there are things I must tell you that should not be committed to paper. The roads have grown wild since the War of the Worm, and even post-coaches are not guaranteed safe passage. There is no telling who might stumble across our correspondence. Nevertheless, I must ask a favor. Besides Wynce there is no one I trust more, and you may be the only

one who can help. At my mother's request, we will be visiting
my family at Merybourne Manor for a few weeks before Saint
Ellia's Day, and dearest, I would very much like to see you.
Please, if at all possible, come to Merybourne when you receive
this letter and I will tell you what I can.

Safe journey, and gods willing, I'll see you soon.

All my love,
Gwyn

P.S. On a lighter note, you must be curious about the seal, as I
was when I first saw it. Apparently it is the sigil of the right noble
House of Curdred, crafted by Wynce's great-grandfather, who
thought himself most witty when he noticed that his surname
contained the word curd. *Why anyone of sense allowed him to*
think this is beyond me. Nevertheless, it stuck, and we are left
with the attached. Fortunately, it does grow on you.

I turned over the letter. Jotted in red ink below the royal post-master's seal was the date of sending. Nearly three weeks ago. I folded the paper, trying to remember if I'd mentioned our contract to Lake Meera in my letter to her. Had she spent the last fortnight wondering why I refused to answer? Or worse, that her letter had been intercepted as she feared? *But by whom?* Where was the Elsian minister's hand in all this?

Questions burned as hot as the eerie blue flame he'd conjured that dreadful afternoon in the Merybourne gallery. There was more to this affair beyond Master Carlyle's mismanaged funds. Add to that the darker business of the *ghastradi,* and perhaps her fear was well founded. The *ghastradi* of the chief lithosmith in Hatch Ford had known of the minister too. What was it he'd said? *"Little debts all around the kingdom . . ."*

I tucked the letters into my pocket. Alastair wouldn't need much persuading to pay Merybourne Manor a visit on our way south, not if there were answers to be uncovered. I left the study, nursing a tenuous thread of hope. The shadowy web settling over the kingdom was a vast, messy thing, but here at least was the solution to one small knot.

Aye, but untie carefully, a little voice said in the back of my mind. *Pluck one wrong thread, and all of this begins to unravel, and it may loose more than you expect.*

I studiously put the thought from my head and went in search of Alastair.

CHAPTER 7

SONS OF THEIR FATHERS

After a fruitless search through our chambers, Alastair's study, and the great gallery, I gave in and sought out the housekeeper, who was busy directing the stream of servants attending the washing. The laundry was a bright, noisy room at the back of the house hung all around with damp clothes and filled with the sounds of splashing. Steam wreathed half a dozen bright red faces bent over the washing tubs. A handful of the girls looked up as I entered, followed soon by the rest as their neighbors nudged them. The buzz of conversation dropped at once to a scandalized susurrus. I tapped Madam Gretna's shoulder.

"What is it now— Oh! Apologies, my lady. How can I help you?"

I hid my smile at her seamless acceptance of my presence in the laundry. She'd already seen enough of my antics as the *nakla* mistress of Pendragon; after joining Alastair on a contract, I guessed there were few things I could do that would surprise her. It made it a little easier to pretend the servants' stares didn't bother me. "Have you seen Lord Alastair?" I asked.

"No, I'm afraid not. Not since he came in, anyway," she said.

"Sarah, that basket goes to the bluing tubs. I'm so sorry, Lady Aliza," she said as she waved one of the girls to the other side of the laundry. "Is there anything else I can do for you? The bath should be ready in your chambers shortly."

"No, thank you." Disappointed, I started for the stairs when a fragment of Gwyn's letter came to mind. "Actually, there might be. Madam Gretna, has there been any news from Edonarle since we've been gone?"

A few of the maidservants nearest us exchanged a look that I didn't miss. *That's a yes, then.* Madam Gretna fiddled with the keys on her belt, frowning slightly. "Well, I suppose that depends on what you mean by *news*. I only hear rumors, mind."

"Rumors are a start," I said. "We didn't hear much about anything on our contract."

Still she hesitated. "I'm sure Lord Alastair will have better information, what with the letters he's been receiving from around the kingdom, but . . ."

"The *Tekari* are moving, milady." One of the maids stepped forward, wiping her wet hands on her apron and dipping into a curtsy. "That's what Madam Gretna's trying to say."

"Liana!" the housekeeper chided.

"What? We've all heard the stories," Liana said. Several other maids nodded in eager agreement.

"One of my cousins out near Middlemoor swears he seen a ghoul last fortnight," another girl said. "Running south, he says it was, fast as it could. And the next night it was a whole gale of nixies."

"No, I heard it was pixies," a third girl whispered.

"Nixies, silly! Pixies are *Idar*."

"It was *Tekari*," Liana said, "of all kinds. Folk say they're heading south."

"South to where?" I asked.

She shrugged. "No one's sure. We ain't seen any ourselves up here, just heard about it. No *Tekari* is fool enough to pass through Pendragon grounds," she added with a touch of pride.

"As I said, rumors, all of them," Madam Gretna said firmly before Liana could continue. "Now, ladies, back to your chores, please!" The girls returned to their washing with various degrees of reluctance. "And, Lady Aliza, perhaps you'd like to come with me?" she said.

I followed her up the stairs, leaving the maids to continue their argument in peace. "Is it true?" I asked.

"Alas, who knows? Everything's been chaos since the Battle of North Fields, but Miss Liana's right. We see none of it up here at the house, thank the gods. All we can rely on is gossip and the occasional letter from relatives." Her expression grew troubled. "Though now that I think of it, there was some rather odd news out of Ramshead a few weeks back. Town on the southern slope of the mountain," she said at my blank look. "My sister mentioned it in one of her letters. Seems their local lithosmith was robbed blind. Every last heartstone taken and not a trace of the thieves left behind. The local magistrate was at her wit's end!"

My blood ran cold, then hot. An empty lithosmith shop, just like what we'd found in Hatch Ford after the *ghastradi* Erik Tully had been unmasked. I weighed the dreadful import of the question I didn't want to ask against the answers I needed to know. "Madam Gretna, did your sister happen to mention anything about . . . *ghastradi?*"

She stopped on the landing and stared at me in dismay. "The ghast-ridden? Good gods, my lady, of course not! Why on earth should she?"

I sighed. Not that that was any guarantee the *ghastradi* hadn't been involved, but I would take the rumor mill's silence as a good sign, or at least a less terrible one. "No reason."

"You'd best ask the master if he's heard anything more," she said.

"Aye, when I find him I will."

"Have you tried the Sparring grounds up on the hill overlooking the house? Near the Standing Stones. There's a path around the stables. He might be up that way."

I thanked her, told her I knew the place, and took my leave. Tekari *of all kinds on the move, and now heartstones stolen wholesale?* The pieces shuffled around in my mind like a sentient jigsaw, coming together in patterns that made no sense. There was one thing, though, that did: *south.* Whatever war was stirring, whatever plans the *ghastradi* were hatching, the answer lay to the south.

The climb to the hut below the Standing Stones took longer than I expected, and I was winded by the time I reached the lichen-covered pavement. The cold wind sweeping across the mountainside could not suppress the momentary flush that rose to my cheeks as I took in the sight of the hut, remembering our last visit. Unfortunately, even if we had the time, there was no chance of repeating our evening together. Alastair was not there.

Akarra, however, was. She sat on the crag overlooking the hut and the slope below, her tail twining meditatively through the dry stems of ivy clinging to the rocky face. At a gesture of her wing, I sat on the bench next to the hut.

"I don't like the winds, Aliza," she said after a moment of silence. "First the *Al'eketh*, now the *Keth*. The North Wind and the South Wind," she said. "It turned south about an hour ago and has been gaining strength since."

The hairs on the back of my neck pricked up. *The South Wind?* Was it a warning, an invitation, or pure chance? I knew enough of the fickleness of the gods not to trust it as a sign of favor. I knew enough of the gods not to trust them at all. As quickly as I could, I told Akarra of Gwyn's letter and the maidservants' reports. Her wings fluttered at news of the moving *Tekari*.

"Well, at least we know where Wydrick and Tully went," she said.

"Aye."

I wondered how easily the *Tekari* of the kingdom were recruited. Had they leapt at a second chance for vengeance against us, or did they require persuading? Wydrick had gone to murderous lengths to recruit the Green Lady of the Wastes. I feared what he might have instructed other *ghastradi* to do in their campaigns, not only against human and *Shani*, but *Idar* as well. There would be no Indifferent in the war to come. Images of slain *Idar* strewn across the roads of southern Arle filled my mind, their chests cut open and their heartstones removed as a grisly warning to everyone who stood against our unknown enemy.

"Will you be able to fly in the morning?" I asked.

A smile touched Akarra's lips. "Master Groundskeeper was kind enough to set aside a few head of cattle for me this afternoon. I'll be fine."

I made a note to seek out the groundskeeper and give him my personal thanks. We sat for a minute in companionable silence, watching the *Keth* send dead leaves scuttling across the pavement. It felt strange, this little moment of something like calm. The shadow of war hung over Dragonsmoor, just as it did the rest of the kingdom, but here at least it felt distant, even forgettable for minutes at a time. The maid Liana was right; House Pendragon stood like an island in the midst of a tempest. I wondered how long that could last.

"Aliza, I'm worried about Alastair."

I looked up at her. "Me too."

"I've known him through the death of his father and Mar'esh's maiming and the first time he thought he lost you—grief and rage and heartbreak of the kind I thought humans could not bear. Yet bear them he did." Her wings drooped and she let out a fiery sigh. "But this . . ."

"I know."

"Lord Erran may not have been a good man, but he loved Alastair more than life itself. I will never doubt that."

"Not enough to tell him the truth," I said quietly.

She sighed. "Perhaps that is exactly why Lord Erran did not tell him. Perhaps he thought it would spare him pain."

Yet all it did was worsen the pain when he did find out. "I should go find him."

"You don't know where he is?"

"I thought he might've come up here."

"Ah." She gave a humorless chuckle. "As did I. Have you checked with his smith? Or the armory? He'll need a new sword."

"I haven't, but I will."

"There is another place," she said before I could start down the path. "Below the house, where the ashes of the family are kept. He may be there. Barton will know how to find it."

"Thank you, Akarra."

She reached down and touched my cheek lightly with the tip of her wing. "Lend him some of your strength, *shan'ei.* He will need it."

I DIDN'T BOTHER CHECKING WITH THE SMITH OR VISIT-ing the family armory. As soon as she'd said it, I knew. Barton showed me the entrance to the mausoleum at the back of the house. It was through a low stone doorway, a room of plain marble, bare and white and chill, and I didn't wonder why Alastair had neglected to show me this room on our earlier tours. Through the door I caught a glimpse of a short stair and a dim, lamplit passage.

"Thank you, Barton," I said. "If you don't mind, it might be best for me to see him alone."

"Very well, my lady."

The mausoleum of Family Daired was no musty, oppressive tomb, nor was it lavish with expensive monuments to the fallen dragonriders. This was the resting place of those who had no illusions about death. Simple stone plinths lined the long gallery on each side, on which rested the urns of each Daired. The urns varied in style and substance; I saw gold and iron, alabaster, ebony, and oakstone, even one of glass, but what drew my eye first were the tapestries hanging behind each plinth. The Daireds might not have had any illusions about death, but they wanted their lives remembered. The rich colors glowed even in the dim light, the cloth untouched by moths or rot, depicting the battles and great deeds of each Daired, immortalized in woven splendor astride their dragons. In any other moment, the artist in me might have given in to the desire to linger over each one, puzzling out the stories behind the ashes, but there was only one plinth I cared about now, and only one story.

Alastair sat on the ground halfway down the gallery, a new sword resting naked across his knees. The lantern beside him sent long shadows creeping across the floor. I crossed the distance as softly as I could, suddenly conscious of the deep silence that pressed down on this place. This was the hall of the dead; here, it was the living who intruded. Alastair said nothing as I approached and sat down.

Lord Erran's tapestry showed him astride Kaheset, his sword raised against a writhing knot of lamias. The obsidian urn atop the plinth, however, was empty. Alastair had not been able to retrieve his father's body from where he'd fallen in Cloven Cairn.

"Kaheset was right," he said.

"He shouldn't have told you like that."

Silence.

"Alastair—"

"I knew," he said in a quiet voice. "Some part of me always knew. Little things my father would say or do, or the way he'd look at Tristan when he thought no one was watching. I saw as a child but didn't understand, and when I was old enough to understand, I no longer wanted to see."

"Dearest, I'm so sorry."

At last his gaze fell. "Do you know why it took so long for me to ask you to marry me?"

The question surprised me, but I seized the opportunity to draw him out. "You had quite the list, if I recall."

He remained grave. "From our first battle in the Witherwood I knew I'd love you. By the time we left for Edan Rose in the spring I'd decided: either I'd make you my wife or I'd die alone, *nakla* and all our family's traditions be damned." He sighed. "Still, I almost didn't ask. Every time I took up my sword, every time I thought I'd made up my mind, I'd see that heartstone and hear again all my father's lectures about the honor of our house and the strength of our bloodline and our duty to live up to the Daired name. The truth of *tey iskaros* went deeper than feelings, he'd said, and no matter where our hearts lay, *nakla* were forbidden to us. We were better than them." His lips pulled taut as if in a grin, but it was the grin of a death's-head: lifeless, joyless, empty. "My father was a hypocrite."

"Alastair, you are not your father."

He bowed his head. "It doesn't matter. My life has been a waste."

"No. Look at me. *Look* at me, dearest." I touched his cheek, gently but firmly forcing him to face me. "You've sweat, you've bled, you've served, you nearly died to protect this kingdom. Many times. You've saved more people than you know. How can you call that a waste?"

"Everything I've done I've done to uphold our family's honor, to be the man my father was. What is any of that worth when that honor is a lie?"

"Is what you did for Leyda a lie? Or for Cordelia?" *Or for me?* I brushed a loose strand of hair from his forehead. "I understand your family's legacy is important to you, love, as it should be, but you can't live the rest of your life chained to the expectations of the dead."

There was a long silence.

"Then what do I do?"

The hungry, almost desperate way he said it left me feeling as if I'd stumbled naked across the threshold of a house on fire with only a thimble and my tears to quench it. What answer could I give, not to the heir of House Daired, but to the man I loved?

"What the son of every failed father must, I suppose," I said. "He dishonored your family name. You have the chance to redeem it."

The lantern crackled. Alastair's shoulders rose and fell. I took his hand.

"Aliza, I once told you that I wish you'd been able to meet my father," he said at last. "Do you remember?"

"Aye, I remember."

He stood and held out the blade in his hand. It was a plain

sword, without pommel stone or scrollwork. Made for killing and nothing else. "I don't wish that anymore."

He swung the sword. His father's tapestry fluttered to the ground, sheared neatly in half. An anguished scream would not have sounded more terrible or more pained than that faint crumple of ruined cloth.

"I wish he had been able to meet *you*." He drew me closer and kissed the top of my head. "Wherever this leads, whatever horrors are waiting for us in Edonarle, I'm glad you're with me."

It took a second for me to draw back my voice from where it had fled. "Edonarle? Aren't we going to Edan Rose?"

"No." He sheathed his sword and collected the lantern without a second glance at his father's desecrated memorial. "Come. I've had a letter from Aunt Catriona. They're in Edonarle. She, Julienna, Edmund, and the others. They've asked for us to join them."

"All right, but why?"

"Do you remember what Lord Camron warned me about before we left for Lake Meera?"

I cast my mind back to what seemed another life. "The trade agreement?"

"Yes. The guilds have been busy while we were away. They've persuaded the king to call a convocation. Aunt Catriona tells me they expect an Elsian delegation in Edonarle by Saint Ellia's Day. Embassies from the Garhad Islands and the Southern Principalities are already there."

Els. In honesty, I'd forgotten about the details of the proposed agreement, delivered so hastily by Lord General Camron before we'd left for Lake Meera. Now it came flooding back, and with it, a renewed suspicion. The timing was too perfect. Four nations brought together for the first time in decades, in *centuries*, haggling over the terms of Garhadi ale and Elsian steel, distracted and vulnerable—and all the *Tekari* of Arle heading south, toward Edonarle. The puzzle pieces began to fall into place.

"This is it," I said. "This is where the war begins, isn't it?"

He nodded. "Aunt Catriona says tensions are already high. The king wants every ally he has in the city in case something tips it over the edge." The line of his lips took on a familiar grimness. "That's where Tristan will be."

"Then that's where we need to be too." I thought of Gwyn's letter. "But first, there's someone we need to see."

I TOLD HIM ABOUT THE LETTER AS WE RETURNED TO OUR chambers. His frowned deepened as I described Gwyn's cryptic warning. "I agree we should go to her, *khera*, but what do you hope to find out? What more do you think she can tell us?"

"I don't know, but anything is better than nothing. If we're going to face this unrest in Edonarle then so be it, but I don't want to go unarmed."

That drew out a sliver of a smile. "Now you're thinking like a Daired."

We took supper and retired early. Though painfully conscious of the godsforsaken hour Alastair expected us to leave the next morning, I couldn't resist a little teasing before we went to bed. "Alastair?"

"Hmm?" he grunted, tugging off his boots.

"You promised me something at Castle Selwyn."

Guildmaster Tornay herself would've given all the wealth of the Artists Guild for a glimpse of his expression. Its calculated innocence would have served as a model for her paintings of Saint Marten for years to come. "I did?"

"Aye. I distinctly recall a promise in the Lake Hall to 'make amends.'" I unlaced my dressing gown and laid it aside. "Do you remember now?"

The boot fell from his hand as a slow grin spread over his face. "*Thorough* amends, I believe my words were."

I extended my hand but found suddenly that I could not return his smile. For more than one reason I had tried not to dwell on the events leading up to that night in the Lake Hall, but now I felt again that knotted ache of sorrow, that grasping emptiness inside me where our only child had lived and died. "Tomorrow we head into darkness and danger and gods knows what other madness," I said. "I don't know what's going to happen. I don't know if I *want* to know. But right now, tonight, I want you. Whatever we face—"

He crossed the room and kissed me before I could finish. "I keep my promises, *khera*," he whispered in my ear.

And he did. Oh, he did.

CHAPTER 8

A HOWL IN THE DARK

The storm arrived during the night. Cold rain lashed the windows as we dressed the next morning, and by the time we set off, the rain had turned to a fine, sheeting sleet. Half a day into our flight and I'd made up my mind. Given rain like this or a blizzard of the Old Wilds, I'd take the blizzard, and gladly. Snow had no pretensions; it forced you to face the cold head on, and its fury played no games. Not so with sleet. This chill was subtler, more insistent, and once it had taken hold, harder to shake. My oilskin cloak stood as my staunch defender for half an hour before it too fell to the persistent drizzle, and by the time we landed for the night at a village on the southeast border of Middlemoor, my teeth were chattering uncontrollably.

"We're a little out of the way, but this is no weather for sleeping outside," Akarra said as Alastair undid her tack. "We'll make up time in the morning."

The village had no inn, and it took some banging on doors and bleary-eyed residents pointing toward one house or another before we found a farmer willing to lodge us in his barn. It sat at the edge of the village, just outside the wall. The Daired crest made no impression on him, and he held out his hand expectantly at the door to the barn. Alastair counted out ten copper trills into his open palm. The man looked at the coins, looked at our armor, and raised an eyebrow. Alastair added another five trills. The man grunted.

"Ye can afford quality like that, ye can afford me rents for the season. And don't ye be thinking of threats, young master, dragonrider though ye be. Ye don't scare me." He eyed Akarra. "Your fire-breather neither."

Akarra said something in Eth, and Alastair smiled. He pulled out a silver half-dragon and tossed it into the man's hand.

"*That's* more like it."

The farmer showed us to the barn, muttering warnings under his breath to "keep that blasted creature away from my hay." Akarra rolled her eyes and headed for the stretch of pasture beyond the barn.

It was a squelchy business, peeling off our wettest things and hanging them from pegs or over railings. It didn't help that we had to feel our way around in the dark, the farmer having taken the lantern and offered nothing in its place. From around us came sleepy snuffling and the inescapable smell of animals. Either their master made it a practice to shove strangers into their barn at odd hours of the night or they were very placid animals, for our presence disturbed them no more than a few minutes before the noises settled down again. Alastair felt around for the nearest pile of straw and we lay down—me still shivering, him quiet—and listened for a while to the rain on the roof.

"What did Akarra say?" I asked after a minute.

"Hmm?"

"About the farmer."

"She reminded me what the going rate for rams is in these parts."

I could make out only the faint outline of his features in the dark, but even so I fancied he was smiling. "Let me guess. A silver?"

"Two for a silver, actually, but she'll be generous."

"Do you often meet with people like that farmer?"

"More often than we like."

"I always assumed anyone would be happy to lodge a Rider. People at Merybourne Manor talked of it like some sacred duty."

He shifted. "Aye, and despite my, ah, first claims to the contrary, we were grateful for your hospitality," he said. "But our work is bloody, and most decent folk would rather not be reminded why we exist. They may say otherwise, but all Riders know the truth."

"I suppose." I closed my eyes and nestled closer to him, partly for warmth, partly to encourage his touch. He draped an arm around my shoulders. "We'll have a lot— *Did you just say* aye?"

Never before had I thought darkness capable of blushing. His silence had a crimson hue.

I sat up. "You did! You said *aye!*"

"Perhaps it slipped out," he muttered. "So?"

Laughter warmed me better than anything the barn had to offer, and I settled back at his side with a grin. "Oh, don't sound so peeved. It suits you."

"If you say so."

"I do."

For a minute we listened to the rain, our moods considerably lightened.

"Have you ever wondered why I was late that day?" Alastair asked.

"Hmm? What day?"

"The day the Riders came to Merybourne. The day we first met."

I had at the time, but since then it had hardly crossed my mind. I turned toward him and propped myself up on one elbow. "Well, I do now. What happened?"

"The first time Cedric told us about Lord Merybourne's contract, I said no."

"Really?"

"Really. I'd flown through Hart's Run several years before and hadn't found it very impressive. Come now, you can't deny it," he said as I nudged him in the ribs. "I didn't fancy staying there for any longer than a day."

"I'm sure."

"Less than that, if I could help it."

"All right, all right, I get the idea," I said. "What changed your mind?"

"Akarra told you about the fiasco with Cedric's woman in Edonarle, didn't she?"

I thought back to our conversation on the hill outside of Hunter's Forge and the aftermath of his first disastrous proposal. Akarra had set the facts straight afterward on any number of misconceptions I'd formed about her Rider, including his interference in my sister's relationship with Cedric Brysney. That Brysney had only recently had his heart broken by a faithless fiancée when he came to Hart's Run was not something I'd be quick to forget, no matter how much I wished to. I nodded, then, remembering he couldn't see, added, "She did."

"That woman plagued him from the moment she arrived in Edonarle. Lingering around his favorite tavern, inquiring at the guesthouse where he and Charis stayed, that kind of thing. He wanted nothing more to do with her, but she was, ah, determined."

"To do what? Win him back?"

"If possible. She wanted his fortune and his famous name."

I tried out one of the Eth phrases I had heard Alastair mutter on occasion. *"Ahla-na'asheen."*

He laughed.

"Did I say it wrong?" I asked.

"Depends. Were you trying for *accursed* or *arithmetic?*"

"The former."

"Ahla-na'ad-shaheen, in that case," he said. "And I'd agree. When Merybourne's contract came, Cedric couldn't sign it fast enough. Charis too." He paused. "Actually, it was Charis who asked me to join them."

I reached out and found his hand. His voice still caught whenever he talked about his fallen friend. "And you said no?"

"At first. Then Cedric told me everything that the woman from Hallowsdean had done since she arrived in Edonarle. I was . . . well, *angry* may be an understatement."

Having been on the other side of his protective nature, I could understand the reaction. "I can imagine."

"Maybe it was foolish, but I went to find her. I told her to give him up, to return to Hallowsdean while she still had a shred of honor left, or face House Daired and House Brysney in the High Magistrate's Court."

"I gather from your tone that conversation went *extraordinarily* well."

"She, ah, got the wrong impression." He cleared his throat. "Of my intentions."

My eyebrow shot up. *"Oh?"*

"You needn't worry, *khera,* she wasn't as persuasive as she thought she was. But neither was I. She didn't give up. Just found richer quarry."

"So you didn't come to Hart's Run for your friend's sake?"

He shifted and faced me. The rain had lessened and the moon must have been peeping through the clouds, for enough light fell through the barn slats to see his expression. He wore a faint smile. "Well, not *only* for my friend."

Straw poked at my cheek as I moved closer. "Is that why you were late, then? Dodging the attentions of this artful young lady?"

"Hardly. I signed the contract as soon as I next saw Cedric. Akarra and I meant to leave at once, but there was a murder at the docks and Akarra thought it was odd enough to warrant investigation."

I frowned. "Odd? Was it the *Tekari?*"

"We never found out. The first mate of a vessel from the Principalities was found dead in the hold of the ship when it docked, but none of the other sailors saw anything and the captain had already burned the body before we arrived. We had to hand it over to the City Watch."

My curiosity abated with less than the usual twinge of disappointment. If he had stayed any longer in Edonarle, who knew what about our meeting might have changed or if we would have met at all? Dodging the muddy missiles of an inconvenience of hobgoblins might not have been the most auspicious beginning to a relationship, but it was certainly a memorable one. I traced the faint pattern of embroidery along the open collar of his tunic. The sound of rain faded to a steady drip from the eaves. Sleepy animals shuffled in their stalls. We were both flirting with the edges of exhaustion already, but as that was nothing new and as I had no guarantees we'd get time alone like this at Merybourne or Edonarle, I wasn't about to let it go quite yet.

"Alastair?"

"Hmm?"

"What did you think when you finally did get to the Manor?"

"You mean when I met you in the garden?"

"Aye."

He sat up on his elbows. "I don't think you want to know my very first thought, *khera*."

"Fair enough. Your second will do."

"About you or the hobgoblin?"

I gave him a look. "His name's Tobble, and I'll let you guess."

Alastair smiled. He leaned toward me and followed the curve of my cheek with one finger before touching my lips. "I thought you were unruly, provincial, possibly mad, and the most beautiful woman I'd ever seen."

I bit his finger playfully before pulling him in for a kiss. "*That* was the right answer, dearest."

We fell back into the hay a few minutes later, breathless but smiling, Alastair's arm wrapped securely around my shoulders. His breath steadied in seconds, but I found sleep eluded me. I stared up at the darkened ceiling, listening to the quiet sounds of the creatures on the other side of the barn, and thought of all that lay ahead. It felt so distant.

Is this what Edan Daired and Marten and Ellia and all the other saints felt on their great adventures? The stories we told of them were grand, sweeping, epic, the foundation on which we had built our kingdom, but what of the reality? Were there moments when Edan had lodged in a barn like this, wakeful like I was, unsure of what lay ahead? Had Marten, Ellia, and Niaveth shared stories of their growing-up years around their campfire in the wilds of Arle, with only the glow of the flames and their companionship to keep the darkness at bay? I thought again of Mòrag's account of "The Lay of Saint Ellia" at Castle Selwyn and her unflattering description of House Daired. The traditional ballad had surely smoothed over their more human moments, the little disagreements, the indecision and infighting. After all, no one was naive enough to think the legendary lovers had never quarreled. *Did they wonder what lay ahead too?*

My eyes snapped open. I had no memory of falling asleep, but the light streaming through the cracks in the walls was the bleak bone color of just before dawn. For a moment I stared into the gloom, trying to place what woke me. Not Alastair snoring; I was used to that. *A dream? A feeling? A memory?* The animals at the end of the barn shuffled nervously. *Something dangerous?*

I bolted upright as my answer rolled through the chilly air, sending the hairs on the back of my neck sticking straight up. Somewhere in the distance, a wolf howled.

Alastair rolled over with a sleepy grunt, then bolted upright. "Is that . . . ?"

"The second one. Alastair, please tell me those are ordinary wolves."

"They're not."

Direwolves. "Did they follow us?"

"I don't know."

I groped for my knife belt. They hadn't sounded close, but I knew better than to underestimate the speed of a pack. The wall would serve as a staunch defense for the villagers, but the barn door offered us little protection if we were being hunted.

His breath quickened. "We need to go. Get your things together. Quickly. Don't make a sound."

In silence we collected our clothes and weapons, moving as fast as we could while avoiding the squeak of wet leather. It was impossible for me to put my armor on again without help, but Alastair managed both his and mine in the dim light. The nervous noises from the barn animals grew louder and more insistent. One horse pawed at its stall. A few goats bleated quietly.

There was the sound of wings and a thud outside the barn.

"*Khela!*" Akarra hissed.

Alastair drew his sword and unbarred the door, motioning for me to stay behind him. Akarra crouched just outside, her head level with his. "Where are they?" he asked.

"Half mile east," she said. "A dozen or more, and—"

A terrible shriek tore through the early morning air. Alastair dropped his sword and clapped his hands over his ears. I covered mine too, feeling the cry like a needle of poisoned ice. It rose until I thought I could not stand it. My head would burst or my ears rupture or my teeth shatter—

It stopped just as suddenly as it had started, leaving a sucking silence that was almost as painful as the shriek. I drew an unsteady breath and ran an internal inventory. Nothing broken, though my whole body ached as if I'd been running.

"Banshees too," Akarra said as Alastair picked up his sword. "And possibly others."

"They're heading south, aren't they?" I said.

"Unless they change direction, yes."

South from Middlemoor . . . I realized it at the exact moment Alastair did. He looked at me, then at Akarra, horrified.

"Thell. They're heading toward Hart's Run."

CHAPTER 9

THE METTLE OF MANOR-FOLK

Mist hung in chilly clouds above the trees, outlining the early morning shadows in white. We didn't try to talk while we flew. Woods and fields rushed by beneath us, dark at first, then a patchwork of late autumn colors as the sun rose over the hills: rusts and violets and browns and a few stubborn streaks of orange. Over and over I played the logic of our plan, as if by repetition it would grow less mad. Unless the *Tekari* drastically changed course, the horde's path would carry them through Hart's Run and, if they were not stopped, straight on to Edonarle. With the city already stirred up from the upcoming convocation of nations, a ravaging horde of *Tekari* might be exactly the spark the *ghastradi* needed to kindle their war.

I tried not to think how many other hordes like this one were rushing south across the kingdom. We could stop only so many.

It was a risk, though, trying to head them off. Akarra could fly twice as fast as the fastest direwolf could run, and the hills of Hart's Run would slow them down, but even if we arrived at Merybourne Manor before the pack, we'd have little time to prepare. Still, it was a reasonably defensible house, with plenty of room to shelter folk from the surrounding villages, and it offered us the best chance at stopping the creatures.

Just don't change direction, I found myself thinking as we flew southward, racing the daylight, our enemies, and our rapidly waning luck.

I CAUGHT THE FIRST GLIMMER OF THE RIVER MERYLE and Merybourne Manor a few hours later, and for one bright, precious moment all the terrors and fears, heartache and hauntings of the last month fell away and I was a little girl once again, straining for a better look at the beloved chimneys and windows of the Manor House as Uncle Gregory and Aunt Lissa ushered me back from a visit to Edonarle. No matter how much I loved my summers with them, the sight of home had always worked something primal in me, easing the ache of homesickness I'd succeeded for so many months in ignoring. Even in the flat gray light of late autumn that showed nothing at its best, the roofs and lanes of Merybourne seemed for a few minutes the most beautiful thing I'd ever seen.

As we landed in the front courtyard, I realized that our flight had not taken us over the ruin of North Fields. *Good.* A lifetime might pass before I looked again on the bone-picked corpse of the Greater Lindworm and it would still be too short.

"Where is everyone?" Alastair asked.

I looked around. Piles of leaves still damp from the night's rain lay in the corners of the courtyard. A lantern burned beside the door to the Manor House, but I saw no movement through the windows. For one terrible second all my fears came crowding back. *We're too late. The Tekari already passed through, they killed them, oh gods, they killed them all . . .*

Then one of the second-floor windows banged open and a curly-haired head poked out. "Aliza? Merciful Mikla, is that really you?"

I almost laughed in relief. "Henry! Of course it's me, come down and let us in!"

The Merybourne bard withdrew into the house with a muffled exclamation that sounded like *"Aliza's back!"*

"Your poet friend?" Alastair asked as I dismounted.

"He'll help me gather the Manor-folk," I said. "You two warn the other villages. Trollhedge is across the river to the south and Little Dembley is west of here, not more than a mile."

"Good," Alastair said. "Make sure you bring in anyone from the outlying buildings. The lodge, the stables, any place that's not defensible. The hills will force the *Tekari* to fan out, but we need to keep them contained if we're going to stop them. You know what else to do?"

"Barricade doors and windows and round up any weapons." I thought of the banshees. "And make sure someone has a jar of beeswax handy."

The severity of his expression softened a little, and I caught the shadow of the dimple beneath his cheek. "We'll be back soon."

Henry burst through the front door just as Akarra took to the air. Leaves stirred by the rush of her wings slapped wetly against the wall, and he watched in wonder as they disappeared over the bare treetops. I didn't wait for him to recover. He swayed on the threshold as I threw my arms around him.

"My goodness!" He chuckled and returned my embrace. "To what do I owe this pleasure? And where is Master Daired off to?"

I released him. "I'm sorry, Henry, there's not much time. *Tekari* are coming from Middlemoor, a whole horde of them. They're heading for Edonarle, but we need to stop them here."

"They're . . . it's— *What?*"

"We saw them in Middlemoor and flew ahead to stop them here."

"Hold on. You *want* them to come through the Manor?"

"They were headed this way anyway, and it's the only place we know the townsfolk will be safe while we fight. But we can't do it alone." I started inside, but he held me firmly at an arm's length.

"This isn't some kind of dragonrider prank, is it?" he asked.

"Henry!"

He released me. "I'm sorry. I just . . . No, you're right. No time. How close are they?"

"I don't know. We flew fast, but they can't be more than a few hours behind. I'd guess we have until sunset."

"Then we'd best move fast. Tell me what you need."

IF THERE WAS ONE THING I'D NEVER DOUBT AGAIN, IT was the effectiveness of a bard in rousing a house.

"*Tekari!*" Henry bellowed, charging through the halls with a goatskin drum in the crook of one arm, commandeered from his apprentice Davy, whom he'd sent to raise the alarm in the other wing of the house. At every door Henry gave the drum a good thwack. "Everyone to the Great Hall! To arms, Merybourne, to arms!"

One of the doors we passed flung open. "Master Brandon, what is the meaning of . . . Aliza?" Lord Merybourne blinked from me to Henry and back again. "What's going on?"

"The Manor-folk are taking up a council of war! To the Great Hall, Your Lordship," he cried, already halfway down the hall. "*Tekari* are coming!"

Lord Merybourne hesitated for half a second before dashing for the stairs as fast as his legs would carry him. I jogged after Henry.

"Keep at it. I'm going to get my family."

The corridors to my family's apartments felt strange, foreign somehow, though I could make every turning with my eyes closed. It struck me as I touched the smooth brass handle of the door: it wasn't the Manor that had changed at all. It was me.

I slipped inside as quietly as I could, shut the door and leaned against it, breathing in the familiar smells of home. Well-worn wood, lamp oil, and lavender. The cleaning herbs our maid Hilda used to get stubborn stains from the upholstery. The bright astringent scent of bee balm, and over it all, the wafting smell of breakfast. I smiled. In a world where so much had changed, where danger deepened with every step we took, this tiny moment stood like a lighthouse on the shores of chaos. *This.* This was worth fighting for.

And gods help the *Tekari, Idar,* human, or Eldest who would try to take it from us.

"Who's . . . oh!" The housemaid Hilda stopped short in the doorway from the sitting room. Her eyes grew very round. "Bless my soul! Miss Aliza, is it really you?"

"Aye, Hilda, it's really me."

"I suppose I should be calling you Lady Daired now, shouldn't I? But what on earth are you doing back? And what's that commotion I heard downstairs?"

"Just Aliza, Hilda. Always Aliza. Is my family here?"

Raised voices drifted out from the dining room just then, and Hilda gave me a knowing look. "Aye, milady."

"Thank you." I started toward the voices. "You'd better go to the Great Hall. We'll explain everything there."

Hilda looked puzzled but did as I said, leaving me to enjoy, however briefly, the familiar and well-loved sound of a burgeoning argument between my mother and youngest sister.

"But, Mama, it could be *important*!" Leyda cried. "Why else would Henry be carrying on like that?"

"The man's a bard, dear. Carrying on is his full-time occupation."

"Just let me go see!"

"As soon as you finish your breakfast, young lady, and not a moment before," Mama said. "Mari, darling, must you really read at the table?"

My sister Mari mumbled something I couldn't hear.

"Mama, *please*!" Leyda tried again.

I moved into the doorway. "She's right, actually."

Mama spun around in her chair. Papa gave a little start and pulled down his spectacles. Mari shut her book. Leyda beamed.

"Er, sorry I didn't send word," I said. "I'm—"

Mama didn't let me finish. I was nearly bowled over by her embrace, then again as Leyda threw her arms around us both, and for a moment there was nothing but laughter and tears and scoldings and inquiries as to Alastair's health and whereabouts, only to dissolve once more into laughter and a second embrace. It took an iron will to tear myself from them.

"I missed you all too. But there's no time. *Tekari* are on their way!"

Mari gasped and Leyda shot Mama a pointed look, which she ignored. Papa's knuckles grew white where he gripped my shoulder. "You're sure?" he asked.

"Alastair and I saw them. He and Akarra are warning the nearby villages now. The horde'll be here soon. Everyone's gathering in the Great Hall to lay our plans."

"Well then, what are we sitting here for?" Mama cried. "Girls, go with Aliza. Robart, come; we'd best help Madam Farris with her boys. Quickly now!"

I snatched a slice of toast from the table before hurrying after my sisters. We joined a stream of Manor-folk emerging from their rooms with various exclamations of annoyance at Henry, only to sober when they saw me in my Rider's armor. Leyda plucked at my sleeve as we approached the Great Hall. "You and Master Daired *do* have a plan, right?" she asked.

"Working on it," I whispered. "You two go in; I'll be right behind you."

Henry stood at the door, waving the last of the Manor-folk through. "Inside, everyone, quickly!" he cried. "Yes, Master Farris, I'm sure I'm interfering with something terribly important. Quickly now, Madam Moore! Everyone! Jenny, fetch Cook! Ah, Aliza," he said when he saw me. "That's everybody, or nearly everybody."

"Thank you." I cast my eye over the gathered crowd. Familiar faces, mostly. People I had grown up with, played with, argued with, but not warriors. Farmers, tailors, blacksmiths, and apothecaries; scholars, accountants, bards, and children: poor defenders against direwolves and banshees. Then again, I was hardly better. A few battles under my swordless sword-belt only qualified me to properly appreciate the danger, not to stop it.

I caught a glimpse of Madam Carlyle near the front, and next to her, Gwyn stood with her little son in her arms. My friend's expression brightened when she saw me, then grew worried.

"Ladies and gentlemen, please!" Lord Merybourne boomed from the front of the Hall. "We must— No, there's no fire, Martell. And no, no flood either. Listen, we—listen, please!"

I put my fingers together and whistled as I had seen Alastair do when summoning Akarra. The note came out sharp and clear and much, much louder than I'd expected. Every head turned in my direction. Whispers rippled through the crowd as they recognized me.

"Manor-folk!" I cried. "Aye, it's Aliza Bentaine. There's no time for details; *Tekari* are coming. Banshees, direwolves, maybe others." Whispers rose to full panicked conversations and I heard at least one voice mutter something about the rumors being true, but I waved my hands. "Listen to me! My husband and his dragon will be back to guard the Manor House before they get here, but we need to prepare."

"How?" a man I didn't know asked.

I relayed Alastair's instructions. "With any luck they'll pass by the house altogether, but in the meantime, block off any way they could get inside," I said as the crowd dispersed to begin siege preparations.

"What can we do?" Leyda asked.

I looked at my sisters. Mari clutched her bestiary to her chest, eyes wide and wary. Leyda stood with arms folded and chin thrust out, as if defying all the *Tekari* of Arle at once. She'd abandoned the crutches she'd been using when I last saw her and her broken leg seemed to have healed straight, but I didn't for a second imagine that meant she'd forgotten the War of the Worm. Wydrick's betrayal on the battlefield had left scars deeper than the skin.

"Find a mallet and meet me out in the garden in ten minutes," I said.

"Find a *what?*"

"Just come on!" Mari said, and dragged Leyda away.

"Aliza! Over here!"

I dodged the barrel-chested farrier and his son, ducked beneath the angry gesticulations of Madam Moore, and met Gwyn in a tight embrace. Tight but brief; her son at once made clear his disapproval of a stranger commandeering his mother's attention. She released me and took my hand. "I wasn't sure . . . but gods, I'm glad you came."

"I'm sorry it couldn't be sooner. What was it you had to tell me?"

She looked around. Besides the farrier and Madam Moore, Lord Merybourne and a handful of men stood beneath the massive windows debating the best way to barricade them. At the sound of overturning tables, the baby let out a piteous wail. Gwyn sighed. "I'm sorry, dearest. Later."

It took everything in me not to press for answers, but with a fussing baby and the danger hanging over our heads, I knew better than to argue. I saw her back to her family's apartments and waved a hurried hello to Madam Carlyle, Gwyn's little sister Rya, and an astonished Wynce Curdred before jogging back downstairs to meet my sisters in the garden.

"ISN'T THIS SUPPOSED TO WORK?" LEYDA WHISPERED.

"Shush," I said, and hammered the ground again with the mallet. We crouched in a grassy patch of garden near the kitchens, or what would have been a grassy patch before the rain. Mud spattered my arms and trousers at each blow.

Leyda made a face and dodged the next shower of muddy drops. "What if they're already hibernating?"

"Garden-folk don't seal their Underburrow until after Saint Ellia's Day," Mari said from my other side. "Now *shhh!*"

I struck the ground once more, hoping I remembered the correct pattern in Low Gnomic earth-sign. The message *Enemies approaching. Help needed!* should've been traveling through the snug tunnels of the Merybourne Underburrow, stirring all the garden-folk to, if not our immediate assistance, then at least curiosity strong enough to send someone up to the surface to see what was the matter. I repeated the pattern a fourth time and sat back on my heels to stretch my aching arms. Mari shifted beside me, mud squelching beneath her boots. Leyda sighed loudly. I thought of Alastair, who'd returned soon after we'd left our family apartments with word that Trollhedge and Little Dembley were preparing for an attack. As yet neither village had seen any sign of the approaching *Tekari*, but he said they'd agreed to sound a hunting horn when they were spotted and so pass along a warning.

Mari, Leyda, and I had left him to preside over the tiny fighting force Lord Merybourne had cobbled together: three blacksmiths with their hammers and pokers, the woodcutter and carpenter with their axes, Madam Moore the apothecary with her healer's pouch and a pair of silver daggers, a handful of hunters with longbows and crossbows, and to my surprise, Henry Brandon with an elegant and ornately impractical rapier. "A gift," he'd said, reddening when Alastair examined it. "From the theater troupe in Edonarle."

"Do you know how to use it?"

"I have it on reliable authority the sharp end goes toward the enemy, milord."

Alastair only shrugged. "Good enough."

My plan had met at first with exasperation, then with hesitation, but Alastair had at last agreed it was worth a try. Akarra had flown west to scout for any sign of the horde's approach. I could see her in the distance, swooping low over the woods beyond the west pastures.

"What do we do now?" Leyda asked.

There was a rustling behind us. I whipped around, but there was nothing except sodden leaf litter, fallen branches, and the Manor wall. The *drip-drip-drip* of water from the bare shrubs beat like the tick of a clock in my mind. *Late! Late! Too late!* it said. I lowered the mallet for a fifth attempt when Mari tugged my sleeve and pointed.

"*Hgud!*" she said in Gnomic. "Hello!"

A tangle of mossy hair worked its way through the mud to

our left. The hobgoblin blinked and swiveled to see us better, her shoulders still belowground. "Eh? What's this all about?" she asked in Gnomic.

"Is Chief Hobblehilt nearby?" I asked. "We need to speak with him."

The hobgoblin was unmoved. "You just signed *enemies are approaching*. What enemies? Where?"

"That's what we need to talk to him about," Mari said in nearly flawless Low Gnomic. "There's a whole horde of *Tekari* coming from the northwest."

The hobgoblin squeaked and disappeared, only to reappear a few minutes later with the fat, surly chief of the Merybourne Underburrow and a number of other garden-folk, including, to my delight, my old friend Tobble. He squealed when he saw me and jumped into my arms as Mari began explaining the situation to Chief Hobblehilt.

"Aliza! You came back!" Tobble said.

"Of course I did, silly," I murmured. "You didn't think I'd stay away forever, did you?"

"They said that *snudgut*—sorry, that dragonrider of yours took you away to his palace in the mountains. We didn't think we'd ever see you again!"

His words were teasing, but there was a hint of uncertainty in his tone that stirred a guilty pang in my heart. Dealing with the aftermath of the Worm had occupied the inhabitants of Hart's Run for weeks after the battle, both human and *Shani* alike, and with my own time divided between my sister Anjey's wedding preparations and my own, I'd given less thought than I should have to a proper farewell to my friends among the garden-folk. Tobble's chiding was well deserved. I kissed his damp forehead. "I'm sorry. I should have told you."

"Aye, you should've. But *shh*, I want to hear what's going on!"

"You *sure* these creatures will pass through Merybourne?" Hobblehilt was asking Mari. She looked to me.

"No, Your Honor, we're not sure," I told him. "They might go around. I hope they do, but if not, we can't let them pass without a fight."

Chief Hobblehilt stroked his mossy chin and exchanged a glance with his underlings. One of them, a thin gnome in a mud-colored uniform, bent down and whispered a few words in his ear. The chief nodded solemnly. "Well, when you put it like *that*..." He turned back to us. "We were unprepared for the Battle of North Fields. The *Thegegth* monsters won't find us so again. What do you need from us?"

I smiled. "How fast can your people dig?"

CHAPTER 10

SISTERS-IN-ARMS

The sun was angling low in the cloudy sky when we heard the first horn from Little Dembley. Henry tapped my shoulder and pointed up. Just visible in the distance, Akarra wheeled and dove, spitting dragonfire. I swore and threw down the bundle of branches and garden debris I was carrying. It joined a long, low pile stretching the entire length of the west pasture. Lower than it should be, but there wasn't time for anything more. Even with a score of volunteers from the Manor helping build it up, it was hardly an obstacle, let alone a defense.

"Back! All of you, back to your positions," Alastair cried.

The Manor-folk scattered, disappearing beneath the fringe of pines that bordered the pasture. The sounds of grunting and a few curses tumbled down as those with bows hoisted themselves into the lowest branches of the trees. Those with axes, swords, daggers, and hammers retreated beneath the boughs. Henry was the last to vanish, grimly saluting with his rapier before taking cover.

Or nearly the last. A dark braid swung out of sight toward the end of the line. *Oh no you don't!* A foul word slipped out as I dashed toward the figure.

"Watch it!" Leyda cried as I pulled her from the trees. The farrier's hammer in her belt tipped out and landed on the ground with a soggy squelch.

"What are you doing out here? And where did you get that hammer?"

"Master Farris had an extra!"

"He— Oh, never *mind*," I hissed. "You're supposed to be inside with the others!"

"You told Henry that everyone who can fight should fight," she said. "Well, I can fight! I *want* to fight, Aliza."

"No."

"Why not? You're out here, aren't you?"

"Aye, but I'm . . ." I stopped. *I was what, exactly?* A Daired? Hardly, at least not in any way that counted on the battlefield. Here and now, though, that was beside the point. I would not lose another sister to the *Tekari.* "We'll be fine. Get back to the house."

Alastair jogged up. "What's going on? Miss Leyda, what are you doing?"

"She was just leaving," I said, but Leyda sidestepped my grasp and snatched up her hammer.

"I'm going to help, Master Daired," she said firmly.

He took the hammer from her and gave it an experimental swing. "With this?"

"It's all I could get my hands on, sir."

"Badly weighted for you, Miss Leyda."

"Exactly. Thank you, Alastair," I said. "*Now* will you—?"

"You'd better use this instead." He drew a long knife from the sheath strapped to his calf and handed it to her.

"*Alastair!*"

Leyda turned an even deeper shade of red. "Are you—? I mean, thank—*thank you*, my lord!" She took the knife, bowed, and vanished into the trees before I could stop her.

"Are you mad?" I said. "Alastair, she's seventeen! She doesn't know how to fight."

"Most of the people here don't know how to fight, and your sister's seen more of the battlefield than all of them combined. Besides," he added with a shadow of a smile, "you should know better. Bentaine women are notoriously hard to dissuade."

I clenched my teeth, hating him for being right, hating myself for handing him the one argument I couldn't stand against, but before I could rally fresh protests, a second horn sounded from the west. The *Tekari* were getting closer. Fear swept anger clean away and I gripped Alastair's arm, thinking suddenly of the scar on his shoulder and his maimed hand and the numbing doubt that weighed down his sword arm. *What if all this wasn't enough?*

He covered my hand with his. "Aliza, it's all right. They won't get through." He nodded to the line of brush and overturned earth before us. "It was a good plan."

"And if they do?"

"Then I'll be waiting."

"What if they go around?"

"Akarra will make sure they don't."

I looked up. Akarra had stopped flaming and was flying toward us. Alastair leaned down and kissed me softly. *"Myet av-bakhan, khera."*

"Aye, you be on your guard too." I slipped my hand into the pocket beneath his hauberk and drew out the little bottle of beeswax. "Don't forget this."

I left him warming the vial in his hand and retreated to the trees. The branches were dense and it took a moment to find Leyda crouched beside one of the largest trunks. "You have no idea how much trouble you're in," I murmured, settling next to her. "Mama and Papa must be worried sick."

"Papa knows I'm here, Aliza," she said calmly. "I told him I was coming."

I looked at her then, really looked at her. She had told him—told, not asked. *And he'd agreed?* What must she have said to persuade him that she belonged out here on the front lines, that she was no longer a child in need of protecting? What arguments must have raged before Papa was at last able to admit that the War of the Worm had done away with his wide-eyed, carefree little girl forever? I blinked, and blinked again. So much had changed since I'd last seen my family, but this? This *hurt*. Leyda, my baby sister, was my baby sister no longer. *And if not that, then what?*

The answer came with equal parts pride and sadness. *An ally.* Not only that; she was an ally who'd once been closer to our enemy than any of us except Alastair. I glanced around. One of the blacksmiths stood two trees away, glaring through the boughs at the empty pasture beyond. On the other side, several branches above the ground, a hunter tested her bowstring.

"Leyda," I said quietly, "before this starts, I need to ask you something. About what happened with Wydrick."

The shock in her eyes hit me like a crossbow bolt to the gut, but her expression hardened before I could take it back. I willed away the memory of the monsters she'd seen, that we'd both seen on the blood-soaked battlefield, and took her hand. She would not meet my gaze.

"I'm sorry. I wouldn't ask if it wasn't important," I said.

"I already told you what I remember."

"Everything?"

"I—" She looked up. There was a long pause. "Tell me why it's important."

The words reeled back and forth in my head. *Tell her—spare her.* Would the truth pour poison or salt into the wound? *Kill or help heal?* Painful either way, but I had no right to keep it from her. As quickly and quietly as I could, I told her about the ghasts we'd encountered in the Old Wilds and of Wydrick's cryptic warning in Morianton. She listened without speaking, her eyes fixed on my face, her expression inscrutable save for the occasional tensing of her jaw.

"Whatever the *ghastradi* are planning, it's going to come to a head in Edonarle, and soon," I said. "Did Wydrick give any hint as to what might be coming when you last spoke?"

"Is that why you were heading south?" she asked. "You didn't come to see us?"

"We *did* come to see you, dearest, but we need to know what we're facing after this, and for that we need all the information we can get. Anything you remember about him. What he did, what he said."

"Ask your husband. He was there too."

"He didn't speak to Wydrick."

She parted the branches with the tip of Alastair's knife and looked out over the fields. He stood guard a few paces from us, sword in hand, watching Akarra's approach. She was very close now, zigzagging just above the treetops, pushing the *Tekari* toward us.

"Leyda?"

"'One of us must make the sacrifice or all Arle will be destroyed,'" she said softly. "That's what Tristan told me before he broke my leg."

"What did he mean?"

"I don't know." She paused, and her next words came with effort. "Aliza, I don't know if it was quite *him* at that point."

"You saw his eyes change?"

"For just a moment." She ran the blade of Alastair's dagger along her sleeve, as if wiping away streaks of nonexistent blood. "It went back and forth. Like he couldn't make up his mind. It scared me, and that's when I decided to run. Only—he stopped me. Or his ghast did, I don't know. I wasn't thinking *ghastradi* then, but I really wasn't thinking much at all after I saw what he meant to do."

"Was that when he broke your leg?"

She shook her head. "Not right away. I remember feeling something . . . cold." She touched her chest, right above her heart. "Cold and angry. It's hard to explain. I didn't know what it was, or where it came from. I just knew I had to fight."

The remembered sting of flesh striking flesh prickled through my palm. Wydrick had hinted at what he intended for my sister in the tavern at Morianton. Another *ghastradi*, born of terror and desperation on the battlefield, feeding on the innocent fear of Leyda's young heart, subservient to Wydrick and Wydrick's mysterious master. I squeezed her hand. Betrayed, crippled, with escape impossible and the Greater Lindworm bearing down on her, and still she had resisted. All the undying strength of the *ghastradi* brotherhood, all their wiles and dark plans, broken by the stubborn heart of one young girl.

A warning rippled through the line and the hunter and the blacksmith both paused to plug their ears with beeswax. Leyda moved to do the same, pulling a little box from her pocket. I caught her hand, pulled her close, and kissed her forehead.

"You're brilliant, Leyda. You know that, right?"

She blinked. "Well, aye. But what was that for?"

A direwolf's howl echoed from the forest to the west. Our smiles evaporated. I nodded to the box of beeswax. "Later. Put that in."

She obeyed, and I did the same. The world of sound shrank,

stoppered like a cork until all I could hear was my own breath and the galloping thud of my heart. It was a strange and unpleasant sensation. I made signs to Leyda to keep her knife at the ready and pushed the branches aside. The sun had dropped below the trees and the shadows along the west side of the pasture were deepening and *moving*. The black shapes of direwolves sprang from the woods in a silent cascade, their fangs bared. A sharp ache jolted through my jaw, my teeth, and I covered my ears. The beeswax blocked the worst of the banshees' screams but could not mitigate its effects entirely, and I gasped in relief when it stopped. The banshees broke the cover of the trees in a line of pale, long-limbed horrors, their mouths gaping open, but it seemed they could no longer spare breath for screaming. Grasses swayed beneath their feet, moved by creatures unseen. *Blast!* Another kind of *Tekari*.

Alastair crouched in a guard position as Akarra burst through the last row of trees, trailing dragonfire. The direwolves straying too far south changed course and bunched together, redoubling their speed as they charged toward our miserable barrier of sticks and the lone figure of a Rider between them and the Manor.

My heart in my throat, I readied my dagger. They were only fifty yards away now, this snarling wave of fangs and fury. Only twenty. Only ten. Now close enough to see the muscles bunch in the lead direwolf's hindquarters. It sprang over the barrier in a single bound, jaws open, eyes fastened on Alastair's throat. It landed a few feet from him—and disappeared.

I didn't need to hear to imagine the wolfish yelp as it crashed headfirst through the layer of sticks and leaves we'd laid over the trench the garden-folk had dug, nor the sickening crack as the angle of its leap brought its neck into fatal contact with the edge of the ditch. Its body slumped out of sight. Others followed, too close to stop, and Akarra drove those that were relentlessly forward with her dragonfire. Leyda punched the air next to me, her mouth open in a soundless cheer. One enormous banshee dodged the flames, sank low, and sprang straight up, only to fall back with an arrow protruding from its bony chest. The huntswoman to our right smiled and notched a second arrow with shaky hands.

A second banshee let out a scream I felt in every bone. It leapt over its fallen comrade, using its corpse as a bridge, and landed next to Alastair. He ducked beneath its claws, fell to one knee, and thrust upward. The banshee swiped with its other claw, but Alastair twisted, drawing the blade out and swinging it back in one motion. The banshee's last scream fell silent as its head slid from its shoulders.

Akarra's roar shook the earth. She swooped low and snapped up a third banshee in midair as it attempted the same leap as its fellow.

Movement in the corner of my eye. I tugged Leyda's sleeve. Small gray-skinned creatures, all knobby arms and legs and marshfire eyes, swarmed over the bodies of their *Tekari* allies. *Hagsprites!* I grabbed her hand and dragged her sideways as one came hurtling through the boughs, narrowly missing our heads. We stabbed at the same time, but the creature dodged our knives and scuttled away, only to fall with a jerk and an arrow in its neck. Leyda crouched and readied her knife as more hagsprites crawled out of the ditch. I caught one down the shoulder, its dull silver blood spraying me, Leyda, and the tree behind us. I felt its shriek reverberating through the steel as it tried to claw itself free. A bloodred tongue snaked from its open mouth, long and thin as a whip as it lashed toward my face. I yanked my dagger free and ducked, just missing the stinging barbs on the underside of its tongue. My upstroke severed it, but not cleanly, and the hagsprite gurgled, spitting silver blood as it tried to flee, only to meet its end on Leyda's blade.

She drew it out and lashed upward, managing another solid hit as a second hagsprite sprang for her throat. A thudding from the left drew my attention; the blacksmith beat back three at a time with his great hammer, mouth open in what I could only imagine was a fearsome war cry. Panting, Leyda shook her knife free from the hagsprite's body and looked around, but there were no more hagsprites in our immediate vicinity.

I turned back to the field just in time to see another direwolf fall with a howl, an arrow protruding from its side. It stumbled into the trench, followed by Alastair's blade. Akarra wheeled overhead and bellowed something that made him fall back. He looked over his shoulder and waved frantically toward the trees. I saw what he meant just in time.

"Get down!" I shouted, and pulled Leyda behind the trunk of the tree.

Akarra checked her flight at the west end of the pasture and dived, exhaling dragonfire as she followed the path of the trench. Flames filled the hollow like water, consuming wood, earth, and any *Tekari* within. The heat hit us like a battering ram as she flew by. Charred pine needles, blazing branches, and smoking clods of earth rained down through the trees. I slapped at the sparks that landed on Leyda's sleeve, and together we stamped out the remaining debris that the damp ground hadn't extinguished. We looked at each other over the steaming earth, both breathing hard. The sound of my own heartbeat rattled in my ears.

"Is it over?" Leyda mouthed.

I shook my head and pointed to Alastair. He stood as close as he dared to the trench, now a smoldering, smoking pit, his sword still at the ready. Akarra landed next to him. He said something and she nodded.

I touched Leyda's shoulder. "Now it's over."

The sounds rushed back as I pulled the beeswax from my ears: the crackle of flames, the sizzle of burning flesh, the sighs and laughter from among the Manor-folk as they too saw the battle was won. The blacksmith came over and clapped me on the back.

"Good thinking with them diggings, Miss Aliza. And Miss Leyda, you've some mite o' luck with a blade! Those little beasties didn't hurt you, did they?"

Leyda shook her head. "We—"

"Look out!" the huntswoman cried. My hand was halfway back to the beeswax in my pocket when I saw it slinking out from the shadows of the trees: the gaunt, bloody form of the largest direwolf I'd ever seen. The silver hair along its spine stood straight up, and its eyes glowed green in the flickering light of the fire. Slowly its massive head swung from side to side, taking in the whole length of the pasture and the smoking ruin that was all that remained of its pack. Its gaze landed at last on Alastair. It lifted its snout to the darkening sky and howled.

Alastair raised his sword.

"*Khela*, that's not wise," Akarra warned. "Let me—"

"Rider!" the direwolf snapped. "I summon you as the ancient customs demand: on the honor of your bloodstained House, if it has any left. You alone and I alone and none to interfere. Face me! Face me and pay for what you've done!"

A stunned silence rolled out across the field, followed by a low growl from Akarra. Leyda looked from me to Alastair and back, her mouth very round. I heard Goryn Mauntell's laughter in my ears and thought of his smile as he had delivered the same formal challenge in Rushless Wood. The tip of Alastair's sword dipped. He looked over his shoulder and caught my eye. There was a question there, a question at once frightening and reassuring, and I swallowed hard, feeling suddenly the terrible weight of the decision he was offering me.

I nodded.

"Take me to him," Alastair said to Akarra.

"*Khela . . .*"

"Take me to him, Akarra."

She grunted. "Very well."

He swung onto her back and she rose into the air, landing just beyond the smoldering ditch. "As you wish, direwolf," Alastair said as he dismounted and drew his sword. "You and I and no other. My dragon will not interfere."

"Good," the direwolf growled, and lunged.

I covered my mouth as Alastair went down. The huntswoman notched another arrow, but before she could shoot he was up again, the direwolf's jaws missing his shoulder by inches. His sword came down in a wide arc, slashing deeply along the wolf's hindquarters. It howled in pain and spun, snapping. Alastair ducked again, but he was a half second too slow. The wolf hit him hard, throwing off his next stroke. The point of his sword swung wide and buried itself in the earth as he fell to one knee. Akarra started forward with a growl, but Alastair kicked up just as the direwolf sprang for him. Iron-shod boot connected with the creature's jaw with a crunch I felt even from the distance. It whined and stumbled back. Alastair staggered upright and pulled his sword from the mud. For a minute they circled each other as each caught their breath, testing, feinting, and, I noted with horror, both limping.

"Master Daired! He's hurt," Leyda cried, and drew her knife. I pulled her back. "Aliza! Someone has to help him!"

"No! Let him do this."

Alastair's voice carried faintly from beyond the crackling

embers, steady but stretched thin with pain. "Tell me, wolf," he said. "Tell me where your pack was headed and I'll give you a clean death."

The direwolf gave a sharp, barking laugh. "You *fool*," it panted. "You meddle in things you know nothing about."

"Then tell me."

"A great and ancient thing is stirring, something you have never dreamed of in your darkest nightmares. It has no name. It has no fears. It will conquer your kingdom and bring your people down to the dust where you belong, and it will begin in Edonarle." Its mouth fell open, tongue lolling in a terrible predatory grin. "But you shall never see it. You will not leave this field alive."

"We'll see."

White flickered under the eaves of the trees. I cried out as a smaller direwolf charged Alastair from behind. Akarra roared and caught it headlong with a blast of dragonfire, but it was all the distraction the first direwolf needed. With a snarl it launched itself at Alastair's exposed throat.

I never saw him bring his sword up. The blade never flashed. The direwolf scarcely made a sound. For one horrible second it was on top of him, then a deep and dreadful shudder ran through its entire body as it slumped sideways. Alastair rolled out from underneath and drew his sword from its belly. It tried to raise its head once, twice, then gave up with a snarl. Alastair limped around its other side, out of reach of its snapping fangs.

"You have no honor, direwolf, but I do." He placed the point of his sword over the creature's heart. "I keep my word," he said, and thrust.

CHAPTER 11

THE RIGHT NOBLE
HOUSE OF CURDRED

I wanted to run to him, to cheer, to shout his triumph to the skies. The blacksmith let out a rumbling laugh and hefted his hammer over one shoulder. "Miss Aliza, you've gone and married a right champion, you have. That's as fine a piece o' work with a sword as ever I seen."

"Aye, very neat, but are we sure they're *all* dead?" the hunter said. She'd not taken her arrow off the string.

The *yes* died on my tongue as a scream rang out from the Manor House. A *human* scream. Leyda and I exchanged a horrified glance before bolting for the house, the hunter and blacksmith hard on our heels.

We heard the sounds of the struggle before we rounded the hedge: grunts and hisses and the shrill, piping shriek of a Gnomic war cry. "Take *that*, you *Thegegth* filth!"

On the path to the kitchens, three gnomes and two hobgoblins wielding tiny spears faced off against a pair of hagsprites. A third hagsprite lay dead in the leaf litter, speared through the eye. One of the gnomes was bleeding heavily from a cut on his forehead.

"Watch out!"

There was a twang and a zip. The largest hagsprite fell just before it could spring, howling in pain and clutching the arrow in its back. Its companion hissed and spun toward the huntswoman following us, but the garden-folk were on it the instant it turned its back. We halted next to them as they finished it off. The bleeding gnome waved frantically toward the house.

"We couldn't stop them all, Miss Aliza. Some of them got in!"

Another scream rang out as we ducked inside. Claw marks raked the wood of the kitchen door, and the lock had been chewed through from the outside. The kitchens were deserted.

"Find Mama and Papa," I told Leyda. "Make sure they're safe. Go with her, please," I asked the huntswoman as she charged up the back stair. "Master Blacksmith, with me."

We followed the sounds of raised voices down the corridor toward the front of the house. Claws had scored the floors here too, and every few feet there were drops of silver blood. A vase on the banister of the main staircase had been smashed against the baseboards. I sprang up the stairs two at a time, the blacksmith huffing along behind me.

"Miss!"

I nearly ran headfirst into one of the kitchen maids at the top. "Jenny! What are you doing? Get inside!"

"They went the other way, miss," she said, and pointed back down the hall toward the family quarters. "They're trying to get into the Carlyles'! I was—"

I was off at a dead run, no longer caring if the blacksmith followed. The corridors were dark, but I'd run these halls countless times before. I breathed a silent prayer of thanks to see my family's door shut and no sounds of struggle within, but my stomach twisted as I rounded the corner. The Carlyles' door hung open, tilted on its hinges, still swinging gently. There was the sound of grunting and scratching from inside.

I bit back a scream as something touched my arm. "Shhh. It's me, Miss Aliza." The hunter nodded to the door and edged forward, one hand at the nearly empty quiver on her hip. The sounds of scratching and grunting grew louder as we approached. She moved to one side and peered around the corner, then drew back quickly and fitted an arrow to the string. "They're at the sitting room door."

"How many?" I whispered.

"Three. Big ones."

Blast. She had only two arrows left, and I no longer trusted my shaking hands to hit anything. The blacksmith puffed up. "Three? Right. One for each of us, eh?" he whispered. "One, two—"

Wood splintered. Madam Carlyle screamed.

"Now!" I cried, and leapt into the Carlyles' front room. Splinters and bits of door littered the floor, which was slick with silver blood. The hagsprites had chewed and clawed a gap in the door just wide enough to slink through, and as we watched, the hindquarters of the last hagsprite wriggled into the room beyond. An arrow bit into the doorframe, just missing it. The huntswoman swore.

More screams. This time it was little Rya.

"Gwyn! Open the door!" I yelled.

The screams stopped.

"Open the door!"

There was a sharp cracking sound from inside. One of the hagsprites shrieked.

"And *that*"—a thump and another shriek—"will teach you"—

crack—"to mind your own"—a howl and the sound of claws tearing at wood—"business!"

A bloody hagsprite pushed its way through the broken door, howling in pain as it hobbled along on three legs. The second followed, in worse shape than the first. There was no third.

They saw us at the same time, but it was too late to retreat. One hissed a challenge, its tongue licking toward the huntswoman like a whip. Her last arrow brought it down before it could lunge. The blacksmith finished the second. I leapt over the bodies before they'd stopped twitching and banged on the broken door. "Gwyn! Madam Carlyle! Are you all right?"

"We're fine," came Gwyn's shaky answer, and the door swung open. She stood on the threshold, her son clutched tightly in her arms, eyes wide with a mixture of fear, astonishment, and to my surprise, delight. "Come in."

Long claw marks scored the floor leading up to the table, where Madam Carlyle, Master Carlyle, and little Rya stood perched, their faces frozen in various degrees of shock. Rya was crying softly into her mother's skirts. In front of them, impeccably cravated as ever, stood Wynce Curdred, wiping the silver blood from his ornate cane-sword. The third hagsprite lay at his feet. When he saw me, he dropped into an elegant bow.

"Lady Aliza! What an unexpected pleasure."

I opened my mouth and found all words had fled.

Gwyn seized my hand. "The other *Tekari*—?"

"Dead, young mistress," the blacksmith said through the crack in the door. "Won't be troubling you again."

"And the battle?" Madam Carlyle said from the table.

"Won."

"Oh, thank Mikla," she breathed, and hugged her daughter

as Master Carlyle wrapped his arms around them both. "There, there, dear. It's all right now."

Still struggling to wrap my mind around the sight before me, I looked from Curdred to Gwyn and back again.

She smiled. "Aye, dearest. We have *much* to talk about."

WORD OF THE BATTLE'S END SPREAD QUICKLY, HELPED along by the blacksmith, Henry, and any number of garden-folk too excited by the evening's events to return to their Underburrow. I found myself running errands to every floor of the Manor, carrying bandages for Madam Moore, herbal unguents for Cook, and reassurance for everyone that the *Tekari* would not trouble them again tonight. To those who didn't believe me, I simply pointed to the columns of smoke rising from the western field, where Akarra and Alastair were burning the bodies. "They won't let anything else through," I promised.

Sunset didn't see any slowing of activity in the Manor House. Lanterns were lit and the bustle continued. Lord and Lady Merybourne worked alongside the servants, sweeping up broken crockery in the kitchens, scraping smooth the scored floors, and tending to the Carlyles' broken doors. Papa trailed after Lord Merybourne, acting as scribe for all the damages. Along with Hilda and Madam Carlyle, Mama presided over the distribution of tea to any and all who wanted it. Sidetracked by the hunger of a fussy baby, Gwyn promised to meet me in my father's study once her son had finished nursing. Eager as I was to hear what she had to tell me, I appreciated the interlude. There were other things I needed to attend to.

I found Leyda back in our family's sitting room, still dressed in her muddy and blood-spattered trousers, eyes bright as she re-counted the story of the battle for Mari, who was furiously transcribing in her journal. Every once in a while she'd pause and look up at Leyda, her mouth round.

"He *didn't*."

"Thell as my witness, he did!" Leyda said. "Ducked right under the direwolf and stabbed it through the heart. Hello, Aliza. Then Akarra . . ."

I smiled and left them to their work.

Fires still smoldered in the trench along the edge of the west pasture, its flickering light filtering in strange shadows through the border of trees and the gardens beyond. I snatched a lantern from the kitchens and slipped outside carefully, my dagger in easy reach at my hip, but as I'd promised the Manor-folk, it was no longer necessary. The *Tekari* were gone. The garden, however, was far from abandoned. I jumped as Tobble trotted into the lamplight.

"Aliza!"

"Goodness, you scared me!" I crouched down and looked him over, but besides some grass stains and streaks of mud, he looked no worse for wear. "You weren't hurt at all, were you? Or any of your folk?"

"No, no, I'm fine. Corporal Thatch took a claw to the forehead, but Old Hedge is patching him up. Were you?"

"I'm all right."

"Good." He brightened and scrambled up into my lap, leaving muddy footprints. "Are you staying for Saint Ellia's Day?"

"Oh, Tobble, I'm sorry. We're heading to Edonarle tomorrow." His face fell.

"We'll . . ." *We'll be back again soon*, I wanted to say, but all that awaited us in Edonarle suddenly weighed down my tongue and left my promise unspoken. What did we know of what was coming or how long it would take to defeat? "I'm sorry we can't stay longer."

He looked up at me and wrinkled his nose. "Dragon business?

More like"—he gestured around to the claw marks on the door—
"this?"

"Aye."

Tobble didn't answer right away, only looked at me searchingly.
A chill wind whistled through the garden, stirring cold, autumnal
sounds in the dark. I shivered. "Are you scared?" he asked at last.

"Yes. I am."

He rose to his tiptoes and planted a kiss on my cheek. "It'll be
all right. You won here; you'll win there too. Whatever trouble
your Rider's gotten you into, you're not in it alone." He made a
face. "Speaking of, you might want to go see him. Hobblehilt said
he's still out in the pasture."

I thanked him and set him down, promising to say goodbye
before we left, and he scurried off into the foliage.

The wind turned, carrying with it the smell of charred flesh
and dragonfire. It grew stronger beyond the barrier of pines and
I paused on the edge of the trench, staring for a moment at the
burning shapes within before tearing my gaze away. A speck of
light shone in the field beyond the trench.

"Alastair?"

He stood, his silhouette dark against the lantern light. I forgot
the makeshift pyre before me, forgot the horror and the fear and the
creeping chill, remembering instead his courage, his battle prowess,
unhampered by fear or pain, the fluidity of his sword in that final
stroke against the direwolf, and the distance between us was suddenly intolerable. The fire lit the path around the trench; I ran as
fast as I dared. Then his hands were on my waist and my hands were
in his hair and I pulled him close for a kiss as desperate as it was delicious, and ten thousand lifetimes weren't long enough for us to get
our fill of each other, so this moment would have to do.

"You were magnificent, Alastair," I said. "*Magnificent.*"

"I want you, *khera*," he growled in my ear. "Here and now, I want you."

I closed my eyes as his kisses grew more insistent. The gods had a cruel sense of timing. There wasn't much of me left that hadn't handed sense over to something much more enjoyable, but the sliver that remained had a loud voice. "Later," I tried.

"Hmm?"

"Alastair, later!"

"Now. Right now."

"We still have—*oh*—we have work to do."

"Thell take our work, Aliza, and Thell take the whole bloody kingdom. I *need* you."

"I need you too." I kissed him, long and deep, before gently pushing him away. "But *later.*"

For an instant he moved as if to kiss me again. Then he drew back, breathing hard, and touched my cheek. The firelight traced his features in glorious golden contour, and the shadows could not disguise the desire in his gaze. It was softer now: less wild, less dangerous, but no less beautiful. All at once he grinned. "Now we're even, aren't we?"

"What?"

"For that night in Castle Selwyn."

I smiled. He'd certainly made amends for his denial in Lake Meera when we'd stopped at House Pendragon, but I was perfectly content to let the debt resurface. "Aye, we are." I took his sword hand and pressed it to my lips. "Don't worry, dearest. I'll make it up to you."

IT TOOK MORE WILLPOWER THAN I THOUGHT I POS-sessed to bring myself back to the task at hand, but the new battle scars decorating the Manor House sobered me. I sat down with Gwyn in Papa's study and poured her a cup of tea. She took it gratefully.

"I must say, this was a more exciting visit than I hoped for," she said. "I can't tell you how glad I am you came, and not just because you and Master Daired saved our lives."

I raised a teasing eyebrow. "Your husband didn't seem to need any help."

"No, he didn't." She took a sip of tea and gave me a sidelong glance.

We burst out laughing.

"That was rather wonderful, wasn't it?" she said when we'd recovered enough to speak. "Not something Wynce has ever done before, but then, there haven't been any opportunities in Hunter's Forge. I always suspected he kept a sword in that cane of his."

"He did splendidly, Gwyn. You make sure to tell him that." I grew serious. "But your letter. What was it you couldn't write to me?"

Instead of answering, she fished in her pocket of her dressing gown and pulled out a crumpled envelope. "Tell me what you think of that."

I unfolded the scrap of paper inside. There was no greeting, no name, simply a tally of figures.

Loan: 70 silver dragonbacks
Interest: 30 silver dragonbacks
Total required: 100 dragonbacks
Payment in heartstones only

It was sealed at the bottom with an imprint of the roaring sphinx of Els.

"They made you pay in heartstones?" I asked.

"Aye. We were to deliver them to a courier from Lithosmith Row."

"Did you know the courier?"

"No. She was just a girl, Leyda's age, maybe, and I don't think she knew anything about it. Just another message to run. That's not all. Turn it over."

I did. It took a moment to find the postscript, smudged as the paper was with soot and ink stains.

> When the time comes, you must stand aside. Do not fight, and you will live. These are the final terms. You will not hear from us again.

A chill ran down my spine. The *ghastradi* of the lithosmith in Hatch Ford had said something similar. *"Stand aside and live—or fight us and die."* Els, the Shadow Minister, debts around the kingdom, war, *ghastradi,* heartstones, the Silent King . . . they were all connected. This confirmed it. *But how?* And perhaps most important, *why?*

"What do you make of it?" Gwyn asked.

"I honestly don't know."

She drew in a shuddering breath "Tonight, with the hagsprites. Maybe I'm losing my mind, but I couldn't help but think it was a warning."

"What?"

"Perhaps they'd seen I'd written to you, that my letter was my way to fight back, and they sent them to frighten us . . ." She covered her face. "Oh, gods, Aliza, what's going on?"

A tap at the door curtailed my attempt at comfort. We looked up to see an abashed Curdred in the doorway, his son squalling in his arms. "I'm so sorry to intrude, my dear, but I'm afraid he's been rather inconsolable."

She sighed and took the baby, whose cries settled at once to happy cooing. Curdred chuckled and rested a hand on her shoulder. Suddenly unsure of how much Gwyn had shared with her husband, I tried to slide the letter out of sight, but Gwyn saw and shook her head.

"No need. He knows."

Curdred's gaze landed on the paper. "Ah. I see."

"I was telling her about the terms," Gwyn said.

"They were paid. Gwyn and her father are free and clear of this, Lady Aliza."

The protective, almost desperate way Curdred said it made me repent of every time I'd judged him in the first days of our acquaintance. This man, for all his oddities, was fiercely devoted to my friend, and for that he had earned my respect.

Still, I had to know. "One hundred dragonbacks in heartstones is a small fortune, Master Curdred."

Gwyn looked up at her husband.

"It is," he said simply.

I smiled and stood. "You're a good man, Wynce Curdred."

"You're kind, Lady Aliza, but every marriage comes with debts," he said thoughtfully, taking his wife's hand. "Perhaps we were fortunate. Ours had the luxury of a ledger."

Fortunate indeed. Understanding the look they exchanged, I thanked Gwyn again and bid them goodnight. After the events of the evening, they had earned some well-deserved time alone.

In any case, I had a debt of my own to settle.

CHAPTER 12

CITY OF KINGS AND QUEENS

Alastair, Akarra, and I left soon after sunrise the next morning, the wind at our backs brisk and biting cold. Despite the fond farewells of family and friends, I climbed into the saddle in a bad mood that Alastair didn't share. Half an hour's search had not turned up even so much as a glimpse of Tobble, and Alastair had finally had to cut short my efforts before I could say goodbye.

Leaving wasn't the only thing that left a bad taste on the back of my tongue. The sweetness of victory soured with the dawn, which put our fight with the *Tekari* firmly in its rightful place: a mere skirmish, a troubling of supply lines to the true battle. We'd sweat and bled, and our real work hadn't even started.

The journey from Merybourne to Edonarle took a full day and the better part of a second. We might have made better time if Akarra hadn't refused to land until we found a suitably hospitable town, but with images of the *Tekari* attack fresh in my mind, I wasn't about to make a fuss over the diversion. Even Alastair seemed eager for an early night. For all his buoyancy after the battle, the flight and the memory of our errand seemed to sober him until he was as grave as he had been at Pendragon.

Akarra touched down outside a walled town on the frosty banks of the River Meryle just over the border of County Nan. The town was a small one, and we shuffled through the now-familiar motions at the door of the nearest inn. So far every innkeeper we'd met had a similar routine: first came the greasy-eyed appraisal of our clothes, weapons, and the dragon crest, followed by mumbled flattery or perhaps, if the innkeeper was tired too, simply an outstretched hand. This innkeeper was one of the latter. Coins passed from purse to hand and a harried servant showed us to our room, which was on the whole indistinguishable from every other we'd seen since our journey through the Old Wilds, save this had the luxury of a dead fire and an absent washbasin. I tossed our panniers onto the floor by the cold hearth and fell face first onto the bed.

There was a faint squeaking sound from the hearth. Alastair looked up from unlacing his boots. "What was that?"

I rose on my elbows and peered at the fireplace with bleary eyes. Whatever it was did not sound again. "Mice," I muttered, rolled over, and, without bothering to undress beyond my boots, promptly fell asleep.

THERE IS AN ART TO SLEEPING IN ONE'S CLOTHES. WAKing up with a knot in my neck and deep imprints in the skin at my forearms from sleeping with my sleeves bunched up, I realized I'd not yet learned it. Alastair had. The dark circles beneath his eyes were the only visible signs of a restless night. He went through his morning exercises without a single mistake, though there was a slight sluggishness to his movements that troubled me. I watched him out of the corner of my eye as I prepared our panniers to leave, keeping well away from the drafty fireplace as I did. Mice had pattered through my dreams all night and I had no desire to meet their counterparts in the daylight.

"How's your shoulder?" I asked when he finished.

He rolled it a few times before easing into his leather jerkin. "Sore."

"It didn't seem to give you any trouble with the direwolf."

"It was an old wolf."

"Do you want me to mix something for it when we get to Edonarle?"

He picked up one of the panniers and slung it over his shoulder. His *left* shoulder, I noticed. "No need. It's fine."

"Alastair—"

"It's fine. We need to get moving. Akarra will be waiting for us."

IT WAS DIFFICULT TO TELL WHEN THE CITY BEGAN AND the countryside ended. Akarra flew south over the River Meryle, then banked west before the waters divided into the eastern Wash and the narrower, deeper River Nan. We followed the latter. Wild lands grew tame beneath a bridle of lanes and fences and the roads widened, showing the pale streak of paving stones under a layer of mud. We passed more towns and villages, some with only short walls, some without walls at all. Farms and homesteads grew thicker around the towns until we no longer flew over a patchwork of fields interrupted by the occasional settlement, but a patchwork of buildings interrupted by the occasional field. The air was still cold, but the sun was bright, and by noon the sweat was starting at my temples.

Then the wind turned and I caught the smell of the sea. In an instant a thousand small childhood memories I hadn't realized I'd forgotten came flooding back: Uncle Gregory guiding me through the maze of Nan's Menagerie, teaching me wood-wightish herblore in the wilder sections of the Royal Park, hunting for shells on the breakwater rocks outside the Low Quarter, Aunt

Lissa and I reading in front of the open windows at their kitchen table and laughing as the wind tried to make us lose our places. They were fleeting images, rolling and tumbling together before sinking back into the past, but for one instant each shone bright and sharp, drawn vividly to life by the salty tang of the ocean. I wiped the sweat from my brow and squinted ahead as Akarra topped the last hill. I could not forget the danger hanging over us, nor the terrible events that had brought us here, but no amount of *ghastradi* could keep me from this little moment of joy. I had *missed* this place.

If the vista of Edonarle was breathtaking when approaching from the ground, then there were no words for the sight from the air. The Bay of Nan spread out before us, blue and sparkling in the sun. Distant wyverns dived and gamboled over the water, their scales flashing like jewels as they snapped at passing seabirds. From the shore rose the walls and towers of Edonarle, stronghold of the kingdom, oldest of Arlean cities, ancient seat of kings and queens. Centuries of architecture built and razed and built up again had formed a hill sloping up from the harbor, with the city fit around it in roughly concentric circles. As Akarra swooped low, I tried to puzzle out the places I knew through the haze of smoke hanging over the city like an industrious blanket.

"What's down there?" I cried, pointing to a quarter near the harbor where the roofs took on a jagged quality and what few streets I could see were clogged with foot traffic.

"Salt Market," Alastair called over the wind.

I looked again, fitting the sight from above into what I knew of Edonarle's famed Salt Market. Aunt Lissa had taken me to visit at least once every summer, but by the look of things it had grown significantly since my last stay, with the vendors' tents and merchants' carts spilling over onto the tree-lined avenues of the Royal Park.

With the arm not wrapped around my waist, Alastair pointed south. "The villas are down on the water," he said in my ear. "That's where Cedric and your sister will be."

I turned my head to follow his finger, but Akarra banked and carried us out of sight before I could fix the place in my mind. We were descending rapidly now. The highest towers of the palace and the looming edifice of the Gray Abbey rose above us, while Akarra's tail just cleared the roofs of the houses below. I began to hear noises beyond the ever-present rush of wind and wingbeats. Shouts drifted up from the streets we passed, happy, familiar shouts of recognition and welcome. A half-dozen wyverns rose from one of the lower streets and flanked Akarra for a few seconds, squawking their greetings in Vernish before shearing off to play in the winds over the harbor.

Quite suddenly Akarra's wings stopped beating, and my stomach flip-flopped as we tilted downward. I gripped Alastair's arm. Walls of warm stone and red-tiled roofs shot up around us on all sides, and it was all I could do not to shut my eyes.

With a thud and the crack of talons against tile, we landed. Savoring for a moment the sensation of not being impaled on the nearest weathercock, I blinked and looked around. We were in a deep, ivy-covered courtyard in the First Circle of the city, high enough for the patch of sky overhead to be free of the smoke and haze that hovered over the lower circles. Alastair swung off and offered me his hand with a grin. "You didn't think we were going to crash, did you?"

"A little warning would have been nice."

"There's an art to it," Akarra said. "I won't tell you how many tiles I took off our neighbors' roofs when I first visited the townhouse."

"Yes, and the Chief Magistrate still hasn't forgiven us." Alastair nodded to the house rising on our right as he helped me down. The tiles on the eaves nearest the courtyard were a slightly different shade of red than the rest.

Akarra laughed. "You know the magistrate is secretly proud of it. Now, what are your plans for tonight?"

"We need to see Cedric and the rest of the Riders in the city," he said. "They'll be able to tell us what's going on."

"Will you need me?" she asked.

He unbuckled her saddle and pulled it free. "Not tonight."

"Good, because I need to hunt. The deer population in the forest west of the city always needs thinning." She spread her wings and crouched as if to spring, but at the last moment checked herself and cocked an eye in Alastair's direction. "Are you sure you won't need me, *khela*? I can't put a talon on it, but there's something here that makes me uneasy. The city is restless. I can't help but feel we've arrived just in time for the storm to break."

"I feel it too."

"I can stay," she offered.

"No, you need to hunt. It's been a long flight and you need your strength back."

She lowered her head and looked at us solemnly. "Just promise me you'll both be careful."

"We promise," we said together.

Alastair patted her neck and added something in Eth, which seemed to reassure her. She touched her snout briefly to his forehead in a dragon's kiss and took to the air in a swirl of wings and dust and dead leaves.

Absent one dragon, I was able to take in the full extent of our surroundings. Ivy wreathed the walls all around us, still trembling in the wake of Akarra's departure. The noises of the city sounded dull and distant here. With the afternoon sun radiating off the pavement and the walls holding it in like a great marble cup, the courtyard was warmer too. Stairs at one end led to a balcony, or rather a series of balconies, which in turn rose into the splendid edifice of the Daired townhouse. I had to tilt my head back to take in the whole sight: carved marble balustrades glowing in the westering light, staircases ascending from pillared colonnades, great metal doors adorned with iron scrollwork, windows shuttered in rich wood panels sheathed in silver, and everywhere the living, fluttering colors of late autumn ivy. Beyond the house I caught a glimpse of the Gray Abbey's belfry, but the towers of the palace were hidden from where we stood.

A man in the dragon-crested livery of House Daired appeared at one of the upper balconies. "Ah, my lord! Welcome home."

"Caldero," Alastair returned his greeting. "Our steward here in the city," he told me as we started for the stairs.

The interior of the townhouse fit what I'd come to associate with typical understated Daired splendor: wide corridors and patterned halls in mosaics of a thousand colors, marble dragons guarding pillared doorways, everywhere the faint but rich scent of dragonfire and—

"Is that *kaf*?" I asked, sniffing.

"There's always *kaf* nearby when Julienna's staying here. Which reminds me. Caldero," he called to the steward, who appeared at the top of the stairs, "where is my sister?"

"In the armory, my lord." He bowed deeply to me. "By the by, it's an honor to meet you, Lady Daired."

"Thank you, sir."

"And my aunt? Lord Edmund?" Alastair asked.

"They just went out, I'm afraid, but they have plans to return for dinner."

"Very well." He handed him Akarra's tack. "Take these to Master Orune and ask him to have the buckles refitted."

"Very good, sir." The steward bustled out.

"Aliza, would you—"

I took the pannier from him. "Go. See your sister. I'll unpack."

"Thank you, *khera*. I'll only be a minute. My chambers—our chambers—are the first door on the right."

He kissed my cheek and headed back down the stairs. His sword clinked faintly in its harness as he moved. My smile faded. That single sound woke again all the fears that had lain latent for the last hour, and the shadow descended once more. As much as I looked forward to seeing Julienna, this was no familial visit. We were Daireds, and we were here for war.

I followed Alastair's directions and found the rooms that were unmistakably his. The shape of the chamber was different, but the furnishings were very like our rooms at Pendragon, from the enormous canopied bed to the embroidered hangings to the splendid dragon-manteled fireplace. A jointed wooden manikin stood by the wardrobe dressed in a spare suit of war armor. A rack of swords, quarterstaves, and spears hung on the far wall next to the balcony, the doors of which were wide open. Curtains twisted and tangled into the room, bringing in with them the strong smell of the ocean. I tossed our panniers on the bed and headed for the washbasin.

"*Gheraph hugh gudg!*"

My hand closed around my dagger before my brain could fit the sounds to words. "Who's there?"

The side of my pannier rose and fell. I readied my knife as the flap was pushed aside and something tumbled out onto the coverlet.

"*Blegh!* Cousin Nobble can tease me all he likes; I am *never* doing that again!"

I nearly dropped the dagger. "*Tobble?*" The little hobgoblin bounced to his feet with more muffled Gnomic curses. "Tobble! What in Thell's name are you doing here?"

He brushed off his jerkin and looked sheepishly up at me. "Aliza! Er . . . hello. Please don't be mad."

"But what are you *doing* here?"

"Well, you said there was dangerous business afoot. I might have mentioned it to Chief Hobblehilt, and he, ah, he sent me to keep an eye on you."

"He did *what?*"

"He wants us garden-folk to help!"

I gave him a long, hard stare. "He told you explicitly not to come, didn't he?"

He avoided my eye. "Maybe."

"Tobble, I wasn't joking when I said it would be dangerous."

"And I wasn't joking when I said I want to help!"

"You can't—"

"You think it's comfortable, hanging off a dragon's saddle for two days? Squished between someone's sweaty shirt and a lump of hard cheese?"

I closed my eyes, silently conceding him that point. Foolhardy and reckless it might have been, but I couldn't fault my friend's commitment. "We don't even know what we're facing here," I tried instead. "How is it you expect to help?"

"Well, I guess we'll find out!"

"Tobble, you are *impossible*. I can't let you put yourself in danger. Please. You need to go home."

"But . . . how?"

"What?"

"Your dragonrider's not going to go all the way back to the Manor just for me."

For a second I stared at him, seriously debating the practicality of scooping him up, tossing him in a box, and posting it back to Merybourne on the fastest coach money could buy. He grinned, showing every flat brown tooth. He was right, of course, and he knew that I knew he was right, but that did nothing to ease my annoyance. I rubbed my temples. "Look, Tobble, you can't stay here."

"Of course not!" he cried, looking mildly scandalized. "Not in your *bedroom*. I'll just be out in the gardens." Before I could clarify that no, that was not what I had meant, he leapt down from the bed, pattered off to the balcony, and swung himself out of sight on the nearest rope of ivy.

Perfect. Darkness and danger and murderous *ghastradi* on the loose, and now I had a hobgoblin to look after as well. I muttered an Eth phrase I'd picked up from Alastair in one of his fouler moods and started unpacking.

CHAPTER 13

REUNION

A knock on the door startled me out of my second rehearsed explanation as to why a Merybourne hobgoblin had taken up residence in the Daired gardens. I kicked our empty panniers under the bed and turned to see a slight, dimpled girl peeking around the open door, her Rider's plait swinging in a dark braid over one shoulder.

"Julienna!"

Alastair's younger sister bounded into the room and threw her arms around me. "So good to see you!" she said. "Alastair told me you had quite the first contract. I'm glad you're all right."

She didn't glance at my belly, didn't give the slightest hint that her brother had mentioned our child. I hoped he hadn't.

"Aye, so am I." I took her hand. "How long have you been in the city?"

"A few weeks. Mar'esh and I have had several contracts along the coast, but Aunt Catriona thought it'd be best if we stayed here until after the treaty talks are finished."

"Alastair said your aunt thinks there might be trouble."

"There already has been trouble. Haven't you heard?"

"We've been a little preoccupied. Tell me."

She fell into one of the chairs by the window with a sigh. "Where to begin? The treaty business is hardly worth mentioning; of course all the guilds are up in arms about that. Some want it, some hate it. Most of the common people are just looking forward to the show." She rolled her eyes. "The Garhadi ambassador's retinue took an *hour* to make it from the docks to the palace. They brought live peacocks, for gods' sakes. The Principalities weren't much better, but at least they didn't have palanquins. Or poultry."

Garhad Islands, Southern Principalities, and Arle. That was three nations accounted for. "And Els?" I asked.

"Oh, their ambassador hasn't arrived yet. If gossip is anything to go by, though, they'll be here soon."

"What about *Tekari?*"

She gave me an odd look. "What about them?"

I told her about the horde and the skirmish at Merybourne, and the maids' reports from Pendragon. "We've heard they're on the move. Have there been more attacks lately?"

"Not in the city," she said slowly, "but yes, I'd say there have been more along the coast in the last few weeks. Mar'esh and I fought off a half-dozen ghouls in Lesser Westwich just after Martenmas. Folk in the nearby towns said they'd never had ghoul problems before. And then there was—" She stopped.

"Then there was what?" I pressed gently.

"It wasn't *Tekari*, but something odd did happen a few days ago. Two of the largest lithosmith shops were robbed. Thousands of dragonbacks' worth of heartstones gone and the City Watch has nothing to show for it." She stood up as Alastair entered. "That's what the Riders are saying. You're back just in time, brother."

"Julienna—"

"No, no, I'm going. I imagine you'll both want to finish unpacking," she said before he could finish. She squeezed my shoulder as she passed. "I'll see you later."

Alastair closed the door after her. "She told you the news?" he asked wearily.

"Aye. *Tekari* attacks around the city, folk in a general frenzy over the treaty talks, and more missing heartstones." I fished my brooch out from beneath my armor and tossed it onto the bed. "What's new?"

"Caldero said the same thing."

"I suppose that means we're in the right place. You think Wydrick and the other *ghastradi* are in the city already?"

"I'm tired of guessing, Aliza. I want to *know*. If we're going to stop this war, we need to understand what we're facing. Tomorrow I'll have a word with my contacts in the palace," he said. "In the meantime, though, I think we should leave these here."

He removed the Greater Lindworm's heartstone from its chain and, after a moment's rummaging through the great wardrobe next to the bed, pulled out a delicate oakstone box. Dragons danced around the border, breathing scrollwork around the figures of the seven great saints of Arle, and a tiny bronze key in the shape of a dragon sat within the lock. He put our heartstones inside, locked it, and threaded the key onto the chain around his neck.

"For the time being." A smile crept back into his face as he offered me his arm. "I have a surprise for you, *khera*."

"Now? What is it?"

"You'll find out at dinner. Until then I'm under strict instructions from Julienna to show you around the townhouse."

I narrowed my eyes in mock suspicion. It was a little game, a blind stab at levity amid all that weighed on us, and I cherished every second like I cherished the warmth of his hand on mine and the dimple below the scar on his cheek. "She wanted to show me herself, didn't she?" I said.

The dimple deepened. "Yes. I told her she couldn't."

I laced my fingers with his. "In that case, lead on."

AS WAS TRUE OF THE DAIREDS THEMSELVES, THERE WAS A great deal more to their townhouse than a cursory glance revealed. Three stories rose above the street, but the building had deep foundations, with room enough for an armory to rival Pendragon's, and even its own small smithy. Alastair introduced me to the smith, a thin, balding Garhadi man called Master Teo, with an address so respectful it made me wonder if the man was a retired Rider. I'd certainly never seen a bow that low for an ordinary *nakla*. Alastair explained as we headed back upstairs.

"Apart from Forgemaster Orordrin, Master Teo is the finest smith in the kingdom. Perhaps in the world," he said, touching the hilt of the sword at his hip with something like reverence. It was new, I noticed, not the unadorned blade he had taken from Pendragon. A silver dragon formed the pommel and guard, its eyes burning like fire opals.

"And he works for your family? Just your family?"

Alastair smiled. "Even House Daired couldn't afford that. Master Teo smiths where he chooses, but he likes Aunt Catriona, so he makes us blades when he can. The forge here is his to use as he pleases."

"Generous of you."

"Generous of *him*."

"I'll bet he's—"

I drew up short at the top of the stairs, whatever conclusion I'd drawn about Master Teo discarded for sheer surprise at the sight awaiting us in the front room. Julienna and her cousin Captain Edmund stood deep in conversation with a flame-haired Rider and a beautiful silver wyvern. Next to them, Lady Catriona and Captain Edmund's wyvern spoke with another Rider with her back to me. Her glossy black ringlets fell over her shoulders in the double plait of an apprentice Rider, which did little to hide the short sword in its scabbard on her back.

"Anjey?"

She spun around. "Aliza!"

Shadows and flames, steel and armor and the looming threat of war evaporated and for one glorious moment, all was right in the world again as I threw my arms around my older sister. She laughed and squeezed me tight.

"Oh, dearest, I've *missed* you!" she said.

"I missed you too." I released her and looked at Alastair. "But how did you know we were here? We only arrived this afternoon."

"Silverwing saw Akarra flying in," Brysney said, and the silver wyvern next to him hooted a greeting in Vernish. "Hello, Aliza," Brysney added with a grin. "Good to see you."

"I sent a note inviting them for dinner as soon as we arrived," Alastair said, sidestepping a gentle elbow to his ribs. "I wanted to surprise you."

You certainly did. Anjey's hair wasn't the only thing she'd changed. She wore a small gold hoop through her left ear, much like her husband, and her cheeks were leaner, her eyes brighter, and I got the impression of hard muscle beneath her sleeves. It was an impression only, as her Rider's leathers prevented anything more. Besides the sword at her back, she wore a long dagger at one hip, twin of the knife Brysney had given me. Gone was the doe-eyed, raven-locked darling of the Merybourne bards. The sister that stood before me had forged a new kind of beauty, a wild, ferocious loveliness full of sharp edges and shadowed in red.

She smiled a little shyly at my obvious astonishment. "Do you like it?"

"Honestly, Anjey, I hardly recognize you."

Brysney draped an arm around his wife's shoulders. "My beautiful Rider-in-training. Anjey's taken to the fighting arts like a phoenix to fire."

"It's true," Lady Catriona said. "I've seen Angelina spar Edmund here. Even made him break a sweat once." She clapped her nephew on the shoulder and he reddened. "Nice to see you again, Miss Aliza."

I dipped into an unthinking curtsy, but she tutted me upright.

"Good gods, girl, we're family. None of that. Now, Alastair, what's this important business you wanted to talk about? And what's it got to do with the negotiations at the palace?"

Like the first winds of winter, her words leached the joviality from the room. "Dinner first," Alastair said. "It's a rather long story."

OVER DINNER, ALASTAIR AND I TOOK TURNS TELLING them about our contract in Lake Meera, our escape from Rushless Wood, and our encounter with the *Tekari* in Hart's Run. When we mentioned the *ghastradi*, even Lady Catriona looked taken aback. "And Wydrick is one of them?"

"He is," Alastair said. "He has been for some time. Since before the Battle of North Fields, at least."

"Thell tear his soul to pieces," Anjey muttered, "if he has one left."

The other Daireds murmured their agreement in Eth curses of various vehemence. Julienna alone said nothing.

"You think Wydrick and the other *ghastradi* are in the city now?" Edmund asked.

"You say 'other *ghastradi*,'" Brysney said before Alastair could answer, "but do we know how many there are? Or *who* they are, besides Wydrick and this lithosmith fellow from Hatch Ford?"

I shook my head. "They hinted that their master had agents around the kingdom, but who and where they are, we have no idea."

Lady Catriona pushed her plate away. "So they could be anyone."

"The Vesh are a good place to start," Alastair said. "Our enemy has a bounty out on my heartstone. Aliza's too. It seems that they need them for some reason, and the sooner we can find out why, the sooner we can end this."

Edmund bent his head close to his wyvern and said a few words in Vernish. Brysney let out a long breath and looked at Anjey, but her attention was elsewhere, eyes fixed on the edge of the table as she idly stroked the leather plates covering her stomach.

"All right. How can we help?" he asked.

"Besides tracking the Vesh? We need to find Wydrick," Alastair said. "Do you know how many Riders are in the city right now?"

"Several dozen, I think," Brysney said.

"Master Doublegray at the Sword and Crown would know for sure," Edmund said. "There are a few companies of the Free Regiments camped down at the barracks too. I can spend some time with them, see what they know."

"Good," Alastair said, "but be careful. Wydrick has Ranger connections; he may have spies in the regiment."

Edmund nodded but said nothing further on the topic as the servants came in to clear away our dishes, turning conversation instead to a tale of his wyvern Whiteheart's encounter with a mischievous gale of pixies in the Royal Park. When he finished, Brysney asked Alastair to describe once more his confrontation with the Green Lady and the loss of his old sword, much to the interest of the other Daireds. Anjey plucked my sleeve under the table.

"Let's leave them to it," she said in my ear. "If Cedric gets them started on weapons, they'll go on for hours. Besides, you and I need to catch up."

I was only too happy to leave recollections of Lake Meera at the table. We excused ourselves and took our cups of sweet *kaf* to the nearest balcony. Cloaks pulled tight against the salty sting of the night air, we leaned against the balustrade and sipped our drinks. For a long minute neither of us said anything, enjoying the vista of the city spread out below us in twinkling torchlight and the cold glow of the moon.

"You're frightened," Anjey said suddenly. "Aren't you?"

I released my breath slowly, watching the white clouds spiral away from me into nothingness. "Yes."

"We can stop this. Whatever's coming, you won't be facing it alone." She rested her hand on mine. "We're Riders now, you and me. Riders-in-training, at least."

I looked up at her sharply. There was no trace of irony in her expression, only an honest sympathy that struck me to my core. *She really believes that.* Her transformation—the hair, the armor, the talk of *we*—it wasn't merely for show. I saw it in an instant, and wondered that I hadn't seen it at once. Anjey had embraced her husband's world beyond the titles and external trappings, never mind her low birth or lack of training. Brysney's name had already erased the former, and if the new muscles I'd felt were any indication, she was in the process of rapidly erasing the latter. My eyes fell to the knife at her hip. I thought of its twin, now sitting sheathed and unused in a corner of my wardrobe, and remembered my clumsy attempts at wielding it in the Old Wilds. Shame, slow at first, then building with the force of an ocean wave, washed over me. Anjey had not wasted months wallowing in her *nakla* identity. She'd abandoned it altogether.

"I suppose so." Groping for a non-Rider topic, I said the first thing that came to mind. "Do you still like your villa?"

She smiled. "Very much. You and Dair—sorry, Alastair—must come for dinner, and soon! We won't be there for much longer."

"What? Why not?"

"Cedric has talked of visiting Selkie's Keep this summer. That's where he grew up, you know." She gave me a sidelong look. "We thought we might like to raise our child there."

The word sent a thrill through me, jarring as a wasp's sting. I stared at her. She laughed at my expression, a sweet, musical laugh that warmed me even as sorrow plunged icy needles through my heart.

"Aye, Aliza. Sorry I didn't write sooner, but I wanted to tell you in person." She clasped my hands. "Congratulations, dearest. Come next summer you're going to be an aunt."

CHAPTER 14

A BRIEF HISTORY OF SPICES

I didn't tell her. Instead I swallowed my grief, smiled, and cried what I hoped would pass as tears of joy. In some ways, they were. I was happy for her and Brysney. That her news tore open the newly healed wound inside me and set it bleeding afresh was none of her concern. My pain was my own business. I tied the threadbare bandage of indifference around my heart and pretended not to notice.

For the rest of the evening I played the part of the overjoyed sister, offering suggestions on how best to break the news to Mama, giving my opinion on names, and praying in silence to Thell not to take this joy from my sister as the gods had taken it from me.

Anjey and Brysney left late, taking their good spirits with them. Alastair and I bid the others goodnight and returned to our chambers.

"Your sister told you, didn't she?" he asked once we were alone.

I nodded.

"Did you tell her?"

"No. And I'm not going to."

He sat heavily on the edge of the bed and let out a sigh, soft but weighted down with feeling. "I wanted to tell Cedric, but I . . . couldn't."

"Then don't."

"It might help."

"Nothing will help," I said flatly. "Alastair, I don't want to talk about this right now."

"Aliza—"

"I said I don't want to talk about it." I undressed and curled on my side of the mattress with my arms around my knees, hugging them to my chest like a shield against sorrow.

"*Khera?*" The bed sank beneath Alastair as he joined me. He rested one hand on my shoulder, his touch warming my cold skin through my shift. I didn't move, didn't say anything. After a moment he rose again. I heard the scrape and click of the balcony door closing, and the chill in the room subsided. He returned to bed and lay down with his back to mine.

Just as well, I thought as sleep closed over me. This way we could not see each other cry.

I WOKE TO THE SMELL OF THE SEA AND A NOTE FROM Alastair on the counterpane. He and his aunt were paying a visit to the palace before their meeting with the Riders at noon, though he doubted even they would be able to get an audience with the king on such short notice. I sent up a hollow prayer for favor to any god who was listening. A face-to-face conversation with King Harrold, unlikely as it was, would save us all a great deal of trouble. *If he believes us.* I folded the note and tucked it into my pocket as I dressed.

The pain of the previous night had faded in the daylight, or perhaps had simply withdrawn into whatever room in my heart had walls strong enough to hold it, but regardless, I felt much less inclined to tears. There was work to be done, and I had a scolding to finish.

The day was bright and surprisingly warm for being so close to Saint Ellia's Day. The ivy trembled in a strong sea breeze as I descended into the courtyard.

"Tobble?" I called.

The shrubbery in the corner of the courtyard parted and Tobble popped out, wearing a devious grin. "Good morning!" he said in Low Gnomic. "Heading somewhere?"

"Aye, and you're coming with me."

"Aliza!" he shrilled. "We talked about this. You *can't* send me home. Chief Hobblehilt will have me cleaning *phgethm* pots for a month!"

I rolled my eyes. "I'm not sending you back to the Manor. Until this business is all over, I don't trust the roads, and you're right, Alastair can't fly you home." I put on my most unnerving smile and Tobble wrinkled his nose suspiciously. "Lucky for you, I know just the place for delinquent hobgoblins."

MY HOPES OF SLIPPING THROUGH THE CITY WITHOUT drawing unnecessary attention were quickly dashed. We made it only to the end of the street. Tobble let out a shriek and my heart skipped a beat as a wall of blue dropped from the roof, blocking the avenue in a flurry of wings and iridescent sapphire scales.

"Well met, Aliza!" Julienna's dragon Mar'esh rumbled, giving both of us a toothy smile. "And Aliza's little friend."

Julienna grinned down at us over his shoulder. "You didn't think Alastair and I would let you wander the city alone, did you?"

I gave her what I hoped was a sisterly glare. Her dimple deepened.

"Where are you headed? We'll keep you company."

Perhaps it was just as well. It'd be foolish enough to run around Edonarle alone when war *didn't* threaten; I'd only thought to now because everyone else was occupied with their own tasks. *Their own, much more important tasks.* Nevertheless, I was grateful for companions.

"Avenue of Gulls," I said. "Do you know the way?"

Mar'esh laughed. "Aliza my dear, I'd know every roof and alley of this city on a night with no moon. Lower Quarter, Third Circle."

"Aye, a house on the corner near Galley Street," I said, accepting Julienna's offered hand up. It felt strange, sitting atop scales instead of leather, but Daired dragons tolerated a saddle only for long journeys or during battle. Mar'esh was smaller than Akarra too, and I clung to Julienna to keep from sliding off. Tobble in turn hung on to my neck with a strength borne of sheer panic.

"Aliza, are you sure about this?" he squeaked.

"You flew with us from Hart's Run, and *this* is what frightens you?"

"I couldn't *see* anything in your baggage!"

"Then close your eyes," I muttered, and Julienna chuckled.

"I'll go carefully, my little friend," Mar'esh said from beneath us. "You won't have to worry. Everyone have a good grip?"

There was much to be said for riding a dragon with all four claws firmly on the ground. Though unable to fly, Mar'esh near made up for it with his agility and uncanny ability to climb almost anything. For such a large creature, he was remarkably graceful. He leapt atop the building next to us in a single fluid bound and set off toward the Lower Quarter.

He needed no directions, weaving through alleys and the narrow spaces between buildings, running lightly along the great retaining walls that divided the city circles, even sometimes on the roofs of the houses themselves. On the latter he used his wings to bear some of our weight, spreading them wide so that we glided from rooftop to rooftop, never landing for more than a few seconds on each. It was a novel way to view the city, above the crowds but not so far away as to lose the texture of the city or the rhythm of its populace.

People on every street gawked at us as we rushed by, though not as many as I would have thought. Julienna, it seemed, was a well-known figure around the Salt Market and the neighborhoods of the Second and Third Circles. Vendors cried their greetings, and one of the fishmongers even offered up a fresh cod to Mar'esh as he passed, which he gratefully accepted, snapping it up whole.

"Saved that man's boat from a swarm of hagsprites last month," Julienna explained. "Mar'esh takes this route whenever he can."

Once we were through the Salt Market, the crowds thinned. Mar'esh bounded through a paved square with a fountain in the center, bubbling anemically out of a basin in the hands of a comely woman robed in white stone and, in obedience to the ancient and solemn traditions of the scholars of the Royal University, a patchwork of crude graffiti.

Tobble groaned in my ear. "Are . . . we . . . there . . . yet?"

"Almost. A few more streets."

That was a slight exaggeration, but Mar'esh made short work of the Third Circle, coming to a halt on the Avenue of Gulls near Galley Street several minutes later. It was a narrow street, cramped even for a small dragon, and he had to keep his wings folded tightly to his sides to let us dismount.

"Friends of yours?" Mar'esh asked as I knocked on the red door on the corner.

"Family," I said as the door opened a crack. "Hello, Uncle."

"Sweet Alyssum?" Uncle Gregory lowered his spectacles, polished them on his shirt, and raised them again. "My . . . my goodness! It is you. And a hobgoblin! And, er . . ."

"Uncle Gregory, you remember Julienna and Mar'esh, don't you?"

"Who is it, dear?" my aunt's voice came faintly from inside.

Uncle Gregory laughed and flung the door open the rest of the way. "Lissa, I think we're going to need another pot of stew."

TOBBLE MADE A MIRACULOUS RECOVERY ONCE INDOORS. Uncle greeted him in fluent Low Gnomic, and after Tobble's hurried and not at all thorough explanation as to what he was doing so far from the Manor, Uncle Gregory bid him take up residence in their gardens for as long as he liked. Tobble bounded down from my shoulder with a rushed "thank you!" and a cheeky grin in my direction. I sighed. *Hobgoblins.*

"He stowed away in our saddlebags," I explained.

"Ah, the antics of garden-folk," Uncle Gregory said. "The hobgoblins here will make him more than welcome, and I daresay old Chief Grimmelgund will be around to visit before the week's out. Tobble will have plenty of stories to take back to the Merybourne Underburrow."

"He'll have a stern talking-to when he gets back, that's what he'll have. But thank you for letting him stay."

"Of course. Lady Julienna, would you like to join us?" he asked, and I realized Julienna had stayed on the doorstep. She smiled shyly and nodded. "And, ah, you're most welcome as well," he said to Mar'esh, "though I'm afraid it might be a bit, er, tight . . ."

Mar'esh chuckled. "You're very kind, Master Greene, I'm quite comfortable outdoors. Julienna, call for me when you're done," he said.

The smell of baking bread filled the house, warm and comforting. I breathed in deeply, savoring the memories that came flooding back. The Greenes' entire house would have easily fit within the walls of the Daireds' courtyard, but it had an earthy, lived-in charm that the townhouse, for all its richness, lacked. The small front room served as dining room and sitting room and pantry all in one, with colorful quilts thrown over overstuffed sofas, ropes of drying herbs hanging from the beams overhead, and a cheery fire crackling on the hearth. It was an open fireplace, and through the flames I could see into the kitchen on the other side, where Aunt Lissa bustled back and forth. She stopped abruptly and bent down.

"Gracious me, Gregory, don't just stand around gawping! If you want this stew ready before Saint Ellia's Day, you're going to need to pitch in. Hello, Aliza!"

Uncle muttered something about *domestic felicity* in Low Gnomic but did as his wife said.

Aunt Lissa greeted Julienna warmly and without the stiffness I'd come to expect from non-Riders. In her eyes, Julienna was family; *whose* family exactly made little difference. She put us to work at once. "There are plates and bowls just above the basin, Julienna dear," she said. "And Aliza, keep an eye on the bread, will you? Are you in town long?"

"For a few weeks." It was a safe enough answer.

"Good! Now where did I— Great gods, Gregory, what is this?"

Uncle Gregory looked up guiltily as she pulled a cloth-covered bowl from a shelf below the washbasin. The smell of stewing nettles wafted from it, sweet and a little astringent. Aunt Lissa gave it a sniff. "Is *that* where the rest of my sugarstem went?"

"I told you, it's for Anjey," he said.

She sighed and replaced the bowl. "Fine, fine. Speaking of . . ."

A twinkle started in her eye as she sidled up to me. "Aliza my love, has she told you?"

Despite the heat of the kitchen, I felt suddenly cold. I forced a smile to my lips. "They're expecting the baby in early summer, aren't they?"

"Wait a moment, Anjey's *pregnant*?" Julienna asked. "Cedric's going to be a father?"

"Aye."

"And Aliza's going to be an aunt! How do you feel about that, my girl?" Uncle Gregory patted me on the shoulder. "Oh, what a day. Yes, dear, I'm stirring the stew. I'll tell you what, though, Sweet Alyssum; I don't envy your sister the task of informing your mother."

"Her shriek will put banshees to shame," Aunt Lissa said.

"I think you underestimate Papa's enthusiasm," I muttered. "He'd have the whole family moved to Edonarle before the Long Night if he knew. Aunt Lissa, have you got any thyme?"

"Should be some above the mantel."

I glanced at the neatly labeled herb bowls on their shelf above the hearth, well aware that the bowl marked *thyme* was empty. "You're out. There's still some in the garden, though, isn't there?"

"I think so, but—"

"I'll pick some," I said, and hurried out before anyone could question my sudden interest in seasonings.

The garden was blessedly empty. Mar'esh must have elected to explore the nearby Royal Park, leaving the narrow sliver of green behind the house unoccupied by all but the plants. Even the garden-folk had made themselves scarce, no doubt plying Tobble with *gphetha* and *thegeti* as he told them wild tales of the Battle of Merybourne. The wind blew cold over the walls, but close to the ground it was warm and quiet and lonely.

I was halfway past Uncle's herb beds before I stopped, ashamed. The sunlight and crisp air washed through me, combing out the sad knots and bringing me back to something like calm. It shouldn't have struck me so, the mention of Anjey's pregnancy. Even if it did, running from it served no purpose but to delay the inevitable. She was my sister. I was happy for her, and that was that.

I looked around. What Uncle Gregory's garden lacked in space, it made up for in sheer enthusiasm. Even with the chill of autumn deadening the otherwise rich colors, it still thrived. Masses of chrysanthemums piled high in stone urns, spilling violet and amber and golden petals across the flagstone path. Cultivated moss with feelers like fern fronds crept in a thick carpet up the walls, and bunches of herbs lined the walk, from thyme and rosemary to parsley and fennel. Winter squashes swelled among the roots of the herbs, orange and white and mottled green. I plucked a few sprigs of thyme, realizing as I did that I'd brought neither knife nor basket.

"Here." I turned to see Uncle Gregory coming toward me, a basket swinging on his arm. "You'll need this."

"Thank you."

For a while we picked herbs in silence, broken only by the distant cawing of gulls beyond the garden wall.

"Something wrong, Sweet Alyssum?" he asked after a minute.

"Hmm?"

"I know that look. Lissa wears it whenever she's upset and trying not to show it. Come now, tell me what's wrong."

I walked a few steps ahead, trailing my fingers through the curly tendrils of the largest pumpkin vine. The words lay on the back of my tongue, neat, simple little words ready for speaking if I could but find the courage. I paused beneath a slender sap-

ling of a Saint Marten's tree. Its petal-like leaves had fallen long
ago, but the sweet scent still hung around it, triggering memories
in unconnected cascades of sounds and colors: a child's laugh,
the angry red of a skinned knee, the sting of unguent. And then
more recent memories. The hiss of breath between clenched
teeth. The purpling welt along Alastair's side, delivered by a
valkyrie's talons after my mistake in the Widdermere Marshes.
The iron voice of midwife Threshmore growing rusty with regret. The hungry emptiness of a wound without remedy and eyes
too full for tears.

Remember, Sweet Alyssum, salt water does a world of good . . .

I opened my mouth. "It's nothing, Uncle," I said.

He looked at me for a long time, and I saw the scales in his eyes,
weighing my lie against what I'm sure he guessed was the reason
for it. *Don't ask me, please. Not now.*

"It's been a while since we've reviewed your herblore, hasn't it?"

I smiled my silent thanks. Someday I would tell him. Someday
I would tell my whole family. Just not today. "Aye."

"We'd best fix that. Now, let's see. Ah!" He bent down and
plucked a fallen flower from the damp grass beneath the tree.
"What's this fine specimen?"

"Saint Marten flower," I said.

He raised an eyebrow. "And . . . ?"

"And what?"

"You'll hardly get far as an herbmaster with just the name,
Sweet Alyssum. I want everything you know about this little beauty.
I shan't have my favorite apprentice putting me to shame out there
in the wider world." He grinned. "I even chose an easy one for you."

My smile returned, and this time it was real. I took the flower
from him and thought back to his lessons in herblore. They were
strangely shaped, the petals of the Saint Marten flower, long and

blade-like and pale yellow. This specimen was wilted and browning, but it had retained all four petals. I crushed one between my fingers and felt, to my surprise, a drop of oil seep out. The sweet smell intensified. "Cleans and soothes injuries."

"And keeps its virtue long after you'd think. Full of surprises, that flower." He folded my hand over the faded blossom. "Never hurts to remember. Now, what about this one?"

For the next quarter hour we wandered the gardens as he quizzed me on the use of various herbs until my head was too full of root and leaf and blossom for sorrow and Aunt Lissa called us in for lunch.

As we ate, I told my aunt and uncle what had brought us to Edonarle. Uncle Gregory and Aunt Lissa grew grave as I spoke of our fears for the king's convocation.

"You know, I wish I could say this surprises me," my uncle said. He propped his feet up on a hassock and chewed thoughtfully on his pipe. The smoke curled like vine tendrils around his beard. "But it makes sense. There've been more *Tekari* sightings around the county than I care to count since the War of the Worm. I'm sure you and your dragon have seen your fair share of contracts down this way, Lady Julienna."

Julienna nodded. "More than we like."

"Not to mention the unrest in the city," Aunt Lissa added. "I swear, for the last month or so it's been like sleeping on a beehive."

"What kind of unrest?" I asked. "What have you seen?"

"Oh, you know, the little things. Bars on the windows. Guards for hire standing at attention instead of slouching like they usually do. And you hear all kinds of things in the market. Those robberies on Lithosmith Row, doubled shifts for the City Watch, riots in the Fourth Circle. Then there was that—Gregory, when was that incident down by the docks?"

"Eh?"

"You know. That captain from the Principalities tossed out of the tavern for raving about, what was it? Ghouls?"

"Ghasts, I think," Uncle Gregory said.

I sat up and looked at Julienna. Her eyes widened. Neither of us had mentioned Wydrick or the *ghastradi*.

"Yes, yes, ghasts. When was that?"

"Last fortnight," Uncle Gregory said. "Or was it last week?"

"What happened?" Julienna asked.

Aunt Lissa leaned forward. "Well, I had it from the greengrocer, who had it from a tavern maid, who had it from the cook. He said that Captain Teg went quite mad, yelling all kinds of things about monsters and murder and ghouls."

"Ghasts, dear," Uncle Gregory murmured.

"Them too. Apparently, the captain even threw her beer at the barkeep." Aunt Lissa waved a hand. "They tossed her out after that, of course, but then from what I hear that's hardly new for her. Teg's supposed to have a vicious temper."

Captain from the Principalities . . . murder . . . monsters . . . A memory stirred at the words, so faint it vanished each time I grasped at it, but something, *something* told me this was important. "Uncle Gregory, Aunt Lissa, this Captain Teg. Do you know if she's still in the city?"

They looked at each other. "I think she has a place in the Street of Salt," Aunt Lissa said after a puzzled pause, "but why on earth do you want to know?"

"Do you know if she's here now?"

"No idea."

I hid my disappointment. Further questions revealed nothing beyond rumors of the kind I'd begun to expect: the market was buzzing with speculation on the approaching trade negotiations, *Tekari* sightings around the outskirts of the city were on the rise, and folk had begun to arm themselves before they went outside. Everything to stoke our fear, and nothing to hint at how we could stop it.

We didn't stay long after finishing lunch. Uncle regretfully told us he had made an appointment to deliver a bellboil draught to an apothecary in the Second Circle that afternoon, and he had yet to finish it. To the background of Aunt Lissa's gentle scolding, we bid them both a fond farewell.

A stiff wind blew dust in little eddies in the doorways as we stepped out into the street, whipping Julienna's whistled summons toward the sea. She pushed her plait out of her face and folded her arms as we waited for Mar'esh. "You want to go poking around, don't you?"

I smiled guiltily. "Is it that obvious?"

"Well, yes, but hardly surprising. Besides, Alastair told me you would."

"He did?"

"Several times."

"What did he say?"

"That bloodhounds are easier to drag off a scent." She laughed at my expression. "Come on, Aliza, why do you think I wanted to stay with you today? Alastair and Edmund and Aunt Catriona can beg and scrape and wheedle for an audience with the king all morning; they're not going to learn anything. The most they'll manage today is warning the rest of the Riders of what's coming, but with you . . ."—she shrugged as Mar'esh appeared over the roofs of Galley Street—"well, we have something, don't we?"

My heart swelled. "We do." Someone else in the city knew about the *ghastradi*. This Captain Teg, whoever she was, might have the answers we needed. It was a little lead, and flimsy, but Julienna was right. It was something.

"Are we meeting the others at the Sword and Crown?" Mar'esh asked as we mounted.

I shook my head. "Not yet. We're going to the Street of Salt."

CHAPTER 15

SALT AND ASHES

The Street of Salt wound through the last circle of the city, close to the docks and the maze of streets that formed the Lower Quarter of Edonarle. Most were too narrow for Mar'esh, so he resorted to running along the rooftops. As we traveled, I told Julienna details about our contract in Lake Meera that Alastair had not shared earlier.

"Let me get this straight," she said as we passed the wheel-and-barrel sign of the Coopers Guild. "A band of Vesh attacked you in Langdred? They knew who you were and they attacked you?"

"Aye."

She whistled under her breath. "I knew Vesh could be unsavory, but I never figured they'd be so stupid."

"Unsavory, yes. Stupid?" That front room in the Langdred tavern swam before my mind's eye and I heard, as clearly as if I was standing there again, the tiny splash and thud of Rookwood's finger falling to the bloodstained floor. "No, I wouldn't call them stupid. They were too well prepared for that. It was just bad luck we walked in the door that night."

She glanced over her shoulder, and I smiled at her look of relief when she realized I wasn't wearing the brooch.

"Don't worry, we learned our lesson. Our heartstones are back at the townhouse," I said.

"Good, because if they weren't we'd be turning around and taking it back right now."

"After all that— Hang on . . ." Mar'esh grunted, and we sailed over a wide avenue. "After all that, I'm amazed Akarra didn't burn that town to the ground," he said. "I would have."

Julienna patted his neck and thanked him in Eth.

"Not everyone there was Vesh," I said.

"Not everyone was innocent either," Julienna said as Mar'esh drew up short at the top of a broad street overlooking the bay.

"The Street of Salt," he said. "Do you know which house is this Captain Teg's?"

My heart sank. I'd not thought this far. "No idea."

"Your uncle said she was from the Principalities, right?" Julienna asked, and I nodded. "Let's try that one first."

I looked where she pointed. Indeed, the house was hard to miss. It had a bright cerulean door, cross-barred and decorated in intricate iron scrollwork in the style of the Southern Principalities. We dismounted and stepped up to the stoop. A heavy iron knocker in the shape of two twined serpents hung from the center of the door. *Please be home,* I thought and tapped the serpents twice. I counted to twenty under my breath. No answer. Julienna glared at a knot of pedestrians who slowed to gawp at Mar'esh.

"Anything?" she asked.

I started to knock again, but just as I touched the serpentine knocker there came the sound of a bolt being drawn on the other side, then another bolt, then a third. There was the rattle of a chain. At last the door swung open and a woman stepped out onto the stoop.

I reminded myself not to stare. The Southron captain, if it was the captain, was a portrait in opposites. It was impossible to tell her age, for one thing. Older than me, certainly, but not old, even though more than one white lock of hair coiled through her black braids. Despite the chill in the air she wore a high-necked sleeveless tunic, which showed off an impressive assortment of tattoos, black against her brown skin. *Arresting.* That was the word. The woman on the threshold was arresting. If the jeweled scimitar on her hip gave any indication, dangerous as well.

She glanced from me to Julienna to Mar'esh, settling at last on Mar'esh. The bangles on her wrists clanged as she folded her arms. "Well?"

"Are you Captain Teg?" I asked.

"Yes."

Julienna stepped forward with the same steely glint I'd seen Alastair use with recalcitrant *nakla*. "The same captain who was thrown out of a tavern last week for talking about *ghastradi*?"

She gave a violent start. "Who told—?"

"Yes or no?"

Teg straightened. "What's it to Family Daired if I am?"

"We have questions, Captain," I said, trying for a more conciliatory tone.

"I have no answers for you, Lady Daired, and I have no wish for more ridicule. Good day," she said, and started to shut the door.

"Wait! We believe you."

The door stopped closing. "What?"

"You think the *ghastradi* have returned, don't you?" I said.

It was a calculated bet, an arrow fired into the dark, but it struck home. Like a coil of wire suddenly unspooled, the captain relaxed. "Yes, I do." She unfolded her arms and drew the fore-fingers of each hand across her collarbone before touching them lightly to her eyelids. "Sacred Twins grant you peace. I am Irina Teg. Forgive my rudeness; this was not the visit I've come to expect from Arleans. Come inside."

I took a half step forward when I felt Julienna's hand on my arm. She looked pointedly at Teg's scimitar, and I fell back to the stoop. Perhaps I hadn't learned the lessons of Langdred as well as I'd thought.

Teg gave us a quizzical glance over her shoulder when she realized we hadn't followed. "Ladies?"

"You wear a sword, madam," Mar'esh said with the barest hint of a growl in his throat.

"Yes, as does your Rider. What of it?"

Julienna unhooked her scabbard from its harness on her back and draped it over Mar'esh's shoulder spikes. "In good faith," she said, and held up her empty hands.

"Ah, I see," Teg said. "Your caution does you credit, my ladies, for these are treacherous times. But you've nothing to fear from me. Here."

She unbuckled her scimitar and laid it aside. From a niche beside the door she withdrew a glass dish the size of her palm, divided in the center into two shallow bowls. One was full of salt, the other of water. She wet her forefinger and touched the salt, then put it to her lips and gestured for us to do the same.

"By the laws of salt, I bring you into my house and under my protection. Ladies Daired, enter and be welcome."

The salt was coarse and tasted of the sea, but the strange ceremony reassured me. I followed her inside, and after a moment's hesitation, Julienna did too, leaving Mar'esh standing guard.

The interior was dim but warm, the blue-tiled floors reflecting the glow of dozens of small lamps in their high sconces. Here and there potted palms entirely unsuited to the climate were kept alive with what must have been exhaustive care. The air smelled of *kaf* and some strange spice I didn't know. Teg led us to a tiny courtyard at the rear of the house. Like the inner corridors, the pavement was tiled in blue and white, and a fountain in the shape of a leaping dolphin poured a cascade into a green basin, reflecting sunlight like diamonds across the walls. More potted palms surrounded the courtyard, trimmed and wrapped for the winter, leaving barely enough room for a squat wooden table and reed mats in the center of the courtyard. Teg gestured to the mats.

"Sit, if you will. I'll bring *kaf*," she said, and disappeared into the house.

The mats were surprisingly comfortable. I sat cross-legged, my knees just brushing the underside of the table, and Julienna sat across from me. Teg returned a moment later with a silver tray laden with matching silver cups and a tall fluted carafe decorated in silver filigree. She set the tray on the table and knelt between us.

"Now. What is it you'd like to know?"

"Why were you talking about *ghastradi* in the tavern the other night?" I asked.

She poured the steaming *kaf* and set cups in front of each of us with a thoughtful look. "Before I answer, permit me a question of my own. What concern is it of yours?"

A fair question. There was no need to hide the reasons behind our interrogation, surely? As quickly as I could, I summed up the events of the last few weeks. Teg's thoughtful look deepened as I spoke. When I spoke of the *ghastradi* we'd seen, she muttered something in a southern tongue and hung her head.

"So," she said, "war is coming to Arle."

"In one form or another," I said, "and if the *ghastradi* are involved, we'd like to know how."

"You were wise not to proclaim this from the towers of the First Circle, Lady Daired. Blood of the Fireborn you may be"—she glanced at Julienna—"but common city-folk will not heed you any more than they did me. The ghost-ridden are nothing but old wives' tales to them now."

"What made you believe them?" Julienna asked.

Teg took a slow sip of *kaf* and pursed her lips. "The *ghastradi* took someone from me, my lady. I wasted a year of my life searching out every other explanation for her death, but there is only one that makes sense. Once the Greater Lindworm rose, I had no doubts. The darkest legends of your kingdom walked once more under the sun; why should ghasts not be among them?"

A year ago? All at once the memory that had nagged me since Uncle Gregory mentioned it surfaced with perfect clarity. Alastair had told me all about it in the barn in Middlemoor. "It was your first mate, wasn't it?" I asked, and Teg looked surprised. "You asked my husband and his dragon to investigate."

"You are Lord Alastair's wife?" she said.

"Aye. He said he couldn't find anything. You burned the body before he saw it."

She bowed her head over her cup. "I was a fool, Lady Daired. Yes, I sent for your husband, but I never spoke with him. And I did not burn the body."

"Tell us about her," I said gently.

"Her name was Sareen Yula. She had worked for me for many years. There was no better sailor in the Principalities, and I trusted her as I trusted myself. Perhaps that was my mistake. I knew she had interests in the Garhad Islands and beyond, interests that Arlean magistrates and Garhadi regents would both frown on, but they never interfered with our business, so I allowed them to continue."

"What kind of interests?" Julienna asked.

"Smuggling," she said. "I did not ask for details, but last year she brought something—*someone* onboard that was not human. It was on our summer run from the Islands to the Port of Nan. I felt when we set sail that something wasn't right, that there was someone on the *Hesperon* who shouldn't be there, but I never found anything no matter how I looked. When I asked Yula about it, she laughed and said I was imagining things. She even reviewed the manifest in my presence. There was nothing there that shouldn't have been." Her voice fell. "That was the last time we spoke at length. The farther north we sailed, the more reticent and reclusive she became. Twins forgive me, I let her be." Teg sipped her *kaf*. "We were nearing the coast when she went belowdecks. It was the last time I saw her alive. When we docked, I was first to open the hold and— Well, there she was."

"Was anyone else with her?" Julienna asked.

"I saw no one."

"Why did Alastair say you burned the body?" I asked.

"I did not burn her, Lady Daired, but she was burned. That was how I found her." Teg looked away. "I pray someday I will forget the sight. Her body, charred on the floor of the hold, and nothing else touched."

My mind raced. Julienna looked at me, a frown creasing her forehead. *Burned alive in the hold of a wooden ship, leaving no trace?*

Teg poured herself another cup of *kaf* and drank it in a single swallow. The silver rang faintly as she replaced the carafe with a trembling hand. "I have had a year to think on it, my ladies, and I have come to one conclusion: Sareen Yula smuggled a *ghastradi* aboard my ship. What other creature could conceal itself so well?

Your legends call these creatures living shadows, and that is what I felt aboard my ship. A shadow over everything, though I could not find its source."

"Ghasts can't control fire," I said.

She shrugged. "Perhaps not, but there are many Oldkind creatures that can. You see, I do not think it was a human *ghastradi* Yula brought aboard my ship. She gave it passage, and it repaid her by taking her life. I can only assume it did not want its errand or identity betrayed." Teg stood. "That is why I was speaking of the *ghastradi* in the tavern, Lady Daired. Yula's killer cannot be the first to arrive on our shores in this manner, but I will do all I can to ensure it is the last. Now I have answered your questions. I cannot help you further."

The blood hummed in my ears. The pieces were there, falling into place. *Late summer of last year, after Midsummer but before Martenmas. Right around the time a certain poor manor had celebrated the arrival of five Riders with a banquet at Hall-Under-Hill.* I swallowed, then swallowed again. It made sense. It was the *only* thing that made sense.

"Thank you for your time, Captain Teg."

We rose and followed her back through the tiled hallways to the front door. Julienna nearly trembled with the need to discuss this new information, but I shook my head and mouthed, *"Wait."*

Teg bowed us through the door. "Sacred Twins show you favor, Ladies Daired. I should prefer it was not necessary, but if it is, know that I will provide what assistance I can in your further inquiries."

We thanked her again. She shut the door after us, and we heard the sound of bolts.

Mar'esh stood. "Well? Any luck?"

I nodded grimly. The answer danced before me with the cold

blue light of the Shadow Minister's conjured flame. He'd needed transport to and from Els. He'd said as much in his note to Gwyn. *That creeping cloak of darkness moving with a mind of its own, hiding him from sight?* He'd even shown me his ghast, though I'd not realized it at the time.

A minister of Els, Tully the lithosmith, Wydrick, the Vesh, our heartstones. The threads binding them together stretched back across the ocean, spreading into the spider web of darkness and silence that lay across the desert of Els.

I swung onto Mar'esh's back. "Head for the Sword and Crown," I said. "We need the Riders."

IT WAS A HARD CLIMB TO THE SECOND CIRCLE, WEIGHED down now by this new, more sharply defined fear. Els had interests in Arle; I'd known that since my first encounter with the minister. After Tully, I was prepared to accept that there was something more sinister than mere profit in the Elsian moneylender's campaign among the desperate of Arle, but to what end? *Heartstones? Why does the Silent Kingdom want heartstones?*

Mar'esh climbed over the wall separating the Third and Second Circles, and for a moment I caught a splendid view of the entire city spread out below us, white and yellow and crosshatched with violet where the streets lay in shadow. A flash of dark gray and burnished red-gold danced like sparks above the dull green swath of the Royal Park. Knowing Akarra and Herreki continued their aerial patrol comforted me a little, but nowhere near enough.

"Julienna," I asked suddenly, "when did Els first suggest opening their ports?"

"Right after"—she ducked sideways and I followed just in time, narrowly missing a rope of laundry—"the Battle of North Fields. I think."

Convenient. With our forces decimated from the Worm's campaign, we had not thought to suspect the offer, so unexpected and fortuitous, even from the kingdom we knew nothing about. And why should we? The war was over. No one suspected we'd fought only the first battle. *Except you.* I gritted my teeth as Mar'esh slipped through a narrow archway and into the broad Avenue of Vines. Perhaps that was why the *ghastradi* brotherhood had spoken so freely in Hatch Ford and Morianton. *They knew you couldn't stop it.*

"Thell!" Julienna cried as a wagon cut in front of us, nearly sending its iron-shod wheels over Mar'esh's claws. "Watch yourself!"

The driver, a slight woman with a hood pulled low over her face, started to make a rude gesture before catching sight of us. With a gasp she snapped the reins, and her horse trotted out of our path.

"Blast the traffic," Julienna growled.

"Is it always this busy in this part of the city?"

"Midday, yes." She pointed up the avenue to a heavily timbered building rising two stories above the street. Leafless trees swayed in front of it next to the battered sign that declared it to be THE SWORD AND CROWN. "We'll walk from here, Mar'esh."

He smiled and I caught the scent of dragonfire. "I could always clear a path, *khela*."

She gave him a look as she dismounted, and he heaved a dramatic sigh.

"Oh, very well. If you insist. Call for me when you're done."

Pedestrians with heads bent to the cobbles jostled us from either side, their attention absorbed by their errands. Vendors shouted their wares all around and dust rose underfoot, stinging my nose with the scent of woodsmoke and manure and overripe fruit well out of season. Carts laden with baskets of vegetables and crates of raw wool wove through the crowd, ushered by the shouts and curses of their drivers. One wagon, the one that had nearly run into us, at last gave up and edged out of the crush of passersby. It rolled up to the curb in front of the tavern to wait out the worst of the traffic.

"I wonder how many Riders Alastair was able to gather," Julienna mused. "Master Doublegray knows all the—"

I gripped Julienna's arm.

"Aliza? What's wrong?"

A man was coming out of the narrow alley around the opposite side of the Sword and Crown, a lantern in one hand. He hailed the wagon driver with a furtive gesture and she swung down from her perch, leaving the cart in front of the door to the tavern. The man's other hand was bandaged. A thrill of horror shot through me.

"Rookwood!"

His head jerked up. His companion spun around, her hood falling away to reveal a tangle of fiery red hair that I'd last seen in the inn at Langdred. Dimly I heard Julienna gasp, and the sounds of wheels, and footsteps, and the shouts of drivers, but all were muted by the thundering rush in my ears, all blood and hatred and heat and terror and rage. A spasm of shock crossed Rookwood's features as he recognized me, but it passed in a moment, and slowly, like a cat gloating over its cornered prey, he smiled.

It was then that I noticed the first curl of smoke rising from the rear of the tavern.

Rookwood raised his maimed hand in salute and swung the lantern into the bed of the wagon. Glass shattered.

"*No!*"

Flames erupted from the bales of cloth, licking along the cart, spreading to the door—*were those rags stuffed around the doorjamb?*—

too quickly, too quickly! Already we could hear the sound of shouts from inside.

"The Riders are in there!" Julienna cried, but I was already running for the alley. There had to be a side door, a back door, something. *There has to be something!*

There was a back door, and it was on fire.

The heat nearly barreled me over. Over the crackle of fire and broken glass I heard the crisping sound of singed hair. Smoke dragged black claws down my throat. I threw my arm up to protect my face and edged closer to the wall of flames that hid the back door. More shouts. Sheets of fire rippled like water down the oil-soaked wood as the trapped Riders beat at the door from the inside, but it didn't budge. My thoughts churned thickly, sluggish in the smoke. *Why won't it open?*

Steel flashed, and I heard a piercing whistle. "Aliza, the bar! He barred it!"

Julienna's shout roused me. Sword drawn, tunic up over her nose, she crouched next to me and pointed to the slim iron bar wedged in the doorframe, just visible through the cascade of flames, which split and reformed like some ghastly lipless mouth.

How long are you willing to watch him burn?

How long? Oh gods, how long?

Julienna and I moved as one, sucking in the last of the good air before plunging toward the inferno. A protest lodged somewhere in the back of my mind, weakly citing the smell of burning flesh and boiling blood and heat and agony. Flames curled along our outstretched arms, driving us back. It was all we could do to see the bar, let alone touch it. Still the door shuddered, the blows from inside becoming increasingly more frantic.

I kicked at the bar. The angle was bad, but I felt the iron rod shift a few inches. "Help me!" I gasped. "Julienna!"

She staggered back, retching. My eyes and lungs burned, but still I kept kicking. Hair crinkled and singed around my face. Flames roared. The Green Lady's prophecy laughed inside me. *How long? How long?* Through a haze of burning tears and blinding pain and the swirl of flames and smoke, I kicked. *Thell, not today!*

"Aliza!" Julienna cried, and coughed. "Get back! Get . . . away!"

Still I kicked. The bar was loosening, I could feel it.

"Aliza!"

A roar louder than the flames swallowed my scream as Mar'esh threw me aside, shattering the iron bar, the door, and most of the wall. I rolled out of the way as a surge of soot-blackened Riders, wyverns, and beoryns poured from the tavern, gasping clean air like drowning creatures. Julienna caught me by the elbow and pulled me clear of the crush, and I clung to her as coughs racked my body. She pressed a hot hand against my forehead.

"Alastair?" I croaked. "Alastair!"

I peered through singed eyelashes at the Riders and *Shani* around us. Most were bent double, coughing so their whole bodies shook, but I didn't see Alastair or Edmund or Lady Catriona. An alarm bell rang in the distance.

"Back! Everyone keep back!" Mar'esh's booming voice rolled like a wave from one end of the street to the other, scattering the horrified pedestrians who had stopped to watch. He leapt from the burning tavern, heedless of the flames, and cleared a wide space around the collapsing walls. "Is everyone out?"

"Cedric?" Julienna called. It came out in a wheezing gasp, and she coughed. "Cedric!" she tried again, louder this time.

Her grip on my shoulders eased as Brysney charged out from the crowd to our left, his red hair streaked with soot and ash. He rushed to us, Silverwing hobbling at his side. "Julienna? Aliza!"

"Is Anjey with you?" I croaked.

"She's gone to your uncle's," he rasped, "but what are *you* doing here?"

"Alastair. Where's Alastair?"

Brysney looked around. "He was right behind me. There! Alastair!"

Even roughened by the smoke, Brysney's voice carried well beyond mine. A moment later a hunchbacked figure stumbled out from among the Riders, shrouded in smoke and a damp cloak. "Cedric, what . . . *Thell*, Aliza, is that you?" Alastair's voice came muffled from beneath the cloak. "And Julienna?"

Brysney stood and helped peel back the dripping cloth. Two heads emerged: Alastair's and the wrinkled, graying head of an ancient half-goblin. The half-goblin crouched on Alastair's shoulder, knees drawn almost up to his enormous, bat-like ears, staring at the fire with glassy eyes. His mouth hung slack, the wisp of a beard around it badly singed. An abrasion on his forehead oozed brownish blood. Alastair set the half-goblin gently on the curb, where he curled into a ball with his arms around his legs, rocking on the stone and crying in silence.

Alastair turned to us, but I didn't let him speak. I flung my arms around him and burst into tears. He hugged me hard. "What are you doing here?"

All of a sudden, I remembered Rookwood. Frantically I looked around, but in the rush of escaping Riders and tumult of the arriving water brigade, he had disappeared.

"Rookwood from Langdred," I panted. "He's in the city, he and his Vesh."

"What?"

"They planned this, Alastair. They set the fire. They must know, they must want the Riders out of the way. We have to find him, we have to stop him!"

"Shh, shh, it's all right," he said, holding me tight. "We'll find him."

"We have to chase him! He'll get away . . ."

"He's made an enemy of every Rider in Edonarle, *khera*. There's nowhere he can run."

A new alarm bell began tolling out over the lower circles. Mar'esh growled in Eth and I looked over my shoulder. A second pillar of smoke rose from the outskirts of the city, beyond the Lower Quarter, black and belching.

"Oh gods. Alastair," Julienna said, "look."

The color drained from Alastair's face.

"What is that?" I asked.

"The camp of the Free Regiments," he said. "Every Ranger posted in Edonarle."

Dread like thick smoke filled my heart. One tavern saved had not stopped Rookwood's accomplices. The Vesh had done what they set out to do.

CHAPTER 16

THE GRAY ABBEY

Ashes stung my eyes and burned my throat. I woke to the screams of trapped men, women, and *Shani*, begging for rescue, for the gods to save them, and then, when no one answered, for a quick death. It took the shock of cold water from the ewer basin to dispel the screaming images, and even then they lingered on the edge of consciousness, sending out poisonous roots into the well-tended earth of my nightmare garden.

I braced myself against the marble basin and looked down at my bandaged arm. *Lucky*, the Daired physician had called me, to have escaped with such minor burns. I did not feel lucky. *Angry* was a better word. I dried my hands and flung the towel to the floor. Livid, actually.

"How are you, *khera?*"

Alastair leaned against the doorway to our chambers, dressed in his riding leathers with his sword on his back. His face had not lost the drawn, anxious look from yesterday, and there were angry red splotches across his forehead and cheek where the flames had licked through the cloth.

"I'll be all right. Are you leaving?"

"Yes, but breakfast first." He motioned to the window. "Out there. Herreki and Aunt Catriona have called a council."

I finished dressing, choosing a tunic with the loosest sleeves I could find. The burns smarted and stung enough to warrant a detour to find Caldero, who was happy to show me where the physician had left his store of poultices. I gathered a few jars and bunches of herbs from the kitchen, stuffed them in my pocket, and headed for the courtyard.

Servants had brought out a table and chairs, arranging them in the center of the pavement and leaving plenty of room around the perimeter. Even so, it was a tight fit. I sat between Alastair and Edmund, who was idly scratching the delicate scales beneath his wyvern's wing. The imposing figure of the Drakaina Herreki presided over the council, her golden gaze licking over each of us in turn before landing on me.

"Good morning, Miss Aliza."

The cool and perfectly formal way she addressed me might have bothered me once, but not anymore. She didn't try to hide her disapproval, but at least she hadn't tried to immolate me this time. Akarra crouched next to her and Mar'esh on her other side, encircling us in a living wall of scales and dragonfire.

Lady Catriona handed me a cup of tea. "How are your burns, my dear?"

"They're fine."

"I should have razed Langdred when we had the chance," Akarra growled. She touched Alastair's shoulder with one wingtip, frowning at the red marks on his cheek. "Rookwood should not have left those shores alive."

"But he did," Herreki said. "What-ifs and what-should-have-beens are not our concern, *kes-ahla*. Now we must decide what to *do*."

"We know what we have to do," Edmund said. "Find the

bastard who set the fire and hang him off the highest tower in Edonarle."

The Drakaina shook her head. "Vengeance is not suited for times of war, Edmund, and we are at war. We must find the Vesh conspirators, yes, but we must find the *ghastradi* too."

"And what then?" Julienna asked.

"Then we'll make them tell us what they know," Edmund said. "Whatever it takes."

I listened as Alastair and Edmund went back and forth as to how they might bring about our enemies' sudden eloquence, interrupted here and there by Julienna's protests and Catriona's flat refusals.

Petals on the stem and leaves on the branches. I pulled the herbs from my pocket and laid them out next to the little poultice jars in front of me. The Vesh were the leaves; the *ghastradi* and creatures like the Shadow Minister were the branches. There would be no victory until we learned what lay at the root.

"Alastair, Lady Catriona, did you have any luck with the king yesterday?" I asked suddenly.

Edmund sat back in his chair as Alastair and his aunt shook their heads. "Though not for lack of trying," Lady Catriona said. "The Master of Appointments was implacable. I even took it to the Lord General, but Camron said there was nothing he could do. Delegations from the trade guilds have been lining up to present their cases for or against the treaty for months. They will not be dissuaded."

"Not even if it's life or death?"

"As far as they're concerned, Aliza, this *is* life or death," she said. "There are guilds with vested interests in keeping Elsian ports closed. If they fail, they lose their livelihood. The king has a duty to listen to them."

My cheeks grew warm. *Blast diplomacy.* I focused on shredding the leaves in my lap. *And damn the king's duty!*

"The City Watch might be able to help," Alastair said after a moment.

Mar'esh snorted. "Some use they've been to us in the past."

"They may have been hesitant to act before, yes, but now we have proof," Akarra said. "Bring the Chief of the Watch to the ruins of the Sword and Crown and ask him to investigate. Show him the charred bodies of the Rangers. Have him walk the Fourth Circle with one of the Riders patrolling on foot because his wyvern's lungs were too smoke damaged to fly, and see if he refuses then."

"You know this Chief of the Watch personally, Alastair?" Herreki asked.

"We've worked together before. He trusts me. I'll have his people combing the city by noon today. All the Riders and Rangers who are fit enough are already out there, but they won't scorn the help. Rookwood, Wydrick, anyone who's had a part in this: if they're in Edonarle, we'll have them by—"

"Who *would* the king listen to?" I asked.

I felt rather than saw Alastair's flicker of annoyance, my eyes fixed instead on Lady Catriona. She looked surprised and considered.

"Well, I would say me, but this is a matter of statecraft as well as war, and I admit I have little experience there. Perhaps . . ." She pursed her lips. "The High Cantor. The Chief Magistrate. Lord Camron, but he's been occupied with the ambassadors of late. If you were able to persuade several of the Guildmasters of the danger, they might ask to postpone the treaty talks long enough to investigate."

"It is a start," the Drakaina said. "Very well. Alastair, you, Edmund, and Whiteheart speak to the City Watch. Julienna, you and Mar'esh continue the patrol of the Fourth Circle with the other Riders, and Akarra, you watch the First Circle. What Riders have we stationed here?"

"Lena var Dooren and Old Hammerhand," Edmund said, "and their wyverns."

"Good. Catriona and I will visit the palace again."

Herreki didn't mention me, didn't look at me again. The others finished breakfast with little conversation and hurried back to the house to prepare. In a few minutes only Alastair, Akarra, and I remained.

"I'm sorry about Herreki, *khera*," Alastair said.

I shrugged and folded the torn hush leaves into the poultice.

"She doesn't do that intentionally," Akarra tried. "The snubbing. It's just many years of habit, and . . . What *are* you doing?"

"There." I daubed the edge of a napkin in the grayish poultice and took Alastair's face in my hands. He looked startled but didn't pull away, and I gently spread the mixture over his burns. "This is war. I'm not about to take offense."

"Aliza . . ."

"You two have your work. I have mine."

"Aliza," Alastair repeated softly, and I stopped spreading the poultice. He took my hand. "Would you *like* to come with us?"

"You don't have to say that."

"I know, but I mean it. Would you like to?"

I looked at him long and hard, conscious of Akarra's deep, steady breath above us as she watched me, watched him. He really did mean it. *Leaf and Lightning, I'll never deserve this man.* I tossed the poultice aside, wrapped my arms around his neck, and kissed him. Akarra chuckled as he returned the embrace with equal enthusiasm, and for one glorious instant the fears and troubles hanging over us like some evil cloud evaporated, leaving only the warmth of his arms and the taste of his kiss. It was a minute before we separated, breathless and bright-eyed, and reality fell once more.

"I'm sorry," I said. "You know I'd be no use to you at the palace."

"*Khera*, that's not true."

"It is. Besides, there's something else I need to do. Something *useful*." He arched an eyebrow and I smiled as, with timing I could have prayed for if only I had the faith, the bells of the Gray Abbey began to chime the hour in the highest circle of the city. "Your aunt says the king will listen to the High Cantor, yes? Then I'll go find the High Cantor."

"It's worth a try," Akarra said.

Alastair kissed my forehead. "It certainly is. Just promise me one thing, *khera*, will you?"

"Aye?"

"Don't go alone."

THE DOOR WARDENS AT THE ENTRANCE TO THE TOWN-house did a terrible job of disguising their astonishment. I put one hand on my hip, hoping the gesture came across as more imperious than petulant.

"Look, I really don't care which one of you it is. Whoever's feeling particularly pious today."

"But we have orders to guard the house!" the younger of the two said, a dark-eyed boy with a Garhadi accent and a short spear in his hand. He swallowed nervously. "Er, my lady."

"Aye, so one of you stay to guard the house. It's within walking distance and I'll have you back by noon."

The elder warden shifted his crossbow to one shoulder and peered down at me through bushy eyebrows. "Are these orders from Lord Alastair, ma'am?"

"They're *my* orders, sir."

The two exchanged a glance. At last the elder shrugged. "Very well. Young Teo, escort my lady Daired to the Abbey. Her safety is your responsibility."

Teo? I looked again at my assigned guard in surprise. *Aye.* I could trace some of the master smith's features in his boyish face. His son, perhaps, or another close relation.

"Yes, sir." Teo the Younger straightened with a cumbersome salute and moved to my side.

I thanked them both and started toward the gate for the highest circle of the city, wondering if they knew how much of that performance had been pure bluster.

Young Master Teo didn't speak as we walked, though from what I caught of his expression he was taking his assignment with deadly seriousness. Each passerby got a grimace if they so much as looked in my direction, and those bold enough to offer a good morning were at once put on the other side of me with Teo in between. Briefly I considered suggesting a less aggressive approach, but as the upper streets were less crowded and the Abbey gates not far, I let him do as he pleased. If yesterday had taught me anything, it was that enemies hid in the most unlikely of places, and if solitary excursions were the price to pay for safety, so be it.

We passed walled courtyards and long, curved avenues lined with trees, their bare branches scratching out an eerie music against the walls. Gone was the bustle and crowd of the Second and Third Circles, replaced by the more dignified march of cantors and subcantors as they tended to the various holdings around the Gray Abbey. The streets too were cleaner and better mended, with fresh flagstones fitted regularly when the old ones cracked beneath the weight of passing carriages. Teo and I had to skirt a knot of masons repairing one such hole before the Abbey gates. The lead mason tipped his hat to me as we entered.

"Fourfold blessings, lady," he called, grinning at Teo's scowl. I gave him and his masons what I hoped was a gracious nod and slipped under the shadow of the arch guarding the great Court of the Four, entryway to the Gray Abbey.

Teo nearly ran into me on the other side. "My lady? Are you all right?"

"Oh, aye. I'm fine."

In truth, I was stunned. I'd forgotten how beautiful the Gray Abbey was. Capturing it in any medium but that of reality was a hopeless task, but my fingers still itched for my sketchbook. Commanding the highest point of the city, it rose from the smooth stone pavement of the Court of the Four like some solemn gray-robed officiant over the comings and goings of the capital. Windows with the diamond-paned motif of fourfold architecture winked in the sun. Before the main steps, a massive four-faced statue rose nearly to the height of the tallest bell tower, the carved lines of the gods' robes clean and well cared for, each chip and crack carefully smoothed and filled by the veritable army of subcantors tasked with the preservation of this great symbol of the Fourfold Faith.

Like the garden at the North Fields lodge and the abbey in Morianton, the names of the gods were carved beneath their stone feet. Janna-Provider was first to greet us, her veiled face pointing eastward toward the rising sun. The beech leaf sigil clasped in her hands was made of some rich gem that caught the sun's light and held it like green fire. Her Eth name flickered golden beneath her: *Ahla-Na Lehal'i*, She-Who-Sustains. I circled slowly around the base of the statue, neck craned in a fruitless effort to see their faces, or what could be seen above their veils. Teo trailed wordlessly behind me. Facing north and the entrance to the Abbey was Odei-Creator, *Ah-Na-al Akhe'at*, He-Who-Begins. His lightning-pierced sigil looked as though it had been carved from a single solid diamond. Westward was Mikla-Protector, *An Tyrekel*, Shield of the Faithful. His shield sigil hung bright with fire opals.

I stopped before the final facet, as was proper. The Unmaker's all-seeing eyes peered south, out over the Bay of Nan and into the blue distance beyond Arlean shores. Her hands, open and empty, faced outward as if waiting to receive the souls of all living creatures. Her Eth name was driven deep into the stone at her feet, the letters forged of cold, unyielding steel. *Ket. Death.*

On the plinth before the statue, hundreds of offerings lay in small piles on the steps, from copper half-trills and perfumed paper flowers to boiled seedcakes and tiny cups of wine. The air shook above us as the bell tower tolled out the hour. Before the last echoes had faded from the court, a young woman in the white robes of a senior acolyte bustled out of the Abbey with a basket in hand and started collecting the offerings.

"Excuse me, miss?" I said. "Is the High Cantor here today?"

She paused beneath Mikla's facet and gave me a sharp look. "Learned Master Pennaret is attending to the High Cantor's duties today. Shall I convey a message?"

"Does Master Pennaret know where the High Cantor is?"

By the expression on the acolyte's face, I might as well have suggested that Learned Master Pennaret hang his holy robes of office on the highest point of the Abbey and run naked through the streets of Edonarle. "And *who*, if I may ask," she said in an acid voice, "are *you*?"

"I'm—"

"This is Lady Daired," Teo cut in, "wife to Lord Alastair Daired and secret bane of the Greater Lindworm, and as far as you're concerned, young lady, she has leave to see whoever she likes in this city."

The acolyte went very red and I gave Teo a sidelong look. *Secret bane of the Greater Lindworm?* I'd not heard that one before. Perhaps Henry Brandon's "Charissong" had gone even further than he intended. With a mumbled apology, the acolyte curtsied and motioned for us to follow her inside.

The shadow of the Abbey cut the warmth of the nearly noon sun like a reaper's scythe as we passed beneath the carved arch that guarded the porch. The inside was cool and dim. Lamps burning scented oil threw flickering light over the four-faced statue standing on the sunken dais in the center of the nave. It was smaller than the one outside, but no less richly adorned, nor less well attended. A handful of the faithful sat on low stone benches surrounding the square. Few looked up as we passed. Most ignored us, their heads bowed, deep in prayer. One young man lay prostrate before Odei, his hands outstretched on the cool marble floors, shoulders shaking with silent sobs. I wondered what he prayed for.

"Keep up, please," the acolyte said.

I hurried after her as she led us to the far side of the nave, where a little door opened into a long pillared gallery hung with tapestries depicting the adventures of the seven great saints of the Fourfold Faith. Part of me wanted to linger, to take in the details and artistry, but the task at hand and our guide's agitation prevented any thought of that. She was fairly trotting now, her basket swinging in time with her footsteps. At the end of the gallery she halted.

"Wait in here, if you would. I'll fetch Master Pennaret," she said, and jogged away.

We watched her go. "Maybe it's her day off," I said.

Teo snorted, then clapped his hand over his mouth and looked at me with an expression of such abject mortification I couldn't help but ease his mind.

"Master Teo, I spent my childhood helping the garden-folk grub up mudroot and threadpotatoes for breakfast. Snorting is practically a compliment."

"But, my lady, you're a *Daired*—"

"I won't tell if you won't."

"They're here, Learned Pennaret," the acolyte said, reappearing with a man in the gray embroidered robes of a subcantor. He was a tall man, surprisingly young, black-skinned and handsome in a bookish, bespectacled way. He peered at the two of us over his spectacles with an amused expression.

"Hmm," he said. "I see. Thank you, Sarianne, you may return to your duties."

I curtsied as the acolyte scurried off. "My name is Aliza Daired, sir, and I was told you could help me. I need to speak with the High Cantor."

"An honor, Lady Daired. I apologize if my acolyte was abrupt. What with preparations for Saint Ellia's Day and everything else going on, all my acolytes have been rather on edge today. I am Tavin Pennaret, High Cantor Tauren's right hand. May I ask why you need to see him?"

For a moment I debated. Master Pennaret seemed a rational sort of man, but given the state of his acolytes, I wondered if it would be wise to inspire unnecessary unease. "Well," I said carefully, "Lord Daired and I have reason to suspect there is a plot against the kingdom."

"A plot? From whom?"

Now to put Captain Teg's theory to the test. "The *ghastradi*."

The subcantor's brow furrowed. "I see," Pennaret said after a moment. "Well, my lady, you'd better come with me. This is no place to talk."

CHAPTER 17

UNMAKER

We followed him down a corridor off the main gallery, this one a good deal less ornate than the last. Teo strode at attention at my side, looking more and more comfortable in his role as body-guard. "Here, my lady," Pennaret said, and ushered me into a small study at the end of the hall. Two lamps burned low on a desk covered in papers, notebooks, and an enormous copy of the *Book of Honored Proverbs*, its pages earmarked and worn with use.

"Lady Daired, I'll wait outside," Teo said in a stiff, formal voice. "By your leave."

"Thank you, yes."

Pennaret closed the door most of the way, leaving, at Teo's glare, a crack wide enough to reassure the young man that I was not in any danger. *And to ensure he hears our conversation,* I thought with a little smile. We were both getting the hang of this.

The subcantor cleared the only chair in the room. "I do apolo-gize for the mess, my lady. Sit, please."

"Is the High Cantor really not here?" I asked as I sat.

"He *is* here," he said, pacing behind his desk, hands clasped behind his back, "but before I take you to see him, there are a few things I need to understand and a few things you may need to understand. When you say *ghastradi*, what exactly do you mean?"

"Exactly what you imagine, sir. Shadow creatures riding the souls of the willing."

"And they're moving against the kingdom?"

"Along with the *Tekari*."

He was silent for a moment before he resumed pacing. "I wish I could say this surprises me, Lady Daired, but it doesn't. For weeks now the city has been uneasy."

"Aye, so I've heard." A new thought struck me. "Learned Master—"

"Please. I'm far from master of anything, and I'm much more learn*ing* than learn*ed*. Master Tavin is fine."

"Master Tavin, are you familiar with creatures called *An-Eskatha*? Eldest, in Arlean."

He tapped a finger against his chin. "It doesn't strike a chord, but that doesn't mean much. Oldkind tongues were not my area of study in Quaternary. What are they?"

"Creatures that came before the Oldkind."

"Many scholars and loremasters would say there is no such thing."

"So do the dragons."

"You have reason to disbelieve them?"

I thought of the Green Lady's dripping, faceless facade, her lips drawn back over that void of a mouth, and the writhing shadows of the weald-wraiths. "I've met them, sir."

There was an uncomfortable pause as he absorbed this.

"Do you know if the High Cantor might know more?" I asked.

"If anyone did, it would be Cantor Tauren, yes." He opened his mouth as if to say something, changed his mind, and then reconsidered. "Lady Daired, I will take you to him. I should not, but this is old lore and well beyond me. Come."

He stood and opened the door. I motioned for Teo to follow the subcantor, intrigued despite my growing apprehension. Instead of returning to the tapestry gallery, Pennaret led us to the right, where the corridor grew narrower, terminating in a broad staircase dimly lit with flickering lanterns. A gate of intricate ironwork across the top stair prevented our going any farther. Pennaret fished among his robes for the key.

"What's down there?" I asked.

"Answers, or at least questions that may mean more to you than they do to me." He touched the gate and drew back as it swung open. "That's odd. I thought he locked it."

The sound of distant voices drifted up to us. Pennaret drew in a sharp breath and fairly flew down the stairs. I looked at Teo, weighed the risk against my growing curiosity, and followed the subcantor.

It was a long staircase, much longer than I expected, and curved slightly so that we soon lost sight of the agitated Pennaret as he plunged downward, his sandals slapping against the stone. Another breathless minute and Teo and I reached the bottom, where yet another wrought-iron gate waited. The familiar diamond pattern wove in and out of the four holy sigils, throwing crosshatched shadows on the steps. It too was unlocked, left ajar by Pennaret's passing. I pushed it open and stopped cold.

"Oh . . . *my*," Teo breathed behind me.

The Abbey had been built on the highest hill in Edonarle, but until now I'd never thought to wonder what lay beneath it. Ruins, I'd assumed, the architectural compost of centuries built up like sediment, in which the foundations of the Abbey and the palace complex were laid. That was partly true. The walls rising on either side of the vaulting hall were rougher at the bottom, pieced together from stone of various colors and textures, but as they stretched toward the ceiling, the uniform gray stone of the outer Abbey took over, arching like the ribs of some gigantic creature high overhead. The light of the lamps barely illuminated the ceiling.

In the center of the hall, a third version of the fourfold statue rose from a perfect square of polished white marble. Unlike the statues in the Court of Four and the inner sanctuary, this was no ornate symbol of prestige or devotion, displayed to the crowds to rekindle the wonder of their gods. This was *real*. The air was heavy with the weight of something intangible but undeniable, sharp as incense, though none burned in the empty braziers at each of the four corners of the dais. My knees trembled and I fought the urge to sink to the ground, overwhelmed by something I could not name.

A small sound made me turn to see Teo trembling at my side, his spear hanging forgotten in one limp hand. His throat worked up and down as he stared at the statue.

"It's all right," Pennaret said, appearing at my elbow. "I'm sorry, Lady Daired, Master Guardsman. I should have warned you."

"What is it?" I asked.

"Not something that can be easily put into words," he said, "and certainly not by me. The High Cantor may be more suited to the task."

With difficulty I tore my gaze from the faces of the Fourfold God high above and looked in the direction Pennaret pointed. At a second glance I realized the ground on which the images of the gods stood was not smooth marble after all. Before each facet a diamond-shaped recess had been carved into the stone, each filled to the brim with the element appropriate to each facet of the god it represented. Rich earth before Janna, smoldering coals before Mikla, and though I couldn't see the north side of the statue, I guessed the ancient faithful had filled the place at Odei's feet with something representing the lightning-pierced clouds of a sacred thunderstorm.

Gathered around the rim of the dais opposite Thell, a small knot of men and women stood with their heads bent close together. One of them stood a little apart, looking intently into the pool of water at Thell's feet. Even from the distance it was clear what caused their unease. The surface of the pool was writhing and roiling as if stirred by a miniature tempest, though there was not a breath of wind in the hall.

One of the men by the pool caught sight of us. He was clad simply in gray, but the look of authority in his aged face was unmistakable. "Master Tavin, who are these people?" High Cantor Tauren asked sharply.

The other cantors fell silent and turned to face us with expressions ranging from shock to suspicion and even, in one of the youngest, panic. "You *dare* bring unconsecrated city-folk into Hallowhall?" one of the lesser cantors sputtered. "High Cantor, this is grounds for immediate dismissal!"

"Peace, please. I'm sure Master Tavin has excellent reasons for this unorthodox visit. Let him explain."

Pennaret bowed his head. "I know the customs, my lord, and I ask your forgiveness for breaking them. I wouldn't do it if it weren't important." Head still bowed, he motioned for me to go forward. When I made no move, he gave me a sidelong glance and mouthed a shaky *tell him!*

I swallowed the lump that had settled in my throat and took a step forward, then another. It was impossible to ignore the weight pressing down on my chest the closer I approached the statue. A few feet from the dais I could go no farther. I curtsied, trembled, and sank to one knee, touching four fingers to my forehead. "High Cantor, my name is Aliza Daired and this is my guardsman, Master Teo." A ripple ran through the cantors at the name *Daired*. "I would like to speak with you about what's coming."

The ripple before Thell deepened to a wave.

Whispers rose in the still air, but at a motion from the High Cantor, the whispers ceased. "Return to your posts, my friends," he said. "I will summon you again if we need to take further council. In the meantime, I would talk with Lady Daired alone."

Amidst various hushed protests the cantors obeyed, all performing the fourfold gesture and touching their foreheads, lips, and heart before backing away to the stair.

"You as well, Master Tavin," the High Cantor said, resting a wrinkled hand on Pennaret's shoulder. "Take the young man here and wait at the gate."

Pennaret bowed and did as he said. So did Teo, albeit with a less graceful bow and a look in my direction that was half question, half a plea for permission. At my nod he fairly jogged toward the stairs.

"Don't misunderstand me, child," the High Cantor said when the two were out of earshot. "It is for Catriona's sake I allow you to stay. Impolitic as it may have been to express it thusly, my learned friend was right: it was wrong of Master Tavin to bring you here, Daired or not." He waved away my mortified look. "But Catriona is a dear friend and trusted to many within the Abbey, and any of her kin are welcome to me. Besides," he said, his face darkening, "you speak of what's coming, and that I must know. So please, speak."

I shifted and looked back at the statue, less of an object and more of a presence than anything, looming white in the gloom of Hallowhall. The waters before Thell still churned in their pool. "Gladly, sir, but wouldn't it be better to speak in the Abbey?"

"More comfortable, certainly, but perhaps not better." He followed my gaze to the statue. "You feel it, then?"

I nodded, my throat suddenly too dry to speak.

"As do any who have allowed the gods a claim on their hearts. The imprint of their touch is not easily smoothed away."

"What *is* it?"

He chuckled. "That feeling, you mean? If I may be perfectly honest, no one really knows. As for myself, I like to think of it as awe: half fear, half wonder, as one should feel before the gods."

"Why here?"

One shoulder moved up and down beneath his robe. "Long commerce with the gods in this place has, so to speak, worn thin the walls between us and them. That does not mean their influence is not felt elsewhere, of course, for their nature seeps in through the blood and bones and breath of the world itself," he said, gesturing to the elemental pools before each facet. "Yet they themselves do not walk in the world as we do." He smiled sadly. "There are those who debate this with me, but I have always thought this a mercy. To see our gods face to face might very well be our undoing. Instead they whisper through cracks like this one, granting favor to those who uphold their sacred harmony and defending against those who would not."

"I'm not sure I understand, sir," I said.

"None do, child, until we pass out of the world altogether, Unmaker grant that be many years hence."

For in the hand of the Unmaker, the scales are ever balanced. The phrase came to mind unbidden, though where from, I had no idea. The faint sound of lapping water drew my attention back to the foot of the statue. "High Cantor, the pool. What's happening to it?"

His expression darkened. "I don't rightly know, my lady. I've never seen it thus in my time, and there are no accounts in the records of my predecessors that mention it. It seems a sign that the Unmaker is troubled." He turned to me with a hopeful expression. "Which is why I consider your arrival so fortuitous. You said you know what's coming?"

Quickly I summed up for him everything I had told Pennaret this morning, adding details about our encounter with Wydrick and Tully that I'd thought prudent not to share with the subcantor. The High Cantor listened patiently, his fingers tapping a steady rhythm on his bearded chin. His frown deepened when I mentioned the Eldest.

"*An-Eskatha*, you say? No, I'm afraid I don't recognize the term." There was a pregnant pause as he wavered over his next words. I could see them hanging on his lips, reeling back and forth like some dangerous fish. "And yet it *does* strike me that I've come across it before. Perhaps something from the Epic of Eldrunna or one of those other blasphemous Eldric epics. Honestly, Lady Daired, Quaternary was so long ago and my eyes aren't what they used to be. It's been a while since I read up on any theological lore. You think these creatures are behind the unrest across the kingdom?"

"One of them, at least, and it's been recruiting allies from among our enemies for a while."

"It would have to be something very powerful to rouse the sleeping lindworms."

I glanced again at the writhing water. *And to trouble a god.* "That's what I'm afraid of. It's one reason we need your help. Lady Catriona hasn't been able to secure an audience with the king to warn him about what's coming."

"She hasn't? He won't see *Catriona*? That's . . . but that's—"

"I know," I said. "There may be someone making sure we can't get through. We're trying everything we can think of, but in the meantime, we need allies. You could help us. Lady Catriona says King Harrold will listen to you."

The High Cantor passed a hand over his brow and heaved a sigh. "Well, yes, of course I will help you, but this troubles me greatly. Someone in the palace—"

A deep, reverberating sound shook the hall, echoing like the heartbeat of a giant. The High Cantor broke off sharply.

"What's that?" I asked.

"The Great Bell from the Tower of Nan," he said. "Something's amiss. The Great Bell does not ring common chimes."

"My lord!" came Pennaret's voice from the staircase, but the High Cantor was already heading for the gate as fast as his ancient legs would carry him.

I was nearly winded by the time we reached the topmost gate, but the High Cantor refused to stop for a rest. He charged down the gallery, sending acolytes and worshippers alike scurrying out of his way. Pennaret, Teo, and I followed. The peals of the Great Bell were louder now, the air trembling with their echoes.

"I don't understand," Pennaret whispered to me. "It's not yet midday. They shouldn't be ringing like this. They shouldn't be ringing at all!"

Teo gripped his spear and moved closer to me. The vague sense of dread that had been hanging over me since we entered Hallowhall began to condense, focusing into a point of cold horror in the pit of my stomach as we reached the main nave.

The sanctuary was awash with confusion. Some people continued in their prayers, or tried to. Others had given up and were whispering among themselves or looking toward the bell tower in bewilderment. The cantors not trailing the huffing High Cantor attempted to reassure the congregants, with limited success.

Without warning, the bells stopped. The silence left in their wake was deafening, and my ears rang with it as we emerged from the Abbey into the high portico overlooking the Court of Four and beyond, the city and the sea. The knot of cantors behind us shaded their eyes to see the bell tower above and, just visible on the outer balustrade, the dark figure of the ringer. He or she waved frantically in the direction of the docks. I turned to look.

Riding high at the mouth of the harbor was a small fleet of ships, black against the bright blue of the water. A great golden sphinx rippled on their sails, mouth open as if to swallow all of Edonarle in one bite. My stomach dropped.

"Is that the Elsian ambassador, Lady Daired?" Teo whispered.

I started to nod, but the High Cantor shook his head, pointing to the pennants waving from the ropes on the foremost ship. They shimmered gold, silver, and bloodred in the sunlight.

"No, young man. An ambassador's ship would not warrant the royal colors," he said. "That is the ship of the Silent King."

CHAPTER 18

DRUMS FROM THE DEEP DESERT

As the echoes of the Great Bell died away, other bells took up the call, cascading from the highest point of the city to the lowest in a waterfall of welcome. A shadow fell over the portico and I looked up. Herreki's red-gold scales shimmered in the sun as she swooped low over the Court of Four, heading for the docks. I caught Teo's eye.

"We should get back."

"And I will request an audience with the king immediately," the High Cantor said.

"Thank you," I said. "Send word to the Daired townhouse when you hear from him and we'll join you at the palace."

He touched his forehead, lips, and heart. "Fourfold blessings on you and yours, and may Mikla himself be a shield to your house." He paused, then clasped my hand and added in an undertone, "The gods do not often deal in blind fortune, but perhaps this time they will grant a foolish old man's prayer. Good luck, my lady."

THE STREETS WERE LESS CROWDED THAN THEY HAD BEEN that morning, the few people we passed all hurrying in the general

direction of the lower city, no doubt eager to witness the historic
landfall in person. I wondered how many of them realized it was
the Silent King they were going to see and not some petty ambassador, and if they did, whether it would make them more or less
eager to get a good view. *Why should it not?* I reminded myself that
few people outside of Family Daired suspected anything of the
arrival beyond a colorful procession and perhaps a change in our
trading policies. *No one in our kingdom is ready for war.* The corollary
chilled me to the core. *Including us.*

The street outside the townhouse was empty of people, save
for the old door warden still standing alert at his post, crossbow in
hand. He received Teo back with a tacit nod and a hint of a smile
that suggested, or I hoped suggested, that this tale would make it
back to his father.

"Master Teo's a natural guardsman, sir," I said on impulse, and
the warden grinned. Teo flushed a little as he took up his position
on the other side of the door.

Steward Caldero met me in the front hall and informed me
that the rest of the family was still out. My heart sank. Unsurpris-
ing given their respective tasks, but disheartening all the same. My
head was full of thoughts I did not want to process alone.

I climbed the stairs to our chambers slowly, weighing out
every possible course of action and cursing the poisonous seeds
Wydrick and Tully had planted. It was true what Alastair had
told the Vehryshi at An-Edannathair. The *ghastradi* had delivered their warnings to taunt us, to make us afraid, to mire us in
indecision as we awaited an enemy we did not yet understand,
and I wondered if all of this had been a wild pixie chase: hopeless and distracting from the true task at hand. I flung open the
doors to the balcony overlooking the courtyard trying not to
think about the fact that Family Daired was, at this moment,

scattered throughout Edonarle. A divided force was a defeated one. I folded my arms tightly across my chest and faced the sea.

The city stretched beneath me in a maze of tiered streets and irregular spires, the haze of woodsmoke and rising dust the only thing that obscured the harbor from view. Slate-blue water churned white beneath the swell of the first ship, its silver, gold, and red pennants whipping back and forth. The rest of the ships followed at a safe distance. Only three, and even with my limited knowledge I could see that none of them were ships of war. A fraction of the weight lifted as the sight effaced a possibility I'd not allowed myself to admit aloud. *No invasion, then.*

A crowd had gathered in the open place before the docks, crammed between the water and the warehouses clustered outside the city walls. They shifted and swelled like a single creature, the breathing anticipation of the entire kingdom condensed into this single dockside mass. I shaded my eyes as the lead ship glided into port and the crowd divided in obedience to some shouted command I couldn't hear. Tiny figures in white and green threaded their way toward the quay as the dockhands bustled to ready the ship for docking. Royal officials, I guessed, hurried to the harbor as fast as King Harrold could order them.

The crowd shuffled, the ship bobbed in its berth, and a handful of wyverns circled above it, their Riders watchful specks against the bright sky. Then at last, action. Dark figures swarmed the deck, laying out a gangplank, tightening ropes, and stowing sails. I squinted as more figures appeared on the Elsian ship, each dressed in sparkling golden armor and carrying large, round items I couldn't make out, though that wasn't the oddest thing about them. Perhaps it was a trick of the distance, or perhaps the other sailors were very short, but the armored figures did not look human-sized. They looked a great deal bigger.

Without warning the figures raised their arms, then brought them down. A great booming sound rolled out across the water, swelling on the crest of the wind from the sea. *Boom. Boom. Ba-boom.* Even half a city away I felt the drums deep in my chest like an external heartbeat. *Boom. Boom. Ba-boom.* The wind off the water was chilly, but in those reverberating echoes I felt the heat of sun-scorched lands, felt the sting of distant sandstorms swirling through dead cities. *Boom. Boom. Ba-boom.*

Still drumming, the armored guards took up their places along the gangplank, and the beat quickened as a veiled palanquin emerged from the depths of the ship, borne by another group of those inhuman guards. The procession descended from the ship to the beat of the drums, halting before the king's representatives.

The drumming ceased.

I wished I was closer, part of that eager knot of common-folk pressing in around the two embassies and listening to their scripted greetings, parsing their words out for hidden meanings. From my viewpoint there was only occasional movement, and I was beginning to wonder how much longer the pleasantries would go on when both retinues turned aside and began their processional toward the main gate of the city. The bulk of the crowd followed, trailing after the now-silent drummers like a flock of drab and curious birds. Chilled by the cold stone of the balustrade, I watched until the last of the Elsian embassy passed through the gate and into Edonarle.

THE WAR SUMMONS FOR HOUSE DAIRED CAME NOT WITH drums and drawn swords, but on the gilded edge of an elegant little envelope.

The family returned one at a time, Akarra first, then Alastair and his cousin, then Julienna and Mar'esh, who perched on the courtyard wall so he could keep an eye on the rest of the city while we talked. They'd each witnessed the procession of the Silent King, most of them from a vantage point better than mine.

"Forge-wights," Alastair confirmed grimly when I asked after the Silent King's guards. "Most of his honor guard, if I had to guess, though it was hard to tell beneath all that armor."

Like the Minister of the Ledger? I wondered. And if so, were they all ghast-ridden, or was there a deeper conspiracy at work, with traitors and *ghastradi* even among the Silent King's ranks? "What did the Watch say?" I asked him.

"The Watch Commander agreed to reinforce the Rider and Ranger patrols. He's doubling their shifts for the next few days."

Julienna and Mar'esh both looked about to say something when the sound of wingbeats interrupted them and Herreki descended into the courtyard. Lady Catriona swung down, and my heart lightened to see her pleased expression. She held an envelope.

"I gather you were discussing the arrival of our friends," she said. "It looked like he had quite the entourage. You saw the forge-wights, didn't you?" She tossed the envelope to Alastair. "As it so happens, we may have a bit of luck at last. Read that."

I leaned over his shoulder as he pulled out the letter. The broken seal flapped from its edge, still showing the quartered shield of the Arlean royal crest. He unfolded the letter and read aloud.

To Lady Catriona Daired, Lord Alastair Daired, Lady Julienna Daired, Captain Edmund Daired, and Lady Aliza Daired, Daired House, Edonarle,

Greetings.

His Majesty King Harrold and Queen Consort Callina request the honor of your presence this evening at a reception in the Winter Palace to welcome the embassies from the Garhad

Islands, the Southern Principalities, and the Kingdom of Els.
Please return your acceptance posthaste.

Sincerely,
His Majesty King Harrold IV of Arle
Her Highness Queen Consort Callina I of the Garhad Islands
His Highness Prince Darragh III of Arle
Edonarle, Saint Ellia's Eve, 1061 SE

He handed the letter to Julienna, who was trying to read it over my shoulder. "They gave this to you this afternoon?" I asked Lady Catriona.

"After the Elsian embassy arrived at the palace," she said, "but they've been preparing this for a while. The steward had it ready when they got there. An official welcome, a chance for diplomacy outside the negotiating chamber, that sort of thing."

Edmund made a face at the word *diplomacy*, and Herreki rumbled her disapproval. "Don't scoff, Edmund," she chided. "The banqueting hall may be no less of a battleground than any other, and if House Daired is called to serve, we go without question."

"Indeed we do," Lady Catriona said, taking the invitation from Julienna's outstretched hand. "This is our chance to warn the king." She caught my eye and winked. "Fortunately, we won't be alone. I ran into High Cantor Tauren outside the Audience Chamber. He'll be there tonight too. He seemed well apprised of the danger."

My heart warmed as Alastair rested his hand on my shoulder. "We'd best get ready," he said.

"I assume you're not asking us to brave this dinner party unarmed, Aunt," Edmund said.

"Don't be absurd, silly boy. Daireds don't win battles with cutlery. I want steel on every hip!"

Whiteheart, Akarra, and Mar'esh let out sighs of relief, and Edmund smiled. "Excellent. Julienna, let's you and I see what manner of dress swords Master Teo has to offer, eh?" He took her arm and headed back toward the house. After a few quiet words with her dragon, Lady Catriona followed, as did Whiteheart.

"I assume I don't need to remind you two how dangerous this could be," Akarra said when they'd gone.

"Of course not," Alastair said.

"I don't like that we can't come with you."

"It is as it must be, *kes-ahla*," Herreki said. "Some battles we cannot share, but that does not give us leave to idly fret. Come now, little one. You and I will rotate in and among the Watch as they make their rounds. Mar'esh, you and Whiteheart will return to the Fourth Circle and support the Brysneys and the other Riders stationed there." Mar'esh bowed his head and scaled the courtyard wall in a single sinuous bound. "Alastair, we will meet you and the others here at dawn," Herreki added before following him.

Akarra turned to us with a grave expression. "*Myet av-bakhan.* Use caution, my *khela*."

"Always, *shan'ei*," Alastair said.

She dipped her head down and pressed her snout to Alastair's forehead. He patted her neck.

"*An-Tyrekel* be your shield," he said quietly.

She withdrew and then, to my surprise, kissed my forehead as well. "And *Ket* take your enemies," she finished. "I'll see you both at dawn."

The ivy tossed madly as she took to the air. I settled back against Alastair's chest as he wrapped his arms around me and watched her shrink against the sky. A thousand trivial fears, ten thousand tiny worries bubbled up inside me, only to die once they reached my tongue. The silence was strangely precious, unbroken by the half-expected plea for me to remain behind. Whatever we faced, we faced together.

After another minute we returned to the house. There was much to prepare.

THE LIGHT OF THE EARLY EVENING SUN FELL FLAT AND heavy along the streets of the First Circle when we set out for the palace. We watched from the windows of our carriage without speaking, reflecting the strange hush that had fallen over Edonarle. By tradition, a Saint Ellia's Eve in the capital should have seen festivities in all corners of the city, with laughing children pursued by fathers in paper sea-serpent masks, who were in turn pursued by the oldest daughter of the house, robed in white and shooting fake arrows from her flimsy wooden bow. Sweetmeat sellers and half-trill traveling bards would lay claim to the available street corners, hawking their wares to wide-eyed, sticky-fingered youngsters, and festive lanterns would have burned in every casement.

Tonight the lanterns still burned, but the cheerful atmosphere that accompanied the holiday was dampened by a vague but weighty sense of apprehension. No children ran in the streets; no costumed Ellias reenacted her legendary last stand to the cheers of her neighbors. We passed a lonely handful of revelers in the Avenue of Kings, already sopping drunk despite the earliness of the hour. They sent up a ragged and rather vulgar cheer at the sight of us but otherwise ignored our little procession.

Just past the revelers, the sound of music and bustle rose to something close to its usual festive volume. The carriage rounded a corner and the avenue opened into the great half-moon courtyard before the palace gates. Hundreds of men and women huddled around a great bonfire in the center of the square, watching the performance of "The Lay of Saint Ellia" by a troupe of street performers, who were in turn watched by the lines of stone-faced palace guards ranged before the main gate. Their attention was rapidly redirected, however, when our carriage rolled to a stop. They saluted as Lady Catriona descended.

"Ah! Hello again, Master Rothwinter," she said.

The head guardsman bowed. "Your Ladyship. My lords and ladies, welcome. You are expected."

I climbed down after Julienna, conscious of every unfamiliar movement of the split skirt she'd insisted I wear. A banquet at the palace demanded finery, of course, but both Julienna and Lady Catriona assured me that the practicality of trousers was a much-cherished privilege of Daired women. We'd settled at last on a compromise: a long soft surcoat embroidered with a pattern of violet and golden leaves, covering a pair of trousers and tall iron-shod boots. An ornate little knife—a dress dagger, Julienna called it—hung at my side.

It took effort not to stare as we entered the main gate. The lingering dread clinging to our errand notwithstanding, the Royal Palace demanded a moment of wonderment. In my summer visits to Edonarle, Aunt Lissa and Uncle Gregory had only ever taken us as far as the Half-Moon Court, and everything I had ever seen of the palace had been through rows of ornate ironwork gates. I resisted the impulse to whistle at this new view. Tiered like the city, the palace took after the Gray Abbey in shape, with diamond-cornered towers rising from each of the cardinal points of the compass. The great main hall thrust its vaulted roof from the ring of towers, capped by a fifth tower, from which a blaze of lights shone, visible even to distant ships. A stone dragon curled around the Tower of Torches, its bared talons clutching the fluttering standard of Arle.

More guards waited on the steep stair leading to the long front portico, pillared and tiered like the rest of the palace. Great urns overflowing with faded autumn foliage, now dull in the waning light, stood between the pillars, alternating with more green-and-white-liveried guards. Two men broke from their stations to open the great doors before us, and not, I noticed, without a good deal of ceremony. The grounds, the staff, the ritual: I couldn't be sure this wasn't the way all guests were welcomed to the palace, but I had the feeling the formality was not for us.

"Welcome, Family Daired." Without the least noise to announce him, an elderly man in the impeccable white suit and golden chain of the Royal Herald appeared at Lady Catriona's elbow. He bowed gravely. "The king, queen consort, and High Cantor await your presence in the reception hall. If it please you to follow me?" he said in a tone that suggested no sane person would be displeased by the idea. I took Alastair's offered arm and followed Lady Catriona after him. The sword on his hip swung in time to our steps, and a sudden fear gripped me.

"Are you allowed to bring weapons before royalty?" I whispered.

"Under normal circumstances, no," he said in my ear, "but Aunt said she had a word with the Captain of the Guard. Tonight they're considered ceremonial necessities."

"What about the guards from the other embassies?"

"They won't be permitted beyond the reception hall. The king offered his own guards for their security."

The fear eased a little. Perhaps King Harrold was not as unprepared as we expected.

The herald ushered us down a wide stair lit by an enormous crystalline chandelier. *Shani* gamboled in delicate marble knots on and around the banisters, to which a handful of jeweled courtiers clung. They bowed deeply, turning on the risers to watch our progress and whispering to themselves. I couldn't help glancing over my shoulder as we passed.

"Just ignore them," Alastair muttered.

At the bottom of the stair the herald motioned for us to stop. A grand doorway opened up before us, flanked by more guards. One of them, an older man with a gray-shot beard and the golden tassels of the Captain of the Guard, cleared his throat nervously as we approached. "Fair evening, Your Ladyship," he said to Lady Catriona. "And to you, my lords and ladies Daired."

"Good evening, Captain," she said. "And how are your grandchildren?"

"Very well, my lady, but . . . ah. *Ahem.* Yes. I'm dreadfully sorry about this, but I must ask that you and your family remove your weapons before entering the reception hall."

Lady Catriona drew up short. "What's this about?"

The captain stared studiously at the chandelier. "Begging your pardon, my lady. Lord General Camron's express orders."

"Captain, I thought we'd discussed this."

The face beneath the beard grew very red. "So we had. Then the lord general and I discussed it further. Er. Apologies."

Alastair frowned and made as if to speak, but Lady Catriona made a sharp motion with one hand and he stepped back. "Very well," she said. "Alastair, Edmund, Julienna, do as he says."

Alastair obeyed reluctantly, exchanging dark looks with Edmund and Julienna. Julienna hefted her blades in each hand and glared at the guard who came to collect them with an expression that suggested she'd put them to good use if he tried to take them from her by force, but her aunt raised an eyebrow and Julienna relented. I handed over my little dagger with almost the same reluctance.

"Take care of these," Alastair said, and handed the captain the knife from his sword-belt.

"I will indeed, sir. With my life."

"Good."

"And the second?"

"What?"

The captain nodded to the glint of a hilt peeping from the top of Alastair's boot. Alastair flushed and removed it, tossing it into the guard's arms.

"Thank you, my lord. My lady." The guard's eyes flickered dismissively over my surcoat, lingered for a moment with a hint of confusion on the brooch that did not contain Alastair's lamia heartstone pinned to my bodice, and bowed slightly. "Herald?" he said, and the herald resumed his responsibility of us.

He motioned toward the open door. "This way, if you please. I shall announce you." He took up his place to the side of the door, bowed to the occupants within, and tapped his staff of office. "Your Royal Majesty, Your Royal Highness, may I present Lady Catriona Daired, Lord Alastair Daired, Captain Edmund Daired, Lady Julienna Daired, and Lady Aliza Daired."

Head held high, gripping Alastair's arm like the last anchor in a storm, I followed the others inside.

CHAPTER 19

THE SILENT KING

Courtiers and council officials in festive clothes swept aside to allow our party through. Candlelight glittered over earrings and necklaces, crests of office and heartstone brooches in every color imaginable. My eye snagged on one figure in plain gray robes, a jarring absence amidst the riot of jewels, and I nodded to High Cantor Tauren. He returned the gesture with a knowing look that took a measure of anxiety off my shoulders. Lady Catriona was right; we weren't here without allies.

"Ah, Daireds!" King Harrold came forward, waving for Lady Catriona to rise from her curtsy. He seized her hand and kissed it. "My friends, welcome."

The queen consort appeared at his side with a smile. Unlike her husband, who wore the traditional white-and-green robes of Arlean royalty, she had dressed in the style of her homeland, in the silk shawl and veiled headdress of a Garhadi-born noblewoman. The cloth shimmered in shades of emerald and peacock-blue. Queen Callina's outfit was calculated, a subtle but meaningful acknowledgment of common ground between the Islands and Arle. I cast a sideways glance toward the tables to my left. Delicacies of half a dozen nations lay among wreaths of winter ivy, and around the tables clustered representatives from the Garhadi embassy. They watched us with expressions that, though not unfriendly, were decidedly cool. *This is where the treaty negotiations begin*, I thought. *In the wardrobe and over the hors d'oeuvres.*

"You honor us with your presence," Queen Callina said, embracing Lady Catriona when the king released her. "You're all *most* welcome." She turned to Alastair and his sister. "You're looking well, my lord. And my goodness, Lady Julienna, how you've grown since I last saw you!"

Julienna, blushing fiercely, ducked her head in a curtsy as embarrassed as it was elegant. King Harrold chuckled. "Lord Alastair, Captain Edmund, come with me. There is someone I'd like you to meet."

Alastair gave me a meaningful look over his shoulder as he followed the king.

"And you must be Lady Aliza."

Julienna's blush had nothing on mine. I felt the weight of Queen Callina's royal attention like some colossal gemstone, rich and heavy, and prayed my nerves would not get the best of me. My wits already felt scattered, my tongue thick. My knee creaked as I curtsied.

"Pleased to meet you, Your Highness."

"And I you, my lady." She studied me for a moment, lips curling upward in an enigmatic smile. "We've all heard *such* stories."

There was a pause: expectant on her end, frantic on mine, as I realized she was waiting for me to seize the offered threads of conversation. Royalty or not, however, I had no desire to talk of old battles. "Your wedding gift was most generous," I said at last, thinking of the beautiful Pelagian mares she and the king had sent us. "Thank you."

"A gift deserved is a delight to the giver as much as the gifted. And this was well deserved," she said, and paused again with that expectant gleam in her eye.

Lady Catriona saved me. "How is your family, Your Highness? Any word from the prince lately?"

"Oh, Darragh is *quite* caught up in his studies. Always forgets to write, but I can't blame him. Stoneholm University is reputed to have a fascinating library."

"Do you expect him to return soon?" Julienna ventured.

"Not until springtime. That is, springtime in Nordenheath. I understand that's nearly summer for us." She heaved a sigh full of maternal worry. "The dear boy has his father's blood. Never minded the cold, either of them, but the thought of a nine-month winter makes *me* tremble. Ah! Halat, there you are."

A Garhadi man in a silken robe dyed bright fuchsia turned from his contemplation of the food, particularly a pair of pixies made from spun sugar. He bowed to Queen Callina, then adjusted the monocle over his left eye and peered at us. "Twins preserve me, what an honor!" he said in crisply accented Arlean. "My ladies Daired, your humble servant."

"The Honorable Master Hallam-Halat is the ambassador from the Islands," the queen-consort explained. "Earlier this afternoon I understand Lady Catriona expressed a desire to bend your ear, Halat. Isn't that right?"

"It is, and thank you, You Highness," Lady Catriona said and moved closer to the ambassador. Unthinkingly, Julienna and I did as well, but before they began to speak, a hand plucked at my sleeve. I turned to see a woman a few years younger than me, Arlean by her complexion but dressed in sweeping Garhadi robes in butter-yellow.

I caught the annoyed *aye?* on the tip of my tongue and reeled it back. "Yes?" I said in what I hoped was a gracious tone.

"Oh! It *is* you. Well, that's a relief and no mistake." She chuckled, eyes crinkling up at the corners. "That 'Charissong' had me fearing you'd be some great and terrible shieldmaiden. Just shows, doesn't it? It's as I tell my boys: you should never trust everything you hear in Taleteller's Circle. Of course, they'd rather—"

"Begging your pardon, madam. Have we met?"

"Leaf and Lightning, look at me! Run off again like the pixie that got into the mead." She curtsied, a very pretty, strange curtsy that involved the corner of the veil she wore half wrapped around her glossy blond curls. "Neira Hallam-Halat, wife to that old pickle yonder," she said fondly, gesturing with another crinkle-eyed smile to the ambassador, who was now deep in conversation with Julienna and Lady Catriona.

I returned her curtsy. "Aliza—"

"Aliza Daired, *nakla* bride of the great Lord Alastair, hero of North Fields and bearer of— Oh," she said, eyes running over my heartstone-less bodice much as the Captain of the Guard's had earlier. "Well, yes. Needless to say, we've heard of you! Even in the Islands the story of the War of the Worm is spreading."

"You're kind, Lady Hallam-Halat."

"Goodness me, Neira, please. You'll choke if you insist on saying that whole thing again."

I smiled and allowed Neira to guide us to the opposite side of the food tables, closer to the windows and farther from listening ears. "Lady Neira, then. You wished to speak to me?"

"I did. I thought, Why, if anyone could tell me what's really going on here, surely Lady Aliza could."

Curiosity pricked me. I schooled my voice into passive interest and decided to feign ignorance. "Why do you think anything's going on, Lady Neira?"

Her bright eyes grew wide. "But surely you've seen it! Haven't you been in the city?"

"We only arrived a few days ago."

"Oh. Still, I would've thought . . ." She shook her head and lowered her voice. "I have no proof, mind. Even my husband will give me only the vaguest assurances, but I suspect there's more to these negotiations than anyone's letting on."

"Like what?"

"Alliances, of course!" she whispered. "Everyone's talking of trade treaties, but what if it's not that at all?" All at once she lifted her chin with a look of defiant triumph, as if she had just solved a riddle that had been confounding the whole court. "It all makes sense when you think about it."

"It does?"

"Of course. This treaty is just a cover for the *marriage* negotiations!"

The word *marriage* nearly came out in a squeal. I blinked. "I'm sorry?"

"Prince Darragh, of course!" She giggled. "He's very marriageable, and the leading princes of the Southern Principalities have more than enough daughters to spare between them. So does the Grand Regent of the Islands."

"And Els?" I asked.

"Oh. Yes, them." Her excitement dimmed a little. "Well, perhaps they really are here for the trade talks. But speaking of, where *are* they?" She stood on slippered toes and looked around. "Dinner should be served soon. Surely they don't need all afternoon to dress?" She tittered again, hiding her mouth behind one slender hand. The cloudy white heartstone of a banshee glittered in its silver band on her finger. "Or perhaps those forge-wights do. Maybe they bathe in fire!"

I murmured something vaguely negative, but she didn't seem to notice. I had to resist the urge to draw back when she put her arm through mine and began a sedate but determined walk toward the main body of courtiers.

Surreptitiously I scanned the hall for Alastair. He and Edmund were still in conversation with the king and a contingent of Southrons from the Principalities. I noticed the familiar bearded face of Lord General Camron hovering nearby, indecisive for a moment before bowing his way into their circle. Lady Catriona and the queen consort had moved with the Garhadi ambassador farther from the tables, but Julienna hovered at the fringes of their little group, clearly uninvolved with the conversation but unsure where else to go. I caught her eye and motioned her over.

"Who are you . . . oh!" Lady Neira said, curtsying as Julienna jogged to us. "My lady!"

"Julienna, this is my new friend Lady Neira," I told her. "We were just discussing—"

"Idle court gossip," Neira said, blushing fiercely, her eyes downcast. "Nothing of consequence, Lady Julienna."

Puzzled for a second by Neira's change in address, it struck me all at once. She'd said as much when she'd introduced herself, not to a Daired, but to his *nakla* bride. I felt suddenly like a fool, coarse-handed, coarse-tongued, and ordinary, an impostor among the Fireborn, good for gossip and little else. The thought twisted in my gut, an old and familiar pain. I swallowed the unexpected thick feeling in my throat. Danger and death and the shadow of war loomed; I could not afford to feel sorry for myself.

Putting on a bright smile, I turned to Julienna again and said,

"Lady Neira's husband is the ambassador from the Islands. She thinks there's more to this treaty than the king is letting on."

A flash of interest lighted in Julienna's eyes and she turned to Neira with new attentiveness. "What do you suspect?"

Neira blushed again, though this time I guessed it had more to do with delight than mortification, as she promptly dropped my arm and moved to Julienna's side to answer in that same confidential tone she'd used with me.

She never got the chance.

The sharp ring of the herald's staff echoed through the hall. "Your Royal Majesty, Your Royal Highness," the herald cried, "may I present His Majesty the Silent King of Els."

Conversation died in a heartbeat. A hundred necks craned to see the newcomers, breathless with anticipation. Old fears coiled inside me as the first forge-wight guards entered, armored but weaponless, trailing their heavy chain mail cloaks after them. Golden fires glowed behind their helms. More followed until six stood in front of the herald, their fiery bulk clearing a wide avenue through the courtiers. The shortest forge-wight was a full head taller than the tallest human present. After them came another two guards, these ones shorter and more human-shaped than their counterparts, though equally armored and helmeted. One bore the standard of Els; the other, a curiously curved staff of office.

"Where's the Silent King?" Neira whispered, rising to her toes again. "Can you see him?"

Julienna made a shushing motion as the forge-wights parted and a figure stepped out.

The Silent King was not what I expected. He was no taller than Neira, compactly built beneath his gilt armor and, to all observation, perfectly human. The foremost of his servants towered above him. Murmurs started across the reception hall, moving like

ripples over a still pond. Like his guards, the Elsian king wore a
helm instead of a crown, though his had all the ornateness those
of his guards lacked. It was made of some dark reddish metal and
shaped like a roaring sphinx, its open mouth forming the faceplate
and flowing down over his head and shoulders in a mane of interwoven plates of red and gold and silver. The sphinx's great fangs all
but obscured the sight of his face. Beneath the helm the king wore
a simple white robe crossed with the red and gold sashes of Els and
bound with a wide leather belt. In the hush that had fallen over the
hall I heard the faint clink of chain mail as he strode, with sure and
deliberate steps, toward the king. As he walked, he scanned the
staring faces around him with the casual gaze of one who not only
didn't mind the attention but had long expected it.

As his slow sweep turned toward our side of the room, he
stopped midstep. There was a moment of frantic reassembly
among his guards as they rearranged themselves, searching for
whatever sight had arrested their sovereign. He ignored them,
changing his course from the king to—

My heart began to pound. *Us.* He was heading straight for us.

The rippling whispers rose to a dull roar as courtiers around
us struggled to make sense of this new turn even as the clanking of
mail and the heavy steps of the forge-wights drew nearer. I glanced
at Julienna, who watched their approach with a steely, set expression. Neira's mouth hung open in a perfect circle. I looked behind
us. A handful of startled courtiers stared back, and beyond them,
the wall.

"Aliza?" Julienna whispered.

"It's all right," I said quietly, though it did not feel all right at
all. My mind raced. *What is this? What's your game?* Movement
from the edge of the crowd. Out of the corner of my eye I saw
Alastair push his way to the front, his expression as alarmed as

his sister's. The Silent King was very close now, and it was then I saw what the distance had obscured before. The helmet alone didn't conceal the king's face; a white veil hung beneath those steel teeth, leaving only the blank smoothness of silk where his eyes should have been. A shiver took hold of me somewhere deep in my gut.

Abruptly the king halted. The shock that had me in its grip loosened a little and my thick wits began to run clear again. *Remember where you are!* I curtsied, pulling Neira down with me. Her hand trembled on my arm, but it was not to her or to me whom the Silent King turned his attention.

Julienna paled a little as he took a step toward her, then stopped. Hesitantly, her eyes never leaving that faceless veil, she curtsied. "Your Majesty."

The Silent King tilted his head.

"The Silent King gifts to you the greeting of the desert, Daughter of the Fireborn," one of the forge-wights said from behind him.

"You are of the bloodline of Edan Daired, are you not?" another forge-wight said.

"I am," she said, glancing between the guard and the king and finally settling on the king. "Julienna Daired, sire."

There was a stirring among the rest of the guards. The Silent King moved closer. Julienna stood her ground as he raised his hand. He wore a spiked gauntlet of the same dark red metal as his helmet, hiding all trace of the flesh beneath. I held my breath as he reached out slowly, hesitantly, and touched Julienna's cheek.

"We are pleased to meet you," the first forge-wight said, in a voice so low only we could hear it.

Sharp and bright as a thunder crack, the sound of the herald's staff echoed again through the hall, oblivious to the strange scene it interrupted. "Your Majesty, Your Highness, dinner is served," the herald cried.

The announcement shattered the breathless silence and the dull roar of a hundred voices all speaking at once rose like a wave and broke over our unexpected tableau. The Silent King let his hand fall from Julienna's face and turned on his heel, his honor guard falling into place around him like a movable fortress of steel and flame as he resumed his original path toward King Harrold.

"Ah . . . yes, well, welcome, friends and honored guests," King Harrold said as the room's stunned silence resolved itself into a dull roar. "To dinner!"

Tall doors opened at the end of the hall, revealing a glimpse of a great table laden with crystal and silver. Delicious smells wafted from the banqueting room, but they served only to turn my stomach. I looked at Julienna. "Dearest, are you all right?"

She said nothing, staring after the Elsian retinue with an inscrutable expression, one hand resting lightly on her cheek.

CHAPTER 20

GAMES OF GODS AND MONSTERS

Alastair was at our side in a moment. "Julienna, what happened? Are you all right?"

"I'm fine," she said. "It didn't hurt."

"Did he say anything?" he asked. "I couldn't hear."

She told him what the forge-wight translators had said, though that only deepened our confusion. None of us had seen the Elsian king speak, nor noticed any other method of communication between him and his translators. "It felt strange, though," she said. "Like he recognized me, or thought he did. I can't explain it."

A movement from across the hall caught my eye. Lady Catriona was motioning for us to join her. "Were you able to warn King Harrold?" I asked Alastair as we made our way after the last of the courtiers.

"No, and neither was the High Cantor." He kept his voice low. "We didn't have the chance. Too many other ears."

Lady Catriona met us and looked down at Julienna with concern. "Are you all right, dear?"

"I'm fine, Aunt. Where's Edmund?"

"The daughter of the Southron ambassador asked him to accompany her to dinner," Lady Catriona said with a flicker of a smile. "Don't worry, I've already told him to be on his guard. I warned Queen Callina too, and Lord Camron. They'll relay our suspicions to the king at the first opportunity. But come, we're called."

She strode into the banqueting hall with head high. Alastair offered me his arm and Julienna his other. The last rays of the setting sun filtered through the narrow stained-glass windows, painting the hall in patches of crimson and violet and rich orange. Lamps suspended from silver chains hung from the vaulted ceilings, bathing the long table in a golden glow. Already most of the courtiers had found their seats, either shown to them by the hovering stewards or assigned according to some court hierarchy that remained inscrutable to me. King Harrold and the queen consort sat in great gilded chairs at the farthest end of the table, flanked by Lord Camron and a handful of high-ranking councilors, including the High Cantor.

Next to them on Queen Callina's side were the ambassadors and their retinues. The Silent King sat beside a pair of very nervous-looking Arlean courtiers whom he did not deign to look at. His honor guard, staff, and standard-bearer stood rigid and unmoving a few steps behind him, watching the banquet with quietly flaming eyes. I noticed the guests made an effort not to look at them. Even the palace guards who'd remained in the banqueting hall stayed farther away from them than deference demanded.

"My lord, my ladies," a servant said, appearing at my elbow. He gestured to the chairs at the opposite end of the table from the king. *The keystone seats*, I remembered, vaguely recalling some etiquette texts Mama had once tried to force me to read, but I didn't need to know the rulebook to guess at the subtle political games still at play. King Harrold was host to three nations tonight, and there must be no signs of favoritism. Family Daired was the closest he had to a neutral choice. I took my seat next to Alastair.

King Harrold stood and raised his hands. "Friends, honored guests, Your Excellencies, Your Royal Majesty! Once again, allow me to welcome you to Arle. Many of you have come a long way to join us for this historic convocation, and for that we thank you. May the blessing of the gods rest on those gathered here tonight, and tomorrow, may we bring about such harmony between our four nations as has never been seen before." He made a motion to the chief steward. "Now to feast! Tonight we—"

He stopped. The Silent King was rising from his place, gauntleted hands on the table, the veiled eyes beneath that fanged helmet fixed on King Harrold. "We crave your indulgence, Your Majesty," one of the Elsian honor guard said. "We should like to say something."

King Harrold blinked. "Er . . . well, yes, by all means."

The Silent King inclined his head.

"You are most gracious," another forge-wight said. "Now, we understand tomorrow is a sacred day in your kingdom. A festival commemorating the bravery of a famous saint."

"Indeed it is, Your Majesty."

"We also understand that on this day it is tradition to tell stories of your past, to remember what has been before you celebrate what is to come. Is this not so?"

"It is," King Harrold said, clearly puzzled. Whispers stirred from around the table as the Silent King pushed back his chair. Out of the corner of my eye I saw Alastair tighten his grip on his fish knife.

"By your gracious leave, Your Majesty, we should like to honor this tradition. We too have a story we would like to share in this honored company."

The king glanced at his wife, who offered an elegant shrug. "Well then, yes. Of course. We'd be delighted to hear your tale." He sat back down.

"Your Majesty is most kind," the Silent King said through his strange translator. He began a slow circuit of the table. "We would like to tell you of Els, for it is a place you Arleans have long wondered at. You have too, Garhadi and Southrons, neighbors though we may be. Our silence, you understand, has been long and zealously preserved. But you do not know why."

"And it is time you learned," a new voice said.

It was not a forge-wight that spoke, nor any of the honor guard. A gasp rose from the table slowly, like a wave breaking, as we realized who was speaking.

The Silent King's voice was soft, but it resonated through the hall, through the table, through my very bones: a high, childlike whisper, sharpened on silence until each syllable formed a razor's edge.

"How is it that your great tale begins?" he said. "Ah, yes. Many years ago, in the dark of the world, the gods shaped great creatures from those elements that were to each facet of the Godself most dear. Of that which you call Creator were born spirits of wind and air, fierce winged creatures that gloried in the storm. Of the Provider were born mountainous spirits and every creature that loved the greenly growing places of the earth. Born from the mind of the Protector were spirits of fire, awesome as they were terrible, and from the Fourth, the Unmaker, there flowed into the world turbulent spirits of water."

A few heads nodded around me. It was a version, albeit a

strange one, of the creation epic Henry Brandon had sung for years at Spring Quarters. Now, however, I recognized another story beneath it: Frega Mauntell's tale of the first beings to walk the world.

"These were the pure beings at the beginning of all things," the Silent King continued, "the great guards over all forms of lesser creation, loving only the facet of the Godself who brought them into being and the creatures who shared their elemental essence. For time beyond measure these Elementari lived in peace, shaping the world as the gods had desired."

I tore my gaze from the pacing figure to look at Alastair. He was watching the Silent King intently. Julienna exchanged a glance with her aunt, who looked equally grim.

"But their peace was not to last," the Silent King said, "for the lesser elemental creatures began to mingle their bloodlines and pollute their purity. The Elementari saw this and grew angry, not only with their adopted children but also with the gods who allowed—nay, *encouraged* such an intermingling."

The Silent King paused and his pacing slowed. The courtiers in front of him turned almost all the way around in their seats to keep him in view. Next to me, Julienna let out a long, tense breath. There was the faint clink from the servants' hallway, but even the chief steward seemed absorbed in the Silent King's tale.

"This was their great folly, for in rising against their Makers they were themselves unmade. The Godself in the form of the Unmaker descended into the world," the Silent King continued. "The lesser Elementari fled before her, abandoning the power they had once wielded and fading into the forgotten shadows of the world as broken and fragmented spirits."

I felt Alastair's hand on my arm. It was Rushless Wood and the *An-Eskatha* all over again. I squeezed his hand.

"The others hid and watched as the gods gathered together the remaining creatures, half-breed disgraces calling themselves the *Oldkind*—for already they had begun to forget the greater spirits who had come before them—and had them bear witness. Before these outrages the Godself then made a new kind of creature, one they hoped would end such conflict forever. From the sand *Ahla-Na Lehal'i* sculpted the first human beings, *Ket* filled them with water and blood, *Ah-Na-al Akhe'at* breathed life into them, and *An-Tyrekel* ignited inside them a fiery spirit, combining in a single creature all the strengths and weaknesses of each element. Thus was humankind born.

"From its hiding places the strongest Elementar looked on this new creation and hated it. In its rage and its folly, the Elementar burst forth, hoping to destroy humankind before it had a chance to spread as the Oldkind had, but it was once again stopped by the Unmaker, who bound the great spirit, once the gods' joy and delight, and cast it into a prison deep within the earth.

"While it remained trapped in its prison of stone, it knew not how the centuries were passing above, but as the ages passed, it writhed and struggled, shaking the earth from the highest gargoyle peaks to the deepest pits of the dark ocean. Though these struggles failed to free it, they were not wholly in vain, for cracks appeared in its prison, and the Elementar sent forth ten thousand arms through those cracks to taste the world above.

"There it found a good green land, full of Oldkind and humans alike, and it despised them. While in its prison it could not devour, it nevertheless began to suck the good land dry, and its inhabitants with it, until the land of Thell's prison was little more than a desert, drained of life by the monstrous spirit trapped beneath its sands.

"But not all things died. Others were drawn to the mouth of

Thell's prison: descendants of those lesser Elementari who thirsted for power, rebellious Oldkind and discontented humans, traitors and the betrayed and every lost creature seeking vengeance."

"Did they find it?" an overeager voice rose from one of the courtiers. The Silent King turned toward her, the bloodred fangs of his helmet-crown glinting with an ominous light. A hiss went up from among the Elsian honor guard.

"Oh yes, they found it. They found much." The Silent King resumed his pacing. He was now quite close to our end of the table. "And in them the imprisoned Elementar found willing servants to carry splinters of its own spirit out beyond the walls of its dungeon and the land it had destroyed. So it was that the dark and doubtful rumors of the desert land spread throughout the world of humans and Oldkind."

I wondered if the rest of the table could hear the thud of my heart as the Silent King passed behind us. I could almost taste the sunburnt sand at the back of my throat, almost see the cracks spreading in the desiccated earth and the darkness seeping out. *Willing servants to carry its splintered spirit into the world.* My hand trembled on the cut-crystal goblet in front of me. The imprisoned Elementar—the bound Fourth that the Mauntells so feared—the first ghost: it was all the same creature.

Alastair's eyes had not left the Silent King. Lady Catriona leaned forward in her chair, hands folded beneath her chin, tense as a harp string. Julienna toyed with her meat knife with the air of someone calculating its effectiveness against enemies larger than a haunch of beef. I glanced down the table. Most courtiers sat enrapt, though a number of faces showed varying degrees of puzzlement as well, King Harrold's and Queen Callina's among them. Edmund, sitting a few chairs down on the opposite side of the table, had the gravest look of the lot. But no one dared interrupt.

"Those rumors spread even to your kingdom," the Silent King continued, "a rich land, blessed by the gods with everything Thell's prison lacked. The Elementar had heard of it in whispers among its servants, even glimpsed it through their eyes, and it wanted to know more of it. When it was that six hundred years ago, an Arlean princess came to the shores of Els, it sensed its chance had come.

"The girl was young and zealous, loyal to her kingdom but weighed down by the overweening ambition of her father. When her ship reached Elsian shores, she did not find the thriving kingdom she was promised, but rather a wasteland, a barren and empty fortress, sustained only by the lies spun out by the servants of the imprisoned Elementar.

"It was there before the gates of the long-abandoned Citadel that her despairing companions turned on her, demanding they return to Arle. With her father's task undone, she refused, and in the heat of their argument they woke the Great Sphinx, sentinel of the waste and guardian of the entrance to Thell's prison.

"This, we believe, is where your Arlean tale catches up," the Silent King said in a drier tone than before. "After a long and dreadful battle, the princess's companions slew the Sphinx, yet not without consequence, for one of them—"

He stopped suddenly and clutched the back of the nearest chair. King Harrold half rose, along with Lord Camron and the Garhadi ambassador, but the Silent King recovered with a shake of his head and resumed his pacing. His voice was softer now, yet still resonant, as if the very air took on the shape of his words, beating it into our minds with every breath.

"One of them fell defending her. The other escaped with the princess and returned to Arle, but even then, they were not free from danger, for the stirring of the old Elementar had woken one of the creatures you call *Tekari*, and the ancient sea-serpent followed the princess's ship. There on the shores of her kingdom they fought, and betrayed and abandoned by her last living companion, she slew the Great *Tekari* alone."

Murmurs chased each other down each side of the table and more than a few heads turned toward us to see Lady Catriona's reaction to this indictment of Niaveth Daired. This was far from "The Lay of Saint Ellia" as we knew it. I thought of Mòrag's recitation at Martenmas. *Or was it?*

"The sea-serpent dead, your princess then returned to Els, for nothing remained for her in Arle, save false friends and the machinations of a king who would only use her to further his own ambitions. She found—"

There was a polite cough from one of the Arlean councilmembers. The Silent King stopped before his honor guard and sought out the source of the interruption, the fangs of his helm scything to and fro along the table until his gaze landed on the red-faced councilwoman. She half rose in an apologetic curtsy. "But surely you are mistaken, Your Majesty," she ventured. "The princess died on the shore that day, slain by the sea-serpent whom she slew."

The Silent King looked at the councilwoman. "Did she?"

The courtier colored, frowned, and sat again.

"A most intriguing tale, Your Majesty," King Harrold began, "and we are much indebted to you for it. Perhaps it would be best now to begin—"

"Only a little more remains, sire," the Silent King replied. "A very little more, we assure you. And you shall wish to hear it, for it concerns you."

Alastair pushed back his chair and stood. "How so?" he demanded.

The Silent King looked up. A dry, withering sound rolled over the table, like the windblown rasp of a shed snakeskin or laughter from a long-dead throat.

"Ah, the Blood of the Fireborn speaks at last! We wondered when you would step forth to the fray, or if you would shrink from it like your forebear. Your princess did indeed return to Els, Fireborn, for she had one last quest to fulfill. Before it died, the Great Sphinx had spoken of what it guarded, of the power hidden deep within the desert, and warned the princess from it. But now, in despair, with neither love nor loyalty left save for one already dead, the princess undertook the journey into the desert to find this power and use it, if she could, to avenge herself on those who betrayed her."

He paused. There was a sudden and terrible silence.

"Did she find it?" The same courtier who had spoken so boldly before sounded now like a frightened mouse.

The Silent King didn't answer. Instead, he reached up and took hold of the sphinx helmet by its long fangs.

"She found me," a new, split voice said, one that drove fear like iron spikes deep into my soul. The helmet fell to the table with a clatter of silver, the clink of shattered crystal, and the sound of a hundred gasps. Darkness roiled out from beneath the veil, splaying out from the Silent King in spindly shadows like a spider's legs. "Millennia spent in darkness: nameless, silent, hungry for the life the gods denied me—until she found me. *Freed* me, and died setting me free. But not in vain, for in her death she gave me new purpose and a new goal: forging a kingdom from that which was her birthright. No longer shall her legacy be a kingdom of lies and silence." Darkness billowed like wings behind the great ghast, and for an instant I saw sulfurous eyes burning deep beneath that bowed head, now crowned in shadow. "We are the Great Elementar, First of the Eldest and Vengeance of Saints, and we will be silent no longer." Those eyes flicked toward us and the split voice spoke again. "The time has come to settle accounts."

One of the shadow-limbs twitched. The Elsian standard-bearer stepped forward and pulled off his helmet, revealing Wydrick's face, grim and haunted. He drew a dagger from somewhere within his armor. A second limb twitched and Lord Camron rose, his eyes shining vicious yellow, glinting like the knife in his hand.

My scream came too late. The *ghastradi* plunged their daggers into the chests of King Harrold and Queen Callina.

CHAPTER 21

NIGHT FALLS

Time slowed like sour honey, hardening around the figures at the end of the table. Everything in me clung to disbelief, willing my eyes to admit their mistake, to confess this wasn't happening. It was the colors that first swam through the haze of shock: bright steel and cold yellow and the sudden, sputtering gush of red, and with it, the dreadful certainty of reality.

King Harrold slumped forward at once, but Queen Callina lived just long enough to utter a gurgling cry. The *ghastradi* of Lord Camron drew out his blade with a little grimace of disappointment and drove it in again, this time into her heart.

The small sound broke the spell of shock. Glass shattered, swept off the table by courtiers and councilors scrambling to get away from the writhing shadow-creature and its minions. The Elementar's split voice drifted lazily through their screams. "Rejoice for your fallen sovereigns, little ones, for their end was merciful. The heirs of the traitor shall pay more dearly." It signaled to its honor guard. Each one drew hidden weapons. "Bring to us all those belonging to the Blood of the Fireborn. We want them alive."

The guards began to advance.

"Back! Back, Julienna!" Lady Catriona cried. Alastair pulled me behind him, a dinner knife clutched in his other hand. I snatched up another from a fallen place setting as Edmund ran to join us, standing shoulder to shoulder with Alastair and his aunt. They made a grim wall between the Elsian guards and the last of the screaming courtiers shoving their way through the door behind us. The Elementar's forces crept forward, smoldering eyes fixed on us, advancing slowly but inexorably down the length of the table, pressing us back toward the far wall.

Darkness billowed around the Elementar like a cloak. On its shadowed head a crown appeared, black as a starless sky, and with one gauntleted hand it beckoned to us. "Come now, Daireds. Let justice be swift."

Edmund and Julienna growled Eth curses in unison.

Like a thousand talons on glass, a scratching, shrieking sound filled the hall. It caught in my chest and clawed at my mind, carrying with it the bitter shock of mirth. The Elementar was laughing.

"Come willingly or not; it makes no matter to us. But you *shall* come. All of you. House Daired shall not live to see the dawn." More shadow tendrils drifted from the dark mass on the creature's back, threading like umbilicals to its guards. Their eyes blazed yellow beneath their helmets when it touched them and they moved forward with renewed purpose. "Give yourselves up and we will show mercy to your city," the Elementar said. "Fight us, and yours will not be the only blood we shed this night."

Alastair spoke a few words to his family in Eth. Lady Catriona and Edmund looked at him. Julienna went very pale.

"What?" I whispered, but before he could answer a glorious sound met our ears: the tramp and shout of palace guards. They burst through the doors, pikes, spears, swords, and crossbows brandished, and the Silent King's forces halted. The foremost guard cried out as he saw the dead king and queen and the butchered bodies of their comrades scattered around them. His gaze landed on Lord Camron.

"Lord General! What—?"

"Enough!" the Elementar cried, and raised a hand as if it were flicking away a fly. Lord Camron and the other *ghastradi* straightened. "Kill the guards. Take the Daireds alive."

"Swords! Your swords!" Alastair cried. The Captain of the Guard drew his sword without taking his eyes from the approaching enemy and handed it to Alastair. A few others did the same, arming Lady Catriona, Edmund, and Julienna and drawing daggers in their place, but it was too late. It would not be a fight. It would not even be a struggle. I saw it in the set of Alastair's jaw, the despairing look in Edmund's eye, the sweat on Lady Catriona's forehead. The Elementar's forces were limited to what weapons they could secrete beneath their armor, but their armor was thick and concealed much. The nearest forge-wight withdrew twin blades from beneath his gauntlets, their edges glowing white-hot. There was a hiss, a scream, and the sudden smell of charred flesh as he plunged them into the belly of a charging guard. The others paled and drew back but did not retreat. They fell into a semicircle around us, preventing the forge-wights from cutting us off from the door.

"Run, my lords!" the Captain of the Guard said between clenched teeth. "My ladies, you must run. We'll hold them off."

Blistering heat and hundreds of years of hatred against flimsy slivers of metal? What chance do you have against this creature? What chance do any of us have?

"Alastair?"

"Do it." He looked at Julienna, then at me. "Both of you. Run and get help." One of the forge-wights dashed forward, his blade exploding in sparks as it met with the edge of the guards' shields. "Now!"

He seized Julienna's arm and pushed us toward the open door. I stumbled a little and stared at him, fighting for understanding, for any of this to make sense, but all I could see were the tears on his cheeks and the hopelessness in his eyes. The Elementar uttered a terrible cry and the forge-wights lunged for us. Another hiss and scream. The dead guard's sword clattered to the floor.

"*Run!*" Alastair cried.

We ran. Blinded by tears, choked by terror, numb with shock, we ran.

The Elementar's shriek of rage and frustration resonated in my bones, carried on preternatural breath from undead lungs. Metal crashed and a chorus of shouts filled the hall behind us as the forge-wights closed in on the guards, but we dared not look back.

Stairs and corridors and pillared colonnades flew by, streaked and salt-stained. Dimly I was aware of Julienna running at my side, her Rider's plait streaming out behind her, choking out muffled sobs between breaths.

I finally slid to a halt at the corner of a long, shadowed corridor. The dark shapes of statues lining the tapestried walls roused me from one terror to a newer, more immediate fear. We'd passed no one in our headlong flight, the courtiers no doubt long fled to warn the rest of the palace. There was a deathly hush in the air, but somewhere ahead torchlight flickered along the walls.

"Julienna! Julienna, stop!" I panted.

She halted and stared at me with wide, unseeing eyes. Her

hands clutched reflexively at her sides for her missing swords. "They're still in there. We left . . . we left them. Aliza, we left them! How could we leave them?"

I seized her by the shoulders. "We're *not* leaving them. You heard your brother—we're getting help. Julienna, listen to me! We need to get out of here. Do you know where we are?"

She looked around. "I . . . don't."

Muffled voices drifted down the corridor. I shoved all feeling behind a steel door, barred and strengthened by Alastair's last request: *get help.* "There are people down there," I whispered. "We need to know if they're friend or foe. We need— Julienna, are you listening?"

"I don't understand. Why does it hate us?"

"Julienna, I need you to focus! Our family's lives depend on it."

Her hand fell. Painful seconds peeled back the veil of shock as she looked up at me and slowly her expression hardened into that look I knew so well. She was Julienna no longer, but a Rider and a Daired, and I'd just shown her the battlefield.

"What do we do?"

"We find Akarra and the others," I said, "but first we have to get out of here. If those people with the torch are palace people, they may be able to help."

"And if they're not?"

"Be ready to run."

We edged down the tapestried hall. The carven eyes and grave faces of ancient kings and queens watched us from above. *Please, gods,* I prayed, *you may have abandoned the crown tonight, but don't leave us now.*

The voices from the other side of the gallery grew louder and clear enough to pick out the words. "Easy," a man's voice said. "Don't put your weight on it."

"Blast and damn, man, hold your tongue!" a woman hissed. "We don't have— *Ahhh!*"

We rounded the corner of the largest statue plinth and almost collided headlong with a pair of guards. The man supported the woman, whose foot was twisted at an odd angle. Pain lined her face, but it was washed clean in a sudden torrent of terror when she saw who we were.

"It's you!" she cried in a voice so high it was nearly a shriek, and pushed the man in the opposite direction. He too paled and fell away, the sword on his hip clanging against the edge of the statue. "Go! Go!" the woman cried again. She looked over her shoulder and made frantic shooing motions in our direction. "Get out of here!"

"We won't hurt you!" I said. "Please, we need to know how—"

"Go *back!*"

"We just—"

"You don't understand! You must go back! They'll kill us all to get to you!"

The flickering light moved closer. It was only then that I realized that neither of them held a torch. "Just tell us how to get out!" I cried.

"You know, Miss Aliza, I expected more of you."

Wydrick stepped out from behind the pillar, a torch in hand. His eyes glittered yellowish-green in the flickering light, his shadow falling twisted and misshapen behind him. The guards gasped in unison. Julienna swore.

"And of you, little dragon," he said to her. "There's no running from this. I've been telling you that for a long time."

There was a clang and I glanced sideways. My heart plummeted. The guards were already halfway down the corridor, hobbling away from us as fast as the woman's injury would allow.

"What, did you think they would *stay*?" Wydrick asked. "Did you think they would defend you, fight to the last to protect the Blood of the Fireborn?" He sneered. "Then you know nothing of the world. Learn as I did: loyalty lasts only so long, and everyone will betray you before the end."

I pushed Julienna behind me. Wydrick's voice had not split yet and there was more green in his eyes than yellow, but that didn't mean his ghast wasn't close to the surface. "That's a lie."

"You're a fool thrice over, Aliza Bentaine."

"That's not my name."

"Four times a fool, then! You never deserved his name, and you never will."

I straightened, and as I did, I caught the faint glimmer of torchlight on steel on the ground near Julienna's feet. Hope blossomed. Either intentionally or by accident, the guard had left us his sword.

"Maybe not," I said, "but neither do you."

He stopped advancing. The shadow dancing behind him took on a human shape again, and green swallowed the last trace of yellow in his eyes. There was a flicker of feeling, so strange and out of place against the hateful sneer of his usual expression. *Hurt.* The Daired name touched a chord.

"Aye, I know who your father is," I said. "And given that you're still alive, I'm guessing your master doesn't."

"*Don't,*" he growled.

Julienna shifted behind me, the tension in her arm telling me what I needed to do. I forced a smile to my lips and prayed this would work. "If Family Daired falls tonight, Tristan, it falls together," I said, and ducked.

The blade hummed above me, silenced by a fleshy *thud*. Wydrick staggered back, the sword buried up to its hilt in his chest. Julienna thrust again, driving him back against the pillar. "That's for Mar'esh, you *bastard*," she spat.

Wydrick sighed.

Quick as a viper he seized Julienna's wrist and twisted the sword from her grip, tossing her to the ground as if she was made of paper. With his free hand he drew the blade from his chest. Its edge dripped darkness. I rushed to pull Julienna to her feet, but he got there first. I swallowed the gasp at the sudden sting of cold metal as he pressed the point of the sword against my chest, right over my heart.

"You two play a dangerous game," he said—but still, it was he who spoke, not his ghast. The steel drifted up toward my collar, then hesitated. "Where is it?"

"Where is what?"

He let the tip of the sword fall and yanked me closer. I slapped him hard, my nails gouging deep furrows in his cheek. Shock flamed yellow, then green again as he released me. "The heart-stones, fool. Alastair did not have his. Where are they?"

"Far from *you*."

Wydrick chuckled and came close again, close enough that I could see the shadows seaming together the gashes on his cheek, so close that his cold lips brushed my ear. "If either of you wish to see Alastair again, bring my master the Daired heartstones," he whispered. "It is the only bargain you have left." He tossed the sword aside and shoved me away. "Go. Now!"

I felt his eyes and the dreadful weight of his words follow us as we turned and ran.

Julienna sobbed quietly at my side, her hand locked in a death grip around my arm. Corridor after corridor twisted on into the depths of the palace. There was a cry and flicker of torchlight as we passed one long hallway and we ran faster, skidding on slick marble. My legs burned. My lungs burned. My head was on fire. At the mouth of a darkened alcove, Julienna drew up short.

"Wait!" she panted through her tears. "Aliza, they'll be—they'll be guarding the main gate."

My mind raced to catch up with the rest of me. I looked around. The alcove opened to a pair of stairs, one leading up, one down. *Where else could we go?* "Kitchens! Where are the kitchens?"

"Lower floors," she said, and started for the downward stair.

The corridor at the bottom was plain, undressed stone, its floors worn smooth by thousands of shuffling servants' feet. Doors left ajar showed glimpses of storerooms and pantries. The corridor turned and we nearly collided with a cowering maid. She threw up her arms to shield her face. "No! Don't hurt me! Don't hurt me!" the girl squeaked.

"Shh! We won't hurt you," I said. "It's all right."

She peeked through her fingers, then relaxed. "Oh, thank the gods! Miladies, what's going on? I heard such yelling and then all them courtiers come pell-mell out of the hall and—"

"Can you show us how to get out of the palace?" I asked.

"Aye, but—"

"Quickly!"

"Right. This way."

She led us through another series of passages, which opened out into the sprawling complex of the palace kitchens. A handful of servants huddled around the fire, speaking in low tones and looking over their shoulders. One or two held butcher knives. They jumped when we entered, then sighed in relief. A few mouths fell open on seeing Julienna. "Lady Daired?" the eldest said. "What's going on?"

"The palace is taken," she said.

"*What?*"

"The Lord General betrayed us," I added. "The king and queen consort are dead. You need to get out, all of you. Find the Riders, the Rangers, whatever army regiments are in the city, and tell them what happened. Hurry!"

There was a moment of breathless silence before the kitchen erupted into chaos. Cooks and scullions seized whatever weapons they could lay their hands on and rushed en masse toward the back.

"Miladies?" Our guide plucked at our sleeves and pointed to a small door next to the hearth. "That there leads to the kitchen gardens. You've gotta do some climbing to get over the wall, but it'll get you to the back grounds of the Gray Abbey."

I seized the girl's hand in silent gratitude before following her directions out the hearth door. It was little and low and we had to bend almost double to get out. It deposited us into a little stone-roofed enclosure. Bundles of drying herbs brushed our heads as we ducked out into the garden and the cold night air. I drank it in like a woman dying of thirst, desperate to keep the sobs at bay, to not think of what we had left behind.

Moonlight fell brightly through a gap in the clouds, filling the garden with silver shadows. The lights of houses shone reddish on the undersides of the clouds, flickering with the steady heartbeat of a city that had yet to realize it had become a battlefield. Julienna pointed to the far wall. Just beyond rose the solemn edifice of the Abbey.

It took a mad scramble up one flimsy trellis and a few yards of climbing ivy to scale the wall between the two. Sharp twigs and the remains of an old wrought-iron grating tore my skirts and I bloodied my elbow on the edge of the stone, but we at last managed to swing ourselves astride the wall. My heart sank when I saw what waited on the other side. It was a long way to the ground, without even the excuse of a bush to break a fall.

"We'll have to jump. It won't— Julienna?" I looked at her, but her eyes were fixed, not on the ground, but on the city. With a grim expression she nodded to the west, and new horror filled my heart as I followed her gaze. It wasn't the lights of houses coloring the clouds red.

Edonarle was burning.

CHAPTER 22

SMOKE RISES

Hitting the ground hurt more than I expected, and for a minute I lay on the paving stones, fighting to get my breath back. There was a thump and a smattering of Eth curses as Julienna landed hard next to me.

"Are you all right?" I asked.

"Fine." She sat up and grimaced. "You?"

I levered up on one elbow and inspected my legs. Nothing broken, though my ankle throbbed terribly and one wrist ached where I'd caught the stone at a bad angle. "I'm all right." I rubbed my wrist and looked around. The Abbey garden was quiet, but the red light beyond the walls was growing brighter and the sounds of distant shouts rose and fell with the wind.

"Where do we go?" Julienna asked.

I struggled to my feet. Wydrick's words still lingered in my ears, poisonous with hope. Edonarle burned around us, the dragons were nowhere in sight, and traitors might lurk at every turn, but one slim advantage remained. Wydrick's master wanted our heartstones. *Badly enough to trade for them?*

"We need weapons," I said, "and armor. Both are back at the townhouse."

"Won't that be the next place they look?"

"Aye, so we'll have to be quick."

She nodded to the Abbey. "Fastest way is through there. We can cut through the Court of Four."

"Do you think you can call the dragons?"

She looked up as I helped her to her feet. No familiar shadows circled in the sky above, or anywhere nearby. "I can try."

"Try on the way. We need to keep moving and I don't want to give away our position."

The garden beyond the paving stones was well tended but thickly grown, with trees and shrubs fighting trellised vines in masses along the narrow pathways. My heart skipped more than one beat as we rounded a corner and alarming shadows loomed ahead of us, only to reveal themselves as statuary or the waving, leafless branches of a beech when the moonlight filtered through the clouds.

The door to the Abbey opened inward on silent hinges and we slipped inside. The back corridors were dark and quiet, but there was light ahead and we groped toward it like blind women. The darkness lessened, rolling back to the dim shadows of the nave pricked in the distance by the light of lanterns. Gray-and-white-robed cantors huddled around the base of the Fourfold statue.

"Who goes there?" Master Pennaret's booming voice rang out. He left the circle of cantors with a lantern in hand, lifting it high so the light fell on our faces. "Identify yourselves!"

"We're friends. Friends!" I said, shielding my eyes. "Julienna and Aliza Daired!"

"Dear gods," he muttered, and lowered the lantern. "Ladies, what's going on? What happened at the palace? Not half an hour ago a hundred courtiers came running from the Half-Moon Court as if their lives depended on it, saying something about assassins . . ." He trailed off as if hoping I would correct him. "Is that true? Is the High Cantor all right?"

"I don't know. I didn't see if he got out." Quickly I told them everything that had happened. There was a chorus of indrawn breath from the cantors as I described the true form of the thing that had been styling itself the Silent King.

"For six hundred years?" one of them said. "This creature has been plotting against Arle all this time? But *why?*"

"Because of Saint Ellia," Julienna said. "She freed it from its prison. Somehow it thinks it's repaying the favor."

"And it has people in the city," I added. "Vesh, lithosmiths, maybe some of the Rangers."

"Are all of them ghast-ridden?" another man asked.

"I don't know."

"Merciful Mikla shield us," Master Pennaret said, signing himself with the fourfold gesture. He turned to one of his acolytes. "Ring the bells. Those who don't know what's happening need to be warned." The acolyte took off running for the stairs to the bell tower. "People will be scared, confused. Some may be hurt. We'll offer them shelter here."

Another murmur from the cantors. "All of them? Sir, what if the ghast-ridden decide to slip in?" the first man asked.

"All of them," Pennaret said firmly. "Open the doors. Bring lanterns, blankets, and water, and send someone to the House of Beeches. We may need physicians close by." He touched my arm as the cantors scuttled away to their various tasks. "Lady Aliza, Lady Julienna, what will you do?"

The crash of the bells shook the Abbey, momentarily deafening us. The air throbbed with the uncoordinated cacophony for a full minute before lesser bells around the city began to pick up the warning peal.

"We're going to fight back."

THE AVENUE OF KINGS STRETCHED BEFORE US LIKE THE last ghastly mile before the gallows. I could see the gates to the Daired townhouse from the Court of Four, white and inviting in the moonlight. Julienna crouched at my side in the shadow of the wall. Her whistled summons had failed to draw the attention of the dragons, swallowed as it was by the shouts of a city wakened to war. Somewhere in the distance a direwolf howled. She gripped my arm.

"*Tekari!* In the city!"

I swore. We ran for the gates, keeping close to the buildings on one side. The townhouse was unlocked, and there was no sign of Teo or the other door warden. The door too hung a little ajar. "Careful," I mouthed as we slipped inside.

Lamps burned low in their sconces, casting the front hall into a dim twilight. At first glance it looked unchanged, but Julienna pointed to the floor. Smears of blood led from the bottom of the stairs toward the back of the house. "Caldero!" she cried, and followed the blood.

We found the steward lying across the threshold of the dining room, his eyes open and staring, his neck and chest scored by dozens of narrow claw marks. Blood pooled beneath him. Julienna covered her mouth. I pulled her away.

"Weapons! Get your swords," I said. "Now!"

She checked herself, starting for the stairs to the armory. My heart pounded in my ears as I ran for our chambers, dulling the sounds of commotion flooding in from nearby streets. The hall upstairs was dark and quiet, the doors closed as we left them. I eased the door to our room open, half expecting overturned tables, slashed and bloody curtains, and waiting *Tekari*, but it too looked untouched. I snatched Brysney's knife from its place on the dresser and knelt to get the oakstone box from the bottom of the wardrobe.

On the other side of the bed, a shadow flitted across the ground. Every hair on the back of my neck stood on end. I snatched the box and stuffed it in my pocket, wielding my knife with the other hand.

"Who's there?" I whispered.

There was a rustle and the sound of chirruping laughter.

"Show yourself!"

A hagsprite loped out from around the bed on all fours, grinning at me. Its long tongue quested out from between silver teeth. I lunged at it, but it avoided my knife with ease, scuttling backward on its grasshopper legs with a throaty chuckle. A second later it dashed out the door and out of sight.

I didn't sheath my knife. There was never just one. A sudden gust of wind sent the curtains blowing into the room, fluttering like ghostly moths in the moonlight and twisting around the racks of weapons near the window. Without turning my back to the door, I pushed aside the curtains and peered out. Nothing but bare balcony and empty courtyard and rising smoke beyond.

I let the curtains fall just as a monstrous pale shape filled the doorway.

The ghoul crouched beneath the lintel, the knotted rise of its shoulders just brushing the stonework. Its head, hunched low on its sinewy neck, quested to and fro, peering through the strands of white hair that streamed down cheeks hollowed and sunken with age. It drew in a long breath through slitted nostrils and shifted on its knuckles.

Fear rooted me to the spot. A ghoul that size could cross the room in a single bound, and I didn't need to see the claws hidden behind those knuckles to know it would take only one swipe to disembowel me. Shouting for Julienna would do neither of us any good; I'd be dead by the time she reached the top of the stairs, and she might already be fighting off enemies of her own. *Blast and damn!*

Sickly marshlight burned in its eyes as its gaze at last landed on me. Its mouth fell open in a ghoulish grin.

"Stay back," I said. "Stay back or I'll scream."

"So scream, pretty human. No one will come for you." It spoke in a child's voice, its Arlean high and shrill. It took one lumbering step forward. "I like it when they scream."

I brandished my knife. "Your last warning."

"Teeth!" It giggled. "Oh, this one has teeth! Better and better and better, mhmm. Teeth for the bleeding, the breaking! Steel teeth that will turn against their pretty mistress soon, yes, soon!"

I reached behind me and snatched up the first weapon that came to hand. My fingers closed around a spear.

The ghoul snarled and sprang. The impact drove me backward, tearing curtains free as it shoved me out onto the balcony. My back struck the stone balustrade and the spear splintered in my hands with a sound like a breaking bone. I felt cold claws and hot breath on my face and the weight of the creature pressing in on me from everywhere at once, and then the pressure gave way as the world turned upside down and I felt myself falling, pushed over the edge of the balustrade.

Ivy rushed past and I snatched at it blindly, desperately. Vines creaked and tore around me, but the largest of them held enough to slow my descent, and for one breathless instant I saw everything with perfect clarity. The ghoul's snarl melted away into a look of pure shock as it tipped over the edge of the balustrade, betrayed by its own eager bloodlust. Shock became panic, and it grabbed for the ivy to slow its fall, but it was too heavy. It struck the pavement of the courtyard below with a crunch I felt in every bone.

The ivy sagged. I buried my fingers in the dry foliage and clung to it for all I was worth. Vines snapped. I slipped, caught, and fell another few feet. The courtyard and the sprawled body of the ghoul loomed below, far, but perhaps not that far. I let go.

I hit the ground with a cry and rolled, coming to a stop next to the ghoul in a shower of shredded ivy. It took a moment to catch my breath and tally all the new aches I couldn't afford to acknowledge. *Still alive.* That was all that mattered. Cautiously I stood. Nothing was broken.

The ghoul stirred.

I backed away as it gripped the shattered remains of the spear lodged in its shoulder, breaking off the haft just above the spearhead. It rolled onto its knees, breathing heavily. Dark blood dribbled from its open mouth. "Pretty human . . . doesn't play . . . nice," it wheezed.

Wingbeats sounded overhead. I looked up, and the ghoul sprang.

Akarra's roar shook the courtyard, drowning out the ghoul's squeal and the fatal snap as her jaws closed around its head. A twist, a crunch, and the creature's body went limp. She tossed it aside as Herreki landed next to her.

"What's going on?" the Drakaina demanded. "Aliza, what

happened? There was fire and sudden chaos in the streets, and *Tekari*, and all the bells ringing an alarm and—" She inhaled sharply. "Where is Catriona?"

"And where is Alastair?" Akarra asked.

"They're still in the palace," Julienna said. I looked up to see her at the top of the stairs to the courtyard, her twin swords strapped to her back. She gasped at the sight of the ghoul's body. "Aliza, are you all right?"

I leaned on Akarra's offered wingtip, suddenly unsure of my legs. "Fine. Did you find Teo? Or any of the servants?"

She descended the stairs two at a time, and only when she was closer did I notice the tear tracks on her cheeks. "They're dead, Aliza. Dead or gone. The *Tekari* got to them first." She wiped her eyes with the heel of her hand. "Akarra, where's Mar'esh?"

"Protecting the Fourth Circle with the other Riders, but for Thell's sake, tell us what *happened*!"

"The Silent King controls the *ghastradi*. We were be—be—" Julienna covered her mouth and turned away, a strangled sob swallowing her words.

"We were betrayed," I said, and told the dragons what had happened in the palace. I hated how easily the story fell from my lips, how cold and callous the words tasted, but I spoke them anyway. If I allowed myself to feel their true weight, I would choke on them. Akarra shifted from foot to foot, her eyes never leaving mine. They burned first with incredulity, then shock, then, for one terrible instant, fear. When I spoke of Alastair's last words, she let out an agonized roar.

"You *left* him?"

"Akarra, we had no choice!" Julienna said. "There were too many and they were closing fast. We had to get help—"

Akarra's growl drowned her out. Flames boiling around her

open mouth as she turned toward the palace. "I'll burn it to the ground. I'll burn them all! *Ket* help me, if they touch him I'll tear them apart, the *shikya-vet*—"

Herreki brought her wingtip down hard on Akarra's snout.

"*Kes-ahla*, for shame!" the Drakaina said. "Your anger may be just, but your words are rash. If you wish to save your *khela*, you must use wisdom now, not force. Act the fool and you sentence Alastair to death."

Akarra whirled on her with a wail in Eth.

"I know what I am asking you to do, *kes-ahla*!" Herreki growled. "I know—" She stopped and drew in a deep breath. As she exhaled, she bent down to touch her snout to Akarra's and spoke in a soft voice, softer than I'd ever heard from the great Drakaina. "Tempest-Bringer, you forget my *khela* is in there too. I would not for heaven and earth see her harmed, but Catriona knows her duty, and I know mine." Her eyes flicked to mine, and for an instant we were Drakaina and *nakla* no longer, but comrades. "All shall be done to save Lord Alastair, I have no doubt of it." Her voice fell still further, just audible above the peal of distant bells, the rising crackle of flames, the howl of direwolves, and the human screams. "Remember, *kes-ahla. Tey iskaros*."

A thin cry escaped from Akarra, the desperate mewl of a frightened kitten, and it took everything within me not to fall down next to her, weeping. She drew her wings over her head and turned away.

The dull pain of the oakstone box digging into my side brought me back to the bitter task. "The Elementar—that thing that called itself the Silent King—it wants our heartstones," I said, forcing myself to speak calmly and ignore Akarra's cries. "Alastair's and mine."

"Why?" Herreki asked.

"I don't know. If it wants them badly enough, though, it may be willing to bargain."

"Do you have any assurance of this?"

"No, but we have to try."

The Drakaina considered it, considered me. "Agreed," she said at last. "You must not go alone." She lifted her head and looked, first to the palace, then to the rest of the city. The shouting beyond the wall had gotten louder. "The Riders are scattered throughout the city, and the fire in the barracks decimated the Free Regiments. Gathering allies will take time our *khelari* may not have."

"And we don't know how to get back in," Julienna said. "Herreki, Lord Camron still commands the king's soldiers throughout the city. They don't know he's a *ghastradi*," she added with a grimace. "They'll follow his orders. He's probably already called up reserves to guard the palace. We'll never make it inside unseen!"

She was right. The truth settled over my waning hope, crushing it like the several hundred tons of stone that now stood between the dragons and their Riders. The only windows I could remember seeing within the palace were no larger than a wyvern, barred with thick iron bars and surrounded by slabs of fortified marble. Nothing wide enough or weak enough for a dragon to burst through there, and we had no guarantee the Elementar's forces would remain in the banqueting hall. King Harrold and Queen Callina were dead and their courtiers and servants had fled; with Lord Camron in its thrall, the Elementar could roam the palace at will, choose any prison it liked. Any outright assault would fail, and there were too many guards to attempt an infiltration by stealth. I hung my head.

"So we draw them out," Akarra said quietly.

I looked up. Herreki turned to Akarra. "What do you mean, *kes-ahla?*" she asked.

"The palace will be well guarded, yes," Akarra said, her face still hidden beneath her wing, "but if this creature has so many soldiers at its disposal, then it will not hesitate to order them into the city."

"Why would it do that?" Herreki asked.

"It wants the Daireds, yes?"

I nodded. "Aye, but—"

"If it thinks you and Julienna are with us, Aliza, they'll go where we'll lead them," she lowered her wings, "and we'll lead them as far from the palace as we can."

Herreki frowned. "It's a terrible risk."

"I know." Akarra met my gaze. "But as Aliza said, we have to try."

It was a thin plan, too flimsy for real hope, but Julienna seized on it with a will. I saw the pieces coming together in the set of her shoulders and the hard gleam in her eyes. "You'll need Riders," she said, "or they'll know we're not with you."

"Lena var Dooren and Old Hammerhand are closest," Akarra said. "They're guarding the First Circle near the University."

Still Herreki wavered. "Aliza and Julienna cannot take the palace alone."

"My sister," I said, and Herreki looked at me. "Anjey and Brysney. They're defending the Westbreakwater near the villas. They'll come with us."

After a long and dreadful pause, the Drakaina at last nodded. "Very well. Akarra, meet Már'esh and me in the University Square after you've delivered them safely to the Brysneys. You will tell us of their plan, and we will draw the guards out. *An-Tyrekel* be the strength in your wings and the fire in your mouth, and *Ket* bring your enemies to the end they deserve. And you two"—she turned to me and Julienna, touching our shoulders lightly with one wingtip—"good luck. Now go. Quickly."

THE AIR WAS THICK WITH SMOKE WHEN WE LANDED IN A deserted street near Seven Saints Way. It was a broad street, weaving in and around the villas clustered along the shoreline west of the city. Manicured trees lined the street, and my imagination twisted their shadows into odd and sinister shapes as we dismounted Akarra and looked cautiously around. The whitewashed arches of the villas glowed silver in the moonlight. It was quieter in this part of the city. There was no sign of the Riders, Rangers, or City Watch.

"Shouldn't they be around here?" Julienna whispered.

"Look!" Akarra hissed. She pointed west, close to where Seven Saints Way met the edge of the Royal Park. A familiar red glow flickered between the houses and I swung up onto Akarra's back after Julienna. Akarra half ran, half flew toward the flames.

"Back! Back, if you value your head!"

Brysney's cry drifted up to us before the speaker came into view. He, Anjey, and Silverwing stood back to back in front of their burning villa with swords drawn, facing a semicircle of dark figures, most of them human-shaped, that were ranged along the edge of the street. One of them stood behind the rest, arms folded beneath a long robe, his helmeted head bent to watch the Brysneys' desperate attempts to dispel their attack. *Another Shadow Minister.* He gestured with one hand and three of the assailants moved toward my sister. Rage boiled up inside me.

"Akarra, *reqet!*"

The Shadow Minister didn't have time to scream. There was a

gasp, a crunch of steel, and a short, fiery blast, and the creature was no more. His minions shrieked and scattered, but not fast enough. Between Brysney's blade, Silverwing's teeth, and Akarra's dragon-fire, none made it more than a few houses away.

Anjey ran to Akarra's side as I slid shakily down. "Aliza! What's going on?"

"The war we feared," I said, and steadied Julienna as she dropped down next to me. "We couldn't stop it."

"We were expecting *Tekari*. Who were those people?"

"The Silent King's soldiers," Akarra said. She snarled at the smoking remains of the Shadow Minister. "That thing was one of its lieutenants."

Brysney touched its armor with the point of his sword. "A forge-wight?"

"Aye," I said, and wondered if I should feel glad or uneasy that none of these soldiers were ghast-ridden. "What happened here?"

Anjey turned to the villa, the light of the flames glinting off the tear-tracks on her cheeks. Her shoulders sagged. "I don't know. We were patrolling the northern end of the street when we heard the lantern shatter." She spat in the direction their attackers had tried to flee. "When we reached the house, they were here waiting for us."

"The Lord General must have caught wind of our plans," Julienna said grimly over Akarra's shoulder. "He's a *ghastradi*," she explained at Anjey's and Brysney's horrified looks. "The Elementar—the Silent King—wants to destroy Arle's defenders, and he'll use Camron to do it."

Brysney sheathed his sword and looked around. "Where's Alastair?"

There was the sound of breaking glass from farther down the street and Akarra growled. "We'll explain, but we cannot stay here."

Brysney cast one more pained look at the burning villa and placed his hand on his wyvern's neck. Silverwing hooted softly and rested his nose on his Rider's shoulder. Anjey took his other hand and looked to me. "Where can we go?" she asked.

I rubbed my forehead. The emotions I'd been shoving back since the Elementar revealed itself were creeping past all my guards, threatening to strangle me with tears. Furiously I pushed them back, pushed everything back except my anger, because right now anger was the only thing that could keep me going. I settled myself on Akarra's shoulders.

"Someplace they won't expect."

CHAPTER 23

TEY ISKAROS

The door flew open at my third knock.

"I'll fight you! Whoever you are, you've— Aliza? Anjey?" Uncle Gregory lowered his shovel and blinked at the small crowd gathered on his front step. "What's this?"

"We need your help, Uncle."

"Come in, quickly!"

Brysney helped Anjey in first, followed by Silverwing. I turned to Akarra. "We'll be safe here for a little while. Long enough to come up with a way into the palace. Go help Herreki and Mar'esh."

"Are you sure? I don't like leaving you."

"We'll be all right."

Her wings twitched uneasily. "I'll return in one hour." She looked up toward the First Circle and the darkened spires of the palace and I felt the sudden surge of heat boiling inside her, all fury and grief and desperation. "Find a way to bring him back to me, Aliza," she said softly. "Please."

"We will," I said. "Whatever it takes."

She leaned down until her head was level with mine. "The

Four watch over you," she pressed a dragon's kiss against my forehead, "my *khela.*"

Khela. Tears coursed down my cheeks as I watched her take to the sky. *Watch over them tonight,* I prayed as she disappeared into the smoky night. *Watch over us all.*

Between six humans and a full-grown wyvern, Uncle Gregory and Aunt Lissa's kitchen was more than a little crowded. After stowing his shovel, which he apologized for profusely, Uncle cleared the table and offered us what chairs they had. Aunt Lissa took one look at us, shook her head, and set about putting the kettle on and warming a pot of leftover stew in the embers of the hearth.

"Now then, what's this all about?" Uncle Gregory asked.

Julienna and I took turns telling them what had happened in the palace. When we finished, Anjey described the attack near the villas, her tale punctuated by the occasional growl or hoot from Silverwing. Uncle Gregory and Aunt Lissa listened without a word, their eyes wide.

"We heard such commotion coming from the docks," Aunt Lissa said when she was done. "We thought it might be members of the trade guilds protesting the treaty or students who'd started their Saint Ellia's Day celebrations too early. Then the fires started and we heard the wolves and . . . Janna preserve us, we didn't know what was going on."

"They won't stop." I pulled out the oakstone box and set it on the table. My aunt and uncle looked at it curiously. "Our heart-stones, Alastair's and mine," I explained. "The Elementar wants them."

There was a murmur of surprise from Aunt Lissa. "Heart-stones? What on earth could it want with those?"

"We don't know," I said, "but these might be our only leverage."

"You can't mean you two are going *back* there? And alone?" Aunt Lissa asked, looking from me to Julienna. "Aliza, love, if this creature is as formidable as you say it is, you'd need an army!"

"They won't be alone," Brysney said. "We're coming too. But, Aliza, there's something I still don't understand. The Elementar, or whatever you called it—*is* it the Silent King?"

"The Silent King is what it called itself in Els."

"Why?"

"Maybe so no one would wonder why we heard so little from it," Julienna said with a shrug.

"But that's ridiculous," Brysney said. "What about Elsian steel? Or their Garhadi brokers? They've been trading with Arle for decades."

"Have they?" I asked. "Are you sure? Or is that just what everyone's always said?"

He frowned and didn't answer.

"This thing has servants everywhere," I said. "Oldkind and human, or at least *ghastradi*. Any forge-wight could produce the steel they needed, and all they'd have to do is tell the merchants it came from Els. It's not as if anyone was about to travel to the Silent Kingdom to check."

Anjey set down her mug. "Then Els as we know it is a lie?"

"I think Els as we know it has been a long game," I said.

Brysney spun his dagger on the table, a deep furrow between his brows. "Let me make sure I have this right. This creature, this Elementar, is the thing Thell imprisoned beneath the desert? This ancient, elemental thing that you tell us witnessed the birth of humans and Oldkind, that made an enemy of the gods, that spawned all ghast-kind. This is the thing you want us to fight?"

There was a taut silence. The stew bubbled on the hearth. Bells tolled outside. The leaves of climbing vines trembled at the window behind Brysney, their silhouettes dark against the red-tinged sky. Julienna bowed her head, avoiding his eye.

"Yes," I said.

He smiled and pulled his chair closer to the table. "All right. So how do we get in?"

OVER BOWLS OF STEW AND BREAD, WE HELD OUR WAR council. "We need more Riders," Brysney said. "Three of us and a wyvern—thank you, Madam Greene, this really is delicious—three of us and a wyvern won't retake the palace."

Anjey gave him a sharp look. "*Four* of us, dearest."

He set down his spoon. "Anjey, you can't be serious. You're pregnant!"

"Yes, and our child will not have a coward for a mother."

"No one would ever think you a coward, my love, but I can't let you—"

"If you never intended me to fight, why bother training me as a Rider?" she said, and he deflated a little. "Besides, I have more reason than you. Alastair may be your friend, but he's my brother-in-law. You can't ask me not to fight for my family."

He pinched the bridge of his nose, his expression wavering between exasperation and pride. "Fine, but my point stands. Four of us and a wyvern won't retake the palace."

"Force won't retake the palace at all," Julienna said. "The guards who know what happened will have fled or been killed by now, and Lord Camron will keep the rest of the guard in the dark as long as he can. If we have any chance of getting to my family, it'll have to be by stealth. We'll need to sneak inside."

"And then what?" Brysney asked.

"We find where they're keeping Alastair and the others," I said.

"If we can get to them without being seen, we may have a chance to free them."

"If we *are* seen? What then? We can't kill *ghastradi*."

I tried not to let the despair of that thought show on my face, nodding instead to the box. "Then we bargain."

There was a long, thoughtful silence. "In all honesty, Aliza, that's a terrible plan," Brysney said at last.

"You don't think I know that?"

"Terrible is better than nothing," Julienna said.

"Any ideas how to get inside?" Brysney asked.

"The cellars," Anjey said. "They've got to have cellars, don't they?"

I thought of the great cavern beneath the Gray Abbey, of that massive faceted statue and the roiling pool at the feet of Thell. The Abbey and the palace were close enough to share a wall; surely they would share an undergallery too? There were bound to be passages, crawl spaces, tunnels, cellars, gods knew what other hidden places beneath an edifice with foundations almost a thousand years old. If we could find another way through the Abbey, perhaps we could get into the palace without alerting any of the Elementar's forces.

"They do indeed," Aunt Lissa said. "Quite large ones, if my memory serves me right." I turned to her hopefully, but she waved a hand. "No, dearest. I can't say I've been there personally, but I've known my share of servants who've worked at the palace through-out the years. They've mentioned it. There's an entrance from the kitchen garden on the west side, but the whole thing's gated."

My heart sank, then rose again at a sudden thought. *Unless . . .*

I shoved back my chair and ran to the window. The sash went up easily, sending a stiff breeze through the kitchen. Clouds hid the moon now, transforming Uncle's garden into masses of shadow. *If ever you had to eavesdrop, let it be tonight.*

"Tobble?"

There was a rustle from the ivy near my elbow. "Whatever Gregory says I did, I didn't!"

I swept up my friend and hugged him tightly. "I was afraid you'd gone."

He gave a little grunt of surprise but returned my embrace with a pat on the arm. I set him down on the sill and sat back so the others could see him. He waved cheerily to my uncle and aunt, only to freeze at the sight of Silverwing, who dipped his head in greeting. Tobble responded by sticking out his tongue.

"Really?" I whispered in Low Gnomic.

"You brought him, not me!" he said.

I put two fingers on his little shoulders and turned him to face me. His grin fell away when he saw my expression. "Tobble, listen. Silverwing is our friend, and right now we need all the friends we can get. Something terrible is happening and we need your help. How much have you heard?"

He looked guilty. "Well . . . most of it. Er, all of it."

"Good. Can the garden-folk get into the palace cellars?"

He brightened. "It's not for nothing that a group of hobgoblins is called an *inconvenience*, you know! We can get *anywhere*."

Brysney leapt up and strode over to the windowsill. "How far does the local Underburrow extend, Master Tobble?"

"Anywhere the city is," he said in Arlean. "Garden-folk here hardly had to do any of their own digging. You big-folk did most of it for us. We've got tunnels and cellars, sewers and passages all the way down to the sea!"

"We just need to get into the palace without being seen," I said.

"Can you spread word on the Underburrow? Tell them what's going on, what we need?"

"Of course!"

"How quickly?"

Tobble straightened and saluted. "Give me an hour and you'll have all the garden-folk of Edonarle on your side. You can count on me!" He leapt down from the sill and vanished.

Fresh peals from bells of the Tower of Nan drowned out the rustle of leaves. Aunt Lissa murmured something under her breath as Uncle Gregory and Brysney moved to the door and peered out, Brysney's hand on his sword hilt.

I felt a cool touch on my hand and nearly yelped before I saw Tobble again, leaning on the edge of the window with a concerned expression, so very different from his usual mischievousness. "Aliza," he said softly, "is your dragonrider really in danger?"

The tears came burning to my eyes, but I willed them away. "Aye."

"Don't worry. We'll bring him back to you."

With that he was gone.

"What is it?" Anjey asked the men at the door.

"Hard to tell," Brysney said. "There's a glow over the First Circle. Looks brighter than before, but—"

"Oh *gods*," Uncle Gregory breathed. "The House of Beeches. They've set it on fire!"

Anjey drew in a sharp breath and Julienna swore. Edonarle's houses of healing, dedicated to Janna, now blazed with the Elementar's borrowed wrath. Uncle Gregory signed himself and touched the beech-leaf sigil hanging over the lintel before closing the door.

Silverwing hooted softly and spoke, for the first time since I'd met him, in Arlean. "Our time is shorter than we feared. Rest and arm yourselves, my friends, and gather your strength. I will find Herreki and the others and tell them what you intend."

Brysney touched his forehead to his wyvern's snout. "Thank you, my friend."

"*Glad hearts and good hunting*, Cedric, and gods go with you." Silverwing murmured the standard of Family Brysney and made his way to the door, which Uncle Gregory opened for him with a passable Vernish farewell.

Brysney rubbed his forehead as he watched Silverwing disappear into the smoky night.

"They'll be all right," Julienna said and gently pulled the door shut. "Now, what weapons do we have?"

Anjey and Brysney unslung their sword-belts and laid them on the table, followed by a dagger each from sheaths strapped to their calves. At the sight Uncle Gregory gave a little exclamation and hurried out of the kitchen, returning a minute later with a dusty crossbow and a quiver full of iron-tipped quarrels. "Never had to use it, and thankful for that," he said, laying it carefully on the table. "But I thought it'd be wise to have on hand."

We all murmured our thanks. I eyed the offerings, ranging the odds in my head. *Two full Riders, one Rider-in-training, one wyvern, an inconvenience of hobgoblins, and a nakla who can't stand the sight of blood, armed with two longswords, three short swords, two daggers, and a crossbow. Us against all the forces of an ancient, elemental evil, hungry for the lifeblood of its enemies, teeth sharpened on six hundred years' hate.*

I studied the faces around the table. Brysney, grim but not despairing. This was not the first battle he'd faced where victory was slim. *But this* slim? Anjey, chewing her lip as she considered the weapons before her, clearly torn between her sword and the crossbow. She ran one finger over the sleek walnut stock with a smile. If there was fear behind that smile, she hid it well. Julienna shared all of Brysney's grimness, but there was none of his hope. Her face was lined in a way that belied her sixteen years, and her movements as she tested the weight of her twin swords, while smooth and practiced, were heavy.

Aunt Lissa must have noticed it too. "Master Brysney, your wyvern was right," she said. "You've only a little time before Tobble returns, and you need to rest while you can. Our home is yours. Gregory, fetch the extra quilts from the closet, will you?" She took Julienna's arm in a very motherly fashion. "Come, dear. And Anjey, you too. There's a couch through here."

Either from exhaustion or because she had no power left to resist, Julienna set the sword down and went with her. After squeezing my hand, Anjey followed, and Brysney after her. The curtains fluttered out over the empty table. It was darker outside; the clouds had thickened and the breeze off the water was stiff and cold, promising rain before the night's end. I leaned forward and shut the window, but the chill of the wind lingered on my lips. I stuffed the oakstone box into my pocket, ducked into the pantry, and slipped out through the garden door.

Dead leaves rustled underfoot and bare branches scratched at the sky, now flickering red and orange over the highest point of the city. I willed myself not to look up, to search the silhouettes of towers for some sign that Alastair and the others had retaken the palace and that we would be going, not as rescuers, but as reinforcements. I did anyway. Black against the Tower of Torches, a winged shape circled, tearing at the stone with ineffectual claws each time she rounded the tower. Akarra was too far away for me to hear the anguish in her roar, but I didn't need to. I felt it in my bones. I turned away.

The sound of trickling water seeped through the cloud of despair and I looked down. A tiny rivulet ran through Uncle's garden, edged in damp moss thick as a carpet. The water burbled in its artificial stream bed around the roots of rhododendrons and curly ferns. I had been following it without thinking toward the stone bench on the far end of the garden, half hidden behind a mass of manicured whitethorn.

Khera . . . khera . . .

The smoky sweet scent of dragonfire lingered on the edge of my imagination, close as a breath but somehow just out of reach. I trembled as images I'd forced from my mind came suddenly crowding thick and fast. Alastair standing beside the cantor on our wedding day, smiling, handsome, nervous as a schoolboy. The shape of his scars and the stories that came with them. The warmth of his hand on mine. The taste of his lips. His dimpled smile. *Khera.* I drew in a shuddering breath.

Then the Elementar was there between us, laughing at him, at his family, at me. That *thing*, that roiling mass of shadow with um-bilicals spread throughout the kingdom like some bloated spider, spewing forth hatred, death, and vengeance. It had spooled out its webs for many centuries, and now it only had to wait a little longer. A creature that had lingered so long in darkness for a fool like Ellia to come free it would have patience to spare.

Did you know what it was you released, Princess-past? Did you know what it would cost?

The stone was cold against my legs as I sat on the bench. I pulled the box from my pocket and set it on my lap, picking at the lock in the dim light. It would not budge, and it took me a sec-ond to remember where I'd last seen the key, hanging on a chain around Alastair's neck.

I threw the box against the garden wall with all my might. It cracked like an eggshell, spilling our heartstones onto the damp grass. I scooped them up and sat again. Their facets gleamed dully in the reflected light of the flame-stained sky. Green and red in the daylight, they now looked black as ink against my palm. *Is this enough to save them?*

I closed my hand around our heartstones, buried my head in my arms, and wept.

Bells tolled. The wind stirred the leaves. Distant fires roared and crackled. A few drops of rain pattered across the garden.

"Aliza?"

I looked up. Aunt Lissa stood by the whitethorn with a lamp. She said nothing, simply sat next to me and stroked my hair. For a long time we stayed this way, silent, miserable, buried under all the weight of what had happened and fear of what was still to come.

"I don't know what waits for us out there tonight, my dear," she said at last. "I wish I did. I wish more than anything I could ease your mind and tell you that all will be well, but this is no time for lies. If what you tell us is right, this enemy may be too strong for any of us."

I raised my head as fresh tears coursed down my cheek. She wiped them away.

"But I can tell you this. When the bards sing about this night, your name will be on their lips. Yours and Anjey's and Brysney's and Tobble's. Arle will never forget you."

"And what if we fail? There might . . ." I turned away. "Aunt Lissa, there might not *be* an Arle to remember."

"There will always be some who remember."

"I don't think I can do this."

"And I *know* you can. You have a reckless heart, my darling." Gently she touched my chin. Our gazes met, and she smiled. "You never learned to love by halves."

The soft sound of overturning earth stopped my reply. Aunt Lissa held up the lantern to see the sharp point of a gnome's head

parting the damp grass near the stream bed. A twiggy beard followed, then stick-thin arms in a mud-colored uniform. He popped
free from the ground with a smart salute. "Ladies!" he piped. "Begging your pardon. One moment."

He turned back to the hole, which was rapidly being widened
by hands below. I stared, first in surprise, then in incredulity, then
delight, at the steady stream of garden-folk emerging from the
earth. Gnomes and hobgoblins and even a few half-goblins, their
squat stony heads rising a handbreadth or more above their smaller
cousins. Some carried spades or pickaxes, others pikes and sharpened sticks. Most of the half-goblins had stocky bows slung over
their shoulders. They grinned when they saw us and made some
variation on the first gnome's salute. Still they kept coming: tens,
dozens, *scores* of them, until Aunt Lissa and I shared the bench with
three hobgoblins, two gnomes, and a half-goblin that held the leash
of something that looked like a toothy newt and eyed me in a very
Pan-like fashion.

A laugh bubbled up from somewhere deep inside me. I'd not
expected hope to look like this.

Tobble was the last to climb out of the hole. He took a running
leap and landed straight on my lap. "May I present the Underburrow
of Edonarle!" The garden-folk raised their weapons and cheered,
and tears filled my eyes once more. Tobble laid a cool hand on my
arm and smiled. "We'll fight for your dragonrider, Aliza."

I picked him up and kissed him. There were hoots and snickers
from the rest of the garden-folk, and even Aunt Lissa chuckled.

"Tobble, you are *wonderful*," I whispered in Arlean. Louder, in
Low Gnomic, I addressed the little crowd. "He's told you what's
happening, aye?"

Nods and murmurs of assent.

"This creature we're facing has allies all over the city. It's already killed the king and queen, and it won't stop until Arle is destroyed." I wrestled with my next words. A lie might rally them better, might be the wiser thing, but I would not lie to them. "I don't know if we can stop it. I don't know if anyone can. You're already the bravest and best of the garden-folk for coming this far, and I won't ask any more of you. Go, if you wish," I said, and held my breath.

Not a single creature moved.

Tobble sighed and rolled his eyes. "I told you once at North Fields, Aliza, and it's just as true now. This is our home too. We may be little and our help might not count for much, but we won't stand aside and watch it burn."

My heart swelled. "Thank you. All of you, *thank you*."

"What's your plan, Lady Daired?" the half-goblin with the attack newt asked.

I placed Tobble on my shoulder and stood. The tears had dried and the fear had shrunk to an academic thing, real but no longer important. *Tey iskaros.*

"We're going to take back the palace."

CHAPTER 24

THE SIEGE OF THE SMALL

The sound of breakers filled the narrow alley on the out-skirts of the Wharf District. The walls on either side blocked the sight of the water but not the wind, and I huddled between Anjey and Julienna in the shallow depression of a boarded-up doorway. Brysney paced the mouth of the alley and glared into the night.

"Will you tell him to stop that?" Tobble whispered in my ear. "If Chief Grimmelgund says they'll be here, they'll be here."

"It's habit," Anjey said. "He's used to being careful."

Tobble sighed and sat on my shoulder. "He's making me edgy," he muttered in Low Gnomic.

I gave him a sideways glance. *You should be,* I wanted to say, but thought better of it. He'd stayed quiet and stealthy enough on our tense journey from my aunt and uncle's house to this forgotten corner of the Westbreakwater, where the chief of the garden-folk, a stout hobgoblin armed to his suitably steel-pointed teeth, had assured us the rest of his people would be waiting. We'd expected an ambush around every corner, but the bulk of the fighting had moved into the Upper Circles, where smoke continued to billow from the House of Beeches. A few times I thought I'd caught another glimpse of a dragon's silhouette against the dark red sky, but each time the smoke would swallow them before I saw who it was. The people who remained in the Low Quarter cowered behind locked doors and drawn curtains, and besides the occasional stray cat and clump of windblown litter, we met no one. Retaking the palace would not be so easy.

I felt the bundle tied securely at my waist and mentally sorted its contents. The Riders had their weapons and I had mine: bandages, salves, poultices, soothing oil, all the tools of a healer's craft, the glass vials carefully wrapped in cotton and tucked in their individual pockets. I only prayed I wouldn't need any of them. The heartstones I'd secured in a leather pouch in my innermost pocket.

"How many more of his people are we expecting?" Julienna asked. She adjusted the weight of the crossbow across her back and surveyed the row of garden-folk ranged along the top of the opposite wall. Nearly fifty at my last count, all of them bristling with miniature weapons.

"Some folk from the Stone Hill District had to dig fresh tunnels to get out. Part of the Underburrow was crushed." Tobble's voice fell. "Big-folk were running panicked, they said. Trampling everything. Those not running were setting fire to anything that would burn."

"I'm sorry," Julienna said.

A motion from the unguarded end of the alley drew my eye. The garden-folk farthest from Brysney shuffled restlessly, and in the diluted moonlight I saw one or two of them pointing at something in the darkness behind them. I stiffened when I saw what it was. "Look out!" I said hoarsely, and nodded to the hooded figure running toward us.

Julienna leapt out into the alley. There was the hiss of a blade leaving its sheath and the dark figure skidded to a halt, her sword poised an inch from its neck. "Identify yourself!"

"Friend! I'm a friend!" a familiar voice said. He held up his hands. "Lady Julienna, Lady Aliza, I've come to help!" The figure threw back his hood with a vigorous nod.

"Master *Teo?*"

"Aye, milady. Here and ready to fight."

It was all I could do not to throw my arms around the young man. "I thought you . . . but how did you escape from the town-house?" I asked.

His throat moved up and down. "Father and Master Caldero told me to get the maids out when we saw the first *Tekari* coming. They—held them off while we ran."

He didn't ask whether his father had made it out. I saw in his face that he knew the answer.

"How did you find us?" Julienna asked.

"Master Brysney's wyvern," Teo said. "I spotted him flying over the Second Circle. Me and a few of the chambermaids were hunkered down in the shops near the townhouse when I saw him going toward the Park, and I said—well, I followed him. Caught up with him at the edge of the Park, him and the garden-folk. He told us what's happening."

"Were the dragons with him?" Brysney asked.

"No, but he said he found them, told them your plan," Teo said. "He's gone off now to round up more allies: Riders, Rangers, soldiers, the like. Told me to get to you and tell you that. Are you really going back to the palace, Lady Aliza?" he said as Julienna sheathed her swords.

"We're going to try," I said.

"I want to help."

Julienna looked over him with a critical eye. "Do you have any weapons?"

Teo reached beneath his cloak and drew out a pair of short knives. With a flick of his wrists the blades sliced through the air and buried themselves in the door across the alley. They'd hardly made a sound. He managed a sad smile at her surprise. "I'm better with a spear, but that was too big to carry."

He drew back his cloak to show a number of knives of various sizes and another short sword strapped to his thigh. Julienna sniffed and turned away as Anjey plucked the knives from the door and handed them back to him. "I think these better stay with you, Master Teo."

"They're here! They're coming!" a high voice said from the mouth of the alley.

More than one hand went to a sword or dagger hilt, then relaxed when we saw the little gnome jumping and pointing excitedly to a gap in the wall. A chipped and broken stone gryphon head poured rainwater onto the street where he pointed, or it would have. It was moving now, its head twisting in little jerks as if being hammered at from behind, until at last with a crack the whole thing came free and the final inconvenience dropped out.

Chief Grimmelgund jumped down from the lintel where he was perched. "Where are the rest?" he demanded of the first hobgoblin.

"We're all that made it, sir," she said, and shuddered. "There are direwolves in the Royal Park! Dunno how they got into the city," the hobgoblin said. "There weren't many, but they were fast. They got Nibble first, and they scooped up old Quibble, and then . . . then . . ." Her chin trembled as she trailed off.

"There, there." Grimmelgund clapped her gruffly on the shoulder. "Earth to earth, little one, and *Hgenna* hold them close."

She sniffed and nodded before her companions led her to the main body of garden-folk.

"You heard her!" the chief said louder in Low Gnomic. "We fight tonight for our friends!"

A cheer went up, instantly smothered as they remembered themselves, replaced by a wave of whispered agreement. Brysney scanned the adjoining street one more time before crouching down to look Grimmelgund in the eye. "Chief, you say your people know a way into the palace. How far is it from here?"

Grimmelgund pointed with the lead-weighted staff in his hand. "Just over the harbor wall. There's a tunnel that empties out onto the break-rocks. It leads into the old sewers that run through the heart of the city. The big-folk don't use those pipes anymore, but my people have seen to it that they stay open."

"And it'll take us under the palace?" I asked.

"As close as you could ask."

Julienna crouched next to Brysney. "Will you show us the way?"

"Show you, my lady?" Grimmelgund bowed. "I'll lead you there myself."

A BOULDER SHIELDED THE TUNNEL FROM THE SEA SPRAY, but the stones were still slick with algae and waterweed. I bent and looked into the mouth of the tunnel, yawning black and ominous before us. The moon fought with the clouds for supremacy of the night, leaving us with a little milky light, just enough to see that this looked like a very bad idea.

"You'll have to crouch at first. It widens in a bit. Stay close to me and keep together," Grimmelgund said before he disappeared into the mouth of the tunnel.

"You're sure this is the only way?" I whispered to Tobble in Low Gnomic.

He nodded and moved around to a more secure position on my back, arms wrapped loosely around my neck. "I ran some of these tunnels while Gregory was working. There's nowhere they don't go."

Somewhere beyond the dark, beyond the death and fire that had taken the city, my husband was waiting for me. I bent double and followed Grimmelgund into the tunnel.

"Oh, *blast*," Anjey murmured behind me. "Come on, love."

Brysney groaned something in Vernish but went after her, followed by Julienna and Teo. In moments I could no longer see them or Grimmelgund or even my own hands. The tunnel sloped gently upward underfoot. The roof scraped my forehead and forced me lower until I was nearly crawling. The pattering footsteps in front of me fell suddenly silent.

"Ho there!" Grimmelgund called out. "Half-goblins, the lights!"

There was a scramble and the sound of splashing from the back of the column before a faint orange glow started up the walls. It grew brighter as the splashing grew louder until the dark shapes of four or five half-goblins stopped in front of us, their leashed newt-creatures wallowing happily in the trickle of water running along the bottom of the tunnel. The orange glow came from the creatures.

"One salamander every few yards along the column," Grimmelgund said, and the half-goblin handlers fanned out to take up their assigned positions. "Good. This way!"

The light made crawling a little easier, but not much. My skirts were torn beyond recognition, the knees of my trousers were soaked and reeking, my palms slimy and my knees sore, and there were things laying in the pools we passed that I'd just as well rather not see. I'd long since given up trying to classify the smell. For a long while there was nothing but the wet chill of stone and cramp and a quiet chorus of panting echoing through the tunnel as we climbed steadily upward in the dim orange light. I caught a few snatches of murmured conversation in Low Gnomic. They were naming their fallen comrades.

Gradually the slope of the tunnel grew steeper and I was able to straighten, not entirely, but enough to move forward in a stooped shuffle instead of a crawl. There were no pools now, just the occasional ooze of what I hoped was water through algae-slicked seams in the stone. The drip-drip layered an arrhythmic heartbeat to the other sounds of our little army, and distracted with listening for any sounds of pursuit, I slipped and went down hard on one knee. A strong hand reached out from my left and gripped my elbow.

"Careful, my lady," Teo said as he helped me up. "I don't think this place was intended for humans."

"I don't think it was intended for *anybody*," I muttered as Grimmelgund at last signaled for us to halt. He pointed just above our heads.

"There."

Teo and I joined the others and peered up at the dark shape in the wall. "Another tunnel?" Julienna asked wearily.

"Aye, and this is the tricky bit," Grimmelgund said. With a running leap he sprang from the upward curve of the adjoining wall, caught the lip of the second passage, and pulled himself up. "The big-folk didn't dig these tunnels. You'll have to keep low. Hurry! We've still a long way to go."

"Let me," Brysney said, and followed the chief. With his height he had no need of a running start, but it was a tight fit. A muffled curse came from within as he squeezed his shoulders through the gap.

"Are you all right?" Anjey asked.

"Yes, but I can't turn around," he said. "Anjey, you next. Carefully."

Julienna and I helped Anjey after him; then Teo and I gave Julienna a boost. "I'll bring up the rear, my lady," Teo said, and offered me his knee as one of the salamanders slithered up the wall behind Julienna, tugging its handler after it. By its light I caught the grim grin on Teo's face. "I'm still your guardsman, after all."

I laid a grateful hand on his shoulder and climbed up. The gap was uneven, clearly dug by creatures much less than human-sized and only vaguely aware of the right proportions. Tobble had to jump down and climb up after me. Brysney was right; once inside, there was no turning back. Even flat on my belly, I felt my head scrape the roof of loose stone. Hand over hand I crawled toward the salamander light in front of me, trying not to think of the thousands of tons of city pressing only inches above my head. The suffocating horror of it tightened invisible hands around my lungs and chest. *Breathe. Don't panic. Breathe.*

There was a whimper ahead of me and the salamander light stopped moving. "My lady?" one of the half-goblins asked.

"I can't. I can't. Oh gods, I can't!" Julienna sobbed.

"You're almost through."

A measure of calm returned, knowing I was not the only one to feel the crushing weight of it all. I extended my hand as far as it would go and touched Julienna's heel. She yelped. "It's me, it's all right," I said. "Julienna, you can do it."

"I don't like . . . small spaces," she moaned.

"Come on, dearest. We're nearly through."

She sniffled and didn't move.

"Julienna, for our family," I said.

The sniffling wavered and stopped. I felt her move again.

A tumbling, earthy sound came from ahead and for one ter-

rible instant I feared the tunnel was collapsing, but before panic
had a chance to paralyze me, I found myself sliding face downward
on a pile of loose scree. I landed hard in a few inches of water. The
salty, metallic taste of blood filled my mouth and I spat, grimacing
at the tooth-marks I could feel on the inside of my cheek.

"Are you all right, Aliza?" Anjey asked.

"Aye, I think so."

She helped me to my feet just in time, as Teo came sliding out
from the mouth of the tunnel and landed where I had, swearing in
Garhadi. Together Anjey and I hauled him upright. Frantically he
checked to make sure he'd not lost any of his knives.

"All there?" I asked him.

"Aye. What *is* this place?"

I looked around. Julienna crouched a little way ahead of us
with her head between her knees, gasping in relief. Brysney squat-
ted next to her with one hand on her back, murmuring comfort in
Eth. Around them clustered the garden-folk, all in various stages
of mud removal, and I heard a number of creative epithets in Low
Gnomic for the original tunnel diggers. A smile, unlooked for but
not unwelcome, touched my lips.

My gaze wandered upward. We stood at the bottom of a cavern, not large, but I blessed every inch the rough-hewn roof rose
above our heads. The salamanders' combined light just carried
to the edges of the space, where the remains of a brick foundation could be seen rising past the ceilings. "The city-between,"
Grimmelgund said. "Quickly now. It's not much farther to the
undergallery."

He struck out upward and a little to the right. The ground
underfoot was uneven, a mixture of broken paving stones and
building rubble that had fallen through the cracks as the palace
and Abbey complex rose above it. In places it sloped upward so

sharply that we had to climb again. Mercifully, the sewer smell had lessened.

A strange feeling descended gradually, though it was the light I noticed first. The salamanders' glow grew brighter with each step, pulsing not only orange but also white and gold and fiery blue. The shadows they cast danced along the walls with edges so sharp it looked as though they might cut. The feeling came soon afterward: a heavy, oppressive sense of *presence*, not evil, but perhaps just as frightening.

"Chief Grimmelgund, are we beneath the Gray Abbey?" I asked.

"We are." His voice drifted back from the front of the column. "You feel it, then?"

"Aye."

Julienna caught my arm. "What *is* it? It feels like—like—something's *there*." She gestured vaguely to the roof to our right.

There is *something there*, I thought with a start. *Or maybe better said, someones.* "It's called Hallowhall," I whispered. "Below the Abbey. It's . . . a holy place, I think."

"We do not tunnel there," the nearest half-goblin said gravely.

There was a muffled shout from the front. Julienna pinched my arm in alarm, but it was only Grimmelgund. "Aha!" he cried. "Here we are. You, Rider. Help me with the stone."

Brysney went forward. The cavern roof dropped sharply, or else we had climbed higher than I thought, for he had to stoop. I couldn't see exactly what he did, but at Grimmelgund's direction there was a grunt, a grinding of stone against stone, and a sudden rush of cool air.

"Oh, *teh-nes an Nymasi*," Julienna breathed.

The last climb was easier than the first. A sloping path of scree led to the opening, which was more of a trapdoor than a tunnel.

Brysney caught my hand and pulled me up before turning to help Julienna and Teo. Anjey wiped the mud and dust from her trousers and moved to my side as we waited for the others. "We're in the palace now, aren't we?" she whispered.

I nodded. Family Daired had a mausoleum beneath their ancient fortress; so too did the royal line of Arle. We stood in a long, vaulted gallery. Pillars of white stone marched proudly along the walls until the darkness and distance of the hall swallowed them. Between the pillars, great solemn statues rose from marble plinths, their hands outstretched. Each statue held something. I had to look closer to make it out. *Urns.*

There was a tug on my skirts and a cool touch on my neck as Tobble swung up onto my shoulder. "The Chamber of Ashes," he said. "That's what the others said, at least. All the old dead kings and queens of Arle."

"I've never heard of this place before," Brysney said.

Grimmelgund gave his hand to the last hobgoblin struggling over the lip of the broken flagstone. "Few humans have, and even fewer *should* have. My people only stumbled on it by accident. A royal secret so their dead can rest in peace."

"Do you know how to get to the palace proper from here?" I asked.

"Alas, this is as far as I have ever gone," the chief said. "I know you must go up, but that's all. I hoped one of you might know the way."

The garden-folk turned hopeful eyes toward us. Anjey, Teo, and I looked to Julienna and Brysney. "You two have seen more of the palace than we have," Anjey said.

Brysney shrugged. "I've only seen the public chambers."

"Julienna?"

She smoothed back the loose strands of her plait from her

mud-spattered forehead. "Aunt Catriona's the Daired who knows the palace. But come on, there's got to be a door here somewhere."

There was. With the garden-folk scattering the full length of the hall it didn't take long to find it. An aisle crossed the middle of the chamber and led to a long stair against the far wall. It was narrow and treacherous without railings or balustrade, and the drop on either side looked very long. My heart sank to see the door at the top: a thick, heavily timbered door reinforced with wrought-iron ornaments, their edges only a little rusty. Brysney tested it cautiously. It would not budge. From behind me Anjey sighed.

"Well, what now?"

"Never fear!"

Tobble leapt down and joined the garden-folk gathered around Brysney's feet. He said something to them in Low Gnomic, speaking so quickly I only caught the words *file* and *lock*. There was a shuffling as two of the half-goblins moved to the front so their salamander's lights shone directly on the panel in the center of the door. With a "Hup!" another two half-goblins hoisted Tobble onto their shoulders. He flashed us a grin as he extended his tiny hand into the lock.

"Didn't I tell you that there's a good reason we're called an inconvenience, Aliza?" he said at my astonished look. "Now shush, I need to focus."

His little face screwed up in concentration. The half-goblins wavered beneath him, alternately muttering encouragement and curses as he shifted to get a better hold of the locking mechanism. One of them squealed as Tobble tread on his ear.

"Oi!"

"Sorry!" Tobble said. "Just one more— Aha!"

Pins fell into place with a dull thunk and the door swung open. I scooped Tobble up and set him back on my shoulder as our tiny force poured from the Chamber of Ashes into a dim corridor of the palace proper. "Thank you," I whispered.

"Careful," Brysney said before Tobble could answer, and motioned for those still on the stair to stay there. The corridor was empty save for a few lamps at the far end. A utility hallway, no doubt somewhere in the servants' wing and far away from prying eyes. Still, he moved carefully, checking twice before he waved us out into the passage. I fought off the trembling that seized my legs. *We're here.* Against all odds we'd made it into the palace, and now the real danger began.

"Where do we start looking?" Anjey asked.

Brysney motioned to the left-hand turning. "I think the banquet hall is this way."

Julienna shook her head. "Throne room. That's where we need to look."

"What? Why?"

She drew her sword and looked at me. "Think about it. The Silent King knows our dragons are in the city. We got away, so it probably figures we found them and told them what's happening. It's not going to keep my family in a room as exposed as the banquet hall."

"We'll check *everything*," I said. "Dungeons to the Tower of Torches."

"What about us?" Chief Grimmelgund asked. "My lord, my ladies, we're yours to command."

"Help us look, please," I said, "but do it *quietly*."

The chief bowed and signaled to his people. They scampered

away, their feet pitter-pattering against the marble floor. I drew my knife.

"Let's go."

THE ATMOSPHERE WITHIN THE PALACE WAS WEIGHTED with silent fear. With no servants left to tend them, the lamps set to light the hallways had burned low, and some had gone out altogether, leaving patches of darkness. I lost count of the turnings as Brysney and Julienna steered us through the barren servants' wing. *Hold on, Alastair,* I thought. *We haven't abandoned you.*

We were passing a curtained gallery when we first heard it, rolling like distant thunder from the opposite side of the palace, the blessed sound of fury and dragonfire. Silverwing had gotten through. The dragons might not be able to get inside, but they would keep the Silent King's soldiers occupied. I imagined Akarra and Herreki, Mar'esh and their temporary Riders scouring the streets of the First Circle, driving *Tekari* before them and drawing out the Silent King's forces from the palace.

Brysney stopped at the end of the gallery and held up a hand. Lights shone beneath the crack of the door, but they were steady and did not move. There was no sound from beyond. "Do we try it?" he whispered. "Or do we go back?"

Julienna unslung the crossbow and handed it to Anjey. Teo shifted behind us, a throwing knife ready in each hand. "Can you see if anyone's inside?" I asked.

Brysney moved to the door. There was no keyhole, just a simple latch. He knelt and peered through the crack at the floor. "Looks like an antechamber, maybe for the council rooms."

"Empty?" Anjey whispered.

"I think so. It's hard to tell from this angle. Weapons ready?"

We nodded. He stood and carefully, noiselessly, lifted the latch. The door swung open on oiled hinges.

It was an antechamber, but not for one of the council rooms. And it was not abandoned. A dozen Vesh sat around a table in the far corner, sorting out piles of heartstones in industrious silence. A pair of guards with crossbows paced behind them, and over them all presided the King of the Langdred Vultures.

One of the Vesh held up a clear blue heartstone with a questioning look.

"Ah, selkie, that one is," Rookwood said. "Fine specimen, too. You can leave that out of the pile for the master," he said with an unpleasant chuckle. "We're entitled to our fee, after all, aren't we, lads? It won't even miss—" He stopped suddenly as he caught sight of Brysney. "What the devil? *Guards!*"

The guard nearest him shouted and raised his crossbow. There was the tiniest possible twang.

Brysney grunted and stumbled backward into Anjey.

"Cedric? What— *Cedric!*"

His name on her lips faded into a wordless scream as he slumped to the ground, eyes open and unseeing, his face splattered with blood from the crossbow bolt buried deep in his heart.

CHAPTER 25

THROUGH THE FIRE

The hiss of steel sliced through Anjey's scream. Dimly I saw flashes of silver as Teo scrabbled for another pair of knives and Julienna raised her sword with a yell, but the small red wound on Brysney's chest filled my vision. Anjey collapsed beneath him, the crossbow hanging forgotten at her side. She had not stopped screaming.

Run. The word came as if from a great distance, swimming up through the choking haze of shock. Another twang. This time Teo cried out and dropped his knife, an arrow piercing his arm at the shoulder. *Run!*

"*Wait!*" Rookwood cried. "Don't touch them! Don't harm them, you fools! Don't you know who they are?"

The dreadful excitement in his voice sent everything snapping back into focus. I grabbed Julienna's arm and dragged her back through the open door. "Julienna, run!" I turned to my sister and tried to pull her to her feet. "Anjey, go!"

"Cedric," she moaned, cradling his body. "They killed him. They killed him." Her voice rose to a scream. "You killed him, you *bastards!*"

"No!"

I reached for her, but she was already on her feet, charging the Vesh with sword drawn. The first man fell with a gurgling cry, clutching the gaping wound in his middle, but the second guard sidestepped her thrust and caught her by the neck, knocking the sword from her hand. She writhed in his grip, screaming hoarsely.

"Go, miladies!" Teo panted. "For gods' sakes, run!"

I whirled around and crashed headlong into a pillar of shadow and flame. The smell of smoke and charred cloth burned my nose as I stumbled back and hit the ground hard. Without taking his eyes off me, the Minister of the Ledger reached out and caught Julienna by the wrist as she tried to dodge him. She cried out as the hot steel gauntlet seared her skin.

"Well done, Master Rookwood," the minister said. "Three birds snared and no blood spilt." He glanced at the fallen guard, then at Brysney's body. "None of importance, anyway. So this was the slayer of the Great Worm, hm? Pity."

Anjey uttered a heartrending cry. I started to my feet, only to feel the cold point of a sword slide around the side of my neck.

"Tsk, Lady Daired," Rookwood said. "None of that."

The minister turned to me. "Ah yes, Lady Daired! I had hoped we would meet again. Little Aliza Bentaine, my fool of Merybourne. We warned you thrice that this war was coming, yet you still blundered straight into the heart of it." He shook his head. "Those who belong to the Blood of the Fireborn will face their fate, but you bring yours on yourself."

There was only one answer I could muster. I spat in his face. It sizzled and evaporated in an instant, and the minister chuckled.

"Bind them," he ordered. "I shall take them to the throne room."

Rookwood sheathed his sword clumsily and frowned at the

minister. "Don't you think *I* should be the one delivering them to the master? Like you said, I did catch them and—"

"Oh, do as you wish. Just do it quickly."

One of Rookwood's Vesh seized my arm in an iron grip and hauled me to my feet. It was hopeless, struggling against the ropes, but I did anyway. The Vesh who stuffed a gag in my mouth nearly lost a finger, and the first man who tried to bind Julienna earned a vicious elbow to his temple. He went down hard, but before she could run three other Vesh seized her. Teo fought too, panting and pale as the blood streamed from the wound in his shoulder, but Anjey no longer resisted. She'd fallen silent, her face expressionless and wet with tears. The Minister of the Ledger watched with a thin smile as the Vesh herded us toward the door.

"Commend yourself to whatever god you think will hear you, Daireds," he said as Julienna passed him. "You are awaited."

Brysney's body stared up at us from the threshold. Tears blurred my vision and the splendors of the palace passed by unseen as I turned inward to the only recourse left, praying to gods four-in-one, though for what I hardly knew. The little leather bag in my pocket burned like the last flicker of hope, weaker and weaker with each step.

Suddenly the Vesh in front of me stopped. The gag tugged at my hair as I looked up to see the ornate green and gold archway of the throne room. Rookwood went forward alone, ducking into a perfunctory bow in the doorway.

"What is this?" Lord Camron's split voice rang out from within. "You dare approach the Silent King empty-handed, Vesh filth? We told you, you are not to weary us with your presence again unless—"

"Unless I bring something worth your while. Yes, yes, I remember," Rookwood drawled. "As it so happens, I have a present for His Majesty."

The man behind me drove the butt of his dagger into my back, pushing me forward. So did the others. Julienna cursed through her gag. Anjey moved like a sleepwalker, eyes unseeing. Teo had gone very pale.

The Elementar sat on the king's throne, its armored shell small and insignificant beneath the bloated shadow that rode it. Wydrick, still dressed in the uniform of an Elsian honor guard, stood on the steps of the dais beside it. He drew aside when he saw us.

My heart gave a great leap. "*Ah-uh-er!*" I cried through the gag.

Alastair, Edmund, and Lady Catriona knelt just behind Wydrick, their arms bound behind their backs, heads bowed. At my cry Alastair looked up. Blood mottled his face, and one eye was swollen shut. He threw himself forward when he saw our bonds. "Aliza! Julienna!" he rasped. "What're you—? No!"

"Silence," the Elementar said with a lazy flick of its wrist. The guard behind Alastair struck him across the back of the head. He fell forward and I bit down hard on the gag, swallowing the obscenities that threatened to strangle me. "Well, Vulture, bring them forward."

Rookwood seized my bound wrists and shoved me closer. "Show a little respect, my *lady*," he chuckled. "You bow before royalty, you know." He kicked my legs out from under me and I collapsed at Julienna's side in front of the throne. Anjey and Teo were tossed just as roughly next to her.

The Elementar leaned forward, fingers steepled beneath its chin as it studied us. Its shadow-tendrils crawled hungrily toward Julienna. "The Last Daughter of House Daired," a quiet voice said from beneath the hood of darkness. "We have waited many lifetimes for this. Well done, Master Vulture."

"My pleasure, Your Majesty. In fact, if you would be amenable to compensation, I might—"

"Peace," the Elementar growled, and Rookwood fell silent. "Who are the others?"

"They are of no consequence," said the Minister of the Ledger.

Hatred pierced my chest like a frozen spear as the Silent King turned to me. "This one looks familiar."

"She was at the banquet, Your Majesty."

"At *his* side." One twining tendril gestured in Alastair's direction, who struggled against the gag his guard had stuffed in his mouth. "I was not told there was another daughter."

Wydrick started forward and leveled his gaze at me, green without a flicker of yellow, even and hateful and unblinking. "His wife. She is not Blood of the Fireborn."

The Elementar drew back. "Then we have no use for her or the Rider."

"What of the guardsman?" Rookwood asked.

"If he will take on a ghast and serve us, very well. Put him with the rest of the kings' guard."

Tears burned on my cheeks and I ground my teeth as the Vesh dragged Teo, kicking and struggling, from the throne room. Ten thousand deaths were too good for this creature, this vile spider sitting at the center of a web spun from human and Oldkind lives, plucking and slicing threads as it saw fit.

"The women, Your Majesty?" the Minister of the Ledger asked.

"Kill them if you wish."

There was a smothered scream from Alastair. One of his guards fell with a shriek, his knee bent at an unnatural angle as Alastair's boot connected with the side, but the other guards leapt on him and doubled his restraints. His screams dulled to desperate grunts.

"If it makes no difference to Your Majesty, I'd like to beg a boon," Lord Camron said suddenly. He stepped forward and rested a hand on Anjey's shoulder. She jerked at the contact and raised her tear-streaked face to stare at him numbly. "Give me this one."

The Elementar tilted its head. "What use have you for a Rider, Gheren? Or is it your human that wants her?"

Camron's eyes flashed yellow as they traveled down to her belly, and with a smirk his ghast spoke. "Oh no, Majesty, my human cares nothing for her. But she carries a great deal of life, and we should like to make use of it."

The meaning dawned slowly over both of us. Flames leapt into Anjey's dead gaze. She drew back from the *ghastradi*, but the guard behind her was immovable.

"You have been a good servant," the Elementar said, "you and the human who bears you. We grant your boon; do with her as you wish. But what of the other?"

Camron shrugged. "We have no use for her."

"Your Majesty," Rookwood began. "As a matter of compensation for my work—"

"I will take her," Wydrick said.

The Elementar turned to him. "Ah, our faithful lieutenant. We had promised you a reward of your choosing, had we not? Very well, she is yours."

Rookwood's protest drowned out Alastair's smothered cries, and Wydrick flashed a triumphant smile. I felt again the press of the leather bag against my chest, weighted down with the unconscionable heft of all our lives. Our last foolish thread of hope—but only if I made the bargain. I could not let Wydrick take them.

"But, Your Majesty, you don't understand!" Rookwood whined. "I've a *right* to her. I owe her a debt!"

A shadow tendril twitched. The Elementar passed its cold gaze over me before making a permissive gesture and settling back on the throne. "State your case, Master Vulture."

Rookwood plunged with delight into a recounting of our encounter in Langdred, much to the enjoyment of the other Vesh. Even the Elementar's forces listened with apparent interest. Only Wydrick ignored him. He didn't look at Rookwood or anyone else as he approached.

"Leave her," he growled to the Vesh guarding me.

The young woman dropped the rope bound around my wrists as if it was red hot. Surprised by the suddenness of it, Wydrick hesitated for a moment before reaching for it, but it was only a moment I needed. Before he could seize the rope, I jerked away, putting a few precious feet between us. I raised my hands and tore at the gag, but the knots were tight and my hands, still tied at the wrists, were clumsy. He followed me with a look of both fury and fear.

"No games, woman!" he whispered. "Do you have the heart-stones? Just nod."

A cold, sick feeling took hold of my gut before I could answer, and I realized we were once again the object of the Elementar's attention. Wydrick, too, froze.

Rookwood had stepped up to the dais and was holding up his bandaged hand. "You're here for justice, aren't you?" he said to the Elementar. The shadows around the throne tightened into coils like snakes, but he plunged on. "Righting wrongs and all that. Well, it was she who did this." With a flourish he unwound the bandage enough to show the Silent King the remains of his mutilated fingers. "I *owe* her."

The Elementar looked at me. "Is this true? Wydrick, let her speak."

He started to reach for my gag, then hesitated. "Your Majesty, does this concern us?" he said. "The thief is not part of our brotherhood and the girl is no Daired."

"No," the creature on the throne said slowly, "nevertheless, Master Vulture is right. We came to bring justice on the faithless dragonriders and all those belonging to their house. Blood for blood." Its hooded gaze swept across Alastair and the others, landing on Julienna. "It is the only language they understand."

"But, master—"

"You shall have other rewards for your service, Wydrick, and greater ones than this. Release her to the Vulture."

Furiously I tugged at the gag as Wydrick moved closer. It slipped, caught, and slipped again. He reached for me as the other guards leapt forward, prepared to block my escape, but it was not the door I wanted. I threw myself out of his reach and collapsed to the first step of the dais as the gag at last gave way.

"The heartstones!" I gasped. "I have the heartstones you've been looking for."

"*What?*"

"Your Majesty, she—"

"Silence," it demanded, and Rookwood scuttled back like a dog with its tail between its legs. The Elementar rose, towering over me in a pillar of shadow and steel. "What heartstones?"

"Let my family go and I'll show you," I panted.

The shadows writhed. Darkness like a wave of bilious ink crept toward me, then stopped. "You speak dangerous words, little *nakla*," it whispered. "But we should like to see what you think is worth their lives."

The Elementar nodded and Wydrick drew a knife. He said

nothing as he cut the ropes around my wrists, avoiding my eyes, his cheeks strangely flushed. The ropes fell away and I rubbed feeling back into my hands.

"Show us the heartstones," it said.

I reached into my inner pocket and pulled out the leather bag. The gems tumbled into my palm, sparkling brilliant green and bloodred in the torchlight. The gentle tink sounded loud in the sudden silence that settled over the room.

"Ah," the Elementar said in a soft voice. "Now we understand. The heartstone of the Greater Lindworm, the last of the Great *Tekari.*" Its shadow-tendrils licked out toward me hungrily.

"Consume it and you will have the strength of centuries, master," Wydrick said with lowered head. "As you wished."

The darkness swirled together over the Elementar's mouth and deepened as if in a frown. "As we *wished?* I am first of the Eldest, old before the Lindworm was dreamt of in the depths of the earth. Why should we desire its heartstone?"

Wydrick's smile faltered. The blood ran like ice in my veins.

"You are thinking of the bounty, are you not?" it asked softly. "Ten thousand dragonbacks for the one to bring us the heartstones of the Daireds."

"Aye, it was." Rookwood stepped forward. "And lest we forget, seeing as I was the one who actually *caught* the girl—"

One of the Elementar's shadow tendrils pulled taut. Lord Camron's eyes blazed yellow.

"—I think I should be the one to—"

Camron buried his dagger in Rookwood's back. The King of the Vultures managed one last gurgling grunt before he fell.

"We tired of his insolence," the Elementar said. "But, Wydrick, you disappoint me."

"Master?"

"And you, little one." A bone-deep shudder took me as one of those shadows brushed my cheek, burning like poisoned ice. "A brave and foolish bargain you have made."

Quicker than a viper striking it seized my wrist, closed my hand around the heartstones, and wrenched. The burning ice drove knives deep into my hand, my arm, my shoulder, my entire body. A strange noise came from somewhere nearby, strange and thin and high. Like someone screaming. *Screaming.*

I was screaming.

The Elementar raised my arm, holding it aloft for all the room to see. My voice broke on the third scream. "Tiresome and insolent as he was, Master Vulture was right," the Elementar said. "We came for justice, and it is justice we shall bring."

It released me. My knees gave way and I collapsed on the dais. Tears filled my eyes, blurring everything into shades of pain and helplessness and the swelling, mangled mess of broken bones that was my right hand. The heartstones fell from my grasp and rolled away.

"Master, I don't understand." Wydrick's voice came faintly through the haze of shock.

I raised tear-blurred eyes as the Elementar turned to him.

"When we asked for the heartstones of the Daireds, did you think that we meant those dead things your people wear as jewelry?" it said. "Oldkind heartstones have their uses, yes, but we can get them from our agents any time we wish." It pointed to Alastair and the others. "It was *their* heartstones we wanted."

A thunderstruck silence fell over the throne room. Even my pain gave way before it. Wydrick had gone white as the corpse he was.

"You . . . Master, you didn't tell me . . ."

"Why should we? You are as much a fool as all the others. Now stand aside. We have business to attend to."

Wydrick fell back, mute, staring, his face the bloodless cast of a man who had made a terrible gamble and lost. I saw it through the burning haze of tears, his expression fixing me like an anchor. *Betrayal.* Utter, profound, and agonizing.

"Enough delay," the Elementar said. "The time of accounting has come."

Someone seized my shoulders and yanked me to my feet. The ground swam and pain like lightning seared through my right arm, and suddenly, with terrible clarity, everything came into focus.

Wydrick, trembling with his hands gripping my shoulders. The traitor betrayed, breaking beneath the weight of his misplaced loyalty.

Anjey, tears streaming down her cheeks, held helpless between two of Camron's guards.

Camron cleaning his dagger of Rookwood's blood and watching in ghastly delight as the Elementar made for the Daireds.

Catriona, her face white as salt, grim and hopeless.

Edmund breathing heavily, his head bent, blood dripping from a split lip.

Alastair, one eye swollen shut, still struggling against his captors.

Julienna, fighting like a cornered banshee as the column of shadow approached. Her *ghastradi* guards brushed off her hobbled blows like they were nothing. The Elementar stopped in front of her.

"Remarkable, isn't it?" it said. "After all this time, the Blood still runs true. Niaveth's form and features live again in you, child. We have seen this face in our dreams for six hundred years, the treacherous, smiling *filth*. She, the pride of Arle, Daughter of the Fireborn, Heir to House Daired, Rider of the South Wind—and what was she truly? A base, faithless coward. She failed to serve her penance, so you must do so in her stead. It is what justice demands. Wydrick, give us your sword."

Wydrick released me and unsheathed his dragon-clawed blade. The Elementar studied it thoughtfully for a moment.

"Dragons again. How fitting. Your father's gift, wasn't it?" Wydrick started as if thunderstruck, and a cruel smile split the shadow. "You think we didn't know of your heritage? Of the corrupted blood that runs in your veins? We know you better than you think. Where else would we find such a fit blade to use against House Daired but from the traitor's own armory?"

"Master . . ."

"Be thankful your father fulfilled his family legacy, or you would be kneeling there with the true sons of the Fireborn. He was a faithless coward as well." The Elementar signaled the guards, who pulled Alastair, Edmund, and Catriona to their knees. The man behind Alastair seized his plait and tugged his head back, exposing his throat, and the Elementar turned again to Julienna. "Let her speak," it said, and the Vesh holding her removed her gag. "Which will it be?" The point of the sword traveled in a lazy arc from Alastair to Edmund to Catriona and back. "You will choose the price, Niaveth."

"If you touch them, I swear I will kill you. Thell as my witness, I will kill you!" Julienna choked through her tears.

A gap appeared in the darkness covering the Elementar's face, and a pair of lips curled into a smile, bloodless and withered. "Three of your gods are blind, child, and Thell turned her gaze from us a long time ago. You will find no help among the Four. Your friends and allies have failed you too, as they always will. You can no longer escape the choice. Whose blood shall pay your debt?"

Julienna spat.

"No? Still you will take the coward's way out?" The shadowy mass billowed out behind the Elementar. "*Ahla-na'shaalk,*" it growled and laid the sword against Edmund's throat. "Very well. We shall choose for you."

"*Do not touch him!*" Lady Catriona cried hoarsely, and the Elementar turned to her in surprise. Her gag hung loose around her chin, damp with blood. The guard behind her snarled and reached out to replace it, only to stop at a motion from his master.

"Let her speak," the Elementar said. "What is your defense, old woman?"

"If you would have Daired blood, then take mine," she panted. "Leave the children alone."

"As you wish."

Wydrick's sword whistled through the air. There was a damp crunching sound, and Catriona's head rolled from her shoulders and onto the floor.

CHAPTER 26

SAINT ELLIA'S DAY

Julienna screamed.

"Who next, Niaveth? This one?" the Elementar said, and raised the sword to Alastair's throat.

I saw the glint of steel, the beads of sweat rolling from Alastair's forehead, the warm creep of blood pooling beneath Catriona's body. Julienna's cry hung in the air, oddly muted through the humming in my ears. Alastair would die. Alastair would die, and no amount of heartstones could save him. I knew it as I knew my next breath, hanging suspended on parted lips in that timeless instant before the blow fell. Alastair would die, and Edmund would die, then Julienna, and then Anjey, and me, and I couldn't stop it, and the whole of the kingdom would fall to this creature—this *thing*—this—

"Speak her name."

It was a whisper, hardly above a breath, hardly louder than thought. I felt each word like the throb of my hammering heart, like I felt Wydrick's eyes on me, angry and desperate and very, very green.

"We cannot say it, but you can," he whispered in my ear. *"You must. Aliza, speak her name."*

Her? Through the haze of horror, my brain churned to life.

The Elementar called Julienna Niaveth. It *remembered* Niaveth. But Niaveth Daired had never made it past the Silent Citadel, never seen the heart of Thell's prison and the ancient evil that dwelt inside, and it had never seen her. The Elementar could never have dreamt of her face . . . unless the creature had taken more from Ellia than her desire for vengeance.

A willing heart. A *living* heart. Ghasts did not ride corpses.

Then I understood. I felt a weight on my hip, the tiny pull of the pouch slung across my chest. Any healer in Arle would have known the contents without opening it. Bandages, needles, strong thread. Dried circlets of hallowsweed, hush, and beggar's balm. A tincture of moly, ground ashwine root, and tucked away in its own pocket, a small vial of oil of the Saint Marten flower.

Time ran to a point, crystallized like a diamond heartstone on the tip of the sword, and shattered. I exhaled. The sword fell.

"ELLIA!" I screamed.

The sword stopped in midair.

The Elementar twisted around to see who had spoken, its shadow stuff roiling in anger. "You *DARE?* Wydrick, kill her!"

There was a muffled cry from Alastair. Wydrick looked at me, looked at Alastair, looked at his master. His eyes flickered yellow as he drew his dagger, then green. He sheathed it.

"No."

The Elementar screamed.

I felt it in every fiber of my being, a scream drawing strength from six centuries of anguish so deep, even the present pain could not stand before it. Swords clattered to the ground around us as Vesh and Elsian guards alike threw down their weapons to cover their ears. I clutched my mangled hand to my chest and dragged myself toward the boiling column of shadow. Blood spread in a warm stain across my shirt. The world narrowed. There were no more Vesh, no Shadow Ministers, no *ghastradi*. Even Anjey, Julienna, and Alastair faded from view. Darkness flickered at the edge of my vision, and I was alone with this creature.

"Who are you?" the Elementar cried, though the scream carried on. "Who are you to speak to me? You are no Daired!"

My head throbbed as I felt inside the pouch with my one good hand. The words came like the slow drip of blood, like the thaw in winter, like the long-looked-for truth. "You're right," I said quietly. "I'm not. I don't have the Blood of the Fireborn in my veins." I looked up, seeking the human eyes beneath that ghastly hood, but there was only darkness. "I have the blood of a country clerk, and do you know what that means, Ellia?"

"Do not call us that!"

"It means you're not the only one who knows how to keep accounts."

My fingers closed around the vial of Saint Marten's oil. I held it aloft, steeled myself, and crushed the vial in my good hand.

Slivers of glass dug into my palm, but the pain came slowly, distantly, as if it was happening to someone else far away. Greenish oil dripped from my fingers, filling the air with the soft scent of the Saint Marten flower. I edged closer and squeezed harder. Red drops began to fall with the green, staining the marble before the Elementar's feet. The scent grew stronger.

"The green and the red, Ellia," I said, and the Elementar went rigid. I hardly knew where the words came from; they poured from my lips, faster now. "You remember it, don't you? The Silent King, the Elementar, First of the Eldest—that thing inside you has many names, but that's not who *you* are. You are Ellia of the Shattered Bow, princess and saint of Arle. Aren't you?"

"You know nothing. *Nothing!*" it hissed, but its voice no longer sounded as it had. It was cracked, broken, and I could hear it now beneath the seething hatred: a second voice, higher, weaker, and human. The sound carried images with it, fractured glimpses of a past I'd not lived. The salt spray of the sea, high yellow cliffs, dunes of silver sand stretching to the horizon. Dust. Heat. Sweat, hunger, thirst. Desperation and a desire for vengeance, boiling bloodred and hotter than the desert sands.

"You freed it, and it said it killed you," I rasped. My throat had gone dry. "But it couldn't kill you. It *needed* you, didn't it?"

The Elementar didn't speak, didn't move. Even its shadow-stuff was still. Then, very slowly, the darkness hooding its face retreated, and like a swimmer emerging from the deep water, a face emerged. It was a thin face, with gaunt, hollow cheeks and enormous eyes shot through with yellow, but they were familiar eyes. For six centuries those eyes had watched over every Arlean in tapestries and stained glass and statuary of the saint to whom our kingdom owed so much.

"It never asked for my life," Ellia said. "It only wanted my heart."

Only a willing heart. It can only hold a willing heart. I struggled to my feet, fell, and stood again. Fresh blood welled up around the glass slivers as I opened my hand and stretched it toward, not it, but *her*. The thing before me, that knot of hunger and desperation, of hate and misery, coiled in and around on itself until nothing remained but this poisonous loop, some horrible parody of the Unmaker's circle. Ellia had been entombed within it, living but not alive, watching and envying the world that moved on without her, the world that remembered a lie. "The stories say you only ever gave your heart to one person, Ellia."

The sword drooped at her side.

"Remember Marten," I whispered and reached out, reached *into* the heaving mass of darkness, and touched four fingers to that cold forehead. "The world may be full of the faithless, but he never betrayed you. Remember that, Ellia. Remember your love."

Dark tendrils billowed and twisted into twice, three times the size of Ellia's body. My knees gave way and I fell back, pulling myself to the edge of the dais. A new voice, entirely its own, dripped from the darkness in slithering syllables filled with poison.

"These thoughts, Princess. What are these thoughts?"

The shadow retreated. Gray eyes bent to the ground, where the red of my blood and the green of the Saint Marten's oil flowed in eddies around shards of glass. Ellia raised a hand to her forehead. "It has been many centuries since I have smelled that flower," she said softly. "It would not grow in the desert."

"Nothing so weak and needy grows in the desert," the Elementar said. *"It is the forge of the Fourth, the crucible where wasteful things are burned away. Have you forgotten so quickly?"*

"It was a desert you made."

"And you chose to walk it, Princess. Never forget that. You chose this path, this power, this unlife, and your heart was willing when I took it."

"So Thell's prison became Ellia's prison," she said. With the point of the blade in her hand, she traced a pattern in the blood. "No, I could not forget it."

"A prison that became a kingdom." The shadow unfurled again as the Elementar spoke. *"All we have built, all we have done, we've done together. Consider that when your thoughts would wander to this long-dead Marten, and imagine what he would say to see what we have become. Now—"*

"He found those flowers by accident."

"What?"

"Jadewing landed badly outside a town in Lower Tyne." Ellia's voice came faintly, as if from a great distance of time as well as space. "We were forced to make camp there while he healed. I was annoyed, but Marten found a grove there with the strangest little trees. They had petals instead of leaves, and they smelt of . . . honey. Honey and summertime."

"*It matters not what they* smelt *of! Do you not hear what I—?*"

"Niaveth was the one who found what it could do," Ellia continued as if the Elementar hadn't spoken. The shadow shrank until it was no more than a ripple of darkness over her golden armor. "The flowers. She crushed them and made a poultice for my leg. I'd twisted my ankle looking for water. She carried me back to the others."

"*Yes,*" the Elementar said scornfully. "*Niaveth grew kind. She became your friend, your confidante, your trusted ally. And then she betrayed you.*"

Ellia did not answer.

"*Your friend abandoned you and your lover in your hour of need. Before the teeth of the sphinx on the steps of the Desert Gate she lost heart, and her cowardice proved his death.*" The dark hood fell. Ellia's face disappeared and the Elementar turned once more to Alastair, Edmund, and Julienna. "*We have killed kings and built false kingdoms and broken the circle of the Unmaker for six hundred years to deliver the Fireborn's faithless bloodline to your hand, and now they kneel before us. Strike, Princess! Pluck their heartstones from their still-beating hearts, consume them as you have so many before, and you will taste your revenge.*"

The Elementar took a step forward.

Ellia took a step back. She looked again at the red and green stain at her feet, looked at me, looked at the oil and blood on her fingertips.

"And then what?" she asked.

"*What?*"

"You have fulfilled the terms of our agreement; you have brought me my vengeance." Her words came slowly, as if pushed through a barrier. "What remains then?"

"*I have told you, Princess. What your heartless father could never give you, I shall.*"

"What is that?"

"*A kingdom. An empire. The green islands of the south, the pastures of Pelagios, the mountains of Nordenheath, even the brimstone ruins of Old Eldrun to the far east: all will kneel at our feet. We will taste the heartstones of every living creature beneath the sun.*"

The small *snick-snick* of the sword swinging back and forth at her side sounded deafening in the silence.

"That was not what I wished from my father."

Her voice was so low I hardly realized I was hearing it at all, but its meaning sank into the stone, into my bones like the chill of the marble. There was a knot writhing at the center of the Elementar's shadow-stuff, visible not to the eye but to what lay behind it, shifting and boiling like a nest of angry vipers. Something was changing.

"I never wanted an empire," she said. "I never even wanted my father's kingdom."

The Elementar laughed. "*That is because your ambition was little and weak. Take your revenge, Princess, and I will give you what neither Rhydian, nor Niaveth, nor even your precious Marten could offer. I shall give you the world.*"

The darkness condensed.

"You're right," Ellia said. Her voice wavered, splitting and rejoining with the Elementar's with each word. "Marten could not give me the world." She turned once more to the red and green stain on the stone. "All he had to offer was a flower. A flower, and his heart."

A strangled cry tore free from her throat as two voices fought for control of the same tongue. The shadow within her condensed to a point of pure black, pulsing like a heartbeat and so dark it hurt to look at.

"You dare?" the Elementar screamed. *"You dare fight me, foolish girl? I—agh!—I—"*

"I had forgotten," Ellia snatched her voice back from the creature. "You *made* me forget. For six hundred years you nursed me on thoughts of revenge until I knew nothing else. Not the taste of water or the touch of a hand or the smell of a flower. You took—took—*you*—"

"You gave it to me! You gave me your heart! And I—no—"

One hand flew to her mouth, the steel-tipped fingers digging into the flesh of her cheek in an effort to keep Ellia silent. The other hand peeled it back.

"I gave you what was never mine to give away. Marten had my heart, and in death, in life, in unlife, he will have it still."

"No! You cannot take it from me! You will *not take it from me."*

The shadow billowed, and the darkness retreated from the edge of my vision. With painful clarity I saw the Elsian guards, dumb with horror. Several had begun to back away from their master. The Minister of the Ledger stood with mouth agape, his fire low and dull, half turned toward the door. Camron stood behind him, holding a bound and struggling Anjey in front of him like a shield against the swelling darkness. Fear burned in those yellow eyes. Wydrick alone was unmoved.

A deeper voice spoke from the darkness, a voice with no trace of Ellia in it at all. *"I am the first and strongest of the Elementari, and I have seen eons beyond your comprehension, foolish girl. You shall not defy me!"*

"I do not defy you," she said. "I will only take back what is mine."

"It is not yours! It is mine!"

"You cannot keep hold of an unwilling heart."

"I can and I shall."

"It will take all your strength—"

Dark umbilicals flung out from its shadow-mass, striking out toward the hearts of its *ghastradi*. One by one they stumbled forward, screamed, writhed, and lay still as their ghasts were torn from them, sucked back to the creature they came from. The guards behind Alastair, Edmund, and Julienna fell together. Metal clanged behind me; Lord Camron collapsed, clutching at his chest as a dark thread streamed away to meet the Elementar's summons. He gasped as gashes opened over his heart, his neck, his arms, remnants of wounds his absent ghast could no longer heal. He fell forward with one arm outstretched toward the Elementar, twitched once, and was still.

"As you said, Princess. Now stop this childish charade! Kill the girl and finish our work."

I saw it just in time. Like a whip a coil of shadow hissed toward me. Desperately I rolled. It missed by inches, leaving an evil inky stain on the marble where it struck. It rose again, then reeled back.

Ellia uttered a terrible cry. "It will take more strength than that."

"So be it."

More threads flowed into it, drawn out of the *ghastradi* in the room like a weaver carding black wool.

"Aliza! Come *on*." Anjey appeared at my side, her voice hoarse in my ear. She seized my arm, ignoring my yelp of pain, and dragged me away from the Elementar. She stopped next to Camron's corpse and plucked his fallen dagger from its sheath. "Can you cut?" she whispered, and offered me her bound hands. Fresh blood welled up between my fingers as I clumsily sawed through the ropes, and once free, I pressed the knife into her hands.

"Alastair. The others!"

Stumbling, panting, shaking with pain and fear and sudden overwhelming weakness, I followed Anjey across the throne room, over the corpses of dead and dying *ghastradi*, skirting the cloud of utter black that spat and crackled like a miniature lightning storm, whirling and writhing around a fixed point somewhere in its center. There was no human shape visible anymore where Ellia had stood.

The Daireds' guards had fled or fallen, and Anjey made short work of Alastair's bonds. He threw his arms around me as Anjey freed Edmund and Julienna. "*Khera*," he gasped in my ear. "Run!"

"NO," the Elementar boomed. "*There will be no running.*"

Alastair pushed me behind him as the pillar of shadow loomed over us.

"*Now I have all my strength. Now, Princess, you will take your vengeance, and I—*"

The darkness twisted in on itself as if suddenly confused. Its eyes burned sulfur yellow as it shrank back to Ellia's human shape, and it looked with puzzlement at the sword protruding through the chink in its breastplate. Wydrick clutched the dragon-twined hilt, his face deathly white. A black thread coiled around his neck, writhing like a snake trying to escape its charmer, but something pulled it back each time. His eyes flashed green, then yellow, then green again.

Next to me, Alastair reached for the fallen guard's sword.

"*What is this treachery?*" the Elementar demanded. "*Ghethel, I have called you. Take your human and come back to me!*"

"I cannot," Wydrick's ghast wheezed. "Oh, master, you under-estimated him."

"*Wydrick?*"

"Not . . . Wydrick," he said, his voice loud and terrible and very much his own. "My name is Tristan Daired, son of Merranda and Erran, and my father was no coward. I have done terrible things, unforgivable things in your service, but I will not go to him unworthy of his name."

The Elementar's eyes blazed and the black thread tightened around Wydrick's throat. He screamed.

Alastair lunged, driving his sword deep into the shadow's heart.

The black thread loosened and Wydrick gasped. Darkness pooled around Ellia's feet and licked at the edge of the dais, but it could climb no farther. A stain spread across her chest, pouring from the heart transfixed by the brothers' blades. She bowed her head. Black tears streamed down her withered cheeks.

"Marten said he loved me," she said in an undertone, and raised her head. "I remember it now." Her clouded eyes fell on me. "Is that enough?"

I met that gaze and saw, not the princess, nor the saint, nor the Silent King, nor the monster she had become, but a woman, not much older than I was, scared and scarred and heartbroken, and I did the only thing I could. I told her the truth.

"It's enough."

The darkness gathered around her, rose once, twice—and scattered with a scream that shattered every window in the throne room. Glass fell in diamond showers from the high panes. A black mist gathered above us like the shadows of carrion birds, darkened, and dispelled, rushing out the open windows into the lightening sky. Ellia's body collapsed at the foot of the throne. It held its shape for a moment, lips turned up in a faint smile, before it too crumbled to dust.

The dragon-hilt sword clattered to the stone next to Alastair's as Wydrick slumped against the dais, the black thread twisting into nothingness. His head lolled to one side, eyes open, staring, and a clear, piercing green. He did not move again.

There was perfect silence.

Alastair pulled me close as we watched the morning light filter through the broken windows. Somewhere in the distance, a bird began to sing. Bells tolled, welcoming the dawn as the sun rose on Saint Ellia's Day.

CHAPTER 27

THE GUARDIANS OF ARLE

My vision swam. My knees buckled and I gave way, almost folding in half as Alastair picked me up. "It's all right, *khera*, it's all right," he murmured in my ear. Louder he said, "Edmund, Julienna, arm yourselves. We don't know—"

The door to the throne room burst open with a bang. "Let them go! Let them go, you *ghnash-hleben-ghak*!"

I opened blurry eyes to see the last thing I expected: a flood of garden-folk, led by Tobble and Teo, all brandishing various weapons and shrieking battle cries in Low Gnomic and Garhadi. They skidded to a halt when they saw we were the only ones moving in the room.

"Master Teo!" Julienna cried. "But you— How did you escape?"

Teo sheathed his knives and pressed a hand to his shoulder, where part of a crossbow bolt still stuck out from his blood-soaked jerkin. He swayed a little on his feet. "Your friends—came and found me. There were *ghastradi*, but then there was a great howling sound and their ghasts left them. What happened?"

"We won." Edmund glanced toward his aunt's body and quickly looked away. "We paid the price, but we won."

The garden-folk lowered their weapons as they followed his gaze. One or two removed their little caps. Alastair started; a moment later Tobble scrambled up onto his shoulder. "Oh, Aliza," he murmured, and put a cool hand against my cheek.

A grave stream of garden-folk waded in among the dead, and I watched over Alastair's shoulder as they moved through the bodies. They closed the eyes of the Arlean guards and folded their hands over their unmoving chests. The smoldering corpses of the forge-wights and Lord Camron's body they left alone. When they came to Lady Catriona they paused, and a ripple of debate ran through their ranks before a consensus was reached. Dozens of tiny hands gently lifted her body from the ground as a pair of half-goblins retrieved her head. One of them hummed the first notes of a Gnomic lament, and the others soon took it up as they marched solemnly toward us.

Anjey bent down to the nearest hobgoblin and whispered something in her ear. The hobgoblin gave her a stricken look and touched her hand before signaling the remaining garden-folk to follow her. Anjey straightened and watched them go. Tears streamed down her cheeks.

"What did you tell them?" I asked, realizing as I did how near the end of my strength I really was. My voice came out in a croaking whisper.

"They're bringing Cedric's body."

I felt shock rolling through Alastair like a wave, taut and painful, but he said nothing, only held me closer and started after the garden-folk. I curled up against his chest and closed my eyes, listening to his heartbeat as darkness took me.

I WOKE TO THE BLUR OF BRIGHT SUNLIGHT. EVERYTHING ached. It took several attempts to keep my eyes open, crusted as they were with sleep and the salty residue of dried tears. A vaulted roof rose overhead. I lay on clean sheets, crisp and snowy white and smelling faintly of launderer's soap. Puzzled, I tried to sit up, only to abandon the attempt as my head spun and the room shifted around me. Instead I contented myself with squinting at the ceiling, wondering fuzzily where I was, what had happened, and why the roof was mottled with black streaks. *And smoke? Was that smoke?* I sniffed. The smell of smoke hung in the air, not strong but noticeable enough to put me on edge, though at the moment I couldn't remember why. I groaned. *Was there a fire?*

"Sweet Alyssum?" My uncle's face swam into view.

"Uncle Gregory? Where—?"

"Hush, hush. Here. Drink this," he said, and lifted a cup to my mouth. I tasted lukewarm water and mint, and drank greedily. Uncle Gregory eased my head back onto the pillow when I finished.

"Where's Alastair?" I asked.

"He's all right. So are Julienna and Captain Edmund and Tobble and all the rest. You needn't worry."

"Where . . . where am I?"

"The House of Beeches," Aunt Lissa said, coming into view. She sat at the other side of the bed and put a hand on my arm. "Or what's left of it."

All at once it came flooding back. I bolted upright, or tried to. "The Vesh! The city—they're in the city, the *ghastradi* are in the streets—"

"Aliza, Aliza, shh! It's all right." Uncle Gregory gently but firmly pushed me back onto the pillows. "You've been asleep most of the day."

I blinked.

"The *ghastradi* have fled," Aunt Lissa said. "Something happened just before dawn on Saint Ellia's Day. We're not sure what, but they just suddenly—stopped. Some of them screamed, some of them pleaded, but they all started shaking as this . . . this . . ."

"It's hard to explain," Uncle Gregory finished. "Truth is, we don't rightly know what we saw."

"Their ghosts were called back," I said.

"Maybe that was it," he said. "Whatever happened, their forces were scattered. Not all of them were *ghastradi*, and there were *Tekari* roaming the streets plain as you like, so the battle was far from over, but when their lieutenants dropped, we started to feel as if we had a chance." He smiled at his wife. "As it turns out, your aunt is very handy with a frying pan."

Aunt Lissa feigned embarrassment. "It was self-defense, dear."

"It was splendid, that's what it was."

I heard a twang, saw the flash of a crossbow bolt and a splash of red. My hands jerked up to protect my face, and the pain in my right arm dispelled the illusion. There was no crossbow, no blood, no more enemies, just the ruin and the memories they had left in their wake. I swallowed hard. "Where's Anjey?"

"She's fine. Ah, that is, she wasn't injured." Aunt Lissa's voice dropped. "We were so sorry to hear about dear Cedric. The dedicats laid him out in the lower halls. Laid out in all honor, mind, but Anjey asked to be alone for a while. She and Silver-wing both."

I could hardly begrudge her that. "I understand."

"She may— Aliza, no, you'd best lay down."

I ignored Uncle Gregory's admonition and pushed myself upright. Though the cuts in my palm pained me, my left arm was the only one that could take any weight. For a minute or so I stared at the bandaged mass of my right hand as it emerged from the sheets. The ache of broken bones hurt less than the unspoken understanding: the Elementar had mangled my fingers beyond the skill of the dedicats to fix. They would heal hopelessly crooked, if they healed at all. *I'll never hold a paintbrush again.* I turned away.

"Alastair," I said. "Is he close?"

"He was. He's been by your side almost all day," Aunt Lissa said. "The chief physician finally convinced him to let her see to his wounds. One of the guards gave him a bad gash on the shoulder, and the physician had to stitch up that cut on his brow," Uncle said. "It seems he and the others weren't taken in the banquet hall without a fight. The dedicats are seeing him next door."

"Take me to him, please."

"It's better if you stay— Oh, why do I bother?" he muttered as I peeled back the covers and slipped out of bed. Aunt Lissa took my elbow and helped me to a fresh shift and dressing gown, then guided me to the room across the hall. It was open and airy, the windows thrown up to the sills and curtains fluttering in the stiff sea breeze, which lessened the smell of smoke. Beds scattered around the room were filled with humans and *Shani* of all kinds, and dedicats of Janna in habits of green and white bustled in the narrow aisles carrying bandages, blankets, poultices, pots of unguents, and pitchers of water.

"He's there," Aunt Lissa said.

Alastair sat on a cot in the corner, attended by an older woman in the stiff robes of the chief physician, who was busy tying off the last stitches in the ragged cut along his upper shoulder. He didn't watch the operation, staring instead out the window to his right. The swelling around his eye had begun to go down, but his brow and cheek were still mottled an angry red. I wound my way through the cots between us and, at a nod from the chief physician, sat quietly on his other side.

"You know, it'll be quite some time before folk will be able to put this behind them," the physician said to no one in particular. "What with the assassinations and all."

"They'll find their feet," Alastair said without turning his head.

"Aye, no doubt, no doubt. Saint Ellia's Day celebrations will never be the same again, though. You mark my words."

"Perhaps it's time we started telling the true story," I said.

Alastair turned. The chief physician clucked her tongue as the motion tugged at his stitches, but he ignored her. He looked at me for a long time, eyes too full for tears, before touching my arm just above the bandage.

"All right, Lord Daired, I think that should do." The matron wiped away the last of the herbal poultice and tied a square of linen over the wound. "Keep it dry and change the dressings once a day and you'll be back to yourself in no time."

He thanked her as she left to attend her other patients. Aunt Lissa, after a knowing nod in my direction, followed her. I moved closer to Alastair.

"How are the others?" I asked.

"They're all right." What he didn't say, I heard. *Physically.* "Julienna and Edmund met the dragons back at the townhouse this morning. What's left of it."

"I'd like to see them."

"Are you sure you're feeling up to it?"

I eyed his bandages with a smile I didn't feel. "Are *you*?"

He nodded solemnly.

The dedicats had laid out a fresh tunic on the end of the cot. My efforts to help him into it were curtailed in seconds; tears welled up at the corners of my eyes each time I raised my right arm, trying to grasp for things with fingers that no longer worked as they should. Alastair gently disentangled my hand from his and finished dressing by himself.

The murmur of conversation slowed as we rose and passed through the hall. Injured city-folk and *Shani* looked up from their cots, human and nonhuman eyes alike wide with unfathomable expressions. There were a few bows from those who were able, but not many, and I was glad of that. I wanted no one's praise, no one's veneration. I knew now how soon memory could twist and sour into a lie, and after one fallen saint, I wanted no part in building another. Alastair kept his eyes bent to the ground, gripping my arm protectively in the crook of his elbow.

The smell of burning wood hung in the air outside, and over some portions of the city columns of smoke still rose, staining the sky a bruised yellow. My heart felt heavier with every step as we passed houses with broken windows, toppled statues, and public gardens with plants torn up by the roots. City-folk picked through the rubble. Busy with their own grief, they paid us no attention.

The townhouse door was burned through, the windows shattered, and the roof little more than a charred husk left open to the sky, but then, like a spark in the darkness, a familiar face ducked out of the dimness within and stood on the threshold.

"Master Teo!" I cried. "Why are you not resting?"

He saluted clumsily with one hand. The other was tied up in a sling. "It wasn't as bad as it looked, milady," he said with a smile. "Mostly. The physicians said I could take up my post. I'm still your guardsman, after all." He bowed to Alastair. "Sir."

Alastair rested a hand on his good shoulder. "Thank you for all you have done, Master Teo. We'll never be able to repay you."

Teo reddened and dipped his head again. "My lord, there's no debt. But, ah, I am to tell you that your family is waiting in the courtyard."

We picked our way slowly through the remains of the townhouse, pausing here and there to turn over the blackened remains of furniture, searching for anything salvageable. There was more than I feared, though less than I hoped. We lingered over everything and nothing, not speaking and not needing to. Facing our family meant facing the loss, facing the pain, facing all we had not been able to save, and at the moment, neither of us was strong enough for that. I saw my husband: a man whose pride in his family name had been shaken to its core, if not shattered altogether, and who no longer knew if he should risk the pain of picking up the pieces—yet still alive and whole and mine. It was a gift I would never again take for granted. I wondered what he saw in me.

As if he had heard my unspoken question, he drew me close and I rested my head on his uninjured shoulder. The throbbing ache in my right arm needled toward the forefront of my mind, but I pushed it down. I didn't want to think of that now. I didn't want to think of anything else. The road ahead of us crossed a new and unfamiliar Arle, but in this moment there was only us.

We held each other and wept.

AFTER THE TEARS CAME A STRANGE CALMNESS. ALASTAIR helped me navigate the soot-stained hallways to the courtyard stair. I dashed the tears from my eyes and surveyed the scene from the balustrade. With little to burn, it had escaped mostly unscathed save for some charred patches of ivy and piles of broken stone and glass fallen from the upper part of the house. The ghoul's body had been carried off and burned somewhere.

Julienna and Mar'esh sat in the far corner, his head over her shoulder, her arms wrapped tightly around his neck. Edmund moved methodically back and forth near the stairs, kicking bits of rubble into a pile. Whiteheart followed him, sweeping up the rest with her tail. She walked with a limp. A bandage fluttered from one wingtip. Akarra sat alone, perched on the courtyard wall facing the sea. Her wings drooped and her tail lay still on the flagstones. I could not see her claws well, but those I could see were bloodied and torn, the talons broken in some places to the bone. Edmund and Whiteheart looked up as we descended.

"Aliza!" Edmund said. "Shield and Circle, I'm glad you're all right."

Not trusting my voice yet, I nodded.

"Where's Herreki?" Alastair asked.

"She's gone to the headland," Akarra said without turning. "To prepare the pyre."

Edmund rested his head against Whiteheart's neck, and she nuzzled his cheek affectionately. "It's what Aunt wanted."

"When is the ceremony?" Alastair asked.

"Dusk," Akarra said. "The Drakaina will keep watch through the night and scatter her ashes at dawn."

There was a pause.

"And then what?" Julienna asked.

Mar'esh nosed her upright. "The king and queen are dead. The prince hasn't set foot on Arlean soil for years, and our alliance with the south is shattered. Much must change, Julienna."

She looked to Mar'esh, then to Edmund, then to her brother. "What do we do?"

The pressure of Alastair's hand increased for a moment before he released me and pressed four fingers to his head, lips, and heart. "We're Daireds, Julienna. All of us. We'll do what Daireds do."

I smiled. "*Tey iskaros.*"

SPRAY DASHED AGAINST THE ROCKS OF THE HEADLAND, stinging faces, hands, any exposed skin. The lights of the West-breakwater District burned low on the shore, and I was possessed by the sudden fleeting image of tunnels and scree and the terrible weight of earth and stone pressing overhead. A gentle tug on my skirt dispelled the image. Tobble looked up at me, his worried expression just visible in the dusk and flickering torchlight.

"You all right?" he asked in Low Gnomic.

"I will be," I said. "I'm glad you came, Tobble."

He looked over his shoulder at the silent columns of garden-folk ranged behind us. Torches in hand, they stood solemn as honor guards on either side of the headland. "We know what you did, Aliza. You and your dragonrider and Lady Catriona and all you big-folk. This is the least we can do."

We stopped near the end of the headland. The sea spread around us on three sides, dark and choppy in the first winds of a winter gale. My hair whipped around my face, and I pushed it back to see Herreki standing by the pyre she had built for Lady Catriona. It was simple, only a few flat stones, and her head and body lay atop wrapped in a plain white shroud. Three small metal discs rested on her body, each carved with the symbol of the Four-fold God: lightning sigil on her forehead, beech-leaf sigil on her lips, and the shield of Mikla over her heart. Her wrapped hands formed the final sigil, an empty circle just below her breast.

Akarra stepped forward first. She folded her wings over her head and bowed so that her snout touched the earth. "*Shurraneth shan*, may *Ket* welcome you with open arms at the gate of the Four-fold Hall. You died as you lived: with honor and valor, kindness and courage. You will not be forgotten."

Mar'esh followed her and added his own tribute in Eth. When he moved back, Alastair, Edmund, and Julienna stepped forward together. Alastair spoke his final words quietly over the pyre, as did his sister. Edmund knelt before the pyre and signed himself with the fourfold gesture. "Thank you, Aunt Catriona," he said before rising again. "Drakaina, the honor is yours."

"*Av Em teh-nes*," she said. "I have— But who goes there?"

I turned to see a figure coming slowly down the aisle of lights. Her unbound hair streamed behind her like black streamers, her pale gray gown shining in the twilight. "Anjey," I said softly, and reached for her. Her eyes were wide and wet, but no tears fell. She took my arm and stood next to me with bowed head as Herreki bent to the pyre.

"*Shan'ei, senna an Nymasi kerranna av te avn shean.* To your rest, my friend," the Drakaina whispered, and exhaled a column of dragonfire.

Shroud and kindling went up at once, and we had to step back to avoid the sudden heat. The spray from the breakwater hissed and steamed. Herreki threw her head back and trumpeted her sorrow to the skies, wailing a note that resonated in my bones. Alastair, Edmund, and Julienna drew their swords as one and let them fall to the ground, joining her lament with the wild cries of the Riders. Akarra, Mar'esh, and Whiteheart added their voices. Then I found myself crying out with them, mingled rage and grief screaming out a challenge to the sea, the sky, to death itself.

It was all we could do, and somehow it was enough.

ONE BY ONE WE DREW BACK FROM THE PYRE UNTIL HER-reki alone remained, standing guard over her Rider one last time, her silhouette black against the roaring flames. The garden-folk fell into step as we walked along the headland. Alastair walked a little ahead, his head bent close to Akarra's, one hand on her shoulder. Anjey had not let go of my arm.

"I'd like to have Cedric's pyre in North Fields," she said suddenly. "Close to Charis. I know that's what he would have wanted."

"Are you sure?"

"I've already made the arrangements. Silverwing left for the

Manor this afternoon. He took Cedric's . . . body." She lifted her chin, and I saw tears shining unshed in the corner of her eyes. "Lord Merybourne won't deny us this."

"Then North Fields is where it'll be, dearest," I said. "We'll leave at first light. But who is that?"

We slowed behind Alastair and Akarra as they neared the place where the headland met the shore. A small crowd had gathered before the breakwater gate, and not all of them were idle passersby. I caught sight of Master Pennaret and next to him, leaning heavily on his arm, a limping High Cantor Tauren. At the sight of him, I felt a bubble of anger swell inside me. *How many would have lived if we'd warned the king in time?* The bubble burst just as quickly. The High Cantor had tried as we had, and failed as we had, and by the look of his damaged leg, he too had paid a price. Anger solved nothing. I turned instead to his companions, men and women in the robes of high-ranking council members. They bowed as we approached.

"Is there something wrong, High Cantor?" Alastair asked.

"Forgive us, Your Lordship," Tauren said. "Captain Daired, my ladies, honored dragons, honored wyvern. It was not our wish to intrude, but there are matters of urgency we must discuss with you. Matters of state."

Edmund pushed forward with a frown. "If you have matters of state, High Cantor, then call the Royal Council. It has nothing to do with us."

"Begging your pardon, sir," Pennaret said, gesturing to the little crowd around him, "but this *is* the Council. All that's left of it."

I counted their pinched and anxious faces. *Fourteen.* Fourteen of what had been a council of at least thirty. Even in defeat, the Elementar had done its work well. I wondered if it had sent its *ghastradi* after them first.

"What matters do you have to discuss?" Akarra asked.

The High Cantor spread his hands. "The king is dead. The queen consort is dead. Chaos threatens, and we are leaderless."

"What about the prince?" Julienna asked.

"Prince Darragh is a long way away and our need is immediate, my lady."

"What do you want from us?" Alastair asked. "House Daired serves, High Cantor. We do not rule."

"Of course not, sir, and I would not ask such a thing, but your wisdom, your insight would be greatly appreciated." His gaze landed on Anjey and me, and very slightly he nodded. "All of you."

"I understand your request, sir," Alastair said after a moment's pause, "but we have lost a great deal in the last few days. Give us leave to mourn our dead."

The High Cantor exchanged a nervous glance with his fellow councilmembers, but no one dared protest. "Naturally, my lord. Er, forgive me, but if I may ask, how—"

"A week, High Cantor," I said. "Give us a week, for pity's sake."

"A week. Yes. Of course. You shall have it, my lady, with our gratitude." He bowed again and backed away, leading the Council and the rest of the onlookers back toward the city.

Alastair and the others looked at me as soon as they'd gone.

"Are you sure, Aliza?" Akarra asked.

"Would you rather we said no?"

"No, she's right," Alastair said. "A week is time enough, and our duty is to the kingdom. There's still work to be done here."

Aye. I raised my eyes to the darkened city and there, beyond the haze of smoke, the first stars of the evening pricking the blackness with their diamond lights. *There is.*

CHAPTER 28

THE CIRCLE COMPLETED

It was strange, I reflected as Akarra landed, how I could no longer look on my old home without feelings of mingled grief and gladness. Cheery lights shone in the windows of the Manor House, and the signs of the passing *Tekari* had been all but erased. Even the crisp autumn air carried with it the scent of home, but the Manor was not the same unbreachable fortress it had been to me when I was a child. Too many monsters had crept through the cracks; too many memories stained the cobblestones red. *Rina, Charis, the Riders at North Fields, and now Cedric.* Hart's Run had played host to too many pyres.

Silverwing's arrival the night before had roused the whole Manor, Lord and Lady Merybourne and my entire family were waiting for us in the courtyard when we arrived. Mama wasted no time. She was at Akarra's side before my feet touched the ground.

"Oh! Oh, my girl," she murmured at the sight of my maimed fingers. She reached up to Anjey, who released her hold on a very airsick Tobble to take her hand. "My precious girls."

Papa nodded to Alastair before embracing Anjey and me.

There were tears in his eyes when he drew back, and he tucked a loose strand of hair behind Anjey's ear. "I'm so sorry, my dear."

"We heard about everything that happened," Mama said.

"And we've made preparations for the funeral procession," Lord Merybourne added with a bow. "With your permission, of course."

"Aye." Anjey's voice was hollow. "Thank you."

Lord Merybourne turned to Edmund, who was just dismounting Whiteheart behind us. "Captain Daired, welcome. But Master Dair—er, Lord Alastair, where is your sister? Silverwing told us there would be three."

"She and Mar'esh will be here by sunset," Alastair said. "They do not fly."

Lord Merybourne, who I gathered had not heard of Mar'esh's wounded wing, wisely did not ask. Instead he motioned us into the Manor House with admonitions to rest, and to Akarra and Whiteheart to take their fill of chickens from the east yard.

I felt a touch on my knee and looked down to see Tobble gazing up at me with wide, solemn eyes. "I'm going back to the Underburrow," he said in Low Gnomic. "The garden-folk need to know what happened."

I crouched down and smoothed the mossy hair from his forehead. "Thank you for all you've done, my friend."

"Of course." His expression grew a little less solemn. "And if Chief Hobblehilt *does* try to assign me *phgethm* pots duty, would you, er, perhaps . . . ?"

"You send him to me, Tobble Turn-of-the-Leaves, and I'll make sure you never have to clean another *phgethm* pot in your entire life."

He brightened, sprang up, and kissed my cheek before scurrying off into the undergrowth. I smiled and followed the others into the house.

Leyda and Mari led the way to our family apartments, Leyda scowling at any intrepid Manor-folk who peeped through open doorways and casements to get a glimpse of the battle-scarred Daireds.

I paused at the threshold, astonished in spite of myself that there remained some corner of Arle unaffected by everything that had happened, at least on the outside. A fire crackled quietly on the hearth. The chairs sat in their regular places: Papa's nearest the fire, Mama's across from his, Mari's pulled close to the window for the best light, and Leyda's discreet pile of pillows on the floor, which she preferred to a chair. Bunches of drying herbs hung above the mantelpiece, and I caught the sweet scent of Saint Marten's flower among them. My hand throbbed. A sharp motion from Anjey drew my gaze, and I saw I was not the only one affected by the reminder of the throne room. She turned from the mantel, biting her lip. Edmund wore a pained expression. Alastair looked to me as if anticipating a sudden flood of tears, but my tears were long shed. I carefully unhooked the herbs, laid them in the basket beside Mama's chair, and closed the lid.

"Everything all right, dear?" she asked.

"Aye, Mama."

She and Papa exchanged a glance, but they said nothing more about it. "I'll have Hilda make some tea. Robart, Leyda, Mari, come."

Edmund and Anjey sat as they filed out and fell to quiet discussion of the practical matters that awaited us that evening. Alastair stood with arms crossed by the hearth, watching the fire. The green facets of the lindworm's heartstone glinted through his open collar, and I felt the equal weight of the lamia brooch tug at my bodice. They were the last things we'd retrieved before leaving Edonarle.

I did not sit. Before Mama could reemerge with tea, I slipped into the old room I'd shared with Anjey and shut the door behind me. Here at last there had been some changes. Imagining the sisterly battle that had led to Leyda taking over our room instead of Mari drew out the shadow of a smile. Gowns and shawls lay strewn over the bed, the nightstand, and the floor. Teacups and saucers littered the windowsill. I almost tripped over a pair of tangled trousers.

The door opened and closed softly behind me. "Are you all right, *khera*?" Alastair asked.

"I'm . . ." I looked down at my hand. "I don't know."

He took me in his arms and rested his chin on my shoulder. "Was this your room?"

"Mine and Anjey's. Leyda's claimed it now."

"I can see that."

I looked at him out of the corner of my eye. His face was serious, but there was the threat of a dimple just below the scar on his cheek, and it broke down a wall in me I'd not realized I'd built. From somewhere deep inside, beyond grief and fear and pain, a laugh bubbled up. It was a little thing, hardly more than a chuckle, but bright and heartfelt and, in its way, defiant. Alastair smiled and kissed my forehead. We had looked into the dark, we had fought through the night, and we had lived to see the dawn. It was worth celebrating.

THE DAY PASSED IN A QUIET BUSTLE. AFTER TEA BEGAN A steady stream of visitors, their tentative knocks growing bolder as the morning turned to afternoon and afternoon to evening. Master and Madam Carlyle came with Rya to deliver their condolences to Anjey. Despite the efforts of her mother to disguise it, Rya could not tear her eyes from my bandaged hand. Master Carlyle did not meet my eye. They did not stay long.

Henry Brandon joined us for lunch, hungry for our version of what had happened at Edonarle but doing his best to restrain himself. I took him aside after we finished and promised to tell him more about it at the first opportunity. He took my arm carefully and pressed a gentle kiss to the back of my good hand. "It was not in vain, my lady. I take it as my life's work to make sure all of Arle knows what you've done."

"Thank you, Henry."

Something approaching a smile alighted on Anjey's lips as she closed the door after him. "Aliza, do you need help with that?" she asked, noting my surreptitious struggle to tighten the loosening strip of bandages with one hand. "Here, let me." We moved closer to the windows. "You're very dear to him, you know," she said in an undertone.

"Hmm?"

"Henry. I wouldn't be surprised if he has the 'Alizasong' ringing in every tavern in every city in the kingdom by the Winter Quarters."

"Alizasong"? The name sat uncomfortably, all rough edges and ill-fitting corners and the dangerous gloss of praise. I looked across the room, where Alastair and Edmund were in quiet discussion with Papa. Leyda and Mari sat on the fringes of their little circle, trying desperately not to look like they were hanging on every word. I wondered if Alastair was giving them the details of the story that Silverwing's report had lacked. *Death came in the shape of our brightest legend, soul-sucked and nursed on six centuries of hatred by a godsforsaken creature older than the earth.* The shadow of the Elementar lifted a little at a new thought. *Six centuries of hatred that could not stand before a flower.*

"No, not that," I said.

"What do you mean?"

"There will be songs, aye, but they won't be mine."

"Well, they certainly won't be Ellia's." She tugged hard on the bandage, making me gasp. "Sorry!"

"It's all right."

There was a long pause. "Aliza, would you do something for me?"

"Anything, dearest."

She opened her mouth, frowned, and seemed to change her mind. "I've asked Lord Merybourne if I can stay in the North Fields lodge for—well, for a while. I know you and Alastair have duties back in Edonarle, but I can't go back there. Not yet."

"No one would ask you to."

"I want to stay there tonight, but I don't think—I don't want to stay alone. Would you and Alastair stay with me?"

"Aye, of course we'll stay with you."

"Thank you." She nodded to the door. "Edmund and Julienna too, if they like."

I turned to see Julienna enter, her wind-burned cheeks flushing even redder under Mama's greeting. She and Mar'esh had made good time. I sighed. With the last of us assembled, there was no more putting it off.

AS THE SUN BEGAN TO DESCEND, WE STARTED OFF ON the familiar road to North Fields. Anjey and Silverwing led, drawing the bier with Brysney's shrouded body slowly over the now-well-marked path. In the hand that wasn't gripping Silverwing's neck, Anjey held a lantern, its flame just visible in the setting sun. Alastair and I followed on Akarra, with Julienna and Mar'esh and Edmund and Whiteheart on either side. After them came what felt like most of the Manor: Lord and Lady Merybourne, the Carlyles, Henry and his apprentice, both carrying their lutes, Gwyn and Curdred and their little son, my family, and the rest of our friends. The procession stretched for nearly a quarter mile behind us. The Manor-folk talked freely, but among the Riders nobody said much. There wasn't much to say.

I felt a familiar catch in my throat as we broke through the eaves of the forest and looked out over North Fields. Where there had once been tossing green, there was now gold and brown, amber and rust, as if the woods had licked up the funeral fires from the Battle of North Fields and preserved them in a new and living medium. The earth at the northeastern end of the fields lay unevenly in humps and hollows around the great curving bones of the lindworm. Fire and scavengers had eaten away its flesh, leaving only the skeleton, raw and white and horrible. I glanced at Anjey in alarm, but against the flinty resolution in her expression, there would be no argument. This would be Cedric Brysney's final resting place and no other. Charis and her brother would at last be reunited.

The pyre was simple, just a mound of kindling piled atop a small cairn of stones. Silverwing's talons and wingtips bore the scratches from having gathered them. We joined him and Anjey as they bought his bier to a halt. Alastair dismounted, and along with Edmund and Silverwing, they moved Brysney's body onto the pyre. Each bowed deeply as they stepped away. Alastair returned to my side and took my arm. I didn't need to look to know he was crying.

Anjey paused for a moment at the end of the pyre with her head bent over his, fingers brushing his shrouded temples. Her lips moved as she placed the gods' sigils on his forehead, lips, and heart. Then gently, lovingly, she opened the lantern, drew out the candle within, and laid it in the kindling.

Silverwing was the first to cry out, lamenting his Rider's passing in agonized Vernish. We added our voices, wordless but no less heartfelt, bidding farewell to friend, brother, Rider, and husband as the smoke of his pyre twisted into the evening sky.

IT WAS A QUIET PARTY THAT RETIRED TO THE LODGE that night. The windows were dark and the hearth cold, and it looked as though it had been several weeks since anyone had visited, but I didn't think any of us minded. Lighting lamps, starting a fire, and airing out the bed linens gave us all something to do. Between the five of us, it took less time than I expected, and Anjey was soon curled before the crackling fire, one hand on the wing Silverwing had draped over the edge of her chair. Edmund watched the kettle swinging over the flames. Julienna pulled out her panpipes and played a quiet, solemn tune. I stood in the doorway, suddenly overwhelmed by it all, and fought off a fresh wave of tears.

Alastair slipped a hand over my shoulder and pulled me against his chest. The hard edge of his heartstone dug into my back as I leaned into him. "I know," he whispered into my hair.

"Does it ever get easier?" I asked.

"No."

"Alastair, there's something I want—something we need to do." I turned to face him. "Come with me."

He didn't question, only followed. The sun had disappeared behind the treetops and dusk was falling rapidly, but there was still enough light to navigate the overgrown path to the walled garden beyond the lodge. Dead, damp leaves made squelching sounds beneath our feet, giving way to the noiseless carpet of moss that spread from the stone dais in the center of the garden, where the statue of the Fourfold God stood silent and watchful.

I looked at Thell's facet facing the southern wall, no longer wondering why the ancient sculptors had arranged it so. She had always been watching over her distant prison and the terrible creature she had trapped there. *Trapped and freed and now sent back.* I unpinned the heartstone brooch from my dress with difficulty.

"Alastair, do you remember the centaur we met in the Widdermere?" I asked.

"I do."

"He asked me why our people hold death close to our hearts." I lowered the brooch. "After all that's happened, I'm starting to think he was right to wonder."

Alastair hesitated for a moment before pulling the lindworm's heartstone from its chain around his neck. "It's curious you should say that. I've been thinking too. We wear heartstones as signs of devotion." He closed my hand around the brooch and rested his forehead on mine. "But we don't need them, *khera*. We bear our own heartstones." He touched four fingers to his chest, right above his heart. "All the world knows this beats for you."

"Aye, and mine for you. *Qon vet qerrek, khera'ei.*" Now and always, my love.

A smile broke over his features. "You've been learning."

"I have." I took both our heartstones and turned to the statue, to the all-seeing eyes of the Unmaker, and knelt. *"Av Em teh-nes."*

It was a simple thank-you, without ornament or explanation, but it felt right. As I rose, I placed the heartstones in Thell's outstretched hands. To the gods belonged the first beginning and the final end, and with the passing of the princess who refused to die, the Unmaker's eternal circle was now once more unbroken. I took Alastair's arm.

A wind stirred the dying grass and rustled the ivy. The hair on the back of my neck prickled and I stopped, gasping for air under the sudden weight that pressed down on us, unseen, intolerable, *ageless.* It lasted only a moment. The wind stilled, the weight lifted, and Alastair and I looked at each other. It took another second for me to remember where I'd felt something like that before. *Hallowhall.*

"Aliza," Alastair said quietly, and pointed to the statue.

The heartstones no longer lay on Thell's open palms, for her hands were no longer open. She held the heartstones tightly, and her lips curved upward in a contented smile. Tears filled my eyes as I knelt next to Alastair.

She was missing two fingers on her left hand, and the fingers on her right were hopelessly crooked.

ACKNOWLEDGMENTS

Thanks first belongs to God, who gives life and breath and makes all things possible.

Thanks also to my incredible agent, Thao Le, and Vedika Khanna, editor extraordinaire and maintainer of authorial sanity, for helping bring this story to life.

To my beta-readers, sounding boards, brainstorming buddies, and everyone who refused to let me give up: Amanda, Crystal, Ryan, Kelsey, Dana, Colleen, Arleen, Leanna, and so many others. Thank you for the check-ins, the spontaneous proofreading, the honest feedback, and most of all, for always being there. This story quite simply wouldn't exist without you.

ABOUT THE AUTHOR

Elle Katharine White grew up in Buffalo, New York, where she learned valuable life skills, like how to clear a snowy driveway in under twenty minutes and how to cheer for the perennial underdog. She now lives in Pennsylvania, where she drinks entirely too much tea and dreams of traveling the world.

www.ellekatharinewhite.com
Twitter: @elle_k_writes